...how ...men who kno... ...theory ...them off their feet!

Kelly Hunter has always had a weakness for fairy tales, fantasy worlds and losing herself in a good book. She has two children, avoids cooking and cleaning and, despite the best efforts of her family, is no sports fan. Kelly is, however, a keen gardener and has a fondness for roses. Kelly was born in Australia and has travelled extensively. Although she enjoys living and working in different parts of the world, she still calls Australia home.

Also by Tara Pammi

Born into Bollywood miniseries

Claiming His Bollywood Cinderella
The Surprise Bollywood Baby

Once Upon a Temptation collection

The Flaw in His Marriage Plan

The Scandalous Brunetti Brothers miniseries

An Innocent to Tame the Italian
A Deal to Carry the Italian's Heir

Also by Kelly Hunter

Claimed by a King miniseries

Shock Heir for the Crown Prince
Convenient Bride for the King
Untouched Queen by Royal Command

Discover more at millsandboon.co.uk.

THE PLAYBOY'S 'I DO' DEAL

TARA PAMMI

PREGNANT IN THE KING'S PALACE

KELLY HUNTER

MILLS & BOON

First Published in Great Britain 2021
by Mills & Boon, an imprint of HarperCollins*Publishers* Ltd,
1 London Bridge Street, London, SE1 9GF

www.harpercollins.co.uk

HarperCollins*Publishers*
1st Floor, Watermarque Building,
Ringsend Road, Dublin 4, Ireland

The Playboy's 'I Do' Deal © 2021 Harlequin Books S.A.

Special thanks and acknowledgement are given to Tara Pammi
for her contribution to the Signed, Sealed…Seduced miniseries.

Pregnant in the King's Palace © 2021 Kelly Hunter

ISBN: 978-0-263-28246-7

05/21

Printed and bound in Spain
by CPI, Barcelona

THE PLAYBOY'S 'I DO' DEAL

TARA PAMMI

MILLS & BOON

CHAPTER ONE

HIDING OUT FROM thugs who'd kidnap her in a heartbeat and cart her off to marry some beer-bellied, gold-toothed creepy old man who gave out loans in exchange for *desirable assets* wasn't how Clare Roberts had imagined her life playing out.

Not even as a girl with the extraordinary imagination that had been needed for transforming her feckless father, who'd dumped her at her unwilling aunt's doorstep when she'd been five, into an emotionally available superhero for years.

But just when she thought she'd hit rock-bottom, life decided to show her the green icky stuff beneath the nasty pond scum.

*Desirable asset...*the very phrase made her want to throw up.

To escape Goon Number One, who had made it clear he'd collect her instead of the money she owed his Mob boss—because when her dad had borrowed money from them he'd used *her* as collateral and then died before he could pay it back—the only option left to her was hiding out on board the superyacht of the man she'd slept with not a month ago. While the night had been everything she'd hoped for and more, the morning after had been entirely too awkward. Her one-night stand had neatly deleted her from his life as easily as spam email.

Served her right for taking an imprudent dive into the roller-coaster world of sex and romance with CEO and unapologetic bachelor playboy Dev Kohli. A former gold-medal-winning swimmer who had gone on to create the world's most contemporary sports brand Athleta. A billionaire before he'd turned thirty and a self-made man, the latter quality being something Clare had admired enormously for a long time after she'd first met him at a PR event she'd organized for one of his friends. As well as his wide shoulders and rock-hard abs, that was.

She should've known her own PR company, The London Connection, might do business with him in the future. After all, he was a man who was reputed to be more loyal to his clients than his lovers.

While Clare completely agreed with the sentiment for a business-only relationship, it pricked a little when, as an ex-lover, one fell into the former category. Not that she was still moping after him.

But the heart wanted what it wanted…or in her case, it was her lady bits that had done all the wanting, after being firmly denied until the ripe old age of twenty-eight.

A hysterical giggle—fueled by the two glasses of champagne she'd guzzled in panic—escaped her mouth. Her two best friends and business partners Amy and Bea would've teased her no end if she'd said "lady bits" within their hearing. Well, Amy definitely would. Bea would've simply fallen into giggles. But they were both on the other side of the world at that moment, trying to keep their business afloat. Apart from the odd text, they'd hardly heard from one another recently.

God, she missed them like an ache in her champagne-sloshed belly. Desperately wanted to hear at least one of their voices. Tell them what her dad had done to her and then have a cry while they cursed him to hell and back. He'd known he was dying and had sent her money to start

The London Connection, which had gone from strength to strength in the last two years. He'd only lived for days afterward, and she hadn't even fully processed what it meant to discover now that, far from thinking her father had finally done something good for her, he'd actually betrayed her in the worst possible way, just to salve his own conscience for having ignored her for her whole life.

But contacting them while she was on the run from a mobster who was intent on kidnapping her and dragging her off to his cave was definitely not a good idea. What if he threatened Amy or Bea because he couldn't locate Clare? After all, anyone who'd done even a bit of digging into her life would know Amy and Bea were her true family. The only people who cared about her in the whole wide world.

No, she couldn't take the risk of endangering their lives too. So she'd decided it was better for them if neither of knew where she was—or who she was with. Her friends knew how determined she could be when she was on the scent of a new client, so she figured that when they didn't hear from her for a while, that's what they'd assume she was doing.

What her friends also didn't know, and Clare wasn't about to tell them, was that their new client was the same man she'd had a one-night stand with recently. She'd never shared his identity with them, feeling a strange sense of protectiveness about that night. Also, because if she talked to them, then she'd have to own up that she'd mostly failed at abiding by the most important rule of one-night stands— keeping it strictly casual. Especially as Dev had clearly had no such problem doing that himself.

Athleta was far too big a fish for Clare to walk away from just because its CEO hadn't proclaimed that he'd love her forever. And tonight had been her one chance to impress on him that her small PR firm could clean up his recently tarnished image.

Only the mobster's goons had trailed her all the way from London to a conference in New York and then to São Paulo, and it was terrifying. Today the mobster's intentions had been made crystal clear. He intended to simply...*take* her in lieu of the money he insisted she owed him.

For two weeks, she'd lived in terror of being snatched from wherever she was.

She'd been meaning to hightail it back to her hotel room when she'd spotted Goon Number One with a drink in hand on the main deck of the superyacht this evening. The short, blond, chubby-faced man had smiled angelically—clearly his cheerful appearance was a useful tool in nabbing unsuspecting women. It was the same man she'd seen leaning near the newspaper stand on the street where The London Connection's offices were located, looking up at the sole window. The very same posh and supposedly secure street that they paid astronomical rent for.

He'd even bumped into her late one evening when she'd been rushing to catch the Tube after work. Apologized profusely. When she'd then seen him lounging in the foyer of her New York hotel, she'd wondered if she was hallucinating.

Now, he was here, aboard Dev's yacht. Looking just as posh as the rest of the designer-suited men. Wearing an affable smile, chitchatting away. He'd almost touched her. Tried to talk to her as if they were long-lost friends. She didn't have time to wonder how he'd got on board. She needed to hide. Now.

She ran her hand over her hips, contemplating the rounds the uniformed security guard was making. The emerald green silk skirt she was wearing had been a gift from Bea, and it gave her some much-needed courage. Without looking back, she stepped gingerly down the spiral staircase— who knew yachts could have staircases like this one?—and tried to not trip in her four-inch heels.

The champagne sloshed around in her belly again as she passed door after door. Peeked into one expansive lounge after another. Even in her panic, Clare couldn't help marveling at the airy, contemporary spaces, the chic stylish interiors. The click-click of her stilettos on the gleaming floors sounded like a sinister countdown.

Heart pounding, she walked into the biggest cabin. For a second, she was thrown at the sheer size of it. A large bed with a navy-blue duvet looked so welcoming that she took an involuntary step toward it longingly.

It was the feel of the luxuriously soft cotton underneath her fingertips that made her realize she was pawing it. Her eyelids felt heavy, her entire body swooning with exhaustion. She'd been traveling nonstop for a week. Hadn't slept a wink ever since that ghastly man had started following her. But she couldn't sleep now. Not if she wanted to remain undetected until after the party wound down.

After one last wistful glance at the bed, she shook off the lethargic fog that threatened to engulf her. She was crashing from the shock of seeing that mobster's henchman again. Moving like an automaton, she walked into a massive closet.

It was about the size of her bedroom at her tiny flat. A faint scent of sandalwood and something else reached her nostrils. Her belly swooped, with a more pleasurable sensation this time. The memory of Dev's hard body driving into hers, the feel of the taut, sweat-slicked skin of his back under her greedy fingers… Clare couldn't help but cling to the memory of the utter feeling of ecstasy he'd brought her to. That moment of sheer intimacy when he'd looked into her eyes and simply…*seen* her. All of her vulnerability displayed on her face. And he'd just held her tenderly and kissed her temple.

The sense of well-being that arose from that memory suddenly calmed the fear brewing in her belly.

She sat down in the vast window seat and looked at the ocean. The expanse of blue was a symbol of how far away she was from her home, her friends and the business she'd built up with her own blood, sweat and tears.

But also on the other side of it was the man who claimed he owned her as if she were cattle.

Clare kicked off her heeled sandals and pulled her knees up to her chest. Leaning back against the plush upholstery, she closed her eyes and waited for her heart to slow its pounding beat.

For the party to be over.

For the yacht to start moving.

Every inch of her rebelled at the idea of traveling to a destination unknown with a man who'd walked away from her without a backward glance after the best night of her life. Who'd told her in no uncertain terms that while it had been pleasurable, their...association was over.

But the billionaire playboy meant safety for now. Even if that meant she'd be clinging to him like an unwanted piece of flotsam.

"Promise me you'll make it to the wedding, Dev. Please."

Dev Kohli pressed a long finger to his throbbing temple, his mild headache becoming aggravated by his twin sister's shrill pleading.

But since Dev didn't lie to himself—it was the only way he'd been able to survive in the military school environment his father had placed him in—he acknowledged that it was guilt that was turning one of the worst months of his life into something much...worse.

"You haven't even met Richard. I mean, Rich and I've been engaged for eight months and my twin brother hasn't met him yet. That's a bit much, even for you, Dev. Don't you want to make sure..."

Diya went on, without needing any more response from him than his grunts peppered throughout the conversation.

The fact that his sister—younger than him by a whole two and a half minutes—was piling on the guilt didn't mean that it was unwarranted.

He hadn't been back to his family's home in California since military school. He hadn't seen Diya in eighteen months. But, even throughout the nearly two-decades-long rift he and Papa had sustained, he'd always made it a priority to see his siblings. Even if all his attorney general older brother and renowned pediatric neurosurgeon older sister did was try to talk him into coming home.

It was Diya who had always been the one to check on him. Even when he'd turned his back on all the rest of them, Diya had been his only connection to his roots. His estranged family. To the one person he'd loved and lost— their mama.

"When's the wedding?" Dev asked, just to interrupt the barrage of English and Hindi building up momentum, spewing at him from across the Atlantic. He'd stared at the date for long enough in the last few weeks.

"You know exactly when it is," Diya snapped.

"This isn't the right time for me to visit California, Diya," he explained softly. "You know what I've been facing in the media. This sexual harassment scandal that's threatening my company's name is not a trivial matter.

"I've got people working around the clock to make sure something like that never happens again. And if I show my face at the wedding right in the middle of this…messy scandal, you know what *he* will say."

His sister didn't need to ask who "he" was.

"The last thing I need right now is to hear his negative voice preaching at me," Dev said, bitter even now. After all these years. Even after he'd proved his despotic father wrong on so many fronts.

"Dev, you can't let the past—"

"I just don't have the bandwidth to sit through another episode of family drama. If I stay far enough away, we can continue to pretend that we're the embodiment of the wealthy, successful Indian American family he's always wanted to be. Do you want to have your wedding upstaged by one of our dirty fights?"

Diya sighed. "If I have to spend every minute leading up to the ceremony keeping you and Papa apart, then I'll do it. In fact, I'll recruit Richard to play referee between you two. Papa adores Richard."

That little fact came at him like a bolt he hadn't even seen coming, lodging painfully in his chest. Dev wanted to bang his cell phone against the glittering glass bar and forget all about the wedding. Of course, his father approved of Diya's investment banker fiancé.

And at twenty-nine, here he was, still envious of something a stranger had—his father's admiration. As if he was that pathetic twelve-year-old boy again, desperate to please his father and utterly failing.

"I'm so sorry, Dev."

Dev sighed. "Not your fault, D."

No one understood how deep the scars of his childhood were, not even Diya. Not his obediently perfect older brother or his genius older sister either. It was like they'd had a father different from the one he'd been given.

Sometimes, he resented them all so much. But mostly for expecting him to just…get over it. To forget that he'd always felt like an outsider among his famous family's overachieving members. Especially after Mama had died.

No, he'd been made to feel like that. By Papa. Until he'd been sent away to the military school at twelve—which had turned out to be a blessing in disguise—Dev had been yelled at by his father, bullied into believing that he was nothing. That he was a cuckoo in a crow's nest.

And that was something he could neither forgive nor forget.

"I promise you, Dev," Diya said, launching into dire warnings now, "if you don't show up for my wedding, I'll... forbid you from seeing your future niece or nephew. Cut you out of my life. There will be epic poems written about the estranged uncle." Dev could hear the calming tones of a man speaking in the background, undoubtedly Richard. He smiled, despite the tightness in his chest.

He wondered what kind of a man had willingly signed up for a lifetime with his firecracker of a younger sister.

Damn it, this wasn't how it should be. Him thousands of miles away from his brother and two sisters and nieces and nephews. Mama would've been immensely saddened by this family rift that had left him utterly alone. She'd have wanted so much more for him than this solitary, no-madic lifestyle.

"Let me sort through the mess my company's in right now," Dev said, making up his mind, "and I'll be there at your wedding."

"You know that we all have faith in you, don't you? Whatever those trashy websites said about you knowing that female executive was being harassed... We know you'd have never tolerated something like that." He had no idea how she'd known, but Diya had just said the one thing that Dev had so badly needed to hear.

"Now, clean up the mess, Dev. And show up at my wedding with your billionaire halo all freshly polished."

Dev smiled.

"Also, it would be awesome if you could bring a date to the wedding."

The sudden image of silky dark brown hair and intel-ligent blue eyes boldly holding his gaze as he moved inside her was so vivid in his mind that for a moment Dev stayed mute.

Diya whistled. "So you've met someone! Who is she? What does she do? I can't wait to tell Deedi—"

The excited tone of his twin's voice sent alarm bells ringing in his head. "No one out of the ordinary," he muttered, feeling horrible for saying it.

Clare Roberts had been so far out of the ordinary that he hadn't quite recovered yet. He'd tried to tell himself during the last few weeks that she'd been just the same as his usual one-night stands, but he hadn't quite managed to convince himself of that yet.

"Continuing with the *love them and leave them* policy then, huh?"

"Don't push it," he warned her.

Diya giggled. "Fine. It's on your own head when you show up all single and handsome… Seema Auntie's been asking about you."

Dev groaned. Seema Auntie had been Mama's oldest, dearest friend and the most notoriously ambitious matchmaker on both sides of the Atlantic. With a horde of daughters, she regularly embarrassed eligible men without discrimination.

He quickly hung up after promising to update Diya on his plans.

Talking to his twin always left him feeling restless. As if he was back in his unhappy childhood. As if he hadn't achieved enough, conquered enough. As if he still didn't have enough. The feeling had been returning more and more frequently, and now it had been amplified by the man he'd trusted most using and betraying Dev's name in the worst possible way and endangering the company he'd worked so hard to build.

With a sigh, Dev looked around at the stunning sight of his yacht leaving the Port of Santos behind. He been visiting the nearby city of São Paulo, but he never stayed anywhere longer than a month. His sports merchandise was manufactured all over the world, and he preferred not basing himself permanently in one place.

In his heart, he knew he didn't really want to miss Diya's wedding.

Which meant he had no choice but to hasten the mass cleanup he'd already instigated in the company. There was no way he was showing up in front of his father with a harassment scandal weighing him down.

He was going to show up with his halo shining so bright that even Papa would be blinded by it. Preferably with a gorgeous, accomplished woman on his arm to ward off Seema Auntie, at least. As if waiting for the slightest signal, his mind once again instantly conjured the image of the woman he had determinedly pushed aside from his thoughts for the last three weeks.

While their night together had resulted in one of those rare connections that even the cynic in him had noticed, his behavior the morning after had been less than impeccable.

All the toxic rubbish that had been written over the past three weeks about his company and him at the center of it—a billionaire playboy who treated women with less care than he did his luxury toys—stung sharply when he thought of how he'd behaved toward Clare Roberts.

Granted, his company's name had just been plastered all over the media when he'd woken up that morning with *her* wrapped around him. He'd barely untangled her warm limbs before switching on his phone to find hundreds of messages from his PR team and board of directors. The female executive who'd not only been harassed but then hounded into leaving his company, had released an interview that had gone viral overnight.

A disaster of epic proportions had ensued.

Dev couldn't forgive himself for not realizing what had been going on under his very nose. He'd immediately launched an investigation, firing the man responsible for the harassment within twenty-four hours and offering a rehiring package to the female executive. But it was nowhere near enough.

He'd messed up big time.

He'd been so busy with launching the next product, chasing the next billion-dollar deal that he'd been distracted from his responsibilities toward the people who worked for him. It was the one thing Mama had tried to instill in all her four children.

That with privilege and power came responsibilities.

Dev had completely failed in taking care of his employees. He also knew that the solutions he'd already implemented were not enough to save his company's reputation. And that's where Clare Roberts was supposed to come in.

Walking through his empty yacht, he wondered why she'd disappeared tonight without approaching him. Especially after she'd hounded his secretary for an appointment to see him this very evening. When the initial request had come forward that the CEO of the PR firm The London Connection wished to see him, he'd done his own research.

He hadn't exchanged anything beyond first names with her that night. So, it had been a surprise to see that intelligent face stare back at him from her company's website.

For a second, he'd wondered if she meant to prolong their…association. Hot and memorable as it had been, the last thing Dev needed was a passionate affair distracting him. But he had pushed the arrogant assumption away.

The London Connection was a small firm that had made great strides in the last two years. It had a reputation of being one of the foremost, woman-led companies that conducted PR for big brand names. Also well-known for their charitable efforts and female entrepreneur empowerment initiatives.

Dev had instantly known it was the kind of company he

needed to reinvigorate Athleta's reputation. Clearly, Clare had seen the potential in the opportunity too.

Then why disappear before he'd even had a chance to greet her?

Why make all the effort to fly to São Paulo from New York, travel out to the Port of Santos where his yacht was moored, and then leave without even speaking to him?

Dev finished his drink and walked into his closet. Thanks to the call with Diya and now this woman not turning up for their meeting, his skin hummed with restlessness. He needed a vigorous swim. Even as a young boy, swimming had helped him work off the frustration he couldn't verbalize to his parents. He had felt free, as if he could communicate with his limbs instead of his words.

As an adolescent carted off to military school, his athleticism in the pool had been his saving grace.

He discarded his shirt. He was about to grab a towel from the neatly folded pile when he spotted a bright piece of emerald silk fluttering at the back.

He was very sure he didn't own a piece of fabric in that striking color. He also remembered thinking how well the emerald silk highlighted Clare's deliciously round bottom.

Was she here—still aboard his yacht, in his closet?

He walked past the rows and rows of suits and looked down.

Shock held him rooted for a few seconds, followed by a gamut of emotions he couldn't check. Anger, disillusionment, even humor traveled through him, ending in pure disbelief.

What the hell was she doing here?

She was curled up neatly in the window seat, her white handbag clutched to her cheek and completely...asleep. Her hair made a shiny mess around her face. A curly lock blew away from her face every time she exhaled. Her wide, pink mouth—perhaps a little too wide for her small face—was slightly open.

Dev reached out and gently shook her shoulder.

The last thing he needed was a mishap with another woman—even though she was the one invading his privacy and hiding in his damned closet.

Especially a woman he'd slept with…and hadn't been able to get out of his mind.

CHAPTER TWO

I T WAS A lovely dream.

Naughtily lovely and just what she needed to escape the nightmare reality of her life.

It featured a man's taut buttocks—the kind that athletes had—round and hard. The kind that spawned internet memes. The kind that Clare wouldn't mind sinking her teeth into. And thighs that would have no trouble holding her up against a wall making her sex damp with the raw muscular power in them. And, oh, Lord…that nicely defined V of muscles at his groin and the happy trail that lead to it…

Clare was desperate to hold on to the dream. She knew exactly who she was dreaming about.

Dev Kohli of the tight butt and the broad shoulders and the charming grin and the surprisingly kind eyes.

A loud curse and a hand on her shoulder ripped open the flimsy curtain between dream and reality. Clare sat up jerkily. Jarred into wakefulness, her limbs protested, after having been cramped tight into the window seat.

She looked up to discover Dev Kohli staring down at her with murder in his eyes.

Well, not quite murder precisely, but something close to it.

Clare swallowed. Blast it, had she actually fallen asleep in the man's closet? This was so not how she intended for him to find her. She'd meant to wait until the party was over and walk out and present her case to him like a rational woman.

He stepped back from her as if she was demented. And she couldn't really blame him. In quick movements, he grabbed a shirt and slipped it on.

If one could burn of embarrassment, Clare was sure she should be a steaming pile of ash on his lush carpet.

"Would you like to tell me what you're doing here?" Ice had nothing on his voice. "Or should I call security to handle you?"

Clare rubbed her palm over her temples. "I'm so sorry, Mr. Kohli," she muttered, straightening her skirt awkwardly. Her head felt like it was stuffed full of cotton wool and her belly ready to eat itself in hunger. Yet despite that, there was that prickle of awareness under her skin at his nearness.

"Why are you here, *Ms. Roberts*?" he asked, a wealth of meaning buried in how he said her last name. A little mocking. A lot annoyed.

Clare met his gaze without hesitation. "I promise, I don't usually go about sneaking into men's cabins. I had the most unbelievably horrid day and then I just… I can't believe I fell asleep. I think it was the scent of you that did it," she said, inanely pointing to rows and rows of Armani shirts.

"I have no idea what that means," he said, the scowl not lessening in intensity.

"I was terrified for my life. And the scent of you in here… I think, it lulled me into thinking I was safe. Because it's familiar, you know. After that night…" She flushed and sighed. "I'm making this worse, aren't I?"

"With every tall tale you're spinning to justify this intrusion, yes. Much, much worse."

"I'm not lying."

"I really doubt that."

It was the disdain in his voice that did it. That made her usually even-keel temper explode. "You think a lot of yourself, don't you? You think you're such a *studly stud* that no woman can stop herself from throwing herself at you? That no woman can keep her clothes on or maintain her dignity around you? That we're all falling over ourselves to get at that tightly packed muscular body of yours?"

Damn, girl, she could hear Amy's admiring laughter in her head.

Her face heating, Clare readied herself to be thrown out of the very window where she'd been hiding. It was shock, she told herself. Shock was making her mouth off like this.

Into the stunned silence came his laughter. Deep, low laughter that enveloped Clare like a comfortingly warm blanket. His face had broken into attractive grooves and lines, the flash of his white teeth rendering him even more gorgeous. If that was possible.

She looked away, needing a respite from all his irresistible masculinity. The dark hollow of his throat made her belly somersault. She had a vivid memory of burying her face there when she'd climaxed. And he'd held her afterward, as if she was precious to him.

The taste of his skin—sweat and salt and so deliciously male—practically hovered on her tongue.

Slowly, praying that her thoughts weren't betrayed on her face, Clare met his gaze. There was chagrin and impatience and more than a hint of humor lurking in the brown depths.

"That wasn't what I'd intended to say."

"Clearly. But that's probably the most truthful you've been just now, huh?" he said, agreeing with a grace she wasn't sure she deserved.

Clare couldn't summon a smile. "Just give me a minute to gather my bearings, please. I'll explain everything properly. And then—" she swallowed the fear "—if you still want to throw me out, you can just toss me into the ocean. It's probably safer for me anyway."

"Two minutes," he said, moving away.

He returned with an opened bottle of sparkling water and Clare took it gratefully. His gaze didn't move from her as she finished the bottle. It wasn't…roguish or obvious but she had a feeling he'd done a thorough sweep of her, from her bare feet to her short dark brown hair, still in disarray.

She fiddled with the empty bottle for a few seconds and then cleared her throat. "I'm not usually this unprofessional. I've had a really bad day, Mr. Kohli and—"

"Dev," he prompted.

"What?" she said, blinking.

His jaw tightened. "It's silly to insist on calling me Mr. Kohli when you've snuck into my yacht, into my bedroom, no less. Ridiculous to pretend that we don't know each other. On a level that strangers don't."

"That night has nothing to do with…today. Or now." At least her tone was steady even if her heartbeat wasn't.

He raised a perfect eyebrow. The man was more articulate with one gesture of his face than she was with all her words today, apparently. But then, it wasn't every day that Clare found herself riding a roller coaster of emotions, swinging from fear to betrayal to sheer lust.

"I'm having a hard time believing that."

Clare straightened, her hackles rising. "If you think I stowed away so that we could get…so that I can…" She could feel her face heating up again and cursed herself. "You've got this all wrong."

"Do I?"

"Yes. Absolutely. That night was a…one-off. I didn't hound your assistant for this meeting just so that I could wait for you in your bedroom. I'm not some sex-obsessed—"

"Then why are you here?" he hastily cut in.

"You need me," Clare said firmly. "That's why I'm here."

He stilled. "Excuse me?"

If she weren't stuck in a ridiculous predicament that threatened her very life, Clare would've found the outrage on his face hilarious. As if the world had turned upside down for him to need her.

"I need you?" he repeated, pushing his fingers through his hair.

Clare forged on, determined to keep his attention now that she had it. "What my company can do for you, I mean. This was supposed to be a business meeting tonight."

He shrugged. It caused all those delicious muscles in his chest to move in perfect harmony. The man shouldn't be allowed to wear his shirt open like that without a warning sign. "That's what I thought too," he said in a dry voice. Wary distrust was written all over his face. "Look, Clare. The last thing I need is to muddy the line between business and pleasure after what's happened to my company recently. I should've shut this meeting down the minute I realized we'd slept together."

She flinched.

"This—" he moved his hand between them, all masculine grace "—over."

And with that, he simply turned and walked away.

For a few seconds, Clare just stood there. She'd never been dismissed with such finality before. At least, not since she'd built The London Connection and made a name for herself in the world of PR.

After the cold indifference with which her aunt had welcomed her when her dad had dumped a five-year-old Clare on her unwilling doorstep like unwanted baggage, she'd made herself tougher. Grown a thick skin out of necessity. Day in, day out, she'd poured all that hurt and loneliness into getting good A-levels and then a business qualification. Into getting away from her aunt's long-suffering attitude.

And yet this stung.

Maybe because he was the one man Clare had ever let her guard down with.

Maybe because she wanted to see admiration and respect in those beautiful brown eyes of his, rather than contempt.

The last thing she wanted after her father had abandoned her was to run after another man who didn't care about her. Who thought she amounted to nothing.

The self-disgust turned to much-needed anger. That fresh burst of emotion propelled her forward before she realized what she was doing. Her hand landed on a warm, hard shoulder.

Clare pulled away abruptly, feeling as if she'd been electrocuted.

He turned, his frown morphing into a full-blown scowl.

Clare raised her palms and backed down. But not before the scent of warm, male skin invaded her nostrils and filled her with that strange longing once more. "Look, Dev," she said, ignoring his expression, "I know this looks bad, okay? But I had a reason for invading your privacy and hiding here. Stepping off the yacht tonight was literally the most dangerous thing I could have done. If you can give me just a few minutes, I'll explain everything."

"I'm not sure—"

"I took a chance on you. I went with my gut instinct instead of listening to what the rest of the world's saying about you right now. At the very least, you can afford me that same chance."

His jaw tight, he rubbed one long finger against his brow. As if he was at the end of his tether. "Explain yourself. About taking a chance on me," he said, as if it was the most outrageous thing he'd heard so far out of her mouth.

"I pitched for a meeting with you even though the entire world's gleefully painting you as a no-conscience, sexist monster who created a toxic work environment for women. Because I thought you should be given a chance to present your side too."

Despite the tension in his face, his mouth twitched at the corners. "So this is an altruistic effort on your part to save my backside?"

Clare shrugged. Trying very hard to not think of the backside in question. The very same one she'd so recently been dreaming of. "Not altruistic, no. I want my company to take over Athleta's PR on this side of the pond. I want a long, nicely padded contract that will put The London Connection on the map in North America. It will be a mutually beneficial arrangement."

A mutually pleasurable arrangement…that was what she'd said when she'd propositioned him that night.

The moment the words left her mouth, Clare knew she should literally have put it any other way. From the flare of awareness that lit up his eyes, he remembered it too.

After months of lusting over him from afar, she'd finally made her move at the charity gala for Women Entrepreneurs. They'd crossed paths a few times at parties and conventions before that, but he'd always been with a different woman on his arm. Despite that, she'd heard about his reputation as a fair and kind man through the grapevine. On that night, Clare had won an award and had been feeling on top of the world. When she'd gone to get a drink, he'd been there. Offering congratulations with warm eyes and that mobile, laughing mouth. Taking her in.

"You don't know who I am, do you?" she'd asked laughingly. "Or what I've won the award for."

He'd dipped his head in acknowledgment. "No, sorry. They were giving out those awards faster than glasses of pink champagne."

She'd swatted his shoulder with her clutch. "Hey, mine

was a shiny gold plaque, you know. The others were only silver."

"Well of course, that puts you a cut above the rest." The devilish charmer that he was, he'd batted those eyes at her. He had ridiculously long lashes and pretty eyes for a…well, for a man. Hand pressed to his chest, he'd mock bowed. "Not that the award isn't deserved. I've just had a long week and the details are a little fuzzy right now."

"Ahh…as long as you aren't seeing multiples of me," she'd quipped, shaking her head as the uniformed staff walked by with a tray of champagne. She'd already had bubbles in her belly and a pounding heart thanks to the man bending down to her from his impressive height.

Her belly had swooped even though his shoulder barely touched hers. He was so broad that he'd filled her entire view. His gaze held hers, front teeth digging into the way too lush lower lip of his. "Why do I have a feeling that it would be even more delightful to have multiples of you?"

Clare had blushed then. "How about you make it up to me for mocking my award?"

He'd finished his drink and turned to her. Shining the full blast of his attention on her. That gaze of his had turned perceptive and thoughtful. Less roguish and more… curious. Even admiring in a way that had sent tingles up and down her skin. "I don't remember your firm's name. But I did hear the emcee say you're a self-starter. A woman who forged her own path, despite an initial struggle. No one can take that away from you, can they?"

She'd been absolutely glowing by then. Inside and out. "No, they can't. As a self-starter yourself, you also know then that we have to milk every opportunity to the max. As I know who you are, but you don't have a clue about me, I have the upper hand between the two of us, right now."

"You're bloodthirsty," he said, leaning closer.

"Does that scare you?" she said, raising a brow, feeling a thrill she'd never known.

Another heart-stopping smile. "On the contrary, I have a weakness for a bloodthirsty woman who goes after what she wants."

"So?"

"So, your wish is my command, my lady," he'd said finally.

"Dance with me," she'd said boldly.

To her eternal delight, he'd taken her hand in his and led them to the dance floor. He'd asked her about the initiative that had garnered her the award. Her views on women in high positions and the obstacles they faced in a company's hierarchy.

With his arm warm and solid around her, his questions peppered with real interest, Clare had never felt so wanted. So…seen for herself.

A successful, moderately attractive woman who could hold her own with a brilliant, self-made entrepreneur. A man who could laugh at himself. A man who could admit he was wrong, apparently.

High on her success, determined to see if the attraction she felt was more than one-sided, Clare had wrapped her arms around his nape. And then she'd asked him directly, the words coming out of her mouth as if the torrent of desire couldn't be denied.

"Are you interested in taking this further?" She'd been so forthright, so honest.

His fingers had tightened on her waist, just a fraction. Sending an arrow of pleasure straight down to her belly. "How much further, exactly?"

"One whole night further."

There'd been a few long seconds where he'd just stared at her. Clare had felt as if she was standing on the cliff-edge of the entire world, ready to jump into the unknown with this man. "No strings?" he'd eventually said with a raised eyebrow.

"No strings," she'd confirmed with a bright smile.

And that had been it. No more words had been needed. At least not until he'd brought her to his suite and had asked her one tormenting question after the other about what she wanted. How she wanted it. When and where and how slow…or how fast or how deep…

Her wish had been his command, literally.

Clare didn't regret it for one moment. Not even now, when he was looking at her so suspiciously. He'd made their night together spectacular on more than one level— he'd been gentle and exploratory and funny…the perfect man. Just what Clare had needed.

Which was why she kept flinching at his nearness. It was a little hard to separate that perfectly wonderful man from this distrustful stranger who doubted her motives for being here.

But in spite of the wariness in his eyes, the knowledge of that night shimmered in the air around them. How hot and hard he'd been under her questing fingers. How he'd used those wickedly clever fingers to learn her rhythm. How deliciously heavy he'd felt over her when he'd ground his lean hips against hers.

A slow hum of heat built up under her skin but Clare ignored the feeling. Whatever had been between them was definitely over. This was all business now.

"Why are you so ready to help me?"

This she could answer with a certainty that had stayed with her despite how awkward things had become between them. "Because I saw how devastated you were when you looked at your phone that morning. How upset you were that something so awful had happened right under your nose." Even though she'd been hurt by his cold dismissal of her, she'd seen on his face the devastation the news had caused. That he was a man of integrity, just as she'd always known, made his ability to walk away from her so easily that much more…cutting.

When his gaze met hers, Clare rolled her eyes. "In the few moments before you threw me out of the hotel room, that is."

"I never threw you out. I said I was leaving."

"It was your suite," Clare said tartly, and then took a deep breath. "After I asked, in the most pathetic voice, if I had done something wrong." Heat flushed her neck and face, but Clare was determined to have it all out in the open. "You said it had been 'nice' but that's all it could be."

Dev rubbed a hand over his face, looking pained.

"The point is that…in those few minutes, before you replaced your mask of jaded billionaire playboy, I saw how genuinely shocked you were. I've followed the story as it exploded all over the media. The harm that was caused happened under your leadership. Everything you've said publicly since that interview, you've never once tried to get out of the fact that you'd failed your employee. Which made me believe that you should be given a chance to turn this around."

"And you're the one to do it?"

When it came to business, Clare never second-guessed herself. She'd built her company to be the best. "Your current PR firm sucks. I can do a much better job. The London Connection has a reputation of women empowerment initiatives. A good record of dragging draconic policies into the twenty-first century. Making companies equitable for all."

"How would this benefit you?" he asked, his gaze pinned on her face.

"Launched our North American branch with a bang?

Built our reputation? Turned a big ship like Athleta around and made it a better place for women to work? Take your pick."

Irritation flickered in his gaze. "I don't need you to teach me how to fix this."

"No. I believe you've already implemented several measures."

"How would you know that?"

"Because, as I said, ever since that morning, I've kept an eye on you. You've hired an independent agency to comb through your HR. You've already promoted three different female executives into more senior positions. You've got an equality and diversity agency doing a private audit on your board of directors."

Again, one brow rose. Clare stared right back. She may have started this meeting on the wrong foot, but she'd never been second-rate when it came to her job.

"But you still need me to put a good spin on it. To make everyone, especially women, believe that Athleta will never make those mistakes again. In simple terms, I will validate your efforts. Isn't that why you finally agreed to see me, Dev?"

He leaned against one wall, his gaze thoughtful. "I'll give you points for thorough research."

Clare shrugged. "But you still don't trust me?"

He shook his head "It's not you in particular that I don't trust."

She waited patiently. If she landed this contract, it would be a huge win for The London Connection. Both for their bottom line and their reputation. Not to mention that, right now, she had nowhere else to go. Literally.

When he finally spoke, tight lines bracketed his mouth. The shock and stress she'd seen in his face that morning three weeks ago hadn't left him yet. "The man who harassed and hounded Ms. Lane out of the company, I've known him for fifteen years. He mentored me when I started in this business. He was one of my first seed investors.

"I… I delegated so much of the everyday operations of the company to him and the team he brought in. Mostly corporate bigwigs. Which meant their power and reach in the company was—" a nerve vibrated in his temple "—far more extensive than it should have been. Unchecked, even. Because I was too focused on the next deal, the next product launch. If you'd asked me a month ago, I'd have staked my reputation on the fact that he'd never abuse his power like that with a woman—with anyone. *Never*… And yet he did. While he worked for me." A curse fell from his mouth, echoing around the cabin. Full of anger and disgust and something more. "Trust is very thin on the ground for me right now. No matter who it is. He…"

"He made you doubt your own judgment," Clare said gently, picking the thread up. Knowing exactly how he was feeling right then. "You're wondering if you can ever get it back…that trust in yourself. You're not sure where else you might have made a mistake. You're struggling to come to terms with why you didn't see it when it was right in front of your eyes."

"Do you have a degree in psychology too, Clare?" His gaze shone with reluctant admiration. And despite the frustration on his face, that hint of humor peeked through. "Or are you gleaning all this from my expression too?"

Clare laughed. Because it was easier to laugh it away before the pain set in. Before she was forced to consider at length what all this meant and how it shattered the very foundation of her life. "No, no degree in psychology. Just a lot of life experience. Believe me when I say I perfectly understand where you're coming from." She took a step forward, intent on making him understand. "I'll prove to you without a doubt that I didn't hide in your bedroom just so I could seduce you all over again. Like I already told you, I have reasons of the life-threatening kind for invading your privacy."

"Fine. I'll ask the captain to bring us back into port, and you can explain that rather bizarre statement to me. We'll—"

"Why take us back into port?" she demanded, her thoughts in a panic again.

He stilled. "I'm en route to Rio de Janeiro, and then heading on to my remote villa in the Caribbean. I'm sure the last thing you want is to be stranded there with me for several weeks."

"I absolutely do want to be stranded at some remote villa in the Caribbean with you," she contradicted him urgently. "In fact, right now, that sounds like a heaven-sent solution to all my problems."

He raised a brow, not so much wary as leery of her motives now. "So you're admitting that you wanted to be stranded with me?"

She sighed, knowing that she was doing a horrible job of this. "Not stranded with you in a romantic setting but more stranded on an island where Mob bosses and their cheerful thugs can't get to me. I heard you say during the party that you were going to be sailing around, or whatever the hell you call it, for the next couple of weeks or so. That's the reason I stowed away."

That distrustful look was back in his eyes again. Not that she could blame him. Frustration and that familiar resentment sat like a boulder on Clare's chest. She'd slogged for so many years, carefully building her life so that she didn't need anyone in it. With one move, her father had negated everything she'd achieved. She was going to sound like a certifiable loon for saying what she was about to say.

"Explain, now," Dev said, in a hard tone that did wonders for the quagmire of self-pity that was threatening to engulf her. "And no more beating about the bush. Give it to me straight."

"Straight, right. Here goes... I'd like you to kidnap me."

He rolled his eyes. "Now I know you've lost your mind."

"No, I haven't," Clare said with a laugh. It was the hysterical note in it, she was sure, that finally convinced him. "I'm the original damsel in distress, stuck in one of those ghastly fairy tales that I used to love. It's not really hoots and laughs when you have to depend on someone else to rescue you, you know?" she said, her words full of a bitterness she hadn't even known was festering inside her. "I need to hide out with you until I can figure out how I can avoid becoming the wife or mistress of some Mafia boss. So much for all the women's empowerment I've been a part of, eh?"

CHAPTER THREE

DEV STARED AT the glittering sheen of tears in Clare's eyes. Like a mirage in a desert, the wet shine disappeared as he moved closer to her, despite his resolve to treat her as nothing more than a business colleague. If not for the tightness around that lush mouth of hers, he'd have thought he'd imagined the gleam of tears. If not for the stark fear that was palpably radiating from her—that made him want to wrap her safely in his arms—he'd have called her crazy and thrown off his yacht, ocean or not.

But as wary as he was currently feeling about his ability to judge someone's character, Dev had a feeling she was telling the truth. Or at least the truth as she believed it to be.

He reached out his hand, then pulled it back.

This is not a good idea, Dev, the rational voice in his head said. The one that had tried so many times to curb his wild behavior. The one that was most in touch with his innermost feelings, so to speak.

But, as much as he'd grown a thick, impervious skin over the past almost two decades—thanks to his military school discipline—he wasn't quite the uncaring bastard the media had so recently accused him of being. Or that he sometimes wished he could be, whenever he found himself caring too deeply, about anything. Especially when he was confronted with a woman like Clare Roberts and all the unwanted feelings she evoked in him.

What they both needed was to take a step back and re-group after this strange meeting, in his closet of all places. "Why don't we move this discussion out of here?" When she shot him a wary glance, he said gently, "You look like you need a drink. I definitely do, after getting yelled at by my twin."

"Oh, you have a twin?"

The twinkle in her eyes had him nodding. "Yes. She's incredibly bossy and she's getting married in about a month. She's just warned me that she'll cut me off from any future nieces or nephews she may give me if I don't make it to her wedding. So the deadline to clean up my image just got even tighter."

"Because you don't want the cloud of this scandal to disturb the wedding atmosphere?"

"No, because I can't go if..." Dev checked himself. Big blue eyes watched him curiously. "Doesn't matter why. It's just important to change the narrative on my company before the wedding. If I want to make it, that is."

She nodded, lifting that stubborn chin of hers. "Then our plan needs to be aggressive too."

He still didn't know why she was here. "I'd also like to have this talk while I'm not still standing half-undressed in my own closet and you don't look as if someone's done a thorough job of...mussing you up," he said tightly. For all his numerous girlfriends, he hated the idea of mixing business with pleasure. Even though the pleasure had been in the past in this case. "I trust most of my staff, but there's no guarantee of anyone's loyalty if there's a nice price tag attached to a juicy story."

Her mouth fell open. "You think someone might tell the press that you've trapped me aboard your yacht with the intention of having your wicked way with me?"

She looked so delighted at the prospect that Dev felt his mouth twitching. "You sound like that's not a bad thing."

"Not a bad thing at all, if I was, in reality, a willing partner," she said dreamily, her gaze suddenly far-off.

"Is this one of your fantasies then, Ms. Roberts?" he said, trying and failing to sound serious.

Her gaze swept over his chest, naked longing shining in it. If he wasn't just as hungrily tracing every feature of her face, he'd have missed it. The woman had no idea how arousing her transparent desire for him was. He was both amused and a little annoyed by it.

No, mostly annoyed, he corrected himself.

Because, he was right in his initial estimate of her. It had been sheer madness—accepting her proposition that night. In his defense, she'd looked incredibly sexy and pretty and had been so earnestly direct that he'd found her utterly irresistible.

Clare Roberts—for all she tried to pretend to be a femme fatale—was very much an innocent from the top of her head to the soles of her pretty feet. The kind he usually avoided like the plague.

"Clare?" he said, and cleared his throat. Desire was a constant low thrum under his skin that he had to get used to—because it couldn't be indulged in again.

"What?" she said distractedly, still only half present.

"Maybe this isn't the time to act out one of your fantasies?" Dev suggested, suddenly realizing he was grinning. It was just too much fun to bandy words with her. More fun than he'd had in a long time. "However, you might want to check what my interest level is after we finish our business dealings though."

She drew herself up to her full five feet three inches, glaring daggers at him. "You really think I'm standing here daydreaming about being kidnapped by you, don't you?"

He shrugged, laughing. "Well, there's nothing wrong with kidnapping when we're both consenting adults, is there? And who am I to stand in the way of a woman's sexual fantasy? Thirdly, you're the one who got all dreamy and soft when I mentioned it."

"I was considering it as a story that could be carefully directed so that it reached the right ears, yes. Not getting all hot and bothered about you having your wicked way with me," she denied hotly.

"That's me put in my place then," he said, with a sigh. "As for a story about you and me being stuck together, Clare, forget it. The last thing I need is any unwelcome scrutiny on my love life."

"But what if it serves my purpose?"

"It doesn't serve mine," Dev growled, realizing she was serious. What the hell was she talking about now? "Do you want this deal with my company or do you want salacious stories about us in the media?"

"I want both."

Dev frowned. Maybe he had been too quick to trust this woman. "I think you'd better tell me the reason you're here first," he said. "Everything else can come later."

He saw her take a deep breath.

"I have a Mob boss after me. His hired thug was here, aboard your yacht this evening, watching me. It was why I had to play hide-and-seek in your closet."

"What?" Dev said, incapable of any other response. He arrested the stinging denial that rose to his lips. The stark fear in her eyes couldn't be a lie.

"The same man was camped outside my office in London. Then I saw him when I flew to a conference in New York. Then again here. When I spotted him up there to-night," she said, pointing to the upper deck, her entire body shivering at some invisible draft, "I just had to hide. I'm sorry for thrusting this all on you, especially when you have your own problems, but I had no choice. I'm stuck in a really bad situation."

"I know the man you're referring to. I signaled to my

head of security after I saw him approach you. He was definitely not on the guest list. When I checked again, he'd disappeared."

Clare simply nodded. "I had a call from his boss as I arrived here tonight. He told me that he was going to have me, no matter what. That no one's going to stop him, because he owns me outright."

Dev saw her shiver again and fisted his hands. "You're safe here. My security escorted his henchman off the yacht."

"I'm safe for now," she corrected.

"Why is he after you?"

Her lashes fell down in a curtain, suddenly hiding her expression. "I took money from a man I shouldn't have trusted."

Dev couldn't help sounding incredulous. "You took a loan from a known Mob boss? Why?"

Pink scoured her cheeks. "I told you it was…a bad decision. I was desperate to establish my business. I didn't look closely at who I was trusting."

Dev raised a brow. "So wait, you took out a loan with yourself as collateral? How can a woman specializing in PR not understand what she was signing?"

"Please don't use it as a measure of my efficiency. Let's just say I found myself tricked. Those weren't the terms that were spelled out when I accepted the money. I was just so happy to have a running start on establishing my business. I…" She rubbed her temple with her fingers, her gaze anywhere but on him. "It doesn't matter why or how this happened, okay? That damned man thinks he owns me now."

Clare Roberts was a perplexing combination of innocence and sophistication, with a good measure of idiocy thrown in. Or had she been that desperate to launch her business? To establish her self-sufficiency? To prove her own self-worth?

Because those feelings of desperation were very old friends to Dev.

"I just need some time to figure a way to get out of his clutches. Somewhere he and his goons can't reach me. The last thing I want is to become the prized possession of some Mafia boss who'll delight in punishing me by lending me to his lieutenants whenever he feels like it."

"And how would you know he'd do that?" Dev asked, his mouth twitching again.

She looked at him and away, embarrassment shining in her face. "I binge-watched a show where the main character did that. Fairy tales and fantasies are not really what you'd associate with a practical businesswoman like me, are they?" A bitterness he knew only too well twisted her mouth.

"We all have our guilty pleasures, Clare."

"Like you and your never-ending array of bed partners?" she retorted. But before he could answer her, she shook her head regretfully. "Let's pretend I didn't just say that. And no, I don't need rescuing by anyone. I just need time to rescue myself. So?"

"So what?" he said, wondering what he was signing up for here.

"Will you let me stay aboard for a little while?"

Dev studied her. With her mussed-up hair and clothes, she couldn't have looked less like the CEO of her own PR firm. She looked like trouble. Of the kind that he didn't usually touch with a very long pole.

The last thing he needed right now was another headache. And yet, he couldn't just throw her out, could he? Not when he'd seen the very man she'd mentioned eyeing her like a particularly juicy steak. Not when stark fear at her plight had rendered her so distressingly pale.

He'd already let down one woman who'd been under his protection. Had failed in what he considered to be one of the most important aspects of his own personality—defending those who couldn't defend themselves.

Those who were deemed lesser or weaker, just because they didn't fit a certain definition of perfect or normal. He had been that kid once, with no champion to defend him. With no one to understand how he'd felt being cut off from the world of the written word. Especially not after Mama's death.

How could he ignore Clare's plight now, knowing that her life might be in danger? He didn't want any more women on his conscience.

He looked down to find her gaze resolutely staring back at him. "All I'm asking for is a place to hide. Whether you hire me or not to clean up your image, you can decide that based on my proposal."

More than pleasantly surprised at how fast she'd turned all that emotion into something far more constructive, he impulsively said, "Fine. We'll figure out a way to get you out of this predicament."

He wondered who was more shocked by his ridiculous promise. Playing the hero had never been his forte. Emotional grandstanding of the kind that his father excelled in had always made him wary. So why was he spouting these words to her?

Thankfully, Clare apparently had a lot more sense and gumption than he had given her credit for.

She shook her head. "Now, Mr. Kohli, don't go making promises you can't keep. Even when I buried myself in fairy tales and stories, I knew enough to not think myself the heroine. To not lose my grip on reality." She sounded like a woman who had never had anyone to depend on. She sounded exactly like him. Dev wondered if that was her appeal for him. "This is a problem I'll solve for myself. As I've always done. All I ask is that you buy me some time."

"Are we really back to being Mr. Kohli and Ms. Roberts again then?"

"I think it's safest, don't you? Especially now that you might be one of my biggest clients."

Dev grinned. There was something about the sudden, starchy formality that she was insisting on that made him want to unravel her. Just a little bit. "Afraid you might not be able to resist me while we're stuck together, are you?"

She laughed. "You think this is being stuck together?" Her arms moved around to encompass the vast yacht. "Aboard your gigantic yacht. It's so ridiculously huge that one might be tempted to think the owner was overcompensating for something…"

Dev took a step forward. One step. There was still a lot of distance between them for him to reach her. Her mouth clamped shut. "You're being unfair, Ms. Roberts."

"How?"

"Making wildly absurd claims that I can't rebut without making statements that could be construed as innuendo? You're baiting me, knowing that I can't play along. You're having your own sweet little revenge."

She blushed and looked away, and he smiled in satisfaction.

"As long as we're clear on the fact that this is not some kind of invitation to re—"

"Yes, yes, I know it's not." She cut in, rolling her eyes. "I'm not stupid. Also, I'm not into skittish playboys who have to be convinced what a treasure I am."

"Did you just call me skittish?" Dev let out an outraged growl and now it was her mouth that twitched.

Her blue eyes widened as she considered him. "I'm not going to crimp your style by being here, am I?"

"What do you mean?" he demanded, feeling surly. Because there was that hum of desire under his skin again. Suddenly the idea of being stuck with this woman for however long—without being able to kiss that lovely mouth—was nothing but pure torment.

"Do you have anyone else on board, Mr. Kohli?"

"Other than my staff, no," he said, wondering where she was going with this.

"A girlfriend? An ex? A bunch of guests waiting to participate in an orgy?"

He pursed his lips. "No."

"Good, then I don't have to disillusion some poor girl looking for a good time?"

"Is that comment in general or specific, Ms. Roberts?"

"Both. We have to be really careful about who you choose as your next playmate."

"Ah…so you were bothered by my behavior that morning then?" He had no idea why he was pressing the issue. No idea why this particular woman had been so stubbornly stuck in his thoughts for weeks.

To give her credit, Clare didn't look away this time. Dev thought she was incredibly brave because her eyes shimmered with a truth she didn't give voice to.

He knew he had hurt her that morning. But it wasn't something he could change or even regret. Better she understood the truth about him now rather than build any ridiculous expectations of this…partnership.

It had to be strictly business.

"That's because I wasn't used to the morning after protocol," she said, all dignified effrontery. The twist of her mouth was both a challenge and something more… something that made Dev want to taste and absorb into himself. "And it was quite a hard landing after the ride you took me on that night. A girl should be forgiven for floating about on an endorphin rush. She needs a little time to recover from seducing you."

Dev burst out laughing. "For the sake of honesty, you didn't seduce me. I seduced you."

Clare was shaking her head and advancing on him suddenly. "No way. I had a plan, and I implemented it to perfection." When his eyes twinkled with a wicked mirth, she stopped.

Dev had no idea how she continually opened doors he didn't want to see through. But she did. "Of course, you had a plan." He shook his head, laughing. Remembering how she'd taken the chance he'd given her. How she'd neatly cornered him into a fascinating conversation and then a whole lot more.

"Why do anything without doing it well?"

He met her gaze again. But Clare looked away, as if that one moment of honesty had been indulgent enough. Reality intruded on them, bursting the bubble of awareness.

Clare knew she should be glad. But there was something about this man that made her not only feel hot and bothered but also naive and foolish. "Anyway, that night's done with. We need to move on from it."

But even now, as she studied his hard jaw, there was a part of her—that foolish part again—that wished he'd tell her that despite what he'd said to her that morning, he'd actually wanted to take her in his arms again. That he'd wanted to see her again afterward.

"Do I have your word that this won't become awkward between us?" he asked, interrupting her reverie with a nice heaping dose of reality.

"Of course you do," she said with extra vehemence. "I told you the reason I snuck in here. And now we've cleared that up, I can absolutely assure you I have no romantic notions whatsoever about you, Mr. Kohli. However, not hiring my company to clean up your image just because we slept together is its own kind of…"

His frown turned into a ferocious scowl. "What?"

"Unfairness," she said, amending her words. "Our sexual

history shouldn't affect my career, Mr. Kohli. I shouldn't be penalized for going to bed with you."

"I agree with that a hundred percent," he said, releasing a sigh. He clasped his jaw in his palm, tension radiating from his frame. And then he looked at her. Clare braced herself. "You'll have to forgive me if I'm being extra distrustful of everyone right now," he said honestly, taking the wind from her sails yet again.

"I understand."

They eyed each other carefully—not exactly adversaries, but not friends either. But… Clare couldn't help thinking there was also a certain level of trust between them, even though he'd tried to be all cold and calculating about his decision to work with her. How could there not be a certain warmth between them when they'd been as intimate as they had? When whatever had pulled them together was still tangibly in the air, crackling into life every time they were within touching distance?

She might not have a whole lot of experience with men. But she knew what desire looked like on this particular man's face. She knew him a lot better than he thought, or she liked.

"I promise you that you won't regret taking me on, Mr. Kohli. I'll have my proposal ready for you by first thing tomorrow morning."

Dev shook his head. "Let's make it a bit later in the day. I have a lot of things to get through tomorrow. Why don't you at least take the morning off?"

"And do what?" She looked so dumbstruck by the suggestion that Dev laughed.

"Just lounge about. Recover from the stress of fleeing that man. Take a bath. Catch up on sleep. We'll meet later tomorrow afternoon some time when I'm free."

She nodded. But he knew it was a reluctant acquiescence. "Okay."

Dev stepped aside to let her pass. When she reached the doorway, he called her name, feeling a strange tightness in his chest.

"Yes, Mr. Kohli?" she said, her gaze steady.

"If you want my help getting out of this predicament you've landed yourself in, I'll need the entire truth from you."

And just as Dev had expected, she colored immediately, confirming his suspicions. He knew there had been something wrong with her story.

Her gaze turned stubborn. "There's nothing more to say. I trusted a man I shouldn't have. I…let my heart rule my head and made a stupid decision. I'm willing to help you clean up your mess. All I ask is that you give me a little time to clean up mine."

Dev had never met a woman who could turn the tables on him so well. And she was right. He knew firsthand the price of letting one's guard down. The price of fighting your battles alone. "Fine. We're partners, Ms. Roberts."

"Perfect, Mr. Kohli. You'll see you're right to trust me in this."

With that parting shot, she walked out of his cabin. Confirming his second suspicion that Clare Roberts was anything but the uncomplicated woman he'd thought her to be when he'd taken her to his bed.

CHAPTER FOUR

DURING THE TIME until their meeting—which to Clare felt like an eternity, since she'd been working without a break ever since she'd graduated from university—she explored Dev's gigantic superyacht. She couldn't help but be impressed, even though she'd teased him about the sheer size of it.

Even if she hadn't already known it after their night together, the more she researched his company, and the man himself, the more Clare learned that Dev Kohli didn't have any need whatsoever to prove his masculinity to anyone. So his yacht, other than being a supreme symbol of his success and stamina, was definitely not just a possession to be strutted in front of the world.

In a perverse way, it would have been so much easier to deal with the man if he'd neatly fitted into a preconceived mold.

Playboy—only cares about bedding women, not keeping them safe from evil henchmen.

Billionaire—cares about nothing except making his next billion.

Playboy billionaire—balding, beer-bellied old man with no humor lurking in his brilliant brown eyes.

But it seemed the man was a trendsetter in this too.

Following his advice, Clare had indulged herself last night with a long soak in the huge tub in her cabin's en suite bathroom, consciously reminding herself that she was safe. For now. At least from external events and Mafia villains. Physically, she was safe.

Emotionally…well, she'd survived for years on indifference, using her big dreams to propel her forward. And that's what she was going to do now too—turn this calamity into an opportunity and move forward with nothing but sheer determination.

Simply because there was no other choice except survival. If she had to be on the run, she'd prefer it to be on the luxury yacht of a man she trusted.

Snuggled in a thick robe that dragged on the lush carpet under her feet, she'd arrived in her bedroom to find hot soup and warm, crusty tomato and cheese sandwiches. Luckily, no one had been around to hear the loud growl her stomach had emitted. She'd tucked herself into another window seat that offered a gorgeous nighttime view of the blue ocean and finished her bedtime snack in a matter of seconds.

Digitally blacked out windows and cool, dark navy-blue furnishings had helped her fall asleep in minutes, all thoughts of kidnapping villains dissolving like mist.

When she'd jerked awake the next morning, warm in the nest of soft bedclothes, Clare realized she'd slept for ten hours straight—a miracle in itself. Not counting how normal and in control she felt after another quick shower.

Clearheaded and alert for the first time in days, she wished she'd done her hiding in a different bedroom and not faced Dev yesterday, when she'd been afraid for her life. She'd made a right little numpty of herself.

She hadn't built The London Connection by acting like a witless fool or a dreamy-eyed twit. The future of her company was even more paramount now than it had been before. Since, thanks to her father, she apparently owed a huge amount of money to a mobster. There was no margin for messing this up with Dev. She needed to keep her focus on it being all business between them, as he'd said.

Ten hours of sleep did wonders for a girl. The stern talking-to she gave herself as she blow-dried her hair boosted her confidence. She made do with the lip-gloss, concealer and mascara in her handbag.

Having enveloped herself in another thick towel, she spent the next twenty minutes, looking through the large but mostly vacant closet attached to her cabin. Luckily, she, Amy, Bea all made it a policy to carry spare underwear and all kinds of paraphernalia in their bags for any PR emergency. But she had no clothes.

As she eyed the almost empty wardrobe, she thought of her travel bag sitting in her hotel room in São Paulo, now all but lost. There was no way she could have sneaked it past security onto the yacht last night. For a few seconds, she indulged in the idea of wearing last night's skirt and blouse again. But then she remembered that before she'd got into that lovely warm bath, she'd dropped them into the conveniently placed laundry basket, which was now, of course, empty.

Apparently, the man's yacht ran as efficiently as his sportswear empire.

In the end, Clare ripped the packaging off one of Dev's dress shirts. Apparently, the man had designer dress shirts lying around in all the cabins. Savile Row deserved better, but she didn't care right then. Thinking for too long on why she was here on a stranger's yacht, sailing away to some idyllic island with her company's fate and her own hanging in the balance might lead to falling into the pit of despair and fury she was somehow keeping at bay.

With the shirt hanging almost to her knees, Clare used a belt and turned it into a dress. Back on went her leather stilettos, and she looked halfway decent. Or at least that's what she told herself.

After getting lost in a service elevator and ending up in a theater room, and discovering a neatly stowed away seaplane on the top deck, it began to dawn on Clare that the yacht was also the man's home. And that while he had invited her to explore, it had been mostly a polite response to a distressed and wild-tale-weaving woman he'd found in his closet. Not the welcome mat precisely.

With each space she invaded, it became clearer that he was a man who absolutely protected his privacy at all costs. Because for all the features in the media detailing his jet-setting life and fast girlfriends, no journalist had ever been allowed access to this yacht.

This was where Dev Kohli, former gold-medal-winning swimmer and billionaire playboy, retreated to when the alternately adoring and punishing world's media became all too much.

Like the man himself, while the exterior was all gleaming confidence, the interior had depths she couldn't plumb in a year, much less a day. There was none of the gold accents and veneer, or the traditional nautical motifs she'd imagined from peeking at antiquated travel magazines her dentist had lying around the office.

Up and down, Clare went, fascinated by it all. After getting lost again, she armed herself with a schematic map and a picnic basket from the galley—apparently, they had been given express instructions to look after Mr. Kohli's guest properly—and shamelessly explored the yacht.

Admiring this example of twenty-first-century engineering was definitely better than pondering one's fate as an owned woman. Or even worse, daydreaming about a man's happy trail. In the end, Clare settled into a lounger on the main deck, her picnic basket by her side, her laptop on her knee. The noonday sun glinted off the water in brilliant golden sparkles, while colorful coastal towns were visible in the distance.

If a man was disposed to moving from place to place, disinclined to put roots down…then clearly, Dev Kohli did it in style.

But, she mused, if all this wealth was at her disposal, the last place she'd want to be was on the sea. There was a temporariness to moving from place to place that didn't appeal to Clare. Even having been disillusioned again and again by her dad's unending lies over the years, that he would come for her and that they would be a family again, and by her aunt's indifference toward her, Clare had always wanted a permanent home.

A grand home and an even grander family of noisy sisters and brothers and nieces and nephews, celebrating birthdays and festivals together, prying into each other's business and making up after silly fights and all that sort of thing.

But with each year rolling around and her dad not show-ing up, it had become increasingly distant. Then he'd given her the money she'd used to start up her business, just be-fore he died. She'd thought he would have been proud to know she'd used the money so well, but even that daydream had turned sour. Because the man her father had borrowed that money from had finally discovered her father was dead and couldn't pay it back, and so he'd come after Clare.

She was truly alone in the world and couldn't escape the knowledge that to put her in such danger, her father had never really cared for her at all.

She still couldn't wrap her head around that bit of news. Couldn't get her jumbled feelings to make any kind of sense. They just sat in the pit of her stomach like a knot-ted lump. For years, a foolish part of her had believed that he'd somehow turn into an ideal father one day. When he'd sent her the money, she'd thought her faith in him had fi-nally been validated. That he had loved her in his own way.

But once again, she'd lied to herself.

Her laptop screen blurred in front of her eyes and Clare blinked hard.

No, she couldn't let the past muddle her future. Her vision cleared when she saw a social media photo turn up in her search results. She stared at the tall, gorgeous brunette—a model, of course, who had just revealed her... association with Dev. Clare's mind instantly did a quick calculation of whether she herself had come before or after this model, in his life.

The very idea of being just another night of transient pleasure to him grated on her nerves. But that was who he was. Dev Kohli was clearly allergic to relationships that lasted longer than a couple of weeks—if that.

She'd do well to remember that simple fact.

Pursing her lips, Clare added a bullet point to the list of things she needed to discuss with him.

It was going to take all the finesse she possessed to make sure Dev understood what he needed to do. So Clare once again pushed away the sorrow and grief that was crouching inside her chest and instead poured her energy into outlining the proposal for saving Athleta.

Focusing on her business, on tangible targets and not naive dreams, had always been her lifeline.

Clare blinked and opened her eyes as a short man in a pristine black-and-white uniform informed her that Mr. Kohli was waiting to see her now in his study. She sat up and straightened her shirt, aghast at the fact that she'd fallen asleep again after only a few hours' work. God, what sort of strange inertia and exhaustion had her in its grip?

Before the uniformed man disappeared to wherever it was that people seemed to hide on the monstrous yacht, she begged him to point her in the direction of the study.

Even with his instructions, it took her ages to find her way to there. It seemed the very universe was constantly conspiring to make her look unprofessional in front of the one man she wanted to impress with her smarts and sophistication and efficiency.

Laptop and a folder in hand, Clare walked into an expansive circular room with a dizzyingly high ceiling. Light filtered through the skylight in the center of it, casting a golden glow over the floor-to-ceiling shelves of books. Rows and rows of books were filed with almost military precision. Clare let out a soft sigh, the idea of spending hours and hours lost in the library in this study would be pure heaven to her.

The sound of a throat clearing jerked her attention away from the world of rare first editions.

In a sunken seating area, in the midst of the airy space, was Dev. Looking for all intents and purposes like a king sitting amid his priceless treasures. Except his treasures, it seemed, were books. Clare instantly knew that this space was different from everywhere else on the yacht. That this room somehow reflected his true nature. That if she wanted to know more about Dev Kohli—the real man beneath the billionaire playboy persona—this was where she would find him.

Not that it was something she did want, she told herself.

Still, she felt a totally unnecessary and unbidden spark of excitement at being given a view of his inner sanctum that he hadn't allowed anyone else.

Dressed in black trousers and a white dress shirt that was unbuttoned at his throat, he looked elegant and masculine and somehow edgy at the same time. His carefully cut hair was rumpled and not quite perfect today. He reminded Clare of a restless predator she'd once seen on a documentary. As if there was a constant hum of energy beneath that sleek brown skin and taut muscles. As if at any moment, he might leap up from the beige leather sofa and launch himself into...

"Ms. Roberts?"

The deep timbre of his voice made Clare start. "Yes, Mr. Kohli?" she replied tartly, irritated with her own wool-gathering. Neither did she miss the affected formality in the way he said her name.

"I asked if you were unwell." His gaze swept over her face and body. Had been doing so for a while, she realized. From her hair to the shirt—his shirt that she'd styled into a dress—to the belt and stilettos, he took in every little detail about her. She felt the quick scrutiny like a warm caress, pooling in places she didn't want to think about right now. "We can do this another time if you're still feeling the effects of—"

"Of course not. I'm perfectly fine. Thank you for asking." Her response sounded chillingly polite to her own ears. A bit too chilly, in contrast to the laid-back humor she saw in his eyes.

Suddenly, she had a feeling that he'd caught her napping on the main deck. Her chin lolling against her chest, with drool pooling at the side of her mouth, most probably.

"I've been ready for this meeting for a while." She sighed. "Only I had no idea how to reach you or any other human on this boat. "Did you get a chance to look at the initial contracts I emailed you?"

"No, it will take me to time to get to them. And it's a yacht, not a boat."

"On this oversized yacht," she parroted obediently, something under her skin humming awake at the twitch of that gorgeous mouth. The man often seemed to be on the verge of laughing. At the world, instead of with it, she suspected. And then of course, that thought led her to unwisely mutter, "Are you laughing at me, Mr. Kohli?"

He shook his head, but the mirth in his eyes remained. "Should I find something funny about this?"

"No. That's what I meant to point out. Nothing about this predicament is funny and yet—"

"Of course it's not. But you have to afford me some allowances when you turn up here, your nose high in the air, determined to find something or other about me to disapprove of."

"That's not at all what I was thinking," she hotly denied.

"Then tell me what is it that you don't like about my yacht," he asked, surprising her yet again.

"What's there to not like?" she retorted, trying to keep her tone steady. Dev was so dangerous in how easily he could read her thoughts. "Like I said, it's big and beautiful."

"And yet, you just called it oversized, implying it's ostentatious."

"That was uncalled for," she said, forcing regret into her voice. Why did the man care so much what she thought of his damned yacht?

"I sense that you don't usually make uncalled-for statements, Ms. Roberts. Or that you say anything at all unless you mean it."

Their gazes held, his probing and lazily amused and hers…resisting the pull of his. It seems she was always resisting something or other about this man. Except the one time she'd stopped resisting and given in to desire, it had been glorious. She desperately hoped she wasn't wearing the jumble of her thoughts openly on her face.

"You're right, of course," she said, acquiescing. *Pick your battles, Clare*, came something that sounded very much like Bea's voice in her head. "It just seems like a lot of room for only one man."

"Ahh…you're going to lecture me about the environment and such? In my meager defense, I do travel with two personal assistants, three lawyers, a personal trainer and stylist, two chefs and a variety of other personnel—"

"Who I'm sure all contribute toward the larger-than-life image of you that mere mortal men can only aspire to."

"There it is again, Ms. Roberts." He raised an eyebrow. "That faint whiff of disapproval."

"Even though I've had a glimpse into the jet-setting life-styles of certain celebrities while I've been working, I still find myself in awe of how much social media conceals from our eyes. How one-dimensional we want our celebrities to be. Nothing personal, Mr. Kohli."

His brows drew close as he regarded her thoughtfully, no quick response forming on that gorgeous mouth. That she had surprised him was clear by the sudden silence. But the buzz under her skin that was still there regardless of what he said or did...she so badly wished she could completely smother that involuntary reaction to him.

"You sound disappointed in me." He sounded comically confused. As if it was impossible for any woman to not delight in him!

"Something like that," she said, thankful that he was so far off the mark. It wouldn't do to cater to his giant ego. She had to keep this attraction purely inside her own head. "So you have a veritable army of servants," she said, refusing to let him unsettle her with that silent scrutiny, "who are of course paid to be neither seen nor heard. I can be forgiven, I think, for imagining us to be practically alone on board."

He ran a hand through his hair, looking slightly un-comfortable.

She scrunched her nose. "I wasn't actually intending to lecture you, you know."

"No?"

"I read the interview you did a while ago for that lifestyle magazine. You run a billion-dollar empire that has offices in five different countries. You have eleven thousand three hundred and seventy-six employees around the world. Not counting the personnel you employ here on the yacht and across the two flats, three estates and one palace you have dotted around. What was it that you said...you've created *'an economy all on its own'*? So all of this luxury is simply a place to rest for a man who gives livelihoods to so many. You called it your kingdom. And you said your mother taught you that a king has both duties and privileges. That was a nice personal touch," she added dryly.

"What, that I have duties and privileges?"

"No, mentioning your mother."

A hardness entered his eyes that transformed his face from having an easy charm to a powerful remoteness. "It wasn't scripted to manipulate my audience, Ms. Roberts." His voice could cut through ice.

Clare nodded pacifyingly. Clearly, his family was a sore topic of conversation. She braced herself for the battle ahead. He wasn't going to like her plan one bit if he was ruffled at the mention of an old interview in which he'd referenced his mother.

"I never said there wasn't any truth to your interview." She eyed him as he sprawled on the circular leather sofa, surveying her with those long-lashed eyes. "You certainly do live like a king, Mr. Kohli."

One arm stretched along the sofa. The folded cuffs of his white shirt displayed a smattering of faint hair over strong forearms. Everything about the man was clean lines and masculine elegance. "You remember a lot about that interview."

Clare tried to not bristle at the inherent teasing in his tone. "I've always had a good memory for details. And it was clear that journalist came to you with an agenda."

"What do you think that might have been?"

"To lump you in with the current crop of spoiled, rich billionaires who don't give a damn about the state of the world. And you disarmed her very easily."

Far too easily, if you asked her. There was a unique

quality about Dev—and she didn't just mean his astonishingly good looks—that put women at ease with him. But an inherently welcoming sense of safety and fairness he extended, probably without knowing it himself.

Of course, he wasn't a saint by any means. He rarely dated anyone more than a few times, but Clare didn't blame any woman for succumbing to the fantasy of being this man's lover. Of hoping that she might be the only woman he wanted in his bed, the only woman he allowed into his life. And heart.

Which was definitely a fantasy, all right. But she…she was made of sterner stuff. More importantly, she'd already had her one fantasy night with him, which was apparently all he was going to deign to allow her.

"So what is it in particular that you don't like about the yacht? Or was it just me who riled you up when you walked in just now?"

"I just…fine, yes, it's a lovely yacht. Airy and light—and don't think I haven't noticed in the information brochures about how it's built with recycled wood and other environmentally friendly materials. But it seems so empty."

"Empty?" he said, his gaze shifting to encompass the furniture around them.

"It's just a personal thing."

His elbows dropping to his thighs, he leaned forward invitingly. "Tell me."

"All this wealth on open display…it seems counterintuitive to what we're all supposed to be pursuing, isn't it?"

He frowned. "And what is that?"

"Happiness. Peace. A place to belong."

"And you think that's what we're all looking for?" He didn't sound quite put off by her opinion, but it was clear that he didn't like it much either.

"You did insist on hearing my explanation, Mr. Kohli," she said pointedly. "I just meant that it feels somewhat isolated. Designed to be cut off from the world. The home of a man who doesn't want to put down any roots."

A bleakness entered his eyes then, and Clare was sure she'd crossed some imaginary boundary she shouldn't have. Trespassed where she wasn't invited, much less wanted.

"Ahh…then it's a good thing that you don't know me quite as well as you think you do," he said, that momentary vulnerability disappearing with a slow, lazy blink.

"I quite disagree," she added, something inside her pushing her on. "The thing is, I've spent quite a few hours recently deep diving into your life, and what's in the media does paint quite a cold, clinical picture of you. Flashy affairs that end faster than people change their car tires and business deal upon business deal where you always emerge the winner. In fact, you appear to lead what looks to the outsider like a very…solitary, selfish kind of life."

"So you're telling me you don't approve of my lifestyle?"

"Not at all," Clare retorted. "I admit that I do try to avoid men who tend to forge their own path and leave people behind along the way, yes, but this isn't about me. There's a world of difference between what you've allowed the world to see and what you're really like beneath all that shine and glamor."

"Despite your…deep dive—" his distaste for the term couldn't be clearer and his nostrils flared with a rare show of temper "—into my life, you still don't really know me. I'm not interested in pursuing all those things you mentioned. Why tie yourself to one place when instead you can have the freedom to explore the entire world?" He moved his hand between them dismissively, as if the things she mentioned were totally unimportant. "Belonging anywhere is overrated, Ms. Roberts. The only time the world listens to you is when you dictate to it. On your own terms."

He was drawing clear boundaries, and it would be wise for her to follow them. And yet she couldn't help feeling this impression he was giving right now, of a man who wanted to conquer the entire world, was just a mask he was putting on.

A facade he had to display in public.

But whether her suspicions were true or not, it wasn't her business, Clare reminded herself. The man was telling her who and what he was, and she should stop searching for qualities in him that weren't present. She'd done this with her dad too. Year after year, she'd convinced herself that he would come back for her one day. When the truth was, he'd barely even bothered ringing her on her birthday or at Christmas.

Clare gave her assent with a nod. "Fine, Mr. Kohli. As you say."

"Toeing the line now, Clare?"

She shrugged. "It's not my job to moralize to you, is it? It's to make you look perfect in front of the world. To give this shiny veneer of yours a human element. And for the most part, I'm glad to have followed my instinct about you."

"Which instinct is that?"

Clare lost her patience. "That you aren't the villain the world is calling you, Mr. Kohli," she said sweetly.

He grinned. "So how are you going to improve my image? And for heaven's sake, please can you stop calling me Mr. Kohli in that prissy voice?"

"Fine. Your love life…it's a trail of broken hearts and short affairs that don't paint a homely picture of you."

"I didn't realize we were trying to find me a bride."

Clare rolled her eyes. "This isn't funny, Dev. For example, did you know that one of your exes, Sahara Jones, has taken to posting old pics of you and her on her social media this past week? Apparently, your breakup three months ago didn't suit her. She's got seven and a half million rabid followers who're all dying to know if you're back together as she's been hinting at and who'll turn into an angry mob at just one word from her. Is Ms. Jones going to brew more trouble for you in the coming weeks?"

"What do you mean?" he asked, surprisingly slow for a man who'd cut such a swathe through the worlds of competitive sport and then business with a dangerously irresistible combination of charm and smarts.

"Is she the type to drag your name through the mud? Plaster private information about you all over social media and make you look horrible? Because, right now, your reputation can't take any more hits."

"Of course not."

"And yet I'll point out that she was here on board your yacht last night—I recognized her. Presumably she was there without your knowledge?"

"You miss nothing," he said, jaw tight. Grudgingly.

"I don't. Neither did I miss that you had her escorted out by security with very little ceremony and that she didn't look very happy about it. So details, please."

"Excuse me?"

"I need details of your breakup so that I can gauge the possible consequences for myself."

His muttered something under his breath. "Sahara and I dated for just over two weeks. I ended our relationship, such as it was, when I realized she had no intention of respecting my privacy.

"On our second date, she sprung some talk show host on me so that we could both discuss all the disadvantages we'd each had to overcome to succeed. She was in talks with her agent about writing a book about our relationship. As you know, she's a model, but not massively famous and she had to jump through a lot of hoops to get there."

"And?" Clare prompted.

"She thought she'd ride the wave to stardom with me as her golden ticket. But I wasn't interested in a woman who was trying to probe into aspects of my life that were none of her business."

"What kind of salacious details did she manage to uncover?"

His jaw tightened. "There were no salacious details, Clare. She had no business thinking she could sell my life story as some romantic journey we were on together. I told my lawyers to sue her if she so much as whispers anything about me again. After the show she put on last time, she was fired from her latest contract. She was here last night to convince me that it had never been her idea in the first place. To help her land a different contract."

"Are you going to help her?"

Dev rubbed a hand over his face and sighed. "Yes. I'm not a callous bastard, Clare. I've already put her in touch with a friend of mine. Even though Sahara should've known better than to drag me into her drama."

"So I should count the matter as being resolved for now?"

"Yes."

"Why?"

"How do I know she won't create more trouble?" The frost in his eyes sent a small shiver down her spine. "Because she got what she wanted from me."

Clare nodded, biting back the question that lingered on her lips. "Can I suggest then, Dev, that until we make sure the world is firmly on your side, that you give up…women?"

The dratted man laughed. A full-bodied, rollicking kind of laugh that made her breath hitch in her throat. That transformed his face from a collection of perfectly symmetrical features to something altogether beautiful. A dimple sliced the hollow of his cheek and his eyes shone. "I don't think I've ever been ordered around quite so strictly in my life."

"Not even by your mother?" Clare added, enjoying the beauty of his smile and the warm fuzzies it aroused in her belly far too much.

He sobered instantly, but the warmth in his eyes lingered. "No. Not even by Mama. Not even when I made her life hell. Not even when I frustrated her no end and caused her grief." He gave a sigh that seemed to rock through the solid core of him. "My mother was one of those souls that was all love and patience and kindness itself."

"The point is," Clare said, wanting to chase away the shadows that crossed his face at the mention of his lovely sounding mother, "that when it comes down to it, hiring me to clean up your image is exactly like being in school with a very strict headmistress. This might never work if you balk at every—"

"Ah… I can see now why your company's so successful, Clare."

"Can you?" she said, having forgotten what she was going to say.

"I have no problem whatsoever imagining you as a strict headmistress."

He delivered it very tongue-in-cheek, his dark eyes full of an easy geniality. Clare couldn't blame him for teasing her, but she still flushed all over at his comment. She took a deep breath, hoping a fresh burst of oxygen would clear the miasma of longing that seemed to take over her brain and body.

A timely reminder to herself that Dev wasn't really the hero she was making him out to be in her head.

"I'm not going to apologize every time I have to advise you about your…sex life. In fact, to be on the safe side, I'd say, just don't have any. For a good, long while," she added feeling perversely petty.

Clare had never thought of herself as wicked, but the idea of policing Dev's sex life—because clearly the man was as distrustful of love as she was—filled her with delight. Whoever said there was a silver lining to every cloud was absolutely right.

CHAPTER FIVE

"EXCUSE ME? Did you actually order me to curtail my sex life?" Dev repeated her words, even though he'd heard her perfectly well. More importantly, he also agreed with her 100 percent.

The last thing he wanted or needed right now was to get embroiled with another woman.

He should have expected Sahara to show up after she'd told him she was in São Paulo. To network, she'd said, citing a renowned photographer that Dev was friends with. He had felt a little sorry for her when she'd lost her contract. But he couldn't help wondering if she'd felt anything for him at all. Or had he simply been a rich, powerful, good-looking walking, talking cardboard cutout of a man for her to drape herself over?

Can you blame her for that? a voice whispered inside his head. *When it's exactly what you want from your flings, when you pursue exactly the kind of woman who has no interest in you except your sexual prowess, your fame and your money?*

"Yes, I did," declared the woman in front of him, dragging his attention away from the kind of thoughts he hated. Conscience-stirring thoughts that made a man weak and useless if he listened to them too much.

Clare continued. "As horrendously novel as this might seem to you, I'm the boss of you right now, Dev, until we fix this scandal and your image. Until we show the world that you're a wonderful, conscientious man who cares about women in the workplace, especially yours. I should decide who you see, who you talk to and who you kiss..." she declared, looking diminutive and delicate and decidedly ignoring the pink blush that crept up her neck.

Although there was nothing delicate about the steel in her words or the way she radiated a sort of resolute competence.

Even as she looked ridiculously cute in a makeshift dress styled from his shirt and belt. She was so much shorter than him that the hem of the shirt, thankfully, reached her knees.

Dev moved until he was standing at the foot of the few steps to the sunken seating area while she stood at the top. Her face still only came level with his, just. The wide-open collar of the shirt betrayed the rapidly fluttering pulse at the base of her neck. A prickle of awareness hummed to life under his skin. He studied the sharp curve of her jaw, the straightness of her nose and the blue shadows under her eyes that made them sparkle even more.

Her hair, cut precisely to enhance the line of her jaw, looked decidedly rumpled right now. His mouth twitched at the thought of the ever professional and polished Ms. Roberts sputtering away at the indignity of not being able to don the mask of ruthless efficiency she usually portrayed.

Once he'd had confirmation that there were some truly dangerous men chasing her—his head of security had even mentioned talk of a bounty on her head—he'd felt an immediate urgency to ensure for himself that Clare, with her larger than life smile and prickly demands, was kept safe from harm.

So instead of waiting any longer, he'd gone in search of her. And stared at her sleeping form for a full ten minutes like a horny teenager who was gazing at his first crush.

She'd looked so fragile napping on the main deck, her mouth soft and lush in repose. Except Dev never normally felt the need to pursue women. Not since he'd shot up to his height of six-two at the age of sixteen. They'd done all the chasing.

And he wasn't going to begin now.

It was just that there was something deliciously delightful about riling up Clare Roberts for the simple fact that her blue eyes widened and her lovely little mouth gaped and a myriad of expressions crossed her equally beautiful face. All the while she processed her frantic thoughts and inevitably arrived at an affected indifference that even she herself didn't quite buy.

"So you're going to be like a twenty-first-century chastity belt," he added.

She scrunched her cute nose at the thought, reminding him of a proud, pretty little bird sticking its beak up into the air. But Dev didn't miss the quick sweep of her gaze over his lower abdominal region, as if wondering how such a contraption would work on him.

His nether regions, suitably impressed by her avid perusal, perked up with interest.

"Not quite, but if it helps you get the idea, I say run with the image."

Dev grinned. "I think you're taking your role in my life too far," he added, holding up his hand for her.

After a few seconds' hesitation, she took it. A jolt of sensation clamped him instantly, the memory of those delicate fingers tentatively exploring his body sneaking upon him suddenly. He let go of her hand as soon as her stiletto-clad feet hit the carpet.

"I'm absolutely not. Rich playboy billionaires are just as accountable to the verdict of the masses as we normal people are, thanks to the power of social media. Even a hint of one more scandal right now could be enough to start a domino effect. Believe me, Dev, if there's one thing I know, it's how to manage reputations."

"Fine, I'll try not to attract too many women. Especially if I have to disappoint them with a no access message to—" he moved his hand over his chest "—all this."

Just as he expected, her blue eyes widened and her lush mouth gasped with indignation.

"Shall we get back to the business at hand?" she asked pointedly, her chin lifting.

"Absolutely," Dev said, grinning.

Celibacy might not be such a hard concept with the enchanting Ms. Roberts to entertain him. Clare was so full of complexities that Dev couldn't help but be amused by her. As he settled down on the opposite side of the couch from her, he knew that she was precisely the right woman to fix both his personal image and that of his company.

To bring Athleta back onto the right path.

For all that he'd occasionally caught her gazing at him with a flash of desire, he believed that she would be all business. He could trust her. Dev had known that, even the first night he'd met her at the charity gala. Like all the big decisions he'd taken in life, he'd gone with his gut on that one.

It was why he'd broken his own rule and taken an unknown woman to his bed. Why he'd indulged himself so thoroughly when—despite all the spectacular stories the press wrote about his supposed indiscreet affairs with any woman he pleased—he never usually gave into his desires with such little forethought.

And while Clare fixed his image problem, he was determined to take a good hard look at the choices he'd been making for the last fifteen years.

That the man he'd trusted the most had been able to abuse not only Dev's trust but that of a woman in his employ was a direct consequence of the choices Dev had made years ago, while at military school.

Fueled by resentment and rejection, he'd set a goal for himself. And in the pursuit of that goal, he'd become bed-fellows with a number of men whose principles he didn't always agree with.

Now he had achieved success and wealth beyond his wildest dreams. Maybe enough to even impress his arrogant father, with his ridiculously extravagant expectations for his children. As if they were all trophies and achievements to be polished and put on display instead of breathing, living people with flaws and dreams of their own.

And yet Dev had to admit to himself that somewhere along the path he'd chosen for himself, he'd lost his way.

He'd surrounded himself with people who courted success and wealth while trading in their principles. That had never been him—whether in his personal life or in business.

Which meant this was his chance to find the right path this time—he'd continue to build Athleta into the biggest and best sports brand in the world, but he wasn't going to do that at the cost of losing himself.

"What else is in your plan," he said, nodding at the glossy folder she held in her hands, "other than curtailing my…"

"…extracurricular activities?" Clare finished his sentence, picking up the thread of the conversation again. "Yes, of course."

She had no idea why she was this flustered. Dev wasn't even a difficult client. She'd had to put up with much worse, especially before The London Connection had yet to build the solid reputation it had now. And yet it was only Dev who again and again, tripped her circuits, for want of a better term.

Dev leaned back into the luxury leather seat, a devilish glint in his eyes.

"Right…" Clare opened her laptop and clicked onto the notes file she'd prepared earlier. "I'm just going to pull up this spreadsheet I created of the assets and liabilities we have to work with."

At that, he got up and took the seat next to her. The couch she was sitting on was large enough to provide ample space between them, and yet it felt as if the very air she was breathing was charged with the vitality of the man.

It took Clare a few seconds to focus on the list in front of her. She cleared her throat and then caught him trying to peek at her spreadsheet. "There aren't any secrets here, Dev."

"Oh, I know that. But it's interesting to see one's life so neatly reduced to two columns. I'm especially curious about the liabilities list."

Clare rolled her eyes. And thanked the universe for giving her the sense to remove that list from this sheet. "Don't worry. I'll handle your masculine sensibilities delicately. I know a thing or two about the male ego."

He laughed at that and the sound enveloped Clare. "Absolutely not, Ms. Roberts. Since you have curtailed any and all of my usual entertainments, this could be the only highlight of my week. Or even the month."

"What?"

"Getting dressed down by you for all my various sins."

Clare bared her teeth in a mockery of a smile. "No one was more disappointed than me at the blatant lack of those sins. I might have to write to the ruthless playboy billionaire club and have your title revoked. Instead of shadows of shady deals, all I could find was a veritable halo, which just needs a little polish." Clare didn't wait for him deny it. "We need to shine a light on the charity programs and drives that are sponsored by Athleta."

That mobile mouth narrowed into a straight line. "I don't give to various charities for publicity," he announced in an almost regal way. As if he expected it to be the beginning and end of the matter.

Clare frowned. Usually, with most of her clients—those with either old money or new—she had to work very hard to convince them that not every small bit of charity was something that could be used for PR. "Whether you give all these large amounts of money," she said, pointing a manicured nail at the figures, "for publicity or not doesn't matter anymore. The pertinent fact is that you do. *Give*, that is. Believe it or not, Dev, you're going to be one of my easiest clients."

With his arm snaked over the back of the couch, and his long legs stretched in front of him, she couldn't help thinking he reclined like a maharaja. The corners of his mouth twitched and that dimple—that damned dimple of his—winked at her again. "I do believe that that is the highest compliment you've ever paid me."

Clare snorted. "Don't go strutting around just yet. But, yes, it is. I don't have to manufacture reasons to show you in a good light. Or convince you that your charity work needs to be more than just a sop to your conscience. I've closely followed Athleta's charity work. It's why I wanted to work with you."

"You have made it more than clear that it's only the job that's important to you, Clare. For the record, I'm no longer under any kind of misconception that you hid yourself on my yacht to seduce me."

Clare couldn't quite meet his gaze then. Knowing that he would see how horribly she was still attracted to him. Not that he probably didn't know.

Still there was a difference between him guessing and being given that information explicitly. "The world needs to know that Athleta is not rotten all the way through. That you, at the core of it, are still sound. That it was just one limb that was diseased and you quickly cut it off."

Any hint of humor disappeared from his face. "And I

also severed everything that limb influenced," he retorted instantly. "Isn't that enough?"

Clare gentled her voice. Not just to appease the hint of bitterness she heard in his tone but because she understood where it was coming from. There was something very deep and complex going on with him, however much she wanted to continue believing that he was nothing but another shallow pool. "Would you give your trust back to someone once it was broken so easily?"

He looked away, his jaw tight. But as she'd known already, Dev was a man who faced the truth, always. Whether it painted him in a good light or not. Hand pushing roughly through his hair, he turned to face her, his dark brown gaze full of shadows that she couldn't see past. "No. I would never give my trust back once it was lost."

She'd meant to persuade him that it was going to take time and a little effort to convince the public, because he'd already, and had always done, the things that mattered most for a company's image anyway. But the vehemence with which he talked about his trust being broken… It found an answering echo within Clare.

"The various charities you give to—girls' education and empowerment through Asia, funding learning disabilities research in the US, youth scholarships for inner city kids… All these are things you and your company should be enormously proud of. It's not enough to do good, Dev. Especially now. It's also necessary to set an example. All the public normally sees is that you're basically living a life of extravagance and luxury and that you're this hot, athletic, aspirational figure that every average Joe wants to be and that every average Jane wants to be with."

Clare patiently waited for his laughter to subside. It wasn't a hardship because the man was insanely beautiful, and she was no better than the average Jane she'd just mentioned.

"You have such a way with words, Clare. You're very good for a man's ego."

Clare shook her head. "I'm not pandering to your ego at all. I'm trying to tell you that it's time to show people, especially your female employees, that you're more than some oversexed playboy billionaire."

He winced. "Oversexed playboy billionaire...is that how you see me?"

Clare pursed her lips. Did the man intend to jump on every little thing she said? "How I see you doesn't matter at all. We're going to drip feed as much information about Athleta's various charity activities as we can. Take this recent visit to São Paulo, for example. What the world thinks is you're here to party with some rowdy friends of yours. And yet I know you came here to work with a designer who uses recyclable materials for a new kind of sole for running shoes and that you attended a conference that's addressing the preservation of the rain forest."

"You really have done your research," Dev replied, surprise in his tone.

Clare felt a pang of satisfaction. "I told you, I'm very thorough when it comes to my job. The next item on the agenda... We need to do an interview with Ms. Jones," she said, mentioning the woman who'd exposed the harassment at Athleta with enormous courage.

"That's out of the question." Dev looked as if someone had punched him. "I'm not going to hound the poor woman into giving a statement just to make myself look better in front of the world."

Clare leaned forward, determined to persuade him to see reason. "But what if she agrees? What if—"

"You've already contacted her, haven't you?"

Clare stilled at the outraged look in his eyes. "I'm not going to apologize for doing my job."

He sighed. "Fine. But I don't want Ms. Jones to be pressured in any way that she's not comfortable with. She's been through enough. Is that clear?"

"I understand."

"What do you suggest I do next?" he said, his brow still twisted into a scowl.

"We're going to do a couple of interviews on a sports channel and a major network channel with your sisters."

If she thought he'd been angry before, it was nothing to the fury that etched his face now. This emotion was not hot like before. This was icy cold, brittle, hard, turning his features from simply stunningly handsome to harsh and rugged.

With a curse, he pushed up onto his feet and moved away from the living area. She craned her neck up, her gaze hungrily trailing the economic efficiency with which he moved. The black trousers he wore clung to his powerful thighs, the white shirt highlighting his broad shoulders and lean waist.

She took the time to simply study him. He'd been blessed with inordinately good looks, and yet it was the energy with which he occupied a space that fascinated her.

It was several minutes before he turned back to face her, his temper firmly under control. "I was ready to agree to your suggestions because one of my employees wronged an innocent woman. But the responsibility for that lies with me, as CEO. There is no need to drag my family into this."

"But an illustrious family like yours can only be an advantage," Clare retorted, and then instantly wanted to pull her words back.

It seemed that her ill-thought words had only pierced anew whatever wound Dev was determined to ignore.

"Let's not get into the advantages and disadvantages my illustrious family has afforded me. It's above your pay-grade."

The dismissal was clear and cold. She hadn't been lying when she'd told him that she'd handled a lot of difficult clients in her time. And yet Dev's dismissal stung her deeper than any other. It shouldn't have, considering their "business-only" relationship.

But she refused to let him railroad her, not in this. "I have no interest in digging into matters you deem forbidden, Mr. Kohli," she said haughtily. "But neither will I be told how to do my job. During my research, I discovered that your older sister is a world-renowned neurosurgeon and your younger sister is a state diplomat. We need to show the world that you're not intimidated by powerful women."

"Doesn't the list of women I've dated show that? I've dated several influential, wealthy women in their own right."

"No. That just shows that you're allergic to commitment and that you're pickier than a five-year-old when it comes to what he wants for dinner."

That shut him up promptly. Clare bit her lip to stop smiling. "At this point, it's not just that you and Athleta are being roasted everywhere. But have you wondered why your invitation to the Ethics and Equity in Sports panel has been canceled?"

"How the hell do you know that?" he said incredulously. "It's only just happened!"

Clare shrugged. "I have my sources."

"You don't have to remind me why I hired you," he said dryly.

"Then stop being so difficult, Dev. If you want to bring about change in your company, it has to start with you. No one said it was going to be easy."

"Are you charging me extra for the motivational speech?" he quipped. Humor was his default setting, Clare was beginning to see. But it didn't mean he wasn't hearing what she had to say.

"I'm just as excited as you are by the changes you want to make. I've been out there, in the business world. The glass ceiling is very much alive and thriving, Dev. It's encouraging to see powerful men want to do their part in fostering an equitable environment for women."

"You're quite the force to be reckoned with, aren't you?"

"Why is there a question mark at the end of that?" Clare said, feeling as if the ground was being stolen from under her. It wasn't a bad sensation. Just a floaty one.

He frowned, his gaze sweeping over her features, as if he was searching for something. "Because there's one piece that doesn't really fit."

"What?"

"Why such a smart woman like you would make a deal with an unscrupulous Mafia boss. Even for much-needed capital. With your asset and liability columns and what little I know of you, I just don't see you taking a horrible risk like that."

Clare swallowed and gathered the papers she'd spread out on the coffee table in front of her. The unvarnished grain of the oak table felt like an anchor steadying her. She didn't know why she was hiding the truth from him.

Even Amy and Bea assumed she'd inherited the money after her dad had died, because the two things had happened so close together. She didn't know if it was her own fault for having foolishly trusted her father when he'd said he wanted to help her. She wasn't sure if it was shame or grief that sat like a boulder on her chest every time she thought of herself so full of hope and happiness when her dad had called her and she'd realized she'd be able to start her business.

She just couldn't.

"I told you. That was a naive decision I made." She switched off her laptop and picked it up. She was glad for the steadiness of her tone as she walked up the steps and faced him. "Both your sisters have already got back to me saying that they would be delighted to do it. I'll arrange for the interview through a virtual channel. I imagine that would considerably lessen the stress you're feeling at the prospect?"

He didn't quite give her the smile she wanted but that warmth flooded his eyes again. Clare felt as if she'd won the biggest lottery jackpot.

"Yes, thank you. Make sure any personal tidbits my sisters might mention are edited out. You're going to have a hell of a long conversation on your hands."

She nodded, intensely curious about his sisters, his family, everything about him. "And the contracts? Have they been looked over by your team of lawyers?"

An instant shutter fell over his expression. "Not yet. Don't worry, Clare. The contract is yours." He went on then, as if he wanted to fill the silence. "I'm having dinner in Rio de Janeiro tomorrow evening." His gaze did a quick survey of her, but didn't linger. "It might be a good idea for you to do some shopping in Rio when we arrive."

"Yes, please. Running away from a Mob boss and his thugs is the one disaster scenario I didn't pack for."

"Perfect. Then you can join us for dinner."

Clare's heart did a thump against her rib cage. "Join you? For dinner? You mean, as your partner for the evening?"

He shrugged. As if the matter didn't require further scrutiny. "I'm meeting an old friend and his wife, who's a notorious gossip. Showing up in front of her as my partner is like taking a front-page ad out that we're together."

"Together?" Clare asked, a totally unnecessary, girlish flutter in her chest region. "Like a couple together? Or like a playboy and his PR guard dog together?"

Laughter lines crinkled out from the edges of his eyes as he threw his head back and roared. It was fast becoming one of her favorite sounds. "Your imagination needs to be put to better use than these scenarios you keep thinking up for us."

Clare straightened her shoulders. "If this friend's wife is such a gossip…"

"Then it's not a bad idea to fake it in front of her to help my reputation. A little smoke to start up a rumor that I'm falling head over heels with the mystery lady tucked away on my yacht…" He sighed when she didn't respond. "I thought being linked to me was what you wanted."

"For safety's sake, yes. But pretending in front of an old friend of yours is a completely different matter. Do you want me to flutter my eyelashes at you and simper?"

Dev grinned. "I'm sure you'll be found out in two seconds if you act all sweet and sugary toward me. Just be yourself—your starchy I'm-making-him-a-better-guy self who frequently likes to dress me down and keep my ego in check. Give your spiel about all the charity programs Athleta runs."

"To your friend?"

"I've been asking him to come on board with Athleta for a long time. This might be the push he needs since he's at a crossroads in his life too. I want to snatch him up before someone else does. He's a footballer and a world-class athlete."

Of course, business was at the center of everything for Dev Kohli. Still, Clare felt a flutter of interest at getting a bona fide glimpse into his personal life. "If he's a good friend, won't he know that we're just…faking it?"

"No, he won't. Especially once he meets you."

"And what does that mean, exactly? That I'm not up to the usual standard of your stunning girlfriends, so you must have lost your mind over me?"

Dev lifted his palms, a smile tugging at the corners of his mouth. "Are you fishing for compliments, Clare?"

Her face heated, but she refused to leave it alone. "Of course not."

"Fine. You're just…different," he admitted.

"Different boring?" she pressed.

"Different…complex, okay?" His words had an edge to them now that Clare wanted to spend the rest of the evening teasing out. But that way lay nothing but trouble with a big *T*.

"Fine. I'll talk you up to him. It shouldn't be that hard. Although I don't see why you can't do it yourself."

"Is there anything worse than a man so pleased with himself that he won't stop boasting?"

Clare nodded, a shaft of pain hitting her in the chest. Her dad had been like that—he'd hardly ever called her, but on the few occasions he had, he'd never asked her about her own life. He'd always gone on and on about his next miraculous venture. Forever blowing his own, tarnished horn.

"I can have the chauffeur bring you back to the yacht after your shopping trip instead of joining us for dinner at the hotel, if you're afraid?" he taunted when she didn't respond.

"Of course I'm not afraid," Clare snapped, and the devilish man looked satisfied. He'd neatly cornered her into agreeing. "So are we going to stay overnight in Rio de Janeiro?"

"Yes. The next morning, we'll leave for St. Lucia."

"Okay. I'll meet you in the lounge for dinner."

"Can't wait to get away from me already?"

Clare sighed. "I'm not ungrateful. I just… I need to catch my breath. Can you understand that?"

"Yes."

"If one of your staff can get me a map of the city for tomorrow—"

He was shaking his head even before Clare finished her sentence. "That's not a good idea."

Something about his tone put her back up. "I've no idea when I'll get a chance to see Rio de Janeiro. I'm just going to play tourist. I won't be late and miss the dinner with your friend."

"I don't think you should venture out by yourself."

Fear gripped Clare. "Why? What have you heard?"

He shook his head again, but Clare had a feeling he wasn't telling her the complete truth. And that sent a spiral of fear and anger through her.

"I haven't yet figured out a way to solve your predicament," he said gravely. "Until I do, I'm…responsible for you, so I'll go with you."

She reached out to steady herself, her heart thumping dangerously loud in her chest. "I don't need anybody's protection. I certainly don't—"

"I can tell you're worried." His voice was curt, commanding, and Clare held on to it. "You have dark shadows under your eyes. If you won't talk to me, talk to someone else. Family, or a friend…someone. Or you're just heading for a—"

"I don't have anyone to depend on, okay? I…don't want to worry my friends as they have enough on their plates right now keeping the business going without me. It's just me." Clare fought the sob building in her chest. She knew if she told her friends they'd leap to her defense and might get hurt themselves. They were better off out of it. But with his careful concern for her, Dev was determined to unravel her. "It's always been just me." Suddenly, she felt dizzy.

"Breathe, Clare." Dev's voice was hard in her ears, an anchoring point. "Focus on me, sweetheart."

Clare looked up. His brown gaze held hers—steady and reassuring. His hand reached out and took hers, enveloping her small one. The thump-thump of her heart felt a little slower now, as she focused on the line of heat his thumb traced on the back of her hand. The familiar scent of him wound around her, like a comforting blanket.

As panic misted away, Clare's first instinct was to snatch

her hand away from his. The concern in his face, the gentleness of his touch…felt strange. Alien, almost. She wanted to shake it off and hide. To reject his simple kindness, which sent a lump swimming in her throat.

"Tell me what it is that you're hiding. And I can help you even more."

Her head jerked up. "Why?"

He looked adorably confused as he frowned. "What do you mean why?"

"Why do you want to help me? Other than the fact that I've thrust myself into your life as an unwanted stowaway on your yacht. The last thing I want is your pity. I need something real right now. Like I've never needed it before."

Clare didn't even realize she was speaking the words until she heard them. Until she felt him react by tightening his hand on hers. "God, I sound pathetic, don't I?"

"No," Dev replied. "You sound like someone who's struggling. Who's wary of leaning on anyone other than yourself. You sound…" He released her hand then. And Clare felt only desolation at the loss of his warmth. Long fingers squeezed her shoulders before he moved away from her. As if he needed to put physical distance between them before he did something he regretted.

"There's something in you that reminds me of…me," he said finally. "That's why I was drawn to you that night at the gala. It's why it felt like more than just another one-night stand. And why I had to walk away from you the next morning. Is that real enough for you?"

Clare stared at him, feeling a surge of something powerful in her chest. Her gaze traced the arrogant nose, the high cheekbones, the mouth that was always ready to laugh… his face was as familiar to her now as her own. She nodded automatically, hugging those unexpected words to herself. Still processing them… "I hope you're not pacifying me because you feel sorry for me."

He smiled and her world immediately felt centered again. "There's nothing about you that evokes pity in me, Clare. Exasperation, yes, but definitely not pity."

Clare laughed then, and if she'd had a better handle on herself, she'd have hugged him. Instead, she dipped her head, hoping to swallow the tears in her throat before they escaped. "Thank you. I've had a lot of distressing news of late and it…"

"Catches you out and brings you to your knees just when you thought you had a handle on it?"

"Something like that, yes," said Clare, stunned by his perception.

"Being strong doesn't mean you lean on no one, you know."

She scoffed. "This coming from a man who cuts himself off from the world on a gigantic boat?"

"Yacht," he corrected loudly, and then grinned. "It sounds like I've met my match in you," he said, regarding her with those brilliant brown eyes, as if he could easily see into her soul. One brow raised, and he muttered, "Come to me when you think you can, Clare, and tell me what fills your eyes with such grief. I swear it'll be our secret."

And then he bid her good-night. Leaving her alone in that warm, wonderful library of his. Giving her something that she hadn't even known she'd needed. The temporary respite from fear.

CHAPTER SIX

HOTEL FASANO—the latest playground of the uber-rich in Rio de Janeiro—kept its promise of the understated luxury and elegance that Clare had heard of and never thought of stepping foot in. The sparkling crystal blue of the ocean and the jutting peaks of the mountains calmed something inside her.

It was only when they'd alighted from the helicopter and Clare could breathe in the air that she'd realized how caged she'd been feeling. It wasn't Dev's fault or his yacht's. It was running from her own life that she detested.

If anything, Dev had only made her feel safer and more secure than she'd felt since she'd first seen the mobster's henchman dogging her steps in London. But the problem was, there were other things Clare felt compelled to run from. Dev, for instance.

Something about the concern and warmth in his gaze that felt far more dangerous to her well-being than any thug—her heart's naive longings that there could be more between them.

Clare flinched internally, aghast at her own thoughts and at the same time wishing she'd asked him to share more of his feelings about their night together. Wishing she'd delved deeper into the meaning of his words.

He was, she was coming to learn, quite a considerate man, for all that he tried to show the world only the shallow surface of himself. But just because he might be curious enough to know what secrets she was keeping didn't mean he had any special interest in solving her problems or healing the wounds inside her soul that never seemed to quite go away.

So she didn't like to give up control. Who did? Who was brave and foolish enough—in equal measures—to trust a stranger with their innermost fears? With their silly dreams that they should have long given up by the time they'd reached twenty-eight? Who poured out their inexplicable longings to a man who was stuck with her through no choice of his own?

Last night on the yacht, she'd snuggled into the sofa, not wanting to leave that library.

It was the one space on the entire yacht that had retained any of Dev's true personality. As if all the books remembered him. As if he'd left a warm imprint of himself behind after all the hours he'd spent in there. She hadn't wanted to be alone in her expansive cabin, adrift on the sea.

So, clutching a book to her chest, Clare had curled up and read and dozed. Noticed somewhere in that state between being awake and asleep that every book on the shelf also had an audiobook. Even some really old titles on subjects ranging from science and philosophy to Indian mythology.

On an impulse, she'd reached for a book on Hinduism and once again, there was its accompanying audiobook. Clare flipped through the book only to find that it was absolutely pristine. Each page still possessed an unmistakable crisp newness as if they hadn't ever been turned.

She'd examined older copies of some of the classics and it was the same. While the pages in those books were more yellowed, with the faint scent of aged paper emanating from them, it was apparent that they'd also hardly ever been thumbed through.

And yet, Clare sensed Dev's presence here—almost as if the books could tell her more about the man than he ever would.

Dev Kohli was anything but a one-dimensional playboy. At some point, Clare fell asleep, pondering the fact that it would be quite something to actually get to know him. Not that she could afford to.

She'd jolted awake to find herself cradled in strong arms, the side of her chest crushed against a harder one. And the delicious scent of taut skin covering even tighter muscles invading her nostrils.

He smelled like Clare always imagined warmth and security to smell like.

Sleep heavy in her eyes, she'd looked up. Only to drown in that unfathomable gaze of his. Not even for a second had fear of a strange man holding her touched her. Even before her mind could completely grasp it, her body had recognized his. The strong line of his jaw, the wiry strength of his arms, the breadth of his shoulders…they had after all starred in her fantasy night.

And yet Clare knew it wasn't just her body that had recognized him, but her heart too.

She wondered if the thudding beat she heard was his heart or hers. Wondered how even in the slightly illuminated shadowy corridors through which he carried her, he could make her feel secure.

As she lay now, on a luxurious lounger next to the hotel's infinity pool on the eighth floor, looking out onto the beautiful Ipanema beach, supposedly glad to be escaping Dev's perceptive attentions, Clare was anything but escaping her own thoughts about the man.

Last night, as he'd carried her, she'd simply clasped her fingers tighter around his nape when it had felt like she was slipping out of his grasp.

"You have the habit of falling asleep in the most awkward places, Clare," he'd muttered, his voice husky and touched by sleep too.

A thick lock of hair had fallen forward onto his forehead. With no thought, Clare had pushed it back. Even after she'd done it, she'd felt no awkwardness. No regret or shame. Neither had his steps faltered even one bit. It had felt natural—her touching him so familiarly as if she had every right to do so.

Had he felt the same or had he simply not imposed that cold distance back between them because she was half muddled by sleep?

"I didn't want to be alone," she'd said, all her defenses down. He had seemed like a knight, come to take her away to a place of safety.

Clare cursed now, a flush claiming her skin. Where had her filter disappeared to?

"And the library is full of people?" he'd asked, a tiny line drawing his brows together. "Strange. I've always found it to be full of people's voices clamoring at me to hear them. So much to say, so much to teach…and always beyond my reach. It's like hearing the echo but never reaching the true source."

Clare frowned now, wondering at that cryptic statement he'd made.

"No, I don't think that, but it's not empty or soulless either," she'd said softly. "It's obviously the room you love most. Your presence lingers there."

His nostrils had flared, an enigmatic expression awakening in his eyes. "I don't know if I would quite call it love, Clare. I've always felt strongly about that room, yes. But it's not love," he'd said, a hitch of something—grief, pain—in his words.

Clare desperately wished she'd remembered more of the nuances now. She had this urgent feeling that he'd shared something extremely significant about himself. Something he wouldn't say in the daylight, in the absence of the intimacy and cover that the dark night and her sleepiness had provided.

She'd glanced up at him, his words puncturing a little more of her exhaustion. "Whatever it was, I didn't feel alone in there. Or afraid. I felt…safe."

His arms had tightened around her, more voluble than that gorgeous mouth of his. "I wouldn't think less of you if you'd simply admitted that in the first place, Clare." A soft smile crinkled the corners of his eyes. "In daylight, I mean."

She shrugged. "Care to show me how?" He was moving up steps now, and she was much more firmly held against his solid chest. If she hadn't been so intent on not disrupting the tidbits of himself he was tempting her with, she'd have nuzzled her nose into all that deliciously warm skin. "Because I learn best by example."

He'd thrown his head back and laughed then. And Clare had the weirdest wish that he would simply keep on walking forever and she'd continue to exist in that half-awake, half-aware state forever so that he would keep holding her and talking to her.

Which had prompted her to say, "Why did you come for me?" Hope and curiosity tied a knot in her belly. Hope that maybe he'd wanted her company too. That maybe he'd thought their night together had been remarkable.

"One of my staff heard you as they were coming to tidy up in there, and came to get me, rather than disturb you. You were having a bad dream. You kept saying, 'How could you?'"

And then he was walking into a bedroom and her heart fluttered like a bird caught in a cage.

"You're not alone, Clare," he had whispered then, gently placing her on the bed in a different cabin than she had been initially shown to. He had sat on the edge of the bed and held her hand—his large, calloused one enveloping hers like his body had done to hers once—and in that deep voice of his, commanded she go to sleep.

The traitor that her body was, it had immediately complied. She'd fallen asleep marveling at the novel quality of someone being there to comfort her, holding her hand to remind her that she was safe. Someone caring enough to say even those few words.

Mercifully, as far as she could remember, the night had ended there.

She'd woken up this morning in the vast bed, sunlight slanting onto her face. A quick look through the cabin had revealed the fact that she was now in a room that shared a door with the master cabin. Dev's cabin.

He'd taken her sleep-mumbled words seriously and kept her close by all night.

When she'd faced him this morning, Clare had refused to make eye contact. Embarrassment and something she couldn't define suffused her. That he had seen her like that…at her most vulnerable…it was a very uncomfortable feeling.

As if all that raw longing she sometimes felt inside was now on the outside for him to see. Her deepest, darkest dreams suddenly displayed in all their multicolored gaudiness.

But her fears that he might mock her or worse turned out to be unfounded. Because of course, Dev was the consummate gentleman.

He had perfectly followed her cue this morning, not even hinting at what had happened the previous night by raising his famously expressive brow. He'd simply asked her if she'd slept well. To which she'd focused somewhere over his shoulder and nodded.

So professional, the both of them.

When they'd arrived at the hotel, she'd gone straight

to the boutique on the ground floor. Uncaring of the astronomical price tag for once, she'd bought a white two-piece bikini, as she'd forgotten to purchase one during her shopping trip beforehand. She'd desperately needed a little time to herself. Away from the shadow of the man who was beginning to pierce through her armor like a most determined arrow.

With her laptop in hand, she finished a number of administrative tasks and sent off a questionnaire to Athleta's newly revamped HR department. Looking through the interview questionnaire she'd prepared for Dev himself, she frowned.

He'd sent it back to her with a request to provide audio files of the questions. It wasn't that unusual a request, in the scheme of ridiculous requests that Clare had fulfilled for her clients.

But it made her think of the audiobooks she'd spied in his library aboard the yacht. How he'd said he couldn't immediately read and sign the business contract she'd put together for him based on the usual format she, Amy and Bea kept at the ready. How Clare had thought he was balking at the high price she'd quoted.

When she'd inquired if he was hesitating at how much her firm charged, he'd looked at her seriously. "Underestimating their own worth is often one of the biggest, most frequent mistakes women make in business."

Clare had nodded vehemently. "I learned that very early on in my career. And I never undercharge."

He'd just looked back at her steadily. "Good to know."

Clare had sighed and said, "That's not why you're not signing immediately then."

"No," he'd confirmed in a hard voice that didn't encourage further discussion. "But the contract is yours, Clare. Do you doubt my word?"

Clare had shaken her head. Knowing that to probe further was less than professional.

It had been a couple of hours before the straightforward contracts had been signed and returned to her. At the time, she'd thought he was just being very thorough with the vetting process.

Now, as she pulled out her phone and dictated the questions into it so she could email the audio file to him, Clare thought she was beginning to see the pieces of the man fall into place.

How and why he'd always played up the whole playboy role that the media had created for him. Why he'd trusted the man who'd betrayed him with so much power...

By the time late afternoon started edging into early evening and she needed to go get ready for dinner, Clare realized that however hard she'd tried to thwart her interest in Dev, it didn't make an iota of difference.

The more she learned about him, the more she wanted to know. The more she wanted to make this business partnership into something far more personal. But that way lay madness and hurt.

The sun was streaking the sky in shades of gold and orange, offering one of those unparalleled Rio sunsets that the city was so famous for.

The rooftop restaurant where she and Dev were going to entertain their guests, with its vintage retro lighting and buttery soft leather chairs and red brick facade, created an easy, intimate atmosphere. From the moment Dev had knocked on her door to escort her looking dapper in a casual jacket over tailored trousers, Clare knew she was going to enjoy the evening.

Neither had she missed the short but thorough appraisal Dev had given her sleeveless white sheath dress and suede pumps, and she'd had her hair styled at the hotel salon.

Another expensive extravagance, but the warm admiration in his gaze was worth it.

"My friend has messaged to say they've been slightly delayed and we're to start without them."

After her hasty shopping trip when they'd arrived in Rio and the work she'd done poolside, Clare discovered she was ravenous once they'd been seated. She attacked the appetizer with a gusto she couldn't quite hide.

She looked up to find Dev's eyes on her. With his arm slung lazily over the back of her chair, he hadn't needed to bend too far to murmur, "I'm sorry if I embarrassed you, Clare. I was just…admiring your enjoyment of your food. You looked as if there was no pleasure greater."

The convivial atmosphere and the yummy food and that feeling of being free of thugs and fear—even for one evening—went straight to her head. And because some naughty imp was goading her, she murmured back, "There isn't. Except maybe the delicious weight of a man pressing down on…"

The sudden flare of heat in his eyes told her he knew what she'd been about to say. And yet Clare didn't feel any shame. Which was progress in her mind.

Dev was good in bed. He knew it. And more importantly, he knew that she knew it. It was high time she acted like an adult about it. Instead of looking like a blushing prude or imagining there was some sort of power play going on here.

Dev had never behaved as if this was a game to him. Even at his coldest. Which meant she needed to stop acting as if she was giving something away when she admitted how much that night had meant to her.

"Well, you know what I mean," she added in a breezy voice to cover up the sudden silence.

He didn't have to say anything as his phone pinged just then. "They're not coming."

"Oh…" Clare said, feeling a pang of disappointment. "Is everything okay?"

Dev shrugged. "Marriage problems I'd say. His wife can be a lot to handle sometimes."

Clare snorted. "Is that just conjecture? Or is there any truth to it?"

He sat back in his chair. Moonlight gilded the sharp planes of his features. "You doubt my word?" he said, mock affront lighting up his eyes.

"As a founding member of the playboy club, absolutely, yes. You might be the authority on everything else, but your commentary on marriage…sorry, but you're not likely to be an expert, are you?"

"I'll have you know I'm not against the institution of marriage, per se."

Hand on her chest, Clare pretended to gasp, "I don't believe it."

"I'm sure marriage is a healthy arrangement for people who want that kind of comfortable companionship and children. It's just not for…"

"Just not for you, of course," she said, rolling her eyes. "Why settle for one meal when you can have the whole buffet?"

He smiled, but when he spoke, there was something far from humorous in his eyes. "Those are your words, not mine. And please for all my sins, I'm not so bad as to declare there isn't a woman out there who's good enough for me."

"Then what is it?" Clare asked, unable to keep that question to herself. For too long she'd been wondering about him, and now, finally, here he was, the true Dev Kohli.

"Love requires something from me that I can't give. It's that simple."

Their gazes met and held, in a silent battle of wills. The breeze from the beach, the star-studded sky, with soft jazz playing in the background made for a beautiful night. But Clare knew it was this gorgeous man and the way he looked at her that made every cell in her body run wild. That, despite his professed inability to love, made him still so fascinating to her.

"Should we return to our rooms and finish some of the interviews maybe? If they're not coming, that is," she asked into the gathering silence. Just to bring herself back to earth. Just to cut through the warm cocoon of attraction wrapping around them. "There's still a lot to…"

"Or we could just enjoy the rest of the evening? You're a hard taskmaster, Clare." He raised a hand and their next course was discreetly placed in front of them.

Clare took a sip of her refilled glass of wine, to give her time to get control of her thoughts. "Then you'll have to tell me a little about your swimming career."

"Don't you know enough about me yet?"

"Like I said, I'm building a profile of you for a few magazines. And I don't just want the stuff that everybody already knows. I want the real gold."

"And if there isn't any gold?" he asked curiously.

"Let me be the judge of that. Also, Dev?"

"Yes?"

"You have to trust me enough to know that I won't release anything you consider private information."

She saw him process that. Could imagine him loosening the boundary he held so rigidly around him. "What do you want to know?"

Clare leaned forward and smiled as she speared a baby carrot on her fork. "Tell me how you went from being a world-class swimmer to a billionaire CEO."

"That spans several very boring years."

"I've got time," she retorted.

He told her while they ate the rest of their meal. Peppering the details with funny anecdotes, self-deprecating humor, and more than a hint of anger and pain when he talked about the mentor in his company who had been the instigator of the sexual harassment.

"What about your father? I had a call from his secretary about doing a joint profile on the two of you. As a head of the local chamber of the commerce, your father brings a lot—"

"Absolutely not," Dev said, immediately shutting her down.

"But he—"

"He never had a hand in making me, Clare. Except by forcing me to become a stranger to my own family. In making me doubt myself at every turn. He was instrumental in molding me into the cold, selfish man you have frequently called me. So, no, but I don't need his help in making me look good to the rest of the world, thank you very much."

The sudden silence in the wake of those impassioned words resonated in the air around them. Clare couldn't rush to fill it. Not when she recognized and understood the depth of anger and pain in them.

"I didn't mean to—"

"Don't apologize. That you eventually raised the subject of my father was inevitable. I should've just told you right at the start that he falls firmly into the category of forbidden topics of discussion."

"What will happen when you see him at Diya's wedding?"

"He'll finally see who I've become." The hardness receded from his gaze as he considered her sympathetic eyes. "And I have a plan to defuse any surplus interest in my family dynamics."

"Let me know how I can help," she offered automatically.

Clare saw a sudden flash of something move across his

face. As if he was momentarily stunned at an insight he'd just had.

She had the most intense urge to ask him why he was staring at her like that.

She wanted to ask him about the audiobooks. She wanted to kiss him and ask him to kiss her again. She wanted to see those brown eyes turn infinitely darker as his passion was aroused.

She wanted to…

But she couldn't. He'd made it very clear that he didn't want the traditional dream of home and family that she still did. That he didn't believe in love or that he was even capable of it.

Clare shivered, even though the evening was far from chilly. In the next second, a jacket descended on her shoulders, smelling of his delicious warm male skin.

"Do you want to walk along the beach by the hotel?" Clare asked, turning toward him. "I recorded some questions for you about the press interviews," she added hurriedly. The coward that she was, she didn't want him to think she was asking just to prolong the evening with him. Even though she was.

If he thought she was acting strangely, he didn't say so. "Of course," he said, his brown eyes twinkling. "Won't do for me to forget that you're only putting up with me for a paycheck."

Clare had no chance to answer as their lift door opened onto the expansive lobby of the Fasano where there was a tall, brown, insanely beautiful woman waiting in a peach-colored evening gown that clung to every curve.

"Dev? I thought that was you!" the woman exclaimed. "Oh, my God, I can't tell you how glad I am to have bumped into you…" She swanned across the marble floor toward them, the thigh-high slit in the gown showcasing toned legs that seemed to go on forever and ever.

Dev's mouth split into a stunningly warm smile. "Angelina…what are you doing here?"

He must have braced himself as she approached because he barely exhaled when she threw herself into his arms. Dev held her with what Clare could only call open affection. Angelina clasped his cheeks and kissed him, and Dev let her.

A strange buzzing filled Clare's ears. For which she was immensely thankful because it meant she couldn't hear the gushing words they said to each other.

She knew she should look away, or paste a polite, but inquiring smile on her face. Or just leave. But she did none of those. She simply stood there like some village bumpkin and stared at the bronze goddess, who must surely be a model, feeling as if someone had punched her in the middle.

Had she imagined a one-night stand, followed by an unwilling pity rescue from a nightmare situation, and one evening of pleasurable playacting at dinner equaled the beginning of something more meaningful?

Hadn't she learned her lesson yet about relationships and foolish dreams—the consequences of which she was still dealing with?

This was not her life, she reminded herself. This was a bubble she was living in until she figured out a way to escape the terrible fate that was threatening her.

Without a word, Clare turned away from them. If she could have sprinted to the lift as she was sure Angelina with her endless, graceful legs could have managed, she would have done so. Alas, she had to attempt to convey a dignified retreat on her wobbly, short legs.

"Clare, wait," Dev called behind her.

And since she couldn't just act like she was having a tantrum—even though she really wanted to—Clare turned around. A polite smile shimmered on her lips in its full fake glory.

His arm around the woman, he said, "I'd like you to join us for a coffee."

"Oh, must she, Dev?" The woman pouted, barely even glancing in Clare's direction. "It's not like you'll remember her name a week from now. I was hoping you and I could have a private chat."

"Clare's not one of my..." Dev suddenly stopped, staring at Clare, arrested. As if he couldn't find the words to describe their relationship. "She's..."

Their gazes held, an arc of electricity practically sizzling between them.

"She's what?" Angelina demanded, turning her curious gaze on Clare.

"What I am is very tired. I'm turning in for the night," Clare said, determined to remain polite in the face of the woman's horrible rudeness. After all, why should she be surprised? This was how Dev Kohli lived his life. "My body clock is still all upside down."

He nodded, and the suspicion that he'd only asked her to be nice was confirmed for her. Dammit, what the hell was wrong with her?

A thoughtful frown crossed his face as Clare met his gaze and then skittered away. "Okay. I'll see you tomorrow. We'll leave right after lunch."

Clare bade him a cool good-night.

And yet, as his broad shoulders disappeared into the lift with the woman still clinging to him, all she wanted was to go back and demand answers from him. Answers she had no right to. Because he wasn't hers.

Dev Kohli wasn't the kind of man who could belong to only one woman. Men like him and her father...they needed larger-than-life dreams, variety, constant thrills to challenge them. So maybe he wasn't the shallow, ruthless playboy that she'd initially thought him to be. But neither was he the kind of man who would settle for anything as

pedestrian as marriage and children. And as much as she'd
tried to bury all her dreams, somehow they always took
root again in her heart—dreams of a man loving her forever, of building a family with him, of living the rest of her
life surrounded by people she loved.

The thought of following the couple in the lift made
Clare want to be sick. Instead, she squared her shoulders
and stepped out into the night. At least a walk might clear
her head of her heart's foolish notions.

Dev Kohli wasn't the man for her.

CHAPTER SEVEN

THE REPETITIVE BANG of a fist on the door to his suite brought Dev's head up. He put down the glass tumbler of whiskey he'd poured himself and opened the door.

Her face pale, trembling from head to toe, Clare stood at the entrance to his suite. She looked as if she'd been running for her life. "I'm sorry for interrupting your...date, but can I come in?"

"Yes, of course, you can, Clare," Dev said, pulling her inside. He slammed the door and leaned against it, his own pulse racing at the terror on her face. "What's wrong?"

"I... I went for a walk after you left with...her. Down to the beach. I wanted to clear my head... I..."

She swayed where she stood, and Dev reached for her. Clearly, she was in shock.

He slung his arm around her shoulders seconds before her knees gave way. That she didn't immediately protest made unease curdle in his stomach. He half carried her to the bar, hitching her against his side.

A burst of laughter from her mouth made him look at her, tucked neatly under his arm. There was a near delirious look in her eyes. "You should've been a football player. American football, I mean," she said.

Dev didn't know whether to smile or call for a doctor. "I considered that as a career for a while. I was told I was too small for it."

Another laugh. Less delirious but still with a slight hysterical edge to it. "You were too small? You…" Her gaze swept over his shoulders and his chest and trailed downward. And then back up again. She giggled, a sound that was very unlike the practical Clare he knew. "For what it's worth, in my opinion, you're very much not a small man."

Dev knew that fear had completely wiped away the cloak of control she usually deployed like some kind of invisible shield. Usually, he'd have preened at her admiring glance.

Picking up the drink he'd just poured himself, he held it to her mouth. She didn't quite sag against him, but he could feel involuntary shivers running up and down her spine. "Drink this," he said in a voice that didn't invite argument.

Scrunching that adorable, all too arrogant nose, she shook her head. "I hate whiskey."

"I don't care," he said, that tightness in his chest releasing a little. The matter-of-fact way she'd spoken meant whatever had terrified her was slowly releasing its grip. "You've had a shock and you look…horrible." The pale cast to her skin, the whiteness around her mouth, it was as if all blood had fled from her face.

She grimaced. "Just what a girl likes to hear from the mouth of the man she's lusting over."

His gaze warmed with a heat that was never too far away when she was near. "I can see that shock is having other effects on you."

"I'm tired of acting as if I don't want you."

He laughed and pulled her closer. "Come on, Clare. For once, give in. The whiskey will warm you up, if nothing else."

She didn't argue further. Her fingers shook as she tried to take the tumbler from him. Dev didn't let go. He held the base of the tumbler as she tilted it up and took a couple of resolute sips.

She coughed almost delicately and gave the glass back. But he was glad to see some color climbing back into her face. His own pulse started slowing down from its former erratic pace.

"Now, tell me what happened."

Tears filled those blue eyes and spilled over as she raised them to his face. With a gasp of indignation, she wiped them off her cheeks. As if she found them beneath her dignity. "I think... No, I know I saw him on the beach, so I ran straight back to the lobby immediately and jumped in the lift."

"Who?"

"He got there just as the doors were closing." She closed her eyes, and sagged against the counter, as if her legs were giving out again. Dev tightened his hold on her. "That sweet smile of his... God, I'm going to see it till the day I die."

"Clare, who are you talking about?"

"Goon Number One, of course."

Dev didn't mean to laugh. Not when she looked like she'd shatter if he breathed too hard. But the way she'd said "Goon Number One," with distaste curling her lip, and her courage vying with her fear...he couldn't help it.

He was so surprised by the curse she spat out that it took a few seconds for him to react, and by then she'd slipped from his grasp.

Without having to turn all the way, he shot his arm out and pulled her back toward him. She landed against his chest, her forearms caught between them, blue eyes flashing daggers at him. "Let me go, Dev."

The fierce way she said his name made his pulse leap with excitement.

"Not so fast, darling," he said, adding an extra drawl to the endearment.

"I'm not going to stand here and let you make fun of me

while I…" She shivered, as if on cue again. "I shouldn't have come to you at all."

Something about her reminded him of himself. She was clearly terrified and yet determined to hold her own. This woman was a fighter, just like him. No wonder she kept tripping him up.

Dev tightened his arms around her waist just as she fidgeted inside them. He pressed his mouth to her temple and she instantly stopped struggling. Her chest rose and fell, her breaths labored. He took his time, wanting to do this right. Knowing she needed exactly the right words from him just then.

Holding her like this, he could feel the strength of will it was taking her to prevent complete hysteria from settling in.

The scent of her skin—warmed by her signature lily-of-the-valley perfume—filled his lungs as he took a deep breath. "Take a moment, Clare. If you want me to let you go, I will. But right now, you need to be held. You need to know that you're safe. You need human contact—preferably male and large and able to provide at least an illusion of security. Ergo, someone like me."

Her laughing snort vibrated against his chest.

"I'll happily be the bad guy and hold you prisoner until you decide that it's okay to lean on me."

She whimpered then, and his muscles clenched as she pressed her open mouth to his biceps.

"For once, trust your instincts, Clare. Not your rational mind. You came to me because, despite the fact that you hate my guts sometimes, you knew you could trust me."

He knew firsthand how hard it was to be vulnerable in front of someone else. To let people see you in pain, lost, directionless. To hope that a kind word would be offered instead of humiliation or a tongue-lashing. And he fully understood her reluctance. From the very beginning, he had seen the similarities between them, the need to be strong in front of the world.

"I can't," she whispered, and the grief in her voice made him swallow.

"Of course you can." He pulled her in tighter and closer until her breasts were crushed against his chest, her legs tangled with his. Until he could rest his chin on top of her head and there was no gap between their bodies. "But until you can, let's just agree that I'm encouraging you to lean on me."

"Why are you being so nice to me?" she asked in a small voice that reminded Dev of himself on one of those bleak nights when he'd felt all alone in the world.

"Oh, didn't you guess already, sweetheart? I thought you had my number."

"I did," she whispered then, and he was glad to distract her. "But you keep shifting on me. I can't quite pin you down."

He smiled then, glad that she was too preoccupied to look into his eyes. He didn't like that she saw so much of him that he usually kept hidden from the world. From even his twin.

Slowly, ever so slowly that it felt like an eternity, the stiffness dissolved from her frame. Her breathing relaxed its harsh rhythm.

And then he heard the sniffle. The soft gasp that she swallowed away before he could fully hear it. He didn't let go. Only gave her enough room to adjust her head until her cheek settled against his chest and he could feel the dampness of her tears soaking through his shirt to his skin. For a man who'd always avoided emotional entanglements, he felt no urgency to restore the distance between them or to redraw their professional boundaries.

He had no idea how long he held her like that. He didn't care if an eternity passed. There was something about Clare

Roberts that had appealed to him from the first moment he met her. And the more he got to know the different facets of her, the more he found her irresistible.

Eventually, the sniffles stopped and she let out a small sigh. But she made no move to tell him she wanted him to release her. So Dev didn't.

Slowly, seconds cycled to minutes and the air around them began to fill up with something else.

Dev became more and more aware of the soft press of her breasts against his chest. Of the heat radiating from the line of her spine as he rubbed his thumb up and down her back. The dip of her waist and the flare of her hips under his other palm. Of how small and dainty she was in his arms.

Sensation began to crawl back into his limbs and muscles, in the wake of that awareness. She shifted against him—rubbing her soft belly against his muscled one, and a dart of pleasure shot low into his abdomen.

"I wasn't laughing at you, you know," Dev explained, clearing his throat. Needing to puncture the building heat between them, he gently nudged her shoulders back until she wasn't touching him, so he could think straight again. "When you said Goon Number One, it felt like we were stuck in a…"

She didn't look up, but he felt her mouth open in a smile against his arm. The warmth of her breath felt like a brand on his skin through the thin material of his shirt. "In a nightmarish B-list horror movie? Believe me, I know exactly how that feels. Until I remember that man's smile and everything becomes all too real again."

"He's not going to get you, Clare. I'm not going to let him."

"I want to believe you. I do believe you. I just… How though? How long am I going to have to keep running? How am I going to—"

Dev tipped her chin up. After the tears, her eyes gleamed brightly. As if she'd come out on this side stronger and more determined. "You're sure it's him you saw tonight?"

"Absolutely. I'd give anything to be told that it wasn't."

Dev nodded. He had no reason to doubt her belief that the henchman had tailed her this far. Not when all his sources said the crime lord that Clare owed money to was a seriously dangerous man. Which meant it was time for action.

"You'll stay here tonight. In my suite. We can't take the risk of him nabbing you right out of the lift or even from your own suite."

She opened her mouth as if to argue and then closed it. With a resigned sigh, she nodded. Stepping back, she looked around his suite. Dev didn't miss the wariness that crawled back into her eyes. He knew she was looking for Angelina.

"I… I know that it's inconvenient for you to have me here tonight but I'll keep quiet as a mouse."

"I'm not sure if I can stay quiet however," some devil goaded him to say. "As you very well know, I'm quite voluble when it comes to…"

Her palm pressed against his mouth. "You're playing with me."

Dev tugged her wrist away. "Am I?"

"I jumped to conclusions, yes. The thing is I've never done this before."

"Done what?"

"Tell a man that I want to be the one he kisses. Well, except for the last time. With you. Which was my first time."

He couldn't help but feel slightly shocked. She'd been so responsive he'd never guessed. "I know it's far too late for this, but I hope I…fulfilled at least part of your fantasy that night."

"You did," she said simply, and Dev knew she'd given him something precious and priceless. Something he wasn't sure he deserved.

It was just that every tentative smile and admiring glance that Clare threw his way had to be earned. It felt like he was constantly winning a prize—precious parts of her that she was reluctant to part with.

"Angelina is absolutely not my current squeeze, Clare. You ran away before I could clarify that. Plus, do you think I'd dare break the law laid down by you?"

"It's not funny," she said, coming closer.

His every muscle tightened with want as the scent of her reached him afresh. There was no hesitation or anger or reluctance in her gaze or in her steps just then. She looked as if she was determined to claim something for herself tonight. As if fear had washed away whatever kept her caged, instead of doing the opposite. She looked at him as if he was a prize. And yet he was nothing close to that.

"No, it's not. But you're determined to see me as some kind of rogue."

"You *are* a rogue. You're just not…" She looked away and back at him. There was a new light in her eyes, and Dev knew he should cut this conversation short right now. Knew that things were spiraling out of his control.

But damn it, the woman was irresistible. Even when she was busy thinking the worst of him—again.

"So she isn't your lover?"

"Nope."

Pink flushed her cheeks but she didn't shy from his gaze. His own humor came flooding back as he saw the inherent challenge in the lift of her stubborn chin. "It's just you did promise me that you wouldn't take any chances with your reputation right now."

Dev stared at how easily the damn woman shifted from terrified to assertive.

"So ask me," Dev said, lobbing the ball back at her. "You know you're dying out of curiosity. Ask me who she is, Clare."

If he thought she'd lift her nose into air and tighten that upper lip in fake haughtiness, he wasn't wrong. She did all those delicious things that made Dev like her so much. But she never ceased to surprise him.

Head held high, she demanded, "Who was that woman, Dev?" She looked like she meant to say more, but to his disappointment, she locked those words away.

She was standing so close now that he could see the pulse fluttering away at her neck. Could see the resolve glinting in her eyes.

"That was my best friend Derek Lansang's wife. The one that should have come to dinner with us. Not that I've ever gotten involved with a married woman, I hasten to add."

"She was very possessive of you."

Dev grinned, wondering if she knew how she sounded. "Angelina acts like that with every man she knows. It drives Derek crazy, but it's part of the woman he married. Despite their frequent spats, they do love each other. And I have some scruples, Clare. Just not as many as you."

Her shoulders ramrod straight, her gaze didn't budge from his even when she was in the wrong. Like Mama had done so many times. "I'm sorry. I shouldn't have jumped to that conclusion."

"No, you shouldn't have," Dev repeated, enjoying seeing her squirm.

Had she been jealous? Clingy, drama-creating women had never been his favorite kind, and yet there was something about being wanted by Clare that shredded his control.

"So that was Derek Lansang, the football player's wife," Clare mused. "I thought she looked familiar."

Dev nodded.

Blue eyes met his and held. "I was jealous," she said simply, and Dev wondered if he'd misheard her.

He had released his arms from around her, but her palms still clung to the material of his shirt.

"I… I had a lovely time at the dinner, playing your partner and I…got caught up in the fantasy of it. And when she appeared and you went off together like you were her knight in shining armor, I had this…most distasteful feeling in my belly. I know we laid down all these rules, and I have no right to feel jealous, but—"

Dev had never thought himself a man particularly prone to having an unruly heart. And yet something somersaulted inside his chest as he looked into her blue eyes. The lashes were still tinged with wetness and her straight nose was red; she should have looked ordinary. But the resolute strength of her character made her beautiful instead.

"But what, Clare?" he prompted, his voice hoarse.

"As I stood in that lift, I realized how sick I was of being afraid. How out of control my life has been ever since that man…started dogging my footsteps. How I've been just counting each day, longing for it to be over. How I've always tried to be the quiet, good girl who never demanded anything. Of herself or anyone else." And then she came closer and Dev could see the tremble in her lush pink lips. "I'm so angry. I'm furious about how much this bloody mobster is cheating me out of. I might escape him again tomorrow, but having this shadow always hovering over me, it's really not making much of a difference, is it? I could escape him every day for the rest of my life but still never be free."

"And that makes you mad?" Dev asked.

"That makes me…crazy," she said. And then her gaze focused on the now. On him. Dev felt his heart kicking like a mad thing against his rib cage again, and desire ran thick and heavy in his veins.

"So I've decided I'm not going to be scared anymore. I'm not going to simply lie down and give up. I'm not going to let every moment be consumed by fear. I'm going to seize the damned day."

"How?"

"For starters? I'm going to kiss you very thoroughly, as I've been wanting to ever since I woke up in your closet." Thick lashes flickered up and down his body before she met his gaze again. "If you're willing, that is."

Dev exhaled a long breath. Damn it, did the woman have any idea how arousing her artless honesty was? "Assuming I was—"

She cut his words off by trailing her fingers all over his chest. His heart pounded under her palm. The anticipation of a single kiss lit a fire in his blood like never before. But then something about Clare—that irresistible combination of honest, innocent passion, made his nerves sing.

"You are willing. That's all that matters to me. Yes, I already know your usual disclaimer. I don't care what this leads to or how long it lasts. I just want to feel this moment, live in it. Before all I remember about it is that I ran away from it. Before the only thing that will stay with me about this beautiful evening in this beautiful city is that... that bastard contaminated it for me."

She didn't leave it to chance. No, she hedged her bets to the highest, by tightening her fingers at the nape of his neck, going up on her toes until her breaths were crushed against his chest and she was burying her face in the hollow of his throat.

Dev's pulse pounded when she boldly touched her tongue there. Every muscle contracting on a wave of pleasure as she gently nipped the skin between her teeth. Every intention and rule he'd ever laid down for himself forgotten when she blew softly on the tiny mark she'd given him.

His hands on her hips tightened without conscious

thought, and then he was pulling her even more tightly against him, until he knew she could feel his growing erection against her belly. She was gasping against his chin and then there it was…her luscious mouth against his—finally.

A stab of pure lust coursed through him as he dipped his head and pressed his lips to hers. Her moan fired up every nerve ending as he licked at the seam of those lips, suddenly voracious for more.

He reached for the round curve of her bottom with his fingers and hitched her higher against him. "Yes, please," she whispered against his mouth, and Dev lost the last bit of good sense he possessed.

As he delved deeper into the warm cavern of her mouth, as he tangled his tongue with hers, pressing her against the wall and drinking her in hungrily, the shape of the future—at least the immediate future—seemed to coalesce in his brain.

She needed his help. He couldn't turn away from the fact. So why not marry their problems and come up with the perfect solution?

He could show the world that he was settling down and changing his playboy image, and here was the perfect woman to do it with. If he felt a momentary doubt about whether he should be further involved with a woman who saw far too much of him all too clearly, it evaporated in the heat of their kiss. And anyway, not being tied down to any woman—even one as complex as she waswas his true nature. He'd be able to walk away afterward, just like he always did.

CHAPTER EIGHT

CLARE HAD LONG forgotten what it meant to feel vulnerable. If she'd ever known it as an adult, that was.

Once she'd been dropped off on her unwilling aunt's doorstep, she had, for the most part, learned to bury any emotional needs. She'd learned to keep her head down, work hard; in essence to be a quiet, good child with no demands. Either of her aunt or herself.

All the silly dreams she had kept building about her dad returning, though, she realized now were just those—something to sustain her through a barren childhood. As she had turned into an adult with little contact with him, she'd learned to foresee any need or want that might not be fulfilled and crushed it.

The need to be loved—unconditionally, of course—had to be the first one to die.

Vulnerability, she had realized long ago, was a costly thing for her. Her aunt had been the embodiment of the British stiff upper lip, and after a while, Clare had seen the value in it. But today, as she had walked away from Dev, while Angelina had wrapped herself like a vine around his broad shoulders, Clare had been drenched in a surfeit of emotions. As if everything she'd ever denied herself was determined to fill her up.

When Dev had opened the door to her, even through the spine-chilling fear, she'd felt the urgency to snatch what she could from life. To stop spending it burying herself in pros and cons. To put herself out there and live.

As Dev held her for his devastatingly hot kiss, fingers plunged into her hair, her body sang with spiraling pleasure. If only her every act of vulnerability could be rewarded in such a delicious way...

In the passionate depths of his kiss, she felt as if she was rediscovering the dizzying sense of being alive again. As if she was shedding layer after layer of all those sterile restrictions with which she'd caged herself. As if she was finally seeing the core of her own self on glorious display for the first time in years.

This had the potential to be as vivid and soul shaking as the fear had been. Except this was something she was choosing. This was something she wanted and needed and deserved.

This man and this moment and this...unparalleled, total joy in a kiss.

Pleasure suffused through her every nerve, deepened by a giddy sense of power that he was just as mad for her taste as she was for his.

The shocking carnality of his kiss, because with Dev—a kiss was far more than just the slide of their mouths—it was a hungry, sensual exploration, a prediction of what their bodies could do for each other, and it rocked Clare to her soul. Every sweep of his tongue against hers, every nip of his teeth into the trembling flesh of her lower lip goaded her on. Every groan he let out filled the void she'd knowingly carved into her own life.

No more, she told herself. She was done hiding from life. Once she made up her mind, Clare had never been a passive participant.

The fabric of his shirt bunched satisfyingly within her grip. She snuck her fingers underneath, finding warm, delightfully taut skin. His powerful body shuddered when she raked her nails gently down his chest.

A fresh burst of desire bloomed low in her belly, urgent and grasping.

She set her fingers trailing up and down his chest and down to his abdomen. The clench of the hard muscle, the rough groan that fell from his mouth, the tightening of his fingers over her bottom…everywhere he touched, new pockets of sensation opened up.

There was already a familiarity to how they touched each other. A languid understanding of what the other craved, a rhythm to the give and take they engaged in. Clare delighted in this knowledge. And she used it ruthlessly, no longer bound by her own confining rules.

That first night they had spent together a few weeks ago, she'd let him take the active role. That was nowhere near enough for her anymore. She loved the light dusting of hair on his chest. She wanted to lick the hard slab of his abdominal muscles.

Why had she denied herself the life-affirming sight of that happy trail?

She wasn't going to let the mobster win. She wasn't going to let her father's cruel neglect of her or her aunt's cutting indifference define how she lived the rest of her life. "I've wanted to do this again," she said against his mouth, "ever since I woke up next to you that morning. And now I can't think of one good reason why I denied myself. I wrapped myself up in so many layers of protection that I lost myself. No more."

His hands moved up from her hips to her shoulders with a possessive thoroughness that pinged every cell in her body. Slowly, with a long, rough exhale, Dev pulled back from the kiss. "No," he agreed, his thumbs tracing over her cheeks in an almost tender gesture. "Nothing has ever tasted as sweet as you, Clare. Or been as full of surprising depths."

"Are you complaining?" Clare said, burying her face in his throat again. She loved the rough, bristly texture of his skin there, the taste of him, the scent of him. It was beginning to feel like her safe space. But of course, he wouldn't appreciate it if she said that.

He wouldn't like it if she took this interlude as anything more than what it was—a fragment of time where he was letting her set the pace and tone of this.

One kiss. Not that she'd had any doubts about his desire for her.

His fingers edged into her hair at the nape of her neck, his thumbs rubbing in mindless circles. "Not at all," he said. "Nothing but admiration here."

"Lower please," she said, in defiant demand.

His laughter vibrated through his body, transferring to hers. "Yes, my lady." He obediently moved those clever fingers down her neck and onto her shoulders.

Clare groaned when he pressed them into the tight knots he found there.

He was unraveling her, she knew. On more than one level. But she had no energy to resist. No wish to erect her silly defenses.

"Why?" she asked, wanting to know everything he thought of her.

Now his fingers were gently kneading her arms and her back muscles and reducing her to a blob of good feeling and nothing else. "Why what?"

"Why admiration? Because I kissed you better than I did last time?"

Again, that laughter. It was low and warm, and it made her chest feel full of a comforting quality. Clare wanted to roll around in that sound forever and ever.

"Why not? You took sheer terror for your life and transformed it into passion and determination. You didn't let it diminish you. You used it to find a new you…that, lovely Clare, is cause for admiration and celebration."

Clare clung to him, no inhibitions or reserve left in her. She'd worked hard all her life with no boyfriends or thought to the future except establishing her own business. The money her father had "given" her before he died—at such cost—had finally allowed her to do that. But the driving force had been her determination to build something for herself.

"You know something about dwelling in fear and forging something out of it, don't you?" she said then, knowing that she was crossing that invisible boundary she'd always sensed around him. Knowing that he might put those walls back up again in the beat of a breath and shut this interlude down.

But she was tired of being circumspect. Of settling for less than what she wanted.

She was also aware that patterns built over a lifetime of abandonment couldn't be broken overnight. Sooner or later, she was going to revert to her old habits. To being circumspect with her emotions. To becoming one of life's spectators once again.

But in the meantime, she was simply going to look at this as a forced, but much-needed vacation. And the main feature of her vacation would be doing deliciously wicked things with Dev Kohli.

Pupils darkened, mouth swollen, hair in disarray, the man looked scrumptious. There was none of that suave, unruffled playboy right now. This was a man in the throes of hard lust. She liked seeing him like this—all gorgeously rumpled, thanks to her hungry kisses.

If she could throw off her shackles for anyone, it had to be this man. Who, she was beginning to suspect, was quite the package—inside and out.

There was a sudden pause, but he didn't push her away and tell her that asking such a question was above her pay-grade. Or that their devastatingly sweet kiss didn't give her a right to delve and probe.

Instead, he drew in a long breath and Clare felt the echo of it in the rise and fall of his chest. "Yes, I do know what it feels like when no one hears you. Or sees you. I know what it feels like when the only definition you have of yourself is set by others."

Clare gave up all pretense then. She threw her arms around his waist and held on tight. His large hands moved over her back—in an act of appeasement or need, she had no idea—and then he pulled her close.

"You're a witch," he said gruffly, but his fingers were gentle as they clasped her cheek, and then he was kissing her again.

This kiss was not gentle or sweet or exploratory. It was a fierce taking. It was a toll he demanded for giving a piece of himself. His fingers clasped her bottom, holding her firmly against his hard body, his erection a brand against her belly. Clare felt the most overpowering need to touch herself between her thighs, or beg him to. The ache that built there was so insistent.

"I want more," she said brazenly, determined to ride this high for as long as she could. She could feel a flush climbing her neck at her pouty request, but she didn't care. "I want a repeat of that night."

His sudden curse ripped through the air.

Hands on her shoulders, he gently put her back from him. "Let's think this through for a moment, Ms. Roberts. For one thing, you're in shock. For another..." His brown gaze zeroed in on her lips, and he seemed as though he'd forgotten what he was saying.

Clare licked them, wanting to feel the swollen sensitivity everywhere else too. "Lost your train of thought there, Mr. Kohli?"

"I think first we both need a cold drink and then... I suggest we wait." Another sweep of his eyes over her body, and it was almost like those big hands had stroked her all over again.

Her gaze dropped down. The outline of his erection was clearly visible. An incredible rush of female empowerment hit Clare in her belly. She flicked her gaze up to meet his eyes. Saw desire etched onto his sharp features. "Why wait? I told you, Dev, you don't have to worry that I'll ask for more."

A flush streaked the sharp blades of his cheekbones. "It's not that. We need to discuss something important first. I think I've come up with a way to get you out of this."

"Out of sleeping together?"

A smile split his mouth. "No." He rubbed a hand over his face. "I think I've already made my peace with the fact that you and I'll end up in bed again soon enough."

"That confident of your studly prowess, huh?" Clare interjected, wanting to be miffed but not really succeeding. She couldn't pretend anymore that he was simply a man who looked at women as conquests or mindless entertainment. Neither was she going to turn him into perfect relationship material with her overactive imagination.

The present was all she had, and she was going to revel in it each day she could.

He shrugged. "Not my studly prowess so much as chemistry like ours. It doesn't happen all the time, and this is the strongest I've ever felt. Does that answer satisfy you?"

His tone glinted with humor and challenge, and Clare nodded regally. The answering warmth in his eyes made her heart feel too big for her chest.

"Do you get the sense that our roles are being reversed?" she said then, pulling away from him.

But he didn't let her hand go. Clare's heart jumped at the small gesture that had nothing to do with desire or lust and everything to do with something else. Something she didn't want to define. If she gave it a name, there wouldn't be the chance of an escape. "What do you mean?" he asked curiously.

"Like I'm becoming this devil-may-care woman and you're—" she smiled, loving how he tilted his head and stared at her hungrily "—turning into some kind of honorable man trying to keep me out of trouble."

Dev laughed. "Am I? Don't worry, Clare. This whole honor thing will wear out soon enough. Just listen to me, first."

Clare nodded, a trickle of apprehension diluting the heady sense of excitement that had filled her. She didn't want to face reality just yet. She didn't want to turn into boring old Clare again.

She liked this new, fun, to-hell-with-everything Clare she got to be with Dev. There was something about him that had made her want to push herself, from the first moment she'd laid eyes on him.

A smile creased his cheeks and that damned dimple flashed at her. "Don't look so worried. This should get you out of the Mafia thug's hands permanently."

Her pulse zigzagged through her body. "How?" she demanded.

"We'll simply get married."

Simply get married...

It had sounded simple in his head but as he watched how his suggestion landed on Clare, Dev wondered if he'd made a big mistake. Not about wanting to protect her. One way or another, he was going to get her out of this predicament.

He'd always had an affinity for the underdog. Seeing that he'd been one himself. Or at least he had before his transformation into an…*an oversexed playboy billionaire*, as she'd called him.

His mouth curved at the title.

While he still didn't understand how a smart woman like Clare could have made such a bad error in judgment by borrowing money from a known mobster, he couldn't hold it against her. His company wouldn't have been in this giant mess if he hadn't made a ghastly one himself.

But…given the way all humor fled her face at his words, and the way she stared back at him, he wondered if he'd just made another error.

By assuming that she'd take his idea in her stride. That she'd see it only as a solution to her problem and not something else. Something more.

When several minutes passed and she still didn't say anything, Dev felt more than a hint of irritation. "Do you have a boyfriend tucked away in London who might object to this idea?"

He knew it was the most ridiculous question the moment he heard it. She'd never hinted at any prior relationship, and he'd gotten the sense that Clare kept her relationships carefully vacant of too much attachment. But…the words had stemmed out of jealousy. From a place he didn't even know existed.

Which was ridiculous. Because it wasn't as if he was asking for anything from her, during their proposed arrangement. Nothing that wasn't inevitable anyway.

The very inelegant snort she let out told him the same. "Of course I don't." Then she straightened and he could see anger building in her face. "Do you think I'd be…cavorting around with you if I had someone I loved back home?"

"Cavorting?" he said, raising a brow, hoping to deflect her attention away from his stupid question.

"Don't think you can distract me, Dev," she said, putting paid to that tactic.

"Then what's the problem?"

She took in a deep breath. "The problem is that marriage is a big step. I...it means a lot of big things like trust and fidelity and..."

Dev reached out and rubbed a finger over her cheek. "I do trust you, Clare. Which is why I'm not hyperventilating."

She looked him up and down. "Are you the type to hyperventilate?"

"If the topic of conversation is marriage, yes. Does that make me less manly?"

"Nothing makes you less manly, Dev," she snapped, with more than a bite to her tone.

"Ah...so the hyperventilation would be a symptom of the underlying condition of not wanting to commit, is it? I forgot that you're the founding member of the bachelor playboy club, allergic to all things long term."

He scrunched his nose in distaste. "You make me sound like I have a disease. But no, a traditional marriage isn't in the cards for me." He pushed a hand through his hair, annoyed that she kept making him ponder things he'd never... well, pondered before. Like marriage. And fidelity. And long-term relationships. And how it would feel to have someone permanent in your life who knew you inside out. Who would make you laugh and want and push you to be a better version of yourself.

Who would also have complete control of your emotional health? Who could destroy your self-worth with one well-targeted barb? the sanest part of his brain pointed out.

No woman was worth opening himself up to that kind of risk again. Yes, that meant sometimes his life was lonely. But it wasn't exactly a choice he'd made so much as a defense mechanism. A way he could survive intact. The only way.

"And while, yes, this is bigger than anything we've both done, it is to our mutual benefit."

"How?"

"Firstly, it should stop this mobster from just…taking you. As my wife, you'll be so much more high-profile, and there will be permanent security in place around you. He's unlikely to just kidnap you, which gives us time to negotiate and see if paying off his loan is going to satisfy his desire for vengeance. As for me, it provides me with instant respectability. A distraction for the media to focus on while I sort out Athleta. It's getting tiring hearing my competitors using this scandal to try and get ahead of me. My twin called and told me both my sisters have had paparazzi chasing them. Diya's also had to put up with my dad's lecture about how I'm casting a shadow over Bhai's shining reputation."

"Bhai?"

"My older brother," he explained. It had been only a matter of time before Dev heard his father's opinion on this matter. It didn't mean he'd ever been prepared for it.

"I told you those interviews with your family were important," Clare said, mercifully interrupting the spiral of anger and frustration he got pulled into whenever he thought of his father. "People need to see your face alongside theirs. They need to see different sides of you."

"I agree. And this way, they will see not only a loyal brother, but a happily married man—head over heels in love with his wife. Two birds with one stone… It seems to me like it's the best stopgap measure."

She laughed and Dev sensed the ache she couldn't hide in her words. "I never imagined I'd hear the words 'stopgap measure' in a proposal."

"Does that mean you've imagined getting a proposal?"

He thought she'd shrug and laugh it off. He needed her to. He didn't want to discover at this stage that Clare was the romantic type.

"In a faraway future kind of way, yes. I'm a businesswoman through and through. But it doesn't mean I didn't harbor the hope of a husband and a family someday. I want to be a wife. And a mum." She swallowed and looked away. When she turned and look back at him, her blue eyes glittered in a way he'd never seen before. "I want to belong. To someone. To something. I've always wanted more than just a career."

If she'd kicked him in the chest, Dev would have been less surprised. He didn't know why. He'd heard her talking about her best friends. He'd seen the hurt on her face the morning after their incredible night together when he'd told her they were done.

But somehow he'd thought she'd be more like him. More disinclined to take the traditional path in life. The idea of Clare marrying some stranger and having his children did strange things to his insides. Things he didn't want to dwell on.

He had to make one thing clear. "You're only in your twenties. All those things are still possible for you, Clare. This marriage is only a temporary solution to both our problems, and it doesn't mean you'll have to give up any of your long-term dreams."

"Making sure I know the score?" she said, the earlier ache in her voice gone. "Making sure you're in the clear? Don't worry, I understand."

He should have been glad that she could so easily shelve her hopes for the future. That she could keep that part of herself mostly hidden. Instead, Dev only tasted a perverse bitterness that she'd so clearly decided that he wasn't going to be included in that particular dream.

Even though, that was exactly what he'd already warned her.

He shrugged. "Earlier, on our way to the foyer after dinner, I spotted a photographer from a popular lifestyle magazine watching from behind one of those giant trees in the courtyard when I was giving you my jacket. I have a feeling the shot he took was quite an intimate one."

She gasped. "Why didn't you stop him?"

"It was too late," Dev said with a shrug. "I'm sure that photo of us has already hit the internet. There'll shortly be rabid speculation that I have a new woman. In a day, they'll know it's you. This way, we're staying ahead of the curve and dictating the news. We could get married at my villa in the Caribbean, and by the time we've sailed back to California for Diya's wedding, the news of our own private, top-secret wedding will be all over the news. As I've already said, hopefully, it will at least make your mobster think twice about snatching you openly. Between us all, my family has a lot of clout."

"He's not my mobster."

"You know what I mean."

"And it will only be an arrangement of convenience?" she said cautiously.

Dev nodded. "It can be whatever you want it to be, Clare." He pinned her with his gaze. "Do you trust me?"

"I do." Her instant answer calmed the furor in his head. Dev kept seeing the damned image she'd created in his mind—Clare marrying some staid accountant type. Clare running behind two children. Clare in bed with this boring old accountant who was nevertheless extremely good in bed.

Or was that himself he was imagining in her bed now?

Dev cursed.

Her gaze held his, a question in it.

Dev shook his head.

"I have a few conditions," she said after what felt like a weighty silence.

"Whatever makes you more comfortable," he said.

"I would like for us to have a prenup."

Stunned, Dev stared at her. It was something he'd fully

intended to work into the conversation. With wealth like his, they were as common as summer homes in warm places. But it had felt somehow wrong discussing one with Clare. As if he was questioning her character.

"I'm glad I can still shock you," she said with a small smile.

Dev said nothing.

"I...when this is all over—however long it takes—I'd like to part as friends, Dev. I... I don't have a lot of those but the ones I have, I like to keep them. A prenup guarantees that our divorce will be straightforward, and we'll be more likely to keep in contact, right?"

"If I'd thought otherwise, even for a moment, I wouldn't have suggested this."

She nodded. "I'm realizing that."

"Is that all?" he said, uncomfortable with the look she sent him. It wasn't exactly gratitude. It was the same thing he'd seen in her eyes that morning. And the night when he'd carried her from the library on the yacht.

It was an emotion that Dev didn't know how to accept. Or even how to feel it himself, much less return it.

"Will you have loads and loads of marital sex written into the prenup?"

Dev didn't laugh. Because as sure as he was that she was serious, he was also beginning to understand that this was no small matter. He held out his hand to her.

She looked at it without taking it.

"Come, Clare. Let's get you to bed. You're in shock and I shouldn't have sprung this on you."

She shook her head stubbornly.

"You're angry with me, I get it. We can talk this over after you've had a good night's sleep."

"I'm not angry with you at all. You're going above and beyond for me. It's just... I have a hard time being dependent on anyone. I don't want to be beholden to you, Dev.

At the same time, I don't think I can quite act per some guidelines written down on paper. It would be too much of a farce. It would make it as much of a cage as that mobster was wanting to thrust me into."

Dev held her loosely, her fierce need to be in control of her own destiny striking an echo in him. "What can I do to make this better for you, sweetheart?" he said, pressing his mouth to her temple. "What can I do to make this less a punishment and more of your choice? Other than the lots and lots of sex that we're going to get to have during this marriage, that is."

She laughed then, and he felt as if he'd won a gold medal again.

As if for the first time in his life, there was perfect alignment, perfect harmony between him and another soul.

It was also the first time in his life he'd laid himself open and offered to give someone else everything he could. Emotionally, that was.

CHAPTER NINE

DEV KEPT SURPRISING HER. In a good way. In a fantastic, knee-buckling way. In a come-trust-me-with-your-heart kind of way.

Clare was so tired of freeze-locking her heart. Of pretending it didn't want more. That it hadn't already started thawing in this man's presence a while ago.

She was so tired of pretending that she wanted more out of life.

She looked into Dev's eyes, something solid and immovable lodging in her throat. She kept expecting so little, and he bowled her over every single time. A strange swooping sensation began in her belly, as if she was perpetually in flight. She drew a deep breath. "I need this to be more than just a...sterile agreement on paper."

He curled his upper lip in a deliberately lecherous way. "You mean all the sex won't unsterilize it? Because if I remember rightly, it was explosive."

Clare laughed and tucked away a lock of hair that fell onto his forehead. There it was again—that floaty feeling. It felt like the most natural thing in the world to laugh with him like this. To touch him like this. "Like you said, we'd have done that eventually whether we got hitched or not."

"True," he said with a nod. He sat down on the sofa and pulled her onto his lap with an effortless poise, as if he couldn't go too long without touching her. "Let's see then."

His palm was big and broad against her back, and Clare wanted to melt into it. "I prefer to sleep in the center of the bed. And I hog all the sheets."

Clare slipped her arm around his neck and settled in. "I would have found that out anyway."

He grinned. And tangled his fingers with hers in her lap. "So this is like a toll I have to pay then?" His thumb rubbed at her pulse on her wrist. "For you to marry me?"

They were both smiling and he was touching her so casually, and yet Clare could sense that invisible boundary tightening around him as he spoke. But she wasn't going to give in and let him keep his distance from her.

It had nothing to do with their getting married either. It had everything to do with the fact that she wanted to know more about him. That she wanted him to share in her own life too. That for the first time, she wanted more from life itself.

The strength of that urge sent a shiver of fear through her. An almost familiar echo from when she'd so patiently waited for her dad to show up, although he never did. But Clare pushed it away.

"How about I share something first?" she prompted, not for a game of give and take but because she wanted him to know. Because he'd earned her trust. By giving his own to her.

He looked at her and knew. Just like that. He knew from her face that it wasn't a small or silly thing. "Clare, it doesn't—"

She pressed her finger against his lips. "I want to tell you this." She swallowed the ache in her throat. "I haven't told a soul since I found out. But I want to tell you, Dev."

His fingers tightened over hers. "I'm not going anywhere, sweetheart."

"I didn't borrow the money from that crime lord. In fact, the first I heard of him owning me—" she shuddered, and

Dev's arms came around her like a cocoon "—was when that goon of his accosted me in London. I didn't take the money, Dev. I didn't even know who he was."

His finger under chin, Dev tilted her face up to his. "Then why does he think he owns you?"

Shame filled her chest but Clare pushed on. "My father passed away a few years ago now. We...we were not a normal family."

"Is anyone's family normal, Clare?" he said, and Clare heard the answering ache in his words. It made it so much easier to go on.

"I have no memories of my mother. When I was five, my father dropped me off at my aunt's. With loads of promises of coming back. Of traveling around the world, making his fortune and treating me like a princess."

Dev nodded, encouraging her to go on.

Clare laughed, feeling that hope and disappointment in her chest like it was yesterday. "My aunt was not happy, to say the least. But she gave me shelter and food and for the most part, she was indifferent to my existence. But I hung on to my father's promises. I believed that one day he'd come back for me. It sustained me...that hope."

"But—"

"If you say it was foolish, I'll never forgive you. So please don't."

"I won't," he said with emphasis. "I won't say anything you've done is foolish, Clare. Or wrong. You're a survivor. That's all that matters."

Clare thought she might have fallen a little in love with him then. "I studied hard, got a scholarship to go to an excellent private school. That's where I met Amy and Bea. I found a job I liked, but I always wanted to be my own boss. So one day, Dad contacted me to tell me that he'd discovered he was dying, but that his hard work had finally paid off. That he was sending me a sum of money that I would have inherited after he passed away anyway. He said it was his gift to me—reparation for all the birthdays and holidays he'd missed. I was overjoyed to hear from him after so many years, and devastated he didn't have long left to live. I was foolish enough to think my faith in him had been validated. It was a lot of money, and I used it to set up The London Connection."

Dev's brows pulled together into a ferocious scowl. The tension in him was immediate. "Wait, so he sent you that capital? He took the money from the mobster and gave it to you?"

Her eyes prickling with heat, Clare nodded. "I wondered how that even works, in this day and age. Yes. And of course he died without paying it back. So the mobster eventually discovered what happened to him, and turned his attention to me. How could a man use his own daughter as collateral? Did he think a major crime lord would never find me?"

"I'm so sorry, Clare." His hand around her arm, his mouth pressed to her temple, Dev held her tight. As if he was determined to stop her from falling apart.

"I keep thinking with each day that passes, it'll hurt less. That I'll understand why he did this. That something will make me see the whole thing in a new light. But the cold, hard reality doesn't change. When all his other schemes failed, he took the easy way out. He only sent me that money before he died to salve his own conscience for neglecting me my whole life, and he even managed to mess that up in the worst possible way."

I took money from a man I shouldn't have trusted.

Her words came back to Dev. She'd meant her father, not the mobster. How could anyone hold that against her?

Dev fisted his hands by his side, fury filling him slowly. What the hell kind of a man jeopardized his daughter's life like that? He banked the fury knowing that it had taken Clare everything to tell him that much. Knowing that she needed comfort just then and nothing more.

She didn't want a champion; that much had been clear from the start.

But this... Dev now understood the fear, the need to be in control, the strength of will it had taken her to not only manage her emotions but to use the opportunity to pitch her firm to him.

Having always lived in the world of overachievers, Dev was full of admiration for this woman who'd withstood so much and still remained strong and fierce. All the while retaining a sense of joy in life.

"It's not your shame. Or even your burden, Clare. It's his. It doesn't matter that he repeatedly broke your faith in him. That he betrayed you in the worst way possible. None of it is your fault. You know that, right?"

"I do know that. But I've moved on from anger and hurt. I have to."

Dev frowned. This woman was forever going to surprise him. "What do you mean?"

Clare shifted her head and met his gaze. "If I let it, what he did will become a poison inside of me. It will corrupt my business, my life, my heart. And that isn't something I can afford to allow to happen. I have to choose to forgive him. Or it will become the thing that will consume and corrupt me." She took a deep breath. "So I'm going to try to let it go. I'm going to focus on getting out of this mess. On moving forward with my life. And that means I'll marry you and help polish your tarnished halo—" she scrunched her fingers through his hair, and his scalp prickled with sensation "—playing the part of your adoring wife for a while...and then go back to making The London Connection even better than it already is. There, now I feel mostly in control of this situation."

Pleasure and pride wound through Dev like a rope that couldn't be untangled. At the same time, he also felt a perverse resentment at her inner strength. Of how bravely she was making the choice to not let her father's betrayal ruin her.

He clearly didn't possess the same strength. He didn't have the generosity of spirit that she possessed. Even worse, he had no intention of forgiving anyone for anything.

Holding her like this, watching her choose joy and happiness over resentment and anger, he felt more than a little jaded. At twenty-nine, he felt as if he'd already lived through ten lifetimes of anger and resentment. All his choices in life now looked like they were tainted too.

Because he'd allowed the poison of his childhood to run rampant inside him for his whole life.

"Thank you for listening to me, Dev," she said softly, pulling him back to the present. "For just about everything."

"I didn't do it for your gratitude, Clare."

"No, you did it because it was the right thing to do. Thanks to you, my faith in men isn't completely dashed."

Dev shook his head. "Don't, Clare. This will benefit me too. So don't make me out to be some kind of hero." He pressed on. "But I know how hard it must have been to lay yourself open like that, so thank you for trusting me with the truth."

She looked up then, and the piercing quality of her gaze pinged through him. "I couldn't let you think I was that foolish anymore. It was fine when I thought you were just another only-in-it-for-a-good-time playboy."

He grinned at that. "I love these titles you keep coming up with for me."

"But none of them truly fit, do they?"

Dev frowned. "What do you mean?"

"I mean that I've seen more of the real you than you show the world, Dev. But there's still a lot more lying hidden. What was it you called it? Paying a toll? I don't want you to tell me as if it's a toll you're paying. I want you to want to tell me. I'd like to get to know the part of you that you don't show anyone else."

No one had ever asked him that. No one had ever cared enough to know. Not even his twin knew it all. But to confide in Clare meant something he wasn't prepared to admit to. "You're mistaking me for a deep lake. I'm a shallow pond, remember."

She pushed out of his arms and looked down at him. "All lies. But it's okay, Dev. If my pathetic excuse for a dad has taught me one thing, it's that you can't demand things from people—loyalty or love or even confidences—that they're unwilling to give. But I'd like you to know that I want more from you. From this partnership. More than orgasms, that is," she added candidly.

Dev had no idea how she did it—making demands of him he couldn't fulfill one minute and making him laugh the next. But there was no point in letting her think this was more than it was. His tone was grave when he said, "I've given you everything I'm capable of giving, Clare. Does that help?"

She scrunched her nose and smiled. A sad smile. As if she understood even though he didn't say the words. "Not really. But I'll take that as a win for now. And now, I'm going to shower, eat a tub of ice cream and then your spare bed's got my name on it."

When she'd have slipped away, Dev pulled her back to him. He felt a strange reluctance to let her go, even though she'd be in the next room to his.

For the first time in his adult life, he felt an acute need for companionship. For more whispered confidences. For more of a connection with a woman than just a sexual one.

For all of those things with this particular woman.

And yet he didn't want to fight it. Or shove it away. Or call it a temporary madness.

In this moment, he felt all of that resentment and distance that forced him to stand alone in the world fall away. In this moment, he felt perfectly aligned with the universe and with Clare.

Her arms came around his neck as he pressed his mouth to the upper curve of her breast. He could taste the salt of the ocean, smell the sea breeze and her own distinct floral scent on her skin. Desire thrummed through him as she responded instantly. Her nails raked over his skin, and a shudder went through her.

Dev licked at the thundering pulse at her neck. He let his hands run rampant, caressing the dips and valleys of her body. He didn't even need this to go any deeper than it was right now. There was a sense of contentment in just holding her and in stoking the fire of their mutual desire higher and hotter.

With a muttered curse, she tugged his face to hers and kissed him fiercely.

Laughter and something else he didn't want to name held him in its grip as she devoured his mouth as if there was no end to her hunger for him. Dev had never been appreciated so thoroughly in his life.

When she let him go, he was rock hard, panting and desperate for more.

"Good night then," the minx whispered, a wicked glint in her blue eyes.

The dark shadows under her eyes tugged at him. "You don't have to go to bed alone tonight, Clare." When she smiled slowly, he held up his palm. "I'm not talking about sex. I'm concerned that nightmare you had on the yacht will be back."

"If it does, then you'll pick me up and bring me to your bed, won't you?"

She didn't wait for him to deny her. Not that Dev would have. He had a feeling he wouldn't have to share anything with her. Because the damned woman had seen and knew everything about him already.

More than he felt comfortable sharing with anyone.

"You're putting a lot of trust in me that's not warranted, Clare," he warned. "I'm no hero."

"Ha! Believe me, Dev, the last thing I need is a hero. Because they don't really exist, do they? If there is such a thing, it's people like us who live their lives, day after day, even though they've been dealt a bad hand."

"Then what is it you think you know about me, Clare?" he asked. He suddenly wanted her opinion. He wanted to know what it was that she thought of him.

"I think you're a man who wants more than he realizes. A man who doesn't have as much as he thinks he does. A man who has a lot more to give."

With that parting, perceptive shot, she walked away.

Making Dev wonder and question and doubt all the things he'd always thought were unshakeable truths about himself.

She was getting married in a few minutes.

As she looked at the knee-length, cream A-line dress she'd picked up during the short shopping jaunt that Dev had allowed her back in Rio before they'd spent several days sailing to his villa on St. Lucia, Clare wondered how many times she'd have to say it in her head for it sink in completely.

She was getting married to a man she would have preferred to like a little less than she did, even if that sounded more than a bit twisted. She was getting married without either of her best friends present. At the thought of Amy and Bea, her throat filled up.

The feel of the delicate silk under her fingers gave her

something to anchor herself with, instead of focusing on the looping thoughts inside her head.

"He's really a catch, you know," Angelina Lansang continued her chatter without missing a beat. "Everyone that knows Dev is going to go crazy to discover he's secretly got hitched. The press, the media…" The tall woman laughed, a little bit inanely. As if this was the best thing about Dev getting married.

Do any of them actually know him? Clare wanted to ask. *Do they know that he's kind and far more complex than any interview or article could ever capture?*

But Clare didn't say anything of the sort, because sweet as Angelina had been during the time it had taken to sail to the island, she couldn't betray the fact that this was a fake wedding.

For a few, fleeting seconds, Angelina considered Clare thoughtfully before smiling again. "I hope you're ready for all the attention you're going to get, my dear." Clare resolutely kept her mouth closed.

Not only did she not know Angelina well enough, she didn't trust her own thoughts. Several days of pondering this every which way hadn't untangled her thoughts any better.

Since the other woman was waiting for a response, Clare smiled. "I can't thank you enough for everything, Angelina."

Angelina nodded, and returned her smile.

Ever since Clare and Dev had met up with Derek and Angelina the following day in Rio and he'd introduced Clare as his fiancée, asking them to join them at his villa and witness the ceremony, Angelina had completely changed her attitude. Not that Clare wasn't grateful.

It was, after all, thanks to Angelina's insistence that Dev had reluctantly agreed to Clare shopping for a suitable bridal outfit before leaving Rio. Not that Clare couldn't have fought that particular battle herself.

Even if the agreement between them was that this wedding was nothing but a mutually beneficial arrangement, she'd had no intention of marrying him wearing a trouser suit more suitable for business than pleasure.

Even if it was a designer suit.

It had been while they were having that discussion that Clare had finally lost the battle of pretending that this wedding mattered as little to her as it did to him.

Yes, this was a convenient arrangement that would benefit both of them. But it didn't mean that she couldn't feel some sentiment. That she could treat it as just any other normal day.

The wedding was only a technicality. She had silently recited that fact so often, it was as if it were her life's mantra. But looking at herself in the mirror, dressed as a bride, Clare knew no mantra was going to work on her.

Foolish or not, naive or not, she'd always dreamed of this day.

Because she was marrying Dev, Clare didn't even have to build her castles on the empty promises of a charming man who was all glitter and no substance. And it was this fact that kept tripping her up.

"You look beautiful." The surprise in Angelina's tone brought Clare back to the present.

She knew it didn't really matter how beautiful she looked. This marriage was only temporary and there would no doubt be countless other, far more beautiful women in Dev's life after she'd exited it. The thought darkened her mood, the pit of her stomach suddenly hollow. And that, in turn, flipped her mood back again. She was determined never to operate out of fear or loneliness ever again.

So what if she and Dev weren't going to promise to love

each other for the rest of their lives? So what if their marriage came with a short shelf life?

She liked the man she was going to marry. She also very much liked what he was capable of doing to her with one playful glance from those twinkling eyes, with those clever fingers and with those sculpted lips. She wasn't going to pretend that she could be all matter-of-fact and cold about this. This was no fantasy she had concocted while waiting to escape from under the indifferent roof of her aunt.

This was her life.

Clare adjusted her hair and stared again at her reflection in the mirror. The dress was classy and elegant, but sexy enough as it clung to her curves. Her skillfully styled hair helped highlight her features. Her lipstick—a vibrant red—made her mouth look full and pouty.

She looked beautiful, she was getting married and she had the serious hots for her husband-to-be.

As she turned to leave the room, Clare told herself it was okay that this wedding felt real to her. It was the most real thing that had ever happened to her. And she was going to make the most of it.

"It's just a PR ploy," he'd said when his best friend had asked him what the hell he was playing at the night before his wedding.

"Like hell it is," Derek had said with a deep laugh. "You're in deep trouble, my man."

Now, as Dev watched his intended walk toward him in his airy Caribbean villa, he felt Derek's words reverberate within his chest.

Clare looked nothing like some cheap participant in a PR ploy and everything like deep trouble poured into an enticingly petite frame. Just for him.

She looked stunning and elegant and beautiful in a cream-colored dress. Far too much like a real bride with her smile glowing and her eyes bright and generally radiating a serene kind of joy.

It reached Dev like a wave of emotion, intent on pulling him under.

He'd never given marriage much thought, except for knowing that it wasn't for him. He'd been far too busy building an empire.

But as he stood there, waiting for Clare to reach him, "PR ploy" felt like the most inadequate nonsense he'd ever uttered.

"You're in so much trouble, man," Derek whispered again with a pat on his shoulder.

Whatever retort he wanted to throw back at his friend died as Clare reached him. As he looked into the blue eyes of the woman he'd promised himself he'd look after. He hadn't, when he'd originally suggested the idea to her, thought to paint himself in the role of her hero.

For a long time, even into his adulthood, thinking himself as anything more than a failure had been hard. Even gaining Derek's friendship at military school and then discovering his talent for swimming, he'd struggled to see himself as anything but a disappointment to everyone around him.

Old patterns were hard to break.

It was only after he'd made his first million that Dev had felt a sense of achievement. Which was all kinds of messed up, he knew. Equating wealth and fame and power with self-worth was going down the same poisonous line of thinking Papa had employed when he'd scoured layers of Dev's self-esteem as a child with his harsh words.

You'll amount to nothing if you continue like this.

And the harshest cut of all: *Your mama's lucky to have gone before she saw you like this.*

By the time he'd realized that he'd started measuring himself by the same toxic yardstick as his father had done, it was too late to change. Plus, Dev had never been a hypocrite. He had enjoyed all the fame and wealth and power that his achievements and success had brought him.

Meeting Derek—who was six foot six and had weighed three hundred pounds as a sixteen-year-old, who was constantly viewed as a threat just because of his size and skin color while in actuality, the gentle giant possessed a heart of gold—had taught Dev a lot about how to manage people's perceptions.

So Dev knew there was a good reason Derek was calling him on his nonsense about his marriage being a PR ploy.

But it *was* saving his reputation too, he reminded himself. This was letting up pressure on him, his family, his company and hopefully salvaging Athleta's reputation. They would both simply walk away from this in a few months with their problems solved. He hadn't told Clare yet, but he'd already had his security chief make contact with the mobster to start negotiations to try to pay off her debt.

This would be yet another satisfying business arrangement with a few pleasures thrown in as enjoyable extras. And he knew it wasn't just him thinking about sex.

But, as he glanced at the woman now standing beside him, Dev kept hearing Derek's sarcastic laughter inside his head.

Deep trouble, man...

It wasn't that her simple but stunning dress made her skin shimmer. It wasn't that she was holding a beautiful bouquet of lilies of the valley as a bride usually did. It wasn't even the platinum ring she'd produced in contrast to the plain gold band he'd selected at her suggestion.

It was the look in her blue eyes.

She didn't look at him as if this was a business arrangement. Or as if she was putting on an act. She simply looked as if she were gloriously happy to be marrying him. In that easy, let's-turn-Dev's-world-upside-down way that only she had.

From the first moment they'd met at that charity gala, she had seen him.

Him. Only him.

Dev Kohli. Not the shallow playboy, not the ruthless billionaire, not the *studly stud* as she'd called him, but just him.

It didn't matter that he hadn't given her what she'd asked for. It seemed as if she'd taken a part of him anyway, even without his permission.

As they stood there saying their vows, culminating with him bending his head and taking her mouth in a kiss that sealed her fate with his—at least temporarily—Dev had the uneasy feeling that he'd gone a step too far with this marriage. That he'd tangled himself into something he didn't quite understand.

Because no kiss had ever shaken him to his core like this one did.

Sweet and familiar, her lips molded to his in the exact way he needed them to. Her body pressed against his with that wide-open generosity of hers, her heart thudding against his own.

She felt like she belonged to him. In a way nothing and no one else ever had.

And, as he pulled away from her perceptive gaze, and laughed at some joke that Angelina cracked, his heart beating faster and faster, Dev wondered how he was going to fight it. How he was going to maintain any kind of distance when all he wanted was to steal her away for himself.

How he was going to walk away from her when all this was over.

CHAPTER TEN

"ARE YOU DRUNK?"

Dev looked up from the open book in his lap he'd been flicking through for the last hour. The letters and words jumped and leaped on the page. Even more so than usual since his concentration was shot to hell.

He simply stared at Clare for a few seconds. Wondering if she was the cause or the means of escape from this torture.

She was standing with her back against the door to his bedroom. On the inside, he clarified for himself. The high walls and ceilings of his villa and all the skylights he'd had his architect install meant she was bathed in moonlight. Her freshly washed hair shone, and her eyes glittered with bright curiosity and something else as they swept over his naked chest.

Desire...and she didn't bother hiding it.

Awareness slammed through Dev.

She was his wife and he was her husband. He'd figured that a piece of paper with their signatures on it didn't really stand for much in the greater scheme of things. But he'd found that it did. He was discovering that maybe he was a traditional man at heart, after all.

A man who believed in marriage and family and all the things Mama had believed lay firmly at the center of human existence. But with that realization also came the acute feeling of inadequacy that he didn't like. It left a bad taste in his mouth. Reminded him of how he'd struggled with it for too many years. What if he wasn't any good as a husband?

This discovery about wanting things that he couldn't have, wouldn't be any good at, bothered him. After years of being a physically perfect championship-standard athlete and then his unprecedented success in the business world meant he'd forgotten how it felt to be bad at something. As a result, he was in a roaring bad mood. Which was really rare for him.

He shook his head. "No."

Arms folded against her chest, she rolled her eyes. "Good."

"What's good?" he asked, knowing that he was winding her up but enjoying it anyway. They were hitting that rhythm again. Bandying words while heat built around them. This was something he was exceptionally good at.

"Well, to start with, it's good that Derek and Angelina seem to be getting through this rough patch," she said.

"Why is that good?"

"It's clear that you allow very few people into your life. Derek's happiness matters to you."

He grunted in response. Really, the last thing he wanted to talk about was Derek and Angelina's marriage. He didn't want to talk at all.

He wanted her. Desperately. He wanted to be inside her. He wanted to scratch this itch—as many times as required—and be done with it. He wanted to get rid of this sentimental nonsense that had taken over his head ever since he'd slipped the ring on her finger.

"You're not in a talking mood," she said, licking her lips.

"No."

"If anyone could see us now," she said, her eyes glinting with challenge, "they'd think I was the feudal lord and you my blushing bride."

He raised a brow. With each teasing word, she dispelled his dark mood. "And yet you're the one plastered to the door." He pushed the duvet down and patted the space next to him on the bed. "Care to try that theory by coming closer?"

Dev found his gaze eating her up, any remaining discontent washed away by curiosity and that simmering hum of desire.

"What the hell are you wearing?" he asked hoarsely.

She raised a rounded shoulder and one thin, almost nonexistent strap fell down. "This was the only thing I could find in the little time I had."

It was unlike anything Dev had ever seen, outside of maybe a period drama. It was all white and made of fine cotton. But without any ghastly ruffles.

The V-shaped bodice and the floaty hem that barely touched her knees stopped it from being plain. But, unlike silk that would have hugged her petite curves, this nightgown fluttered in the breeze through the open French doors, hinting at the dips and valleys of her body.

"You disappeared from dinner too soon," she said. "Those were your friends."

"I had things to look over."

"You don't have to run away from me, you know," she said. A hint of the fragility he'd sometimes seen in her peeked out from beneath the fierce scowl she wore.

"I've stopped running away from things that upset me a long time ago."

"So I'm one of those things, am I?"

He grinned. "If you were a thing I could put in a box so I could stop thinking about it, all of this would be easy. But you're not, are you? You're a…"

"What?"

He shrugged.

"I think the word you're looking for is *wife*. With an independent mind and a beating heart and a…" She licked her lips and Dev felt a bolt of lust shoot through him. "I decided to let you be for a little while since you looked like you were upset."

He refused to answer.

Her lower lip trembled. "Regretting this already?"

"Not really," he said, loath to hurt her. "But you're right I'm not…in a good mood."

"Okay, that's fair enough," she said, that lost expression receding from her eyes. And Dev knew in that moment what was bothering him so much.

He didn't want to hurt her. He didn't want to be the reason the fierce light that was at the heart of Clare was diminished or even extinguished. He didn't want to be another man that made her think she was less than she was.

She wasn't that weak, he reminded herself. She'd understood what this arrangement of theirs meant. She'd accepted it.

And yet he couldn't shed this sense of responsibility he suddenly felt toward her. He turned the gold band on his finger, feeling the solid weight of the metal.

Her gaze flicked to the action and then up to his face. But her expression remained steady. And Dev knew he was just being unreasonable now.

"Do you want me to leave?" she asked.

It felt as if even the breeze and the world and time itself stood still to witness his answer. He rubbed a hand over his face. "No. I don't want you to leave, Clare."

She didn't quite smile. Her wide mouth softened.

"If I stay, I have some demands of you."

"Don't push it, sweetheart," he growled.

She laughed then. "If I stay, I'm going to want to exercise my marital rights. If you're not in the mood to accommodate me, or don't have the energy it requires, you should tell me now."

He burst out laughing, just as she'd intended. He licked his lower lip, sending a leisurely, thoroughly lascivious look up and down her body.

To his delight, pink crept up her neck and cheeks. "I'm always in the mood for you, Ms. Roberts," he said with a wicked grin.

She cocked an eyebrow. "You forget that I'm Mrs. Kohli now."

He fell back against the headboard. Warmth and something else suffused his chest. "That used to be Mama. I haven't heard that title in a long time."

Her fingers went to her chest and she bit her lip. "I'm sorry, Dev. I didn't mean to poke fun at it."

"Don't be," Dev said. This time, the mention of his mother didn't leave a painful void in its wake. Not here, with the only other woman who saw through his surface qualities. Who'd always looked at him as if he could be more. As if he was more. More than the world thought him to be. More than he thought himself to be. "I have a feeling she'd have liked you."

Clare's smile put the moonlight to shame. "You think so?"

Dev nodded, feeling a sudden stab of such overpowering grief mixed in with this new feeling of joy. "Yes. She'd have especially liked how often you keep me on my toes."

She smiled. "You miss her a lot."

He shrugged. "Yes, each year, I miss her more."

"She sounds like a wonderful woman."

"She was. She…had the knack of seeing through to a person's heart. And finding something to love in everyone."

"Will you tell me more about her?"

His chest rose and fell as Dev considered this woman… his wife. She always wanted more. More of life. More of herself. More of him. "I will. But some other time. Not to-night." He beckoned her closer. "Tonight is about you and me, Clare. Only you and me." Now that he'd made peace with that fact, the slumbering need in him had risen keenly to the surface.

Why had he even been fighting this so much?

She blushed prettily, even as she demanded he give her what she wanted. "I have a wedding present for you."

Dev felt like he had been knocked over the head. Al-though he didn't know why he should be so surprised. She'd already told him that she wasn't going to pretend this was a cold, dry business arrangement.

"I have nothing for you."

She clearly wasn't disappointed by that. "I didn't expect you to get me anything. I saw this when I went shopping with Angelina and it made me think of you. Don't worry, Dev. I know what I want from you."

He raised a brow, unashamedly eating her alive with his eyes. He could see the shadow of her nipples through the nightgown, the slightly rounded shape of her belly when it was plastered to her body by the friendly breeze, and a darker shadow at the apex of her thighs. "I should tell you, Clare, that I don't have either the patience or the inclina-tion to be overly gentle tonight."

She swallowed and he saw the flutter of her pulse at her neck. "I never asked you to be gentle with me. It's your own fault if you catered to me. But then, that's what you do, don't you?"

He frowned. "I have no idea what you mean."

"That night, I didn't ask you to be gentle with me. I didn't tell you that it was my first time. It was what I needed and you simply gave it to me. That's who you are, Dev. Why fight it?"

"And here I thought you dwelled in reality, Clare."

She was hurt by that. He'd only meant to pierce the false

image of him she was building in her head. Because he sure as hell couldn't be that man.

But instead of backing down, she covered the distance between them. Now she stood close enough that he could smell the lily of the valley on her. The taut buds of her nipples taunted him. "We all need a dose of cold reality most days, I agree. But as I realized recently, a little dreaming never hurt anyone. In fact, it was the thing that sustained me through so many difficult years."

When he opened his mouth, she pressed her palm to his lips. "It's okay. I don't want to argue tonight. I have other plans—devious plans," she said with a naughty grin.

Lust kicked through him. "I should very much like to be part of your plans, Clare."

In one easy movement, he picked her up and brought her onto the bed. She landed on her knees, on the duvet, his legs still buried beneath it. The scent of her skin enveloped him and he breathed it in, like a junkie.

He took the square package with the neat bow and was about to toss it aside when she grabbed it and held it up to him.

"So that's how it's going to be, huh?" he said, burying his face in her neck. The uproar that had begun in his chest hours earlier calmed at the feel of her soft curves in his hands.

"I want you, Dev. I want to spend tonight with you. More than anything in the world. But…"

He pulled back and smiled. "Okay. I guess it's true what they say about marriage, huh?"

Her eyes widened and she played along. The twitch of her mouth made his heart swell in his chest. "What do they say about marriage, Dev?"

"That the sex dries up and your wife rules you."

"Hey," she said, swatting him on the shoulder.

Dev took the wrapped package from her hands. "All right, fine. If this is what it takes..."

Her teeth digging into her lower lip, she looked at him from under her lashes.

Curiosity took over and he ripped the wrapping off.

To find a cardboard box in his hand—an audiobook of an autobiography of a black American athlete who'd found success despite numerous obstacles. Dev had been sent an autographed copy by the gentleman. It was the one book he didn't have in audio.

So of course, he hadn't read it.

Dev stared at it for what felt like interminable seconds, alarm coursing down his spine. Tension burst into life around them, replacing all the desire and humor that he'd felt so drunk on.

He looked up to find Clare watching him.

He had no idea what she saw in his face. A nervous laugh escaped her mouth. "I noticed that you don't have the audiobook for this title."

"When?" he said. Because he had to say something to cut the awkwardness. Because to say nothing at all would betray his shock.

"Oh, I told you, I loved that library of yours. It's so well categorized that it wasn't hard to see that this one was missing."

"Yeah, I meant to get it."

"Are you angry, Dev?" Her mouth was pinched, her eyes wide. "I didn't do it to pry. Like I said, that library...it was like a part of you. I thought I..."

"No, you aren't prying," he said, stunned by how perceptive she was. He rubbed a hand over his face. "And I'm not angry." But there was something in his tone that even he couldn't identify.

Was it still just shock that had him struggling to form thoughts and sentences? Only Derek knew. It had been him who'd insisted that Dev get diagnosed. That it wasn't too late. Never too late. And of course the therapist that Dev had gone to after he'd been diagnosed knew. Not even Diya had guessed or asked.

"It's not something I ever discuss," he said, his voice hoarse. "If I'd had the diagnosis of dyslexia as a child, then it might have been different."

If he thought she'd nod and agree and close the subject, he was wrong.

Clare frowned, her palms on his bare shoulders, grounding him.

"In fact, your success, your company...you're the symbol of what one can accomplish despite being wired differently."

"Before you ask, no, I'm not ashamed of being dyslexic, Clare."

He felt that maybe he should have moderated his curt tone, but right now, the last thing he felt like doing was pacifying her or anybody else for that matter. He had always struggled alone in his life. Nothing was ever going to change that.

"I didn't think you were, Dev."

"I wasn't diagnosed until very late. Not until I was seventeen."

"But you come from such an affluent, educated family."

He laughed then, and it was the hollowest sound he'd ever heard. "You want the whole sorry story then?"

She nodded, still touching him. Still anchoring him.

"I was a very...rambunctious kid. As Deedi tells it—that's my older sister—I was slow to speak. My mother apparently schlepped me around to a lot of speech therapists. So it was decided at a very early age that of the four of us, I wasn't the brightest bulb."

"Who decided that?" Clare asked with such a fierce scowl that Dev rubbed his fingers against her brow.

"My father. But Mama wouldn't listen to him. She tried her best to help me sit down and focus. And I tried. For her, I tried so hard. But letters and words were nothing but a jumble to me. The more I tried to pin them down, the more they escaped me.

"So I started cutting classes. I started paying a friend to do my work for me. I manipulated Diya into doing my homework. I cheated as much as I could. Anything and everything to not disappoint Mama. Anything to avoid telling her the truth. Because the one thing I couldn't do was bring myself to admit that I just couldn't read. That all the books she bought me…she might as well have asked me to walk to the moon.

"After a while, all my schemes were found out. Diya got into big trouble. My friend was forever banished from seeing me. I begged Papa to not have him expelled from school. That it was all my fault. That I had manipulated them all into helping me. Mama was crushed. I've never felt as low as I did that day when she realized I'd been cheating when she'd thought I'd been getting better."

"Oh, Dev. I'm so sorry."

"I hadn't wanted to disappoint her. And I ended up crushing her. Betraying her faith in me."

"Then?"

It felt as if there were shards stuck in his throat. "She still tried. I got expelled from three different private schools for getting into trouble. She tried private tutoring and every other option out there. I'd hear them arguing at night. Hear him call me useless and stupid and her fighting with him to not call her baby boy that. Arguing that academic success wasn't everything. That she'd spend her life helping me if that's what it took. Papa was furious with me. I think more than that, it scared him. He couldn't see why one of his children wasn't like the other three. He couldn't fathom that his son was such a loser. That I resented him and argued with him and gave him attitude at every turn didn't help our relationship, either."

"But you were a kid, Dev. Just a kid. We shouldn't have to make allowances for adults and their feelings." Dev held her, hearing the pain he'd once felt echoing in her voice.

"Please tell me he didn't abuse you to your face," Clare whispered against his shoulder. "Please tell me your mother stopped him."

Dev shook his head. "He didn't call me a dumb loser, no. That was one of the names I called myself. He called me lazy, incompetent. A rogue who didn't appreciate the privileges he had. A boy who was good for nothing. Then when I was twelve, Mama died."

Clare's arms were around his neck now, her own trembling.

Dev pressed his palms to her back, glad to have her here. "The worst part is over, sweetheart."

She pulled back and glared at him. "How can you be so cavalier about this, Dev?"

"Because I can't let it be more, Clare. It's taken me years to not think of myself as a failure. Hours of therapy to realize that my brain's just wired differently. That not being able to read—something my mother loved to do with me—didn't mean the world of books wasn't cut off for me. Whenever I thought about the past, I had to develop a degree of emotional separation from it. Or I'd have ruined my life with my own hands."

"What did your father do then? After she died."

"He packed me off to military school barely a week later. Diya told me Deedi and Bhai had a huge fight with him about it, but he wouldn't listen to anyone. His grief found an outlet in me, I think. And I was happy to leave a place that no longer held the one person who'd loved me unconditionally."

"You haven't been back there since, have you?"

Dev looked into her eyes and shook his head. "No. And the thought of going back now is painful. But for Diya... I have to."

"How was the military school?"

"In retrospect, it was the best place for me. It was rigorous and disciplined and when night came, I was simply too exhausted to think of my shortcomings. I met Derek there. And one of the coaches found something to nurture in the both of us. The rest is history."

"You're a testament to—"

Dev pressed his finger to her lips. "I don't want praise, sweetheart."

She nodded, and he smiled. "I want the wedding night that I was promised. No, that you demanded that I give you. I want you to look at me as you always do."

"You think hearing this has changed how I see you?" she asked with a frown.

"Does it?"

"Of course not, you arrogant man. It only makes me want to jump your bones even more. There, is that what you want to hear?"

"Yes," Dev said, before dipping his mouth to hers.

It shouldn't have made a difference that she knew about his childhood. About the difficulties he'd had to overcome. Some he still lived with to this day.

But as Dev swept his tongue into her welcoming mouth, as he filled his hungry hands with her curves and kissed her harder and deeper, he felt as if for the first time in his life, someone knew who he was. What he'd achieved to get here. He felt...whole. Even though he hadn't realized what he'd been missing.

Hands wrapping around her slender shoulders, he gathered her closer to him.

"Yes, please. God, yes, Dev. Now," she replied. The throaty need in her voice undid Dev just a little bit more.

The taste of her skin under his tongue felt like peace and joy and contentment like he had never known before.

She was trembling as he nipped and kissed his way from her neck to the soft, silky smooth skin of her jaw. He couldn't touch her enough. Couldn't taste her enough. He licked the delicate lobe of her ear.

She shuddered, a long moan rasping out of her throat and pressed herself against him. Her breasts crushed against his chest, her lips sought his. Dev devoured her mouth as if he was a drowning man. As if the taste of her could bring him back to shuddering life from the cold, sterile reality he'd existed in for so many years.

Suddenly his life before she'd come barging into it felt...flat, one-dimensional. A glittering mockery of the real thing.

Dev had no idea who pushed the duvet out from between them. He had no idea if he was the one who pulled up the flimsy little thing that she was wearing and threw it off. He didn't know if she demanded, or he had created a space between his thighs for her.

But as their frenzied kiss deepened, he filled his hands with the slight weight of her breasts. She straddled his hips, moving up and over him, until she was exactly where she wanted to be.

He nipped her lower lip when she rubbed herself against his hardness, and then flicked his tongue over it. Her fingers sneaked into his hair and tugged imperiously.

"Inside me, now, Dev," she whispered frantically.

He suddenly hesitated.

She moved his head so she could see into his eyes, her own feverish with desire. "You said you had no inclination to be slow or gentle tonight. I find that I'm desperate for hard and fast tonight. So how about you make good on your promise?"

Filling his hands with her slender hips, Dev lifted her up.

She moaned as he lowered his thumb to her core. Slowly, he drew it down, down, down until his thumb was notched at the entrance of her sex. Her dampness drenched him. His erection lengthened further as she wound herself around him like a vine, thrusting her pelvis into his hand.

"I love how greedy you are, sweetheart," he whispered, dipping his finger in and out of her, feeling anticipation bunch his muscles rock hard.

"You make me like this. Only you," she whispered, her face buried in his shoulder.

Dev took another few seconds teasing her out, though it felt like an eternity. With his other palm, he stroked the warm, damp planes of her body. Rubbed the tight knot of her nipple between his fingers. Up on her knees, she thrust into his hand with a frantic urgency that made his throat dry.

Her eyes closed, her neck thrown back, she was lost in sensation. "Do you like this?" he growled, wanting to hear her voice.

"Faster, Dev. Damn it, give me what I want. Please."

He laughed, and she opened those blue eyes and bent to kiss him. Hard and rough, winding him up even more.

"I love it when you laugh," she said, and Dev felt like he was drenched in her shy smile.

He flicked at her sensitive bud gently and felt her responsive shudder. She moved forward and back, her breasts rubbing against his chest, pleasure painting her face a lovely pink. He tormented her for little while more, loving her moans and whispers that told him she was getting closer to ecstasy.

Just when she was hovering right on the edge of the abyss, he pulled back to quickly sheathe himself.

Lifting her with one hand on her buttock, Dev took his shaft in the other and slowly, carefully, slid himself inside her soft, wet heat.

She was incredibly snug around him, and he thought he might have died a little with sheer pleasure.

Her long, guttural moan mingled with his.

Her blue eyes deepened into a darker color, glittering with raw pleasure. She brought his palm to her left breast and sighed.

Dev kneaded her breast obediently, the tip of her nipple pressing into his palm. He didn't move his hips for long minutes. He didn't want to move, even though his body was screaming for release. He intended to savor this moment.

He kissed her brow and tasted the dampness from her skin.

Her gaze held his, shining so brightly that Dev wanted to look away.

But he forced himself to hold it. To see this woman who was a fighter just like him.

"You feel like you're inside me, all the way to here," she moaned, and then she threw her arms around his neck and held him tight.

Dev started to build their pace with slow, deep thrusts. He had a feeling he was never going to get enough of her. That one fine morning, he was going to wake up to find she'd changed him forever.

She matched his rhythm perfectly, bearing down when he thrust up, meeting him stroke for stroke. He glided his palms all over her silky back, following the curve of her hips, and chasing a drop of sweat trailing down her cleavage, before moving to take the begging tip of her dark pink nipple into his mouth. He bit back a groan as she shuddered as she approached her own peak.

And when she was close again, this time he pushed her over the edge with his fingers.

She orgasmed with a low cry, her nails clutching his

shoulders, marking him. And in the hold and release of her climax, Dev chased his own.

With one swift movement, he turned her back against the sheets, and then he lost himself in the arms of his wife.

CHAPTER ELEVEN

THE KOHLIS' HOUSE in California was really a mansion. Even knowing that this trip was mostly about Dev and not her—which meant she was hoping she wouldn't be under too much scrutiny from his big family—Clare couldn't help being nervous.

Fake marriages were not easy. Especially when you were married to a gorgeous hunk with kind eyes and complex emotional depths. Especially when she and Dev made it all too real when it came to passion. Especially when during the two weeks since their wedding, she'd seen how much they had in common.

She tried to bury her anxiety by telling herself that he needed her to be confident and charming and perfect. Not because she needed to impress anyone in particular. But because that was the only way his family would believe that he'd fallen for her.

She *was* all of those things, she reminded herself. The only playacting that they needed to engage in was convincing everyone that they were hopelessly in love with each other. That was the part she was looking forward to.

She couldn't wait to see how Dev was going to pull it off.

Tall Oaks stood in solemn welcome, straddling a wide pathway with lush, green vegetation on each side for almost a few kilometers before they arrived at the residence.

By this time, Clare was used to the grandeur and affluence that followed Dev wherever he went. But as she stepped out of the chauffeured Mercedes and stared up at marble facade of the gigantic mansion, Clare wasn't quite as composed as she'd have liked to have been.

A lump filled her throat.

She couldn't stop imagining Dev here as a little boy. Rambunctious and full of energy, yet confused by his incapability to understand the written word. Being surrounded by a genius brother and overachieving sisters, while letters and words escaped him.

And when he'd finally begun to realize that there might be a reason for that, he'd already lost his champion—his mother.

Tears filled her eyes as she recalled what he'd told her about his father's treatment of him, and Clare blinked them back. She could imagine him here, running wild, losing himself in the woods. Trying to free himself from the stifling expectations and his own shortcomings.

Feeling like he could breathe again.

She sent him a sideways glance, knowing he'd hate to be pitied. But Clare had always known herself. Had always faced her truths.

What she felt for Dev wasn't pity at all.

She reached out and took his hand in hers. He was stiff at first, his jaw tightly locked. But slowly, he tangled his long fingers with hers and his breath came out in a long, painful exhale.

He met her gaze only once. But it was enough for Clare. It was more than enough.

He knew she was here, in this moment with him. He knew he wasn't alone. And with that one glance, he acknowledged it. It told her that her presence did make a difference to him.

Clare knew he couldn't give her any more than that.

Knew that he might never look any deeper at what their marriage had morphed into. Knew that she might have to wait a long time, maybe even forever, to hear what he felt for her.

But she didn't care.

She was happy to be here and share this moment with him.

She was relieved to find that her father's betrayal hadn't put her off forging new connections with people.

She was also ecstatic and a little terrified that she might be falling in love with her commitment-phobic husband whose scars ran so deep.

"So how did you and my brother meet?"

Clare looked up from the intricate swirls the henna artist was drawing on her left palm with a dexterity that left her in awe of her talent.

To find about twenty sets of eyes on her.

Her heart beat to the rhythm of the Bollywood Hip Hop fusion music that was blaring out from cleverly hidden speakers in the backyard. Despite the noise, it felt as if everyone and everything around her had fallen silent just to hear her answer.

And there was a lot going on.

Whatever she had read previously about Indian weddings, Clare had discovered that the reality gloriously outmatched the theory. It wasn't just people dressed in beautiful clothes, long-lost cousins greeting each other, kids from old family friends eyeing each other now that they were grown up, interfering aunties sizing up brides for their sons and vice versa, it was the sheer joy that pervaded the atmosphere. Diya had laughed and told Clare that by marrying Dev she'd apparently saved him from a huge peril in the form of a pushy auntie who wanted to matchmake for him.

It was also the ceremony after ceremony of teasing the bride and the groom, of dancing and food, of being a part of something that was much bigger than yourself.

Oh, Clare knew there were bound to be downsides too, but she didn't care. Not when smiling aunties and uncles she didn't know looked her up and down, kissed her cheek and demanded she—Dev's lovely new bride—take their blessings for a long, prosperous marriage.

It had taken a giggling Diya to explain that in this context, prosperity was all the children she and Dev might have in the future.

And at the thought of children—her and Dev's children—of a boy or a girl with their father's twinkling eyes, his beautiful jet-black hair, and that sheer determination to conquer life, Clare had known it was too late for her.

She badly wanted this marriage to be a real one. She wanted that future with Dev. She wanted…so much she knew she couldn't have.

Ever since they'd arrived here, he'd changed. Oh, he'd laughed and joked with people, played the doting uncle to a number of nieces and nephews, chatted with Diya for a bit, sitting in the lighted courtyard while the groom, Richard, and Clare had waited patiently.

There was a sadness in him, Clare could tell. If he had expected to feel different returning here as a successful businessman, as a world-renowned billionaire, she knew he had failed.

She saw it in his eyes.

She felt it in the silence he imposed between them at night when she crawled into bed after a long day of festivities. When he reached for her and made love to her with a dark passion, as if he needed escape.

Clare loved sleeping next to his large, warm body. Loved it when he cuddled her body against his, whispering soft endearments in her ear.

But it was clear that being back in his childhood home had cast a darkening spell on him. Clare knew that his twin looked at him with concern. But he'd shrugged her concern away in front of Clare. Had then evaded a more in-depth conversation with Clare as if he didn't trust his own words.

As if he could only communicate with his mouth and his fingers and his body.

So Clare let him. She let him take whatever he needed from her. Because she loved him with all her heart.

She finally knew it for certain when she washed off her hennaed hand and saw that the artist had inserted Dev's name so cleverly into the swirls on Clare's palm.

She rubbed at his name with her finger and took a deep, shaking breath.

Knew that he'd carved himself into her heart too.

Whatever she told herself, or however well she prepared herself for the worst didn't matter.

She'd fallen in love with Dev Kohli, and there was nothing she could do about it. Most of the time, Clare didn't want to. Because loving him meant being her best self. Seeing herself through his eyes. Seeing the very fabric and future of her life shift with him in it.

God, she wanted him in it so desperately.

"Clare?"

She looked up to see Dev's older sister—and everyone else—still waiting for an answer as to how they'd met. "Sorry, I drifted off there for a moment!" She strained her brain trying to think of the right story to tell while the artist took hold of her other hand.

She spotted the tall figure of Dev's dad hulking against the back wall, listening. to whom apparently, appearances were everything.

When Dev had first introduced her to Anand Kohli, he

had greeted Clare with a warmth she hadn't expected. And when she'd trotted out her qualifications as the CEO of her own company, approval had glinted in the brown eyes that were so much like Dev's.

But the similarities had ended there. The older man didn't appear to have the warmth her husband did. Neither did he seem to possess the kindness and generosity of spirit that was so much a part of Dev's personality.

A tall, broad man like his son, he had retained his good looks and stature. Clare had tried to imagine him angry and impatient with a little boy who couldn't put his troubles into words. As a hard man who demanded perfection instead of seeing the lonely, lost child.

Clare had never felt an anger before like she had felt it then, on behalf of that young Dev.

In a booming voice, he'd prodded Dev about not informing his family about his nuptials.

And Dev had simply shrugged. Refusing to pretend as if everything was normal between them. As if he had any obligation to his father. He's simply walked away, leaving them both staring after his retreating back.

Clare had automatically turned to apologize to the older man for Dev's behavior but managed to swallow it. This man didn't deserve an apology. Not when he was responsible for all the scars that Dev bore.

And yet…as she'd stood there facing him, she'd thought of her own father. Of how angry she'd have been if she had ever laid eyes on him again. How she'd have demanded an explanation for what he'd done.

How, if he'd offered even a tiny excuse, she'd have tried to forgive him. Would he have been genuinely sorry was a question she was never going to get answered.

But Dev's father was here. Alive. Despite everything, there was something about him that had made her feel sorry for him too.

"He likes you," Mr. Kohli had said then, a hint of shock in his voice. Whatever flash of raw ache she'd seen in his eyes gone now.

Her hackles had risen. "The last thing you should be doing now, Mr. Kohli, is criticizing your son's choice of wife."

He'd smiled then, as if he was some maharaja granting a boon to a peon. "Oh, I wasn't criticizing his choice, Clare. I was surprised, that's all."

"By what?" she'd demanded, more curious than angry now.

"I never thought he'd marry. But not only did he tie the knot, he seems to have traveled a different route to it than I or any of his siblings expected him to."

"Again, I'm not sure if you're insulting me or complimenting me."

His gaze dwelled thoughtfully on where Dev had stood not a minute ago. "After all the women that have paraded through his life, I'm glad he's chosen a wife that suits him so well. The real him. His mother would've been happy to see you with him."

Clare had been struck mute that father and son would think the same thing. "Why do you say that?" she'd asked, fishing for more.

Mr. Kohli's dark eyebrows had tied together. "It's clear that he's happy with you. Even though he thinks I don't know him."

"But you don't," Clare had whispered. She'd walked away then, without waiting for his reply.

"Clare?"

Diya's hand on her arm brought Clare back to the present once again. She forced a deep breath in and smiled. Lies were easier if they were mostly truth embroidered, weren't they? Not that she'd ever come back here and see these lovely faces again.

* * *

"Oh, I…snuck onto Dev's yacht," she said with a dramatic roll of her eyes.

A barrage of whoops and questions came back at her.

She laughed. "I had one date with him and after that he blew me off. So when I had the chance to attend a party aboard his yacht, I crept into his bedroom. And demanded that he—"

"She demanded that I either give us another chance or toss her overboard," an amused voice finished behind her.

Clare tilted her head back to find Dev looking down at her from his great height. He was wearing a half-white kurta with gold piping across the Nehru collar, and he looked gorgeous in a more subdued than usual kind of way.

Laughter and cheers surrounded them. More questions came, but Clare couldn't look away from his dark gaze. She must have moved her other hand to keep her balance because the henna artist was suddenly muttering away in Hindi.

Her heart thumped wildly as Dev fell to his knees behind her. His arm came around her waist, taking her weight and keeping her hand steady for the artist. And then he was dipping his head—uncaring of all the eyes watching—and kissing her.

More squeals abounded them, a deafening jumble of catcalls and whistles, and Clare thought she might cry at the tenderness with which he kissed her. Softly, slowly, almost reverently.

As if he were seeking a benediction. As if he were asking for something he couldn't put into words.

Clare wrapped her free hand around his neck and held on. Her heart racing so fiercely that she thought it might pound right out of her chest.

It had been like this ever since their wedding night. One kiss led to more. A hundred kisses led to everything. Everything led to her being suffused by emotions for this man.

His fingers held her jaw for his tongue's foray now. If he weren't holding her steady, Clare knew she'd have melted right onto the marble floor. She sighed when he finally let her go.

"What was that for?" she asked, rubbing her fingers tentatively over her swollen lips.

He jerked his chin back for a second. As if he found the question unexpectedly daunting. As if he couldn't think of the right words. Something shifted in his gaze and then he said, "Did I tell you how lovely you look in your lehenga?" he said, a smooth charm back in his voice.

Disappointment flooded Clare. Not that she believed his compliment to be false; the traditional outfit Diya had presented her with was gorgeous, with gold embroidery enhancing the stunning pale pink color. But because he had pushed away whatever it was that had tugged him to her in this moment. Whatever he'd been silently telling her with that kiss was now neatly forgotten again.

"Thank you," she said inanely. "How did the male bonding go last night?"

He grinned. "It was boring... Bhai doesn't drink. Richard is quiet. Then Derek showed up and it felt like a party."

"Did you and your brother get a chance to talk?" she asked, knowing that Dev had been evading his brother too.

A shutter fell over his expression. "Let it go, Clare."

Clare refused to indulge in the hurt that splintered through her. This wasn't about her. This was about him.

"I came to see if they were bothering you," he said in a loud whisper that was intended to reach his sisters.

Clare leaned back against his broad frame, feeling as if she was being torn between joy and a searing longing for more.

"Oh…pshh…your bride is safe with us," Diya answered her brother, while most of the crowd turned back to the business at hand. And then she dipped her head and planted a kiss on Clare's cheek.

Dev stared at his twin, while Clare felt as if she'd just been given a wonderful gift. She clutched Diya's hand, a prickle of tears in her throat. "What was that for?"

Diya grinned, and her eyes were glittering bright with their own wetness. "Just for coming into his life. He… I haven't seen him like this in a long time. A very long time."

Before Dev or Clare could stay her, Diya walked away, leaving a sudden silence behind.

Clare would've given anything, anything in the world, to have Dev acknowledge what his twin had just said.

She willed him with everything in her to say one word. Something. Anything.

Time ticked away, seconds to minutes, leaving her desperately aching.

She shivered, the chill coming from inside her rather than out. His body was there instantly, warm and hard. She felt his chin touch her head, his kiss at her temple. But this time, Clare wanted the words. Needed them like she needed air to breathe.

She was just beginning to think she was going to have to wait forever again. Just as she'd waited for her father… months upon months, melting away into years after years. Believing. Hoping. Sustaining herself for so long on so very little.

His hands stayed around her waist. "I have something for you."

"My wedding present?" she said, asking the same question for the hundredth time.

It had started as a joke between them. A game. But now, as his gaze met hers and held it, it became something more. Something portentous.

"No," he said, shaking his head. "Even better."

Clare pouted playfully. "Tell me."

"My security team has been in negotiations with the mobster. He's finally agreed to let me…" He trailed off then, looking slightly uneasy for a moment.

"Let you what?" she asked suspiciously.

"Let me buy you off him."

"The absolute gall of the man!" she erupted. "I'm not a camel!"

Taking her chin in his hand, Dev bent and dropped a brief kiss on her lips. "I know, sweetheart. But you're forgetting the bright spot in all this. You'll be free, Clare, very soon. You'll never have to be afraid of anyone again. Ever."

Clare threw her arms around him. He held her through the shiver that went through her at the realization she was finally free. "Thank you," she whispered.

When he let her go and stood up, she couldn't help saying, "But that pushes us one step closer, doesn't it?"

"To what?" he asked, looking confused.

"To dissolving this…arrangement. Once we've sorted out your reputation too, we can be done with each other. And as there are already lots of positive stories in the world's media about your wedding, as well as the interviews we've done with Ms. Jones and your sisters, I'd say we're nearly there already."

For once, Clare didn't wait to see what he would say. She didn't think she could bear it if he simply agreed with her. Or made a joke of it.

So she carefully held the hem of her gorgeous pink skirt with one hand and walked away, wondering why she was feeling so odd when she was on the cusp of having her freedom again.

She'd never wanted more in her life to be called back. Never wanted to hear her name on his lips so badly.

She didn't even have to give up her company. Yes, she'd

pay Dev back what he'd had to pay the mobster, even if it took her years to do it, but it wasn't a deadly sword hanging over her head any longer.

Yet, instead of elation, all she felt was desolation.

As if she'd been left all alone in the world again.

CHAPTER TWELVE

"ARE YOU GOING to talk to him?"

Dev had known this was coming. He'd seen the combative look in Clare's eyes over the last three days. He knew all her looks now.

Her "I'm ready for battle" look.

Her "I want you so I'm going to have you" look.

Her "Do you really want to try me?" look.

And Dev adored them all. But this look indicating that she was going to prod and push, he disliked with a vengeance.

Her chin tilted high, her wide mouth pursed in dissatisfaction; she'd been retreating from him ever since he'd told her that she was going to be free of the crime lord. Irritation flickered through him. He hadn't expected her to fall on him in gratitude but he had expected… What?

She'd reminded them both of their agreement. That they were getting much closer to being able to end this charade. It was a reminder he'd desperately needed.

A reminder he shouldn't have needed, given how busy they'd been continuing to make his halo shine.

They hadn't been free for even one evening.

If it wasn't some wedding ceremony that Diya insisted they both join, it was attending a charity auction where Clare had trumpeted to the media about the annual charity retreat Athleta held with star athletes. Another afternoon had been spent at an inner-city youth hostel that Dev had always supported financially.

Derek and Angelina had been there at the hostel, all their issues resolved. Although he was pleased for his friend, something about how in tune they'd been had grated at Dev, amplifying the disconnect between him and Clare.

They had spent a perfect California afternoon—Derek and he playing flag football with the teens while Clare and Angelina spent more than two hours in conversation with the warden and the press that Clare had invited.

If he wasn't so wrapped up in his own thoughts, Dev would have laughed at how dictatorial his wife could get when she was on a schedule. How dedicated she was to her job of making him look good.

How easily she'd weaved herself into his life. Into his family's affections.

He'd seen his brother—who was even more allergic to having heart-to-hearts than Dev was—have a long, involved talk with her. He'd even seen his father voluntarily strike up conversations with her. Not that it was a big leap to find Clare interesting.

He'd seen Diya and his older sister with her—their heads bent together, laughing at one joke or another. And then Clare would look up—as if she had some kind of sensor for locating him—and they would stare at each other across the room, that ever-present desire shimmering like an arc between them, connecting them.

He would normally have winked and smiled at her, and she'd have blushed. Whatever the time of the day. Wherever they were.

Except she'd stopped smiling and blushing at him during the last three days. She didn't chatter away asking about this aunt who'd run away with her girlfriend twenty years ago creating a huge scandal or that uncle who'd maintained two families for years. She had retreated from him.

Each night, Dev had crawled into bed, expecting to be given the cold shoulder there too. Dreading it, in fact. Because he wasn't sure he could stand if she turned away from him there as well. Not just because he wanted to make love to her again. That desire for her was always there. He'd made peace with that.

But because those nights with her had become his escape from the grief he still felt being back here, in his family home. From the pain of feeling like a stranger among his own family.

Holding her, kissing her, making love to her had become the anchor he needed to shore up his days.

But to his shock and unending relief, her slender body had pressed up against his. Her palm on his chest, she'd burrowed into him.

She'd done it again last night too. The soft warmth of her body had instantly set him on edge.

"Clare, what's—"

She had pressed her palm over his mouth and shook her head. "I don't want to talk, Dev. Please, will you just… make love to me?"

"Yes," he had whispered, taking the easy way out.

Then she'd pulled him on top of her. The dark night had swallowed up his ragged moan as he entered her in one deep thrust. The breeze buried her gasp as he took her with a desire that didn't abate until he'd driven them both to a glorious release.

And when he'd found her cheek damp afterward, Dev had simply held her while her breathing slowly returned to normal. While she slipped into sleep. But he had stayed awake. Thinking.

He had no idea what the hell he was expecting from her or himself. They weren't, after all, truly married.

"Are you just going to pretend that I'm not standing

here haranguing you?" she demanded now, interrupting his thoughts.

"You sound like a proper fishwife, sweetheart," Dev said, determined to make her smile today. He looked up and his own smile disappeared. He felt as if he'd been kicked in the stomach. Hard.

Today, she was wearing a light blue kurta that made her beautiful eyes pop, with a wide round neck and flared pants. A tiny red bindi between her eyebrows sent shock waves through him.

Eyes wide, he stared at the delicate black bead necklace at her throat with a diamond at the center.

His fingers were shaking when he pushed his hair back. "What—" he had to clear her throat "—what are you wearing? I thought all the ceremonies were finished last night."

A wariness entered her eyes, and she touched her fingers to her throat. "They are. Diya and Richard are leaving for Malibu in two hours. This…your aunts and Deedi and Diya…they had a small ceremony for me first thing this morning."

"What?" he barked.

But she didn't back down. "Since we cheated them out of attending our wedding, they sprang a surprise celebration for me. To welcome me as the daughter-in-law of the house. Your father was there too. They all gave me presents—jewelry, clothes. And this…" she said, touching that necklace again.

"It belonged to my mother."

"I know. Diya told me. I told her I couldn't just take it like that. They didn't listen. She kept saying your mother would've wanted me to have it. That she'd have been overjoyed if she'd been here today."

Dev looked away, feeling as if his heart had crawled up into his throat. "Of course."

"You don't have to be upset about this," Clare said to his back, her voice all matter-of-fact. He wondered if she could sense the chaotic mess his heart was in. If she could see how much he wanted her to have it. How much…he was struggling with that want.

He wanted to let this thing between them grow into what it had the potential to be. He wanted to lean into it with all his being and yet…something stopped him. Something always held him back.

Being here, in his childhood home, didn't help.

"I'm not planning to steal it, Dev. I figured it was easier to go along with what they wanted and then just return it to you afterward. Unless you wanted me to tell them that I'm nothing but a fake bride."

He jerked his head back to her and saw the anger in her eyes. "Hell, Clare. I didn't think you were stealing it."

She shrugged and turned away. "It's obvious from your face that it means a great deal to you."

"What does a trinket mean when she's not here? When you can't bear to…" *To even look at me,* he meant to say. But he caught the words. "You should keep it. It's not like I'm going to run out and get another wife anytime soon. Or ever."

"I don't want it," she insisted stubbornly. "Not when it's an empty gesture. Not when it comes without…"

"Without what?"

"Without what it truly represents."

Dev's voice rose. "I can't believe we're fighting about that necklace when there's…" He raised his palms and sighed. "I'm sorry, Clare. I'm not myself. Not in this place."

"I get that, Dev, I do." Her expression softened. "I promised myself I'd be polite and calm with you today."

"As opposed to the sweet and tart woman that pushes and prods?" he said with a laugh.

She walked over to the bedroom door and closed it. "Dev, talk to your father please."

"You really want to pick a fight with me today, don't you?"

She frowned, her beautiful blue eyes not leaving his face. "Not at all. But I'm not going to back down from it, if that's what it takes."

Dev gave in. "Fine. Why would you push me to have a heart-to-heart with the man who crushed me when I was young?"

"Because I think he's finally realized he's made a mistake. Because he doesn't know how to ask you for your forgiveness."

"Why are you on his side, Clare?"

Only when he heard it did Dev realize how pathetic he sounded. How childish. How he seemed to have morphed back into a needy, temperamental pre-teen inside these walls.

Was it this that had been bothering him? That Clare got along so well with his family, with his father? That he... wanted her to be his and no one else's?

She was his. Only his. The first and only woman who'd seen more in him than he himself did.

She came and took hold of one of his hands. Lifted it and pressed her mouth to his knuckles. Cradled his palm to her face. "I'm on your side, Dev. Always."

"Then why do you ask me to do this when you know how impossible I'd find it?"

"Because I care about you." She pressed her hand to his chest, boldly. As if she was staking a claim on his heart. As if she was laying claim to the whole of him. His pulse rushed deafeningly, but the look in her eyes was calm. She was composed and elegant and the most beautiful woman he'd ever seen. "Because I think that talking to him, letting him say his bit...whether it's to ask for forgiveness or to justify his attitude back then… I think it will help you. I think it will finally burn away the resentment and anger that's been building up inside you for so long. Because I think until you face your past and gain closure, there's no possibility of a happy future for you."

"I'm here, aren't I?" he retorted.

"But are you, really? Did you let your brother get close to you? Did you let Diya see the real you? Or did you only come to show off to your father? To prove to him how rich and powerful you've become. To thumb your nose at him. I've spent some time talking to him recently, and for a sixty-five-year-old man stuck inside his own rigid set of values, I think he knows he wronged you and he's really been trying to change."

"Of course he's changed. But only because I've changed, can't you see? I'm not the lazy, useless, rogue he used to call me. I've become something more. I've amassed all this wealth and power and I finally made the family name proud. He can afford to be proud of me now. He can afford to call me his son."

"But it's not just recently, Dev. That's what Deedi was trying to tell you. He's followed your progress for years. Your entire swimming career, your first company, your first takeover, your work with Athleta. He's been proud of you for a very long time now."

The bitterness inside him was so deep and dense that nothing she was saying impacted on it. Dev wanted so badly to shift it. To cleanse himself of the poison. If not for himself, then for her. To be open to whatever it was she was trying to bring into his life. But he couldn't. "It is easy for him to say he's changed, Clare. Easy for him to give me the approval and the love he denied me once."

"But it's you who's denying all those things now, Dev. Don't you see? You're measuring yourself by his standards from back then. You're letting ugly things from the past dictate your present and your future."

A frustrated groan fell from his mouth. He grasped her shoulders. "Why are you forcing this discussion on me?"

"Because I've seen the shadows of loneliness in your eyes these past few days. I've seen how you look at your nieces and nephews, as if you're an ocean away from everyone. I've seen you say no to almost every overture and invitation that Diya and Deedi have made to you. I've seen you shut them all down repeatedly. Hold yourself apart."

"Because I'm angry and hurt and I…want so badly to belong. But I think…" Dev pressed his fingers to his temples, hating the sick churning in his stomach. "I don't know how. I've stayed away for too long. I…"

She wrapped her arms around his waist and held him, this woman who had a core of steel at her center. "Then take the first step, Dev. Talk to him. Try and sort it out. Make peace with your father. For yourself, if no one else. Despite what he did, if I had one more chance to see my dad, I'd take it."

Dev held her for a few seconds but his breath didn't settle. He felt as if he was standing on the outside again. Not knowing how to read or what to say.

"I can't," he said abruptly, letting Clare go. "I can't open myself up to all that pain again. I can't give him or anyone else the chance to…"

"Hurt you again," Clare finished sadly, stepping back from him.

Dev swallowed and shrugged.

"So what does this mean for us then?" she asked quietly.

"What do you mean?" he asked, feeling like a fool. "It doesn't change anything. This was just another part of our agreement, Clare. This was just you…giving me a hand with getting through some difficult days. Nothing has changed."

She didn't answer. And Dev felt a helplessness that he hadn't known in a long time.

He pulled her to him and she came.

"I want to kiss you," he said, plunging his fingers into her hair. "I need to taste you, sweetheart."

"Yes, please," she whispered.

He felt as if he'd conquered the world. He took her mouth, employing all the skill he possessed to push her to the same sense of desperation he felt. She was sweet and warm, like light in a cave of darkness.

And when he let her go, she looked up at him. Her long fingers cradled his cheek with a tenderness he didn't deserve. "I'm planning to leave for London tonight on the red-eye."

Dev's ferocious scowl told Clare everything she needed to know. She knew that she was pushing him when he wasn't himself. But as she'd already learned, there was no right or wrong time to do this.

To tell the man she loved that she…was an absolute fool for him.

"I'll have the jet ready in an hour or two. We can leave together."

"No." She stepped away from him, feeling as if she was cleaving herself in two. "I'd prefer to go alone. I haven't been to the office in weeks, and Amy and Bea, I know, are wondering where the hell I've got to."

"So I'll be in the way of your reunion with your friends?" he asked harshly.

"No. I just want to get my head on straight." She pressed her hand to his mouth, incapable of not touching him.

He pulled her hand away but didn't let go. "I don't understand what you're talking about, Clare."

"I've fallen in love with you, Dev." Her hand went to the black bead necklace at her throat. "I… I want this marriage to be real. I want to be Mrs. Kohli. I want this family to be mine as well as yours. More than anything, I want to share my life with you too. Are you happy to modify our arrangement to suit my needs?"

He didn't blink. He simply stood there, staring at her.

Clare laughed bitterly. "Yeah, I didn't think so. This is why I pushed you. Because I know how it feels for past scars to dictate your future. To have been so hurt badly that you close yourself off to everything. Even love. I waited for my dad to come back to me for years, Dev. Decades. You know he never did. You know what he ended up doing to me. You saw what it took for me to come back from it. You restored my faith in human nature just when it was ready to be completely shattered. But I can't wait around like that again for a man to love me. I can't…because it will break me this time. Because I love you so much and you're just not ready for it—if you ever will be. You don't want love in your life, do you? So, yes, I have to go. I have to start putting the pieces of my life back together again. I have to decide who I want to be…next."

Clare walked up to the man who'd become her entire world in such a short space of time. She kissed his bristly cheek and breathed in the delicious scent of him.

"Loving you has only made my life better, Dev. That will never change," she whispered. "But you have to choose happiness, Dev. With me. You have to decide if I'm worth trusting. If I'm worth taking a chance on. If you can finally let me into your heart."

CHAPTER THIRTEEN

DEV DIDN'T KNOW why he was still there—at his parents' house in California. In this house where he had never felt like he fit.

Derek and Angelina were long gone. Diya and Richard had left for their honeymoon a couple of hours after Clare had left him. His older brother and sister and their boisterous families had left too. His family had all bid him goodbye with a wariness that he knew he was the cause of. Both his sisters had asked why Clare had left so abruptly.

When would he bring her back for a visit?

When was he going to let them throw a party for him and Clare to celebrate their marriage? Had he convinced Clare yet to move to California with him so that they would all be closer together?

As if he were a stranger they couldn't communicate with without the bridge Clare had provided. As if she had... opened up something between him and them again.

As if she'd rekindled a spark in his cold heart.

There were a hundred things requiring his attention, tens of meetings he was missing with each day he didn't leave. And yet he had stayed, a strange lethargy weighing him down.

Instead of that agitated energy he'd felt during the first few days after his return, Dev sensed something different within the house this time. The walls looked brighter.

The sight of him in the family portrait above the giant fireplace—the one he'd tried to get out of being included in—suddenly didn't feel like a joke of the worst kind.

As the hours and days passed, he felt as if the house gradually changed around him. As if for the first time in years, he could breathe here. Or was it him who had changed?

Or was it Clare who had made life so much better for him that the past no longer held such significance anymore?

As he sat down in the huge library with the vaulted ceilings and rows and rows of books that had always seemed like alien things forever out of his reach, Dev realized he didn't feel the resentment that had been his childhood companion for so long. He didn't feel caged anymore.

Because now, whichever wing he walked into, whatever nook or corner he looked into, he saw Clare.

He saw her laughing with Diya and Deedi.

He saw her turning bright pink as she tasted the spicy *pakoda* his nephew had popped into her mouth when she'd been laughing.

He saw her looking up from where she'd been sitting amid all his cousins and relatives on her knees, her lovely, warm gaze finding him wherever he was and smiling at him.

He saw her dragging him through room after room, laughing, asking questions, determined to know all the hijinks he'd gotten into as a mischievous boy. He saw her kissing him, needing him, telling him he was loved with her eyes, her kisses and her generous heart.

But her words…the very words he didn't even know he'd needed to hear so desperately, the very words that were in his own heart…when she'd finally said those words to him out loud, he hadn't been able to hear them.

He hadn't been able to see what it had cost her to say

them to him. How far she'd come to be able to trust him, and want him, and…love him.

His father was still there, Dev knew. The palatial mansion meant he and the old man didn't have to cross paths even once during the day if they so pleased. While Papa had rarely approached Dev, he constantly sensed his father's presence, in the weighty silence that seemed to follow him wherever he walked.

In the pregnant hope that filled the very air.

"The house is yours," his father had declared, the one time Dev had come close enough to him for a conversation.

"I don't want it." The words had risen to Dev's mouth and yet…something had arrested them. No, not something. Someone.

Clare.

"That wife of yours," Papa had continued in his booming voice, "she will like the house, I think. She will want to raise a family here with you."

Dev had looked up, stunned. For the first time in his life, it seemed his father and he had been thinking along the same lines. The picture of her, in this house, with him, was such a clear image that Dev hadn't been capable of responding.

The two of them together in this house, building a family together…

And for the first time in years, Dev saw himself fitting into this house again. Fitting in with his family. Fitting in with who he'd wanted to be all his life—a man worthy of love.

And Clare had made it all possible by simply loving him.

By giving him what he wasn't even sure he'd earned.

"Who the hell are you?"

If Dev didn't feel as if his heart was lodged in his throat, if he hadn't felt like a total idiot, he'd have laughed at the two women who blocked his way as he walked into the offices of The London Connection.

One tall and elegant, the other a little shorter, with strawberry blond hair—they looked like sentinels guarding the gate against him. Guarding their best friend.

A part of him found relief in the fact that Clare had these women to support her. That she wasn't alone. That she…

"I'm here to see Clare," he said, trying to hide the impatience he felt.

"We heard you the first time. Our question was who are you?" asked the blonde.

Dev pushed his hand through his hair. "You damn well know who I am. I'm your best friend's husband."

Shock seemed to quiet them for once. Until he heard one muttering away and the other one squealing. Something like, "Oh, my God, he's here!"

"I don't think you should be here," the taller one said.

"Wait, Bea, we don't know that. She might want to see him. You know what shape she's been in since she returned. Also, he's our biggest client right now."

Before they drove Dev completely crazy, Clare appeared behind them. Peeking out of the back door, leading to a separate office.

"What's going on…?"

Her words fell away as she straightened. Wariness shone in her eyes as she tucked a lock of dark brown hair behind her ear. "Hey, Dev."

Dev swallowed, trying to dislodge the torrent of emotion that seemed to crawl upward from his chest into his throat. He didn't say anything in the end. Just nodded at her. Stared at her hungrily.

She looked a little gaunt but elegant in a white blouse and black skirt. She looked lovely and fierce and his breath came back in a rush, as if he'd been merely functioning until now, instead of living.

"I didn't know you were coming to London." Her tone made it clear she'd have been three continents away if she had. "Did I miss something on the calendar? I thought we'd finished all the PR for Athleta."

"No. That's all wrapped up," he finally said. "I'm sure you've seen the articles. I'm now being praised as a twenty-first-century model CEO."

"With most of his female fans crying over the fact that he secretly married his English wife," added the one called Bea.

Clare flushed. Her arms wound around herself in a gesture of defensiveness that tugged at Dev's heart. "It's okay, Bea. He'll be back on the market soon enough." Her blue gaze pinned him. "In fact, now that you're here, maybe we can finalize—"

"No, I won't," Dev said loudly. Enough was enough!

"You won't what, Mr. Kohli?" asked the blonde who must be Amy.

"I'm not going back on the market," he snapped. "For anything." And before she could shoot him down with another question, he caught up to her. "I want to talk to you in private."

Her breath quickened as he neared her. "I don't see what we have to say to each other. I'm not interested in playing Mr. Kohli's adoring wife anymore."

"No? I thought you were pretty damn good at it," he said, grinning. Gaining a little of his confidence back. He'd have to beg, yes, but she'd forgive him. She loved him. And the one thing he knew about Clare was that she didn't give her heart away easily.

And once she did, she was never going to take it back again. God, he'd been so foolish.

The woman he'd married was not the flaky type. She wasn't going to kick him out of her life just because he'd been slow to see what was right in front of his eyes.

"Did you get the profile of that last magazine interview I sent you?"

Her blue eyes grew huge in her face. "I opened it just now... I...it's a brave, big move publicizing your dyslexia like that."

Dev smiled. "I didn't do it to be brave or big. I did it because I realized you were right. I was still measuring myself by someone else's standards. And failing. In truth, telling the world I'm dyslexic is a selfish act, Clare. Really, I'm doing it to prove to myself and to you that... I choose happiness. That I choose love. That I choose...you. I love you, sweetheart. I want a future with you, if you'll still have me. I'll even give up the monstrous, gigantic, oversized yacht if it means my tomorrows are filled with you..."

Tears filled her eyes and fell across her cheeks. She looked so stricken that Dev felt a flicker of fear.

"Do you still not trust me?" he muttered hoarsely.

She shook her head, and then she was throwing herself into his arms. "I trusted you from that first night. You gave me my heart back, Dev." A world of joy filled her eyes. "You were just so determined to stay a bachelor."

"But that was before you stormed into my life, Clare." He kissed her temple and held her as she trembled in his arms.

Dev heard a couple of masculine voices behind him but ignored them. The only one who mattered to him, the only person he ever wanted to see was here in front of him.

"I love you. I think I fell in love with you when I found you sleeping in my closet. You're so brave and sweet and I can't imagine what my life would be like if you hadn't come storming into it, Clare. Forgive me for being a foolish man. For not seeing what you were giving me, sweetheart." He opened the top couple of buttons on his shirt and there lay the necklace she'd left behind on his nightstand.

"I want you to be my wife, Clare. Forever and ever. My

father has been trying to give me the family home, but if you don't like the idea, I want you to help me pick a house for us wherever you want to live. I want you to have a big family with me. Because I know that's what you've always wanted. I want you to teach our children how to be strong and brave like you. I want you to give me a chance to love you like you've always deserved to be loved, darling. And I promise I'll never again keep you waiting. Not another minute, not another second."

And then she was burying her face in his neck and murmuring through her tears.

"I do love you, Dev. With all my heart. I…"

Dev kissed her quiet. "Shh…sweetheart, no more tears. I'm here. I'll always be here for you."

EPILOGUE

"Do we have to change the name of our company now that we have offices on two continents?"

Clare looked up to find her friend Bea considering the question thoughtfully, the way she did everything else. Her husband Ares was sitting by her, his arm around her on the couch. Amy and Luca, on the other hand, sat squashed up on the opposite recliner together, still arguing over where they were going to spend Christmas.

She smiled as strong arms came around her waist and she was pulled against a hard body. Warmth exploded in her blood as the familiar scent of her husband enveloped her.

"Are you going to answer Bea's question or are you just going to grin like a fool?" Amy demanded, laughing at what Clare was sure was a blissful look on her face.

"Luca, please advise your wife not to call mine a fool."

Luca grinned while Amy continued. "Well, your wife is the CEO of our company and since she's made the executive decision of ditching us and moving to California to open the US branch of our business, Bea and I have been wondering."

Clare straightened, hearing the hint of uncertainty in Amy's voice. When she looked at Bea, she found the same.

Her friends weren't worried about the business or their share of it. But The London Connection had brought them together when they had nothing else in the world. Nothing but each other.

"Of course, we're not going to change the name," Clare said, clearing her throat. "I'm just one flight away from you. And remember, ladies, we're all about the modern woman."

"What Clare means, Amy," Bea chipped in, while smiling at Ares, "is that Ares and Luca and Dev know better than to expect that we'll put them before the business."

Amy laughed and Clare joined in. She couldn't believe all three of them had met and fallen in love with such wonderful men.

With Dev by her side and her friends near enough to see regularly, she finally had everything she had ever wanted—love and a big family and a place to belong.

* * * * *

PREGNANT
IN THE
KING'S PALACE

KELLY HUNTER

MILLS & BOON

PROLOGUE

'YOU'RE NOT FOOLING ANYONE, you know.'

Prince Valentine of Thallasia was eighteen years old, heir to an age-old kingdom and accountable to very few. His father ruled supreme and expected instant obedience and got it. His mother was long dead. His twin sister was the only other person he listened to, on occasion, and she'd definitely upped her scolding of late. Granted, her scolding often served to burst his bubble of entitlement and superiority—and theoretically this was a good thing. Kept him grounded or modest or some such. But he didn't have to like it.

His sister matched him stride for stride as they headed across manicured lawns towards the sprawling stone stable complex. The royal palace employed over a dozen stable hands alongside a dedicated stable master. They currently had over six strings of polo ponies in training at the palace, not to mention a dozen or so racehorses. Their father was a horse-riding fanatic and, until recently, Valentine had remained happily free of that particular bug.

'I have no idea what you're talking about.'

'This sudden interest you have in horses and riding them every chance you get.'

'What can I say? It's spring. I want to be outdoors.'

'It's spring and you want into the new stable girl's pants,' Vala replied dryly. 'Everyone sees it, everyone knows it. You have the subtlety of a stallion around a mare in heat. Not that you've ever seen a stallion around a mare in heat because until recently your interest in our royal horseflesh has been non-existent.'

'And now I'm rectifying that lack.' He smirked because he knew it would irritate her. 'You should be praising me.'

'I'm trying to warn you, you dolt. Father's not going to approve of your choice of plaything.'

'She has a name.'

'And that's exactly the attitude that's going to get you into more trouble than either you or Angelique Cordova can deal with. Yes, I know her name. Don't look so surprised. I like her, she's smart and outspoken and far too beautiful for anyone's good, and if you take things further with her and Father finds out he'll break her and he'll do it in front of you.'

'Just because he hasn't found anyone to replace our mother—'

'Oh, don't even go there!' His sister had a temper and she wasn't shy about showing it. 'Father lost interest in our dear departed mother as soon as he bred her and got us. He goes through mistresses faster than most people go through tissues and there are never any complications. No fuss, no noise, no royal bastards. Ever. Do you want to know what happens to those women foolish enough to try and trap him? Because I hear rumours and they are ugly and I believe them.'

They were almost at the stables, a centuries-old stone building buttressing the palace walls. The palace had been built to withstand sieges, way back when, and although the walls had come down to the east to make way for a grand entry road and gardens, far grimmer sections of the building existed, tucked in behind the beautiful façade. One of the reasons he hadn't liked coming to the stables before now was that he could feel the weight of oppression and ugliness bearing down on him there—no matter how beautiful and expensive the horses. Not that he had any intention of telling his sister he was afraid of ghosts.

Or that, no matter how much he didn't want to believe her savage assessment of his father, she might be right.

He wanted this conversation to be over so he could get on with the business of admiring Angelique, but his twin put her hand to his forearm and forced him to turn and stop. 'Valentine, whatever's wrong with Father, it's getting worse. The rages. The cruelty. And even you: Crown Prince, heir apparent, God's anointed…you're not immune any more, the way you were as a child when you thought he walked on water and wanted to be just like him. He sees you as competition now and nothing good is going to come of it. He will envy you, pull rank on you, and crush her. I can see it coming, plain as day, even if you can't.'

He didn't want to hear it. 'Look, I know he can be hard to please. He's not…good…with women. With you. I see that.'

His sister laughed, bright and bitter. 'I am the prettiest dress-up doll in the room, and as long as I stay that way, he will adore me. I aim to marry early and get gone from here just as soon as I can. Better still if I can make it seem like his idea.' She held his gaze, her dark eyes imploring. 'But you…you need to be careful who you take up with, okay? And how you go about it. Don't play with

your pretty toys in front of him. Don't ever let your infatuation with Angelique turn into something else. Above
all, practise safe sex.'

'Seriously? You're giving me the sex talk?'

'I'm giving you a *warning*. Bad things happen to
women who get pregnant by father. Bad things happen
to women who defy him in other ways. Ask around if
you don't believe me.'

'You have *no* idea what you're talking about.' His sister always had been melodramatic, full of plots and palace intrigues, but of all the undesirable things he *had*
heard, he'd never heard *that*. Their father had his faults,
but he wasn't a monster.

'I am dead serious about this, Valentine.' Her eyes
flashed cold fire. 'Why do you always think you know
better than anyone else? Why can't you just *listen* to what
I'm telling you?'

He was. He did. She'd never knowingly steered him
wrong. 'All right,' he grated. 'I'll be discreet.'

'See that you are.'

Valentine brooded on his sister's opinion of their father as she stormed off towards the new brood mares.
Yes, their father was a distant figure, not given to praise.
Discipline was harsh—his father had no use for weak-
lings because ruling a kingdom took strength. As for his
father's way with women... Valentine didn't see malice
in it. Indifference, yes. High turnover, yes. Wasn't as if
he were cruel in his dismissal of them. They came, they
went. No fanfare, no problem. His father had needs, that
was all. And Valentine was his father's son.

Surely his father would know that Valentine had no
intention of going to his wedding bed a virgin? And that
he had no intention of marrying *anyone* any time soon,

let alone the pretty stable girl? Even Angelique knew that whatever interest he showed in her, an offer of marriage wouldn't be part of it.

She wasn't a permanent employee, she'd be gone within the year, which to his way of thinking would be just about perfect. Angelique had arrived with six of her family's stunning Cordova mares, hand-picked by his father and hers to temporarily become part of the palace's breeding programme. One year, one drop of foals, less than seven months remaining and then the foals would be on the ground and the mares would be gone and Angelique with them.

It wasn't a *bad* thing, his infatuation. More like the perfect opportunity to live a little, love a little, and learn how to please a woman. Because, heaven help him, he dreamed about pleasing Angelique. He dreamed about possessing her so completely she'd never forget him and more often than not he woke in a lather of sweat and spent desire, no matter how often he took himself in hand. How was that *healthy*? If he could just *have* her for a time…get her out of his system…all would be well, and he could get on with the business of finding a suitable queen for Thallasia.

His sister was wrong about their father's viciousness and instability. His father would understand.

Valentine of Thallasia was eighteen years old, first-born son of a king, and used to claiming whatever he wanted.

And he wanted Angelique.

Valentine strode through the main corridor of the stable complex as if he owned it. Which, technically, he one day would. Stable master Alessandro nodded in acknowledgement. Nothing happened in these stables without that man's notice and that was both a good and bad thing.

His sister's words reverberated in his brain like a persistent little hammer. It probably *wouldn't* hurt to avoid Angelique for the time being and pretend actual interest in the horse-breeding programme and see if he could be of any real assistance. He wasn't against learning about the horse-breeding programmes of kings. As for riding, he could always improve. There were lessons to be learned here. Strengths to be gained. At least be discreet—*that* was his sister's take-home message. *That* he could do.

An hour and a half later, Valentine left Alessandro's office, his brain full of bloodlines and horse names and a new appreciation for the mares on loan to Thallasia. The Cordova name was an old one in horse-breeding circles. A fully trained Cordova horse had been a gift fit for a king for the last three centuries and more. Money and power, passion and status, and Angelique was no mere stable girl—she was royalty of a different kind and all the more irresistible because of it.

Finally, he allowed himself to seek her out. Only natural for him to want to approach the source, given the information he'd just inhaled. And there she stood, hosing sweat from the flank of a just-exercised horse—her pale jodhpurs, knee-high black boots and cotton T-shirt wreaking havoc on what little restraint he claimed to have. His father's second-best stallion was currently behaving like a day-old lamb beneath her hands, but that didn't stop him from offering his assistance. Not that she took it. Instead she rolled her eyes and tucked a stray strand of hair behind one ear. Silky black and falling to her waist, her hair fell in waves like the sea, and she plaited it when working—a single thick rope that fell between her shoulder blades and continued to her hips—but he'd seen it undone once, and he would see it like that again if he had his way. Bury his fists in it the better to tilt her face towards his and—

'You keep looking at me like that and I'm going to hose *you* down,' she told him, and it didn't sound like a threat. More like a promise.

'You wouldn't dare.' He summoned his most engaging grin. 'Because if you *did* I'd have to take my wet shirt off in front of you.' Which as far as he was concerned was win-win.

She laughed and reached for the plastic scraper and began applying it to the horse's back. 'I've seen better bodies.'

Doubtful.

She spared him a glance and laughed. 'You are the smuggest boy I've ever met.'

'Man. Smuggest *man* you've ever met,' he corrected, and she laughed again and it was a beautiful sound.

'Angelique,' Alessandro barked from inside a nearby stall. 'Get on with it.'

'See? You've got me into trouble. Some of us are working.' But she didn't sound concerned. Maybe because she was in the unique position of being beholden to her family's horses first and the royal stables of Thallasia second. It gave her a boldness the other grooms didn't have, not to mention that she was the best rider amongst them by far, with an uncanny instinct for getting the best out of any horse beneath her. He knew for a fact that Alessandro used her shamelessly to help train the more advanced horses here.

'How many horses do you still have to exercise?'

'Your father's best stallion and my favourite Cordova mare.'

The two most impressive beasts in the complex. He'd learned that of late, and naturally he wanted to master both of them. 'Want some help there?'

She straightened slowly, taking her sweet time looking him over. She wasn't indifferent to him, far from it, and this game they played was delicious. 'Are you up to it?'

Surely he could be forgiven for groaning his reply. 'Alessandro, I'm taking my father's stallion up to the gamekeeper's lodge. Will that count as his exercise for the day?'

The older man's head and shoulders appeared above a stall wall. 'Do you have your father's permission?'

'Well, he didn't say no.' Possibly because Valentine hadn't yet asked him. 'Can Angelique come with me?'

The horsemaster spared her a hard glance and a string of rapid Spanish. Angelique nodded and replied in kind.

'Was that a yes?' he asked.

'That was a don't encourage you and definitely don't get you killed. There was also a be careful in there and an I hope you know what you're doing.'

'So it *was* a yes.'

'Only if you're the one riding the mare.'

'*Excuse me?*'

'That stallion's crawling out of his skin today on account of servicing a mare yesterday. We sent the mare to pasture at one of your farms this morning and I swear he can still smell her. If we ride, I'm the one who'll be riding him because he's an ill-mannered pig. *You* will have the pleasure of riding a perfectly trained Cordova mare.'

'See, that's what I thought you said the first time. I

just can't comprehend the "you riding the stallion instead of me" part.'

She gave a gallic little shrug and pointed towards the stallion's stall. 'Me, that one.' She pointed towards a different stall. 'You, that one. She's faster than the big brute anyway.'

'Want to bet?' It was the only way he could tolerate the assault on his masculinity.

'I love to bet.'

It took twenty more minutes before they were riding out towards the heavily forested western edges of the palace grounds. Another thirty before they reached the gamekeeper's lodge. He was the first to dismount. He tried not to stare as she slid lightly from the horse and stared at the lodge with her hands on her hips and her head tilted to one side.

'Would you like to go in?' he asked.

'Are there any other people in there?'

'No.'

'Then, no. If you want to bed me—and you do—you might try getting to know me first.'

'I already know a lot about you.' Nothing but the truth. She came from a centuries-old Spanish horse-breeding and training family with extensive holdings in the Pyrenees. Her mother was from Liesendaach originally—the kingdom adjoining his—but had embraced her new country with a wide-open heart. Angelique had an identical twin sister and an older brother. She liked to rise before dawn and take a two-hour lunch at midday and then work again until late. She feared no horse or man—which in his opinion was a mistake. She was beyond beautiful and he wasn't the only one who'd noticed. In his more cynical moments he'd almost convinced himself he'd be doing her a favour by making his interest in her so plain. Some of his father's men had hungry eyes and brutal ways and they were looking, no mistake.

His sister's warning hammered away at his conscience, and something…he didn't know what…made him say, 'You should go home soon. Don't stay.' He had no idea where his chivalrous streak was coming from. 'Let Alessandro look to the welfare of your father's mares. Come back at foaling time. Better still, don't come back here at all.'

'Why?' He had her attention, every last scrap of it. He wanted to preen and puff and show off beneath that breathtaking face and steady gaze.

'It's not safe for you here. You're too—'

She waited, but he didn't know how to phrase what he wanted to say. 'Too what?'

Too wild, too innocent, too beautiful to resist. Too much. 'Too tempting for this court of crows,' he settled for saying instead. 'You've drawn attention and not just mine. Your father should know better than to send you here. He should have sent his son.'

She dropped her gaze to the ground and toed the edge of the manicured grass with her boot. 'And what if my brother would have been even more vulnerable than me?'

'He wouldn't be.'

Such a strange little smile as she stared at him from beneath that stray chunk of hair and he wanted nothing more than to reach out and touch it, push it gently from her face. Slowly, he reached out to do just that.

She didn't pull away.

'You don't know anything about my brother or me. I can take care of myself.' And if her voice trembled almost as much as his fingers had, neither of them made mention of it.

'What's your favourite food?' he asked.

'Mangoes and strawberries.'

'Your favourite drink?'

'Good café solo. Of which you have none!'

He could fix that. 'And where do you like to be kissed?'

Because he'd make that move next. His insides clenched with the promise of it, and the air between them grew syrupy with waiting.

'Here,' she murmured at last, touching her fingers to a place on her neck.

'Got it.' He logged the spot with his fingers, heat pooling low in his body and causing a stir as she arched her neck as if inviting more. She was warm beneath his fingertips, her skin soft to the touch, and her hair held the scent of summer. He could feel her racing pulse—or maybe it was his. 'Where else?'

She slid her fingers towards the place where jaw met ear. 'Here.'

He set his lips to the first place and slowly dragged his way to the next and she trembled for him and made a faint whimper that sounded like encouragement. 'Yes?' He barely recognised his own voice, the rough, needy edge of it.

She turned her head, her lips found his and that was all the answer he needed. He didn't stop until he was sated and neither did she. From the shadow of the lodge to its entrance hall and then the trophy room with its massive leather sofa that they put to wicked use.

Over and over again, in the weeks that followed.

With every sly challenge and laughing touch she dug

beneath his skin until he could barely think of anything but when next he could have her. Never mind his father's men, who watched them with increasing suspicion. Never mind his sister, who covered for his absence on more than one occasion and told him over and over to be careful and discreet and *for God's sake, Valentine, grow some survival skills.*

He was the firstborn son of a king. He couldn't afford to love as he would. He *knew* this.

Angelique knew it too. They'd talked about what he could offer her and it wasn't much. She was the wrong nationality and moreover she worked for a living. Her education was sorely lacking. He would one day marry a well-bred daughter of Thallasia—bonus points if she had political ties the monarchy could use to advantage. Such was the family firm he'd been born to. They *knew* this. Accepted it. They weren't playing for keeps.

They were just playing.

Her favourite city was Salamanca. Her favourite meal was her mother's paella marinera. There was nothing in this world he craved more than the time they spent together, learning how to please her. Her uninhibited cries as he devoured her. The clench and release of her pleasure.

He knew he was neglecting his regular duties. This reckless abandon had to stop before he handed Angelique Cordova the keys to his heart and soul in addition to the ones to his body.

But he didn't say this had to end as Angelique rolled out of his embrace and started putting on her clothes, chiding him to do the same because they had to get back because she'd be missed if they were late. As it was, they'd have to hurry back, and Alessandro the stable master would know it due to the lather of the horses.

'Race you,' he challenged, and she took him at his word. Always the unruly stallion for her and the well-behaved mare for him. Alessandro could overlook many things but risking the Crown Prince's neck on an unreliable horse was not one of them.

Race you and you're on, with the scent of her drying on his skin.

His father was waiting for them.

CHAPTER ONE

KING VALENTINE OF THALLASIA was a wanted man. His royal blood, his country's wealth and his striking looks made sure of that. He'd been angelically pretty as a child and an unrepentantly precocious teen. There'd been a time in his twenties when his reckless reputation had kept all but the most experienced women at bay. At twenty-eight he'd become engaged to a perfectly presentable, blue-blooded heiress with many fine qualities. He'd been pressured to appear steady and ready to ascend the throne in the face of his father's failing health, she'd been present, and he'd liked her well enough. She'd ticked all the boxes his palace courtiers had wanted her to tick. Well bred, well educated, well versed when it came to mixing with the high-born and observing royal protocol. Above all, she'd made him look good.

He'd broken their three-year engagement last night, and the pity had rolled off her in waves as she'd handed back his mother's ring, kissed his cheek and told him to take care. His former beloved had asked that he wait a day before announcing their split in order to give her time to return to her father's private estate. She didn't want to deal with the media and their questions, she'd said. Given the delicacy of the information he might or might not want to reveal, she much preferred to leave the details to him.

He'd yet to decide if her actions had been cowardly or merciful.

Either way she was gone, and the charity polo weekend in the kingdom of Liesendaach was in full swing. He could have gone home this morning, citing some fictitious royal crisis or other, and his host and childhood friend, King Theodosius, would have understood. Instead, he'd chosen to stay on alone, and Theo, as if sensing a ripple in the ether, was sticking close.

They'd managed to find a relatively private spot to watch the current polo match—a cue for a private conversation. Theo had doubtless engineered the moment and Valentine wondered with dark amusement just how long Theo would hold back his questions. Perhaps a pre-empt was in order. It was that or compliment the man on his beautiful gardens and immaculately kept playing fields, and Theo had probably heard that a dozen times already this morning. Of all the four kingdoms in the land, Theo's palace was the prettiest. The fussiest, King Casimir of Byzenmaach often called it with a sly grin. Pretentious, King Augustus of Arun would murmur, joining in. Fact was, their palaces were grey, gloomy and austere in comparison. And for all the improvements he'd made to *his* palace lately, it was still no match for Theo's. 'I'm no longer betrothed.'

Theo didn't so much as blink. 'I figured as much when your former intended made her apologies this morning and left before breakfast, her fingers bare. My condolences. I liked her well enough.'

'Faint praise.'

'I never thought *you* liked her well enough.' Theo shrugged and turned to watch the play. 'So what's next?'

Good question. Great question. But further confession seemed to stick in his throat and stay there.

Silence fell between them after that. The assessing looks his childhood friend kept shooting him made the imaginary bullseye between his shoulders twitch. 'Out with it,' he demanded after one twitch too many. 'I know that look. You're plotting.'

'Not plotting,' Theo denied smoothly. 'Just thinking.'

'About *what*?'

'Do you realise that you and Angelique Cordova never get within a hundred feet of each other? Is that choreographed? Do you practise?'

'I have no idea what you're talking about.' Valentine knew exactly what Theo was talking about, he simply wasn't about to admit it. 'Although I do note, with casual interest, just how close you've become to the Cordova family of late.'

'Moriana has taken Angelique and her sister Luciana under her wing.'

'Is that wise?' Valentine had never quite forgiven Theo for dallying with both Angelique and Luciana Cordova a few years back. Rumour had it they'd regularly taken turns dating him. Rumour had it they'd bet Theo's cousin, Benedict, a horse that Theo would never notice the difference. Rumour had it they'd won that bet. 'Letting your wife befriend your former mistresses?'

Theo's gaze sharpened. 'That would be very unwise. Good thing I claim no such intimacy with either Cordova twin. No, it's a simple matter of indulging my wife. Moriana finds them refreshing.'

Valentine snorted. He still thought putting the ruthlessly efficient Queen Consort Moriana together with the flagrantly wilful and rebellious Cordova twins was courting disaster. What if they decided to co-operate? They'd rule the world...or at the very least, this part of it. 'It's your catastrophe.'

'You have a quarrel with Angelique? Is that why you avoid her so diligently?'

'I don't avoid her.' He simply didn't go out of his way to encounter her. 'I have no quarrel with any of the Cordovas. They breed exceptionally fine horses and I envy your ability to get your hands on them.' The waiting list for a Cordova polo pony was ten years long. If you hailed from Thallasia, you were never going to get one.

'Your father wasn't exactly thinking ahead when he banished Angelique from his stables all those years ago.'

Wrong. Valentine smiled tightly. His father had most definitely been thinking ahead.

'What was it for again? Riding your father's prize stallion without permission?'

'Racing my father's stallion against the fastest thoroughbred mare in the stables.' He should know. He'd been the one riding the mare.

'Your father also labelled her promiscuous, did he not?'

'Yes.' Another accusation Valentine had been partly, if not wholly, responsible for. 'My late father was not always right.' Nor was he missed by many, but that was not a thought Valentine cared to share aloud.

'And yet the accusation stuck,' Theo mused. 'A reputation Angelique decided to own rather than fight, because she knew from the beginning it was a fight she couldn't win. I respect her for that. So does my wife.' Theo turned on him. 'Do you ever wonder what she might have become without that black mark?'

'No.' He wanted to believe that Angelique was exactly who she wanted to be. 'Angelique Cordova is feted by polo players and royalty alike, owned by none, and beholden only unto herself. What's so bad about that?'

At times, he downright envied her.

They were leaning against a rail, sun on their faces and a field full of polo ponies and riders in full view. They'd started out watching the play, although Valentine had abandoned that some time ago in favour of people-watching. If Angelique happened to be one of those people he studied more intently than others, so be it. With her ivory jodhpurs, knee-high black riding boots, fitted black shirt and her raven-black hair swept into a thick plait that started high on her head and finished at the swell of her magnificent rear, Angelique Cordova could command a dead man's attention. 'I'm thinking of renouncing my throne.'

Theo barely spared him a glance. 'Ha-ha.'

'I'm serious.' Theo's royal fields were a robust green, with woodland to one side and the white stone palace of Liesendaach behind them. It was a picture-perfect venue for the charity matches being played and later there would be a glittering ball to round out the day. Fat coffers would open, and at the end of the evening another hospital unit or education programme would be funded. Valentine had weathered a thousand days just like this one. He couldn't stomach the thought of a thousand more. 'I'm serious,' he repeated quietly.

Theo had turned to face him more fully, his expression sharply concerned. 'You can't be.'

And yet he was. 'You speak of that moment when Angelique was dismissed as if it were a turning point in her life. Something that shaped her world from that moment onwards. You speak as if she recognised it as such and embraced it, right or wrong. Angelique Cordova: passionate, headstrong and fallen.' He wondered if Theo had any idea just how much Valentine had wanted to turn his back on everything he'd been raised to do and run away with her. 'I too find myself at a turning point not entirely of my making. And, much like Angelique, I can either fight against these new circumstances and lose, or embrace them and see where it takes me. I'm tired, Theo.' And infertile now too, and therein lay the crux of the matter.

What use an infertile king?

'I know you've been ill, but my people tell me you're fully recovered.'

'You mean, that's what your spies tell you.'

'Were they *wrong*?'

Valentine huffed a laugh at the underlying thread of astonishment in Theo's voice. 'Surely it must happen from time to time, no?'

'No.' Theo glared at him. 'Are you dying?'

'No.'

'Losing your mind?'

'I gather you think it a possibility.'

'I do think it a possibility. And don't try and tell me you're mourning the loss of your perfectly serene fiancée because I won't believe you. She bored you stupid.'

'She enhanced my image.' It really had been as cold-blooded as that. 'She was perfectly pleasant.'

'And. Bored. You. Senseless. And setting aside the possible reasons for your abdication, who would rule Thallasia if not you? Your sister? How can you possibly think that's a viable option?'

'Why not?'

Theo was silent for long seconds as if contemplating just such a future, and then, 'Your sister has many fine qualities but a leader she is not.'

'She can learn. I'll help her.'

'It's not a matter of learning, it's a matter of character.' Frustration lent weight to Theo's voice. 'Your sister is secure only in her beauty, which—while considerable—is already beginning to fade. Indecisiveness plagues her and always has. She's easily swayed by flattery. And for all that her husband loves her, he's not been built to provide the support a ruling queen needs. You want my opinion or you'd never have broached the subject with me in the first place. Listen as I give it. Your sister is not you. All the progress you've made—*we've* made—in the region these past few years since your father's death will be at risk. Is that what you want?'

'I think you underestimate my sister.' People always had.

'Why are you even thinking this?' asked Theo.

Again, Valentine had no answer for him. Funny how impossible it was to talk about the infertility that had resulted from his recent illness. Funny how his ability to sire children was so entwined with his role as King and his identity. Funny, not funny. 'I could still advise her.'

'Or you could remain King.' Theo's patience had reached its limit. 'I am a king. Born, bred and steeped in all that the role entails. So are you. We serve, like it or not. *Never* do we turn our back on crown and country. I don't know what else you want me to say.'

'Nothing. I want you to say nothing.'

'It would help if you actually told me what was behind

your thinking. Because *"I'm tired"* is not exactly cutting it as an excuse for abdication!'

'It's all you're getting.' Valentine's temper itched to be unleashed, but on what he did not know. Theo was right in all he'd said. There was no way out of service for the likes of them. There never had been. And still anger rode him, played him in a way he hadn't allowed himself to be played in years, looking for an outlet, any outlet would do. 'And why on earth do you have amateurs playing with pros here today? I can't even watch this game without cursing the mess that number four is making of the play. Look at the way he's gouging his horse. How is this entertaining?' It wasn't. 'Who is he?'

'He's Europe's latest shipping billionaire, there's twenty seconds left on the clock, and if you'd been watching the game instead of Angelique you'd already know that both teams have deliberately kept him out of play for at least half the chukka. What's more, that's a Cordova pony he's attempting to ride. I fully expect that privilege to be revoked the moment he dismounts.'

The referee called time. The players left the field. The number four on the blue team rode to where Angelique stood waiting. Her shoulders formed a rigid frame, her hands rested on her hips, and even from here Valentine could tell she was livid. Angelique Cordova consumed by her emotions always had been a sight to behold.

Some things never changed.

'Do me a favour, since you've no quarrel with the Cordovas,' Theo challenged dulcetly. 'Get over there and give Angelique some backup. Europe's newest shipping billionaire didn't amass his vast wealth by being tolerant and kindly.'

'Why me? What are you going to do?'

'Me? I'm going to take the man's place on the polo field. Someone has to replace him in the next chukka and it may as well be me.'

'You're a terrible host. I don't know why I humour you.' But they'd already started walking towards the stables.

A flash of teeth and glinting grey eyes. 'I'll make it up to you.'

Leverage. How quaint. 'You certainly will.'

'I'll change your seating arrangements for dinner tonight, how's that?'

He already knew he was seated at the head of a table and across from Theo's current Minister for Agriculture—a happy man and an excellent raconteur. To his right would be the very married, very elderly, former Grand Duchess of the Opera—a woman whose golden voice had been surpassed only by her rapier wit. 'I like where I'm sitting tonight.' He'd already approved the new arrangements swapping his ex-fiancée out and the old Duchess in.

'Trust me—'

'Highly unlikely,' Valentine interrupted.

'—you'll like my seating arrangements more.'

If Angelique's raw beauty had been her downfall in her teens, by her late twenties she'd honed it into a dagger with which to pierce men's hearts. Lush lips in an otherwise finely drawn face. A body full of feminine strength and dangerous curves. Elegant black brows to accompany her masses of black hair. Flashing black eyes full of passion and pride. There was knowledge in her eyes when her gaze swept briefly over Valentine—knowledge of him—and so there should be.

She'd been his first.

And he'd been hers.

'Hello, Valentine. Whatever you want, it's going to have to wait,' she said as she turned back towards the horse and rider she was tending. The reins were in her hands now, not the billionaire's, and Valentine was of the firm belief that that was where they should stay. Up close he could see pink spittle around the horse's mouth and a skittishness about the pony that he was willing to bet hadn't been there seven minutes ago.

'Blood in my horse's mouth,' she muttered. 'Torn skin from the gouging of your spurs.' She turned on the man. 'What were you trying to do? Gut the horse?'

The man puffed up: chest out and a sneer to go with it. 'Do you have anything more responsive?'

'Responsive to you? No.' Angelique eyed the man with undisguised disdain. 'I don't care how much money you paid to be here or who vouched for you—although, believe me, I will be having words with them—you will have no more horses from me. Not today. Not any day.'

'Keep your horse. It was no good anyway. Who's in charge here?'

'In charge of the horses on loan to visitors?' She was practically vibrating with anger. 'That would be me—Horsemaster Cordova—so let me repeat, I have no horses available for your next chukka, or the one after that, or the one after that. I have no horses available for your use, *ever*! I don't care if I am the only one willing to say it to your face. *You can't ride.*'

For a moment, Valentine thought the man might well take his hand to her, but did she back down? No.

She stepped up into the man's space, all five feet five

of her to his substantially taller frame. 'Do it,' she murmured. 'See what happens when you strike *me*.'

A challenge that was more than enough incentive for Valentine to step up and put Angelique behind him. 'Problems?' he asked with a quiet menace of his own.

The man backed down, still livid but no longer within striking distance of either Angelique or the horse.

'I've heard of her and her family,' the man said with an ugly smirk. 'Her father's the one in charge of the horses, not her. She's just the whore. And he will hear of this.'

Valentine could have told him not to waste his breath. Cross one Cordova and you crossed them all. The man didn't know it yet, but he'd just been blacklisted by the family that provided horses to half of Europe's elite. 'I'm sure he will, but here's what you need to remember. There were seven other players out on that field and let's not forget the spectators. And while bad sportsmanship is tolerated on occasion, bad horsemanship is unforgivable. It's exactly as the lady says. That was your first and last ride on a Cordova horse. Nor will you find any other horses available for your use here today.'

'Says who?'

'Ah. Of course. Allow me to introduce myself. King Valentine of Thallasia, sent by your host King Theodosius of Liesendaach, with the message that he has the sudden urge to play the next chukka in the number four position for the blue team. Kings and their whims, what can you do?'

'I know what you could both do,' muttered Angelique, waving a dismissive hand in Valentine's direction. '*You* could go back to being swooned over by your adoring sycophants. *He* could take up golf instead of polo. No horses involved. Just egos and little balls to smack around.'

Valentine watched as the man took his exit without another word. When he turned back to the horse, the bridle was gone and so too was the saddle, both of them unceremoniously dumped in a pile on the floor. The horse stood there, unbound and quivering as Angelique soothed it with her touch and crooned soft reassurances in Spanish. She had a way with wild things.

They probably recognised a kindred spirit.

'C'mon, let's cool her down.' Cool you down too, but at least he had the sense not to say as much aloud. 'Let's walk.'

She walked towards a vacant stall and the horse walked with her. She took the halter hanging from a peg next to the stall and put it on the horse and then they walked some more. No lead rein, she didn't need one. The horse followed, trusting her judgement, her presence, the hand she kept on its neck.

'What do you want, Your Majesty?' she finally asked without looking at him. 'Why are you still here?'

'You called me by my name earlier.'

'I forgot my place. Please accept my humble apologies.'

'Humble? Hardly.' Angelique Cordova was many things. Humble was not one of them. 'You made an enemy just now.'

She shrugged. 'I said what I had to say.'

'Oh, I think you said a little more than that.' Scorn was a powerful blade and she'd used it without mercy. 'He's a powerful man.'

'They usually are.' She led the pony to the wash area and turned on the hose. 'Are you just going to stand there, or do you plan to be of use?'

He didn't move to hold the horse or take the hose.

There were halter clips hanging there if she wished to secure the animal and he knew better than to try and take charge of a horse in Angelique's care. 'I was of use. My presence prevented him from striking you.'

'Maybe.' She seemed wholly unconcerned by the notion. 'I'll mention your belated chivalry to my father. He still has a tendency to curse your existence.'

'You do that.' He should leave now. 'Maybe I'll be forgiven.'

'Don't count on it.'

And there was the rub. Yes, he'd screwed up. He'd been so young at the time and he'd followed his heart, lost it, and been punished accordingly. Could *no one* cut him any slack? 'You were of age, Angelique. And more than willing.'

'I was. And had our obsession with each other been allowed to fade on its own as these things inevitably do, I would have remembered you fondly. As it was, your father stepped in with his baseless accusations and instant dismissal and you didn't fight for me or my honour, not one little bit. You took my gift and then broke my heart and the world moved on. I'd thank you for defending my honour here today only you're a dozen years too late.'

She didn't look at him as she allowed the pony to drink from the hose.

'What makes you think I didn't speak up for you?'

She didn't answer.

'Angelique, what exactly did you think was going to happen? Did you expect us to marry?'

'No.' She scowled at nothing in particular. 'But you let them say those things about me. You let me wear the shame, and for that I don't forgive you.'

'You have no idea what was said behind closed doors.' He'd tried desperately to take the blame. Told his father that none of it was Angelique's fault, that she shouldn't be dismissed on account of his bad judgement, and it had made not a scrap of difference to the way she and her family had been treated. As for him, he'd been whipped until he bled and charged with four years of military service for his trouble, and it hadn't been because he'd bedded the stable girl.

He'd been punished for *defending* her.

Not only had his skin split, so too had his heart when he'd realised that all Vala's dire warnings about their father being a petty tyrant had been true. Cruelty ruled the man. Cruelty, indifference to the plight of others and a soaring sense of entitlement, the last of which Valentine knew he shared.

Angelique might not know it but she'd saved him that day. Ripped the blinkers from his eyes, caused him to examine the privileges he'd taken for granted, and ultimately set him on a path of self-discovery that led him far from his father's cruel shadow.

Even if he did still have a way to go. 'My father gave me two choices on the day he stepped in to put a stop to our dalliance. The first was to let you go. The second was for him to taste what you'd so willingly given me. Would you rather I'd kept you at his mercy? Because I'm telling you, Angelique, just in case you missed the memo. My father was not a pleasant man.'

All the anger that had simmered beneath his skin for years finally broke the surface. The years of being treated like a fiend by her and her family. The judgment his peers had applied to their affair, Theo's thinly veiled criticism. The guilt he carried with him still when it came to the position he'd put her in all those years ago. The thanks he owed her that she didn't want to hear.

The way he wanted her, still. After all those years spent trying to forget the feel of her heart thundering against his and never, ever being able to actually do so.

Anger, sharp and corrosive, was such an old, old friend.

'Take heart from your escape from the royal court of Thallasia, Horsemaster Cordova. Thank your lucky stars I thought enough of you to let you go. You got to be free. You got to be you. It could have been so much worse.' His heels came together in a parody of a military-parade-ground salute and he smiled bleakly and bowed his farewell. 'You could have stayed.'

CHAPTER TWO

'I'M NOT GOING.' Angelique Cordova stared at her twin sister and tried to push down the panic that threatened to overwhelm her. The charity dinner scheduled to begin in an hour would go ahead without her. She could stay right where she was in the pretty blue and bronze guest room of the living quarters Prince Benedict shared with her brother Carlos. They'd been together openly for over a year now, with both Benedict and Carlos taking up residence in Theo's palace. They wouldn't mind if she hid out in their apartment and it wasn't as if she'd be missed at the ball. There were five hundred other people attending, most of them rich, many of them titled, plenty of them self-absorbed. They could pretend interest in each other while she stayed here and unwound. She turned towards her sister, willing her to understand. 'I can't do it.'

Luciana stared back at her, almost identical in looks but for a slightly deeper dimple when she smiled and a crooked pinkie finger courtesy of a bad break when she was a child.

'I could say I'm ill. Exhausted from the events of the day. Which I am.'

'Liar.' Lucia surveyed her solemnly. 'This is about your temperamental King of Thallasia—'

'He's not my King.'

'—and the run-in you had with him earlier.'

'How did you hear about that?'

'Everyone's heard about it. He breaks his engagement in the morning and by lunchtime he's sniffing after you and dredging up the good old days when our name was mud and no one wanted anything to do with us.'

'I hate to break it to you, but our name is still mud.' Even their brother's outing as Prince Benedict of Liesendaach's live-in lover hadn't helped. 'We're just well-connected mud now.'

'Yes, we are, and I for one would like to remain so. You can't let Valentine get to you. He's nothing to you now. A past lover. If he approaches you, turn him down.'

'I don't want to be near him.' It didn't seem to matter how many years had passed. All he had to do was look at her, be in the same room as her, and her heart started trying to crawl out of her chest and make its way towards him. 'I'm still affected by him. And now he's single and looking straight at me so I can't be around him. Lucia, please, can't we do a sister swap? You can pretend to be me and just…insult him…until he goes away. You're better at it than me.'

'Only because I've never forgiven him for the state he left you in all those years ago, whereas you…your heart is too soft and your memory not nearly long enough. No. I know your vulnerability when it comes to the Thallasian King as well as you do, but like it or not you have to find a way to deal with him that doesn't involve making yourself scarce every time he appears.'

'He came to my defence today.' She'd appreciated it more than she'd let on. 'It was unexpected.'

Lucia looked wholly unimpressed. 'You don't need defending.'

'I know. It's just—'

'It's just nothing. So he's not a complete waste of a man. Doesn't matter. You can't let him back into your life—he'll use you as a rebound fling to get over his broken engagement and then marry a dutiful princess. You *know* this. The world at large knows this, and you are not going to play that game. You need to put on your gown and the diamond necklace and earrings that go with it and go out there tonight and be pleasantly indifferent to him should he seek you out.'

Angelique met her sister's gaze in the mirror that ran the full length of the dressing room.

'He's just a man,' her sister said softly. 'A man who once held your heart, but you've taken it back and moved on. You're here at the invitation of a king and his Queen. You had a job to do today and you did it and I heard only praise for you and our horses. So what if Valentine of Thallasia came to your defence? Too little, too late and what's more you don't need his patronage. Let him see you in all your strength and glory. Hell, let him *want* what he so carelessly threw away. Doesn't mean he'll get it.'

Her sister sounded so *sure*.

'He said I had a lucky escape from him and his family.' He'd said it with such bitter conviction.

Her sister moved to drape the diamond necklace over Angelique's collarbones. 'Dear heart, believe him.'

When Theo had promised to change Valentine's dinner seating arrangements for the better, Valentine had stupidly not seen those words for a threat. Banquet seating was a fine art and Theo's wife, Moriana, was the best of the best when it came to seating people to their advantage. The arrangements had been thrown out on account of his ex's departure earlier that morning, but it had been sorted not half an hour later when the Grand Dame of Opera had stepped in to take her place. He truly hadn't thought Theo's threat worth worrying about.

But it wasn't the Grand Dame of Opera who slipped into the seat beside him and turned an almost faultless smile in his direction several minutes later.

Nor was it Angelique.

It was her sister.

'Luciana,' he greeted, not the slightest bit tempted to use her shorter nickname. Angelique's twin had never hidden her utter contempt for him. Loyal to the last. A part of him had always admired that about her. 'Stunning as always.'

'I am, rather,' she murmured. 'And you...' her eyes raked him from ceremonial head to toe, and then she shrugged '...too. All those sashes and impressive little medals on your breast.'

'Chest,' he corrected. 'You have a breast. I have a chest. Would you like some wine?'

No sooner had he said it than a waiter appeared, but she waved him away with a murmur of thanks and then a no. 'You can be sure that once the evening is over, I'll be heading for my brother's finest wine. Until then, no. I have far too many people to watch over this evening to be doing so with a cloudy mind. And while we're on the subject of clear minds, how is it that you always know I'm not my sister?'

'Magic.' In all honesty, he had no idea how he could so easily tell one from another. But he could.

'Better that than saying you imprinted on her young

and have never been able to wash the essence of her from your soul, I suppose.'

'Much better. And not nearly as bloodthirsty.'

'Still. My version's more romantic.'

'In what universe are you a romantic?' Not that he meant to be rude...

'Oh, okay. I'm a ball-breaker.'

That she was. Luciana might not have always had Angelique's tarnished reputation to contend with. People had painted her as the good sister for many years, right up until she'd become the mistress of a married nobleman and then refused to marry him once he was free. Once a cheat, always a cheat, she'd declared, and moved on without a backward glance. Moved on to parties with movie stars and billionaires, princelings and sportsmen and cut a swathe through them all. These days, Luciana's reputation rivalled her sister's. And Theo's court was their new playing field. 'Why are you here?'

'Sisterly love. The seating arrangements were changed at the very last minute, as I'm sure you were aware.' She stopped speaking to regard him more intently. 'Oh. You weren't aware. That's *very* interesting. Anyway, where was I?'

Did the dippy act *ever* work for her? He thought not. 'You were speaking of Angelique.'

'Yes, of course I was. You and your obsessions. It's almost quaint the way you've never forgotten her. Angelique was up before dawn and has spent all day pandering to entitled aristocrats who take one look at her and think she'd like to end the day naked beneath them. She in turn took one look at the changes to tonight's seating arrangement—which seated her next to you—and said, "I have shovelled more excrement today than any being can be expected to shovel in a day and none of it has come from the rear end of a horse. I can't do this. I'm too tired.'" Luciana beamed. 'And so here I am.'

Charming. 'And your host knows about this swap?'

Luciana shrugged. 'Theo does not—in fact—know everything. A disappointment he struggles to contain, I know, but that's just the way it is.'

'You're funny.'

'Oh, stop with your flirting before I castrate you.'

He'd rather flirt with an angry lioness. 'And people wonder why the Cordova twins are still single.'

'No one *I* know wonders that,' she said, dry as dust. 'Do keep up.'

'Still funny.' But he could barely bring himself to be amused. That Angelique had taken one look at the seating arrangements and decided she couldn't abide to be anywhere near him filled him with a strange restlessness. Their earlier encounter had left him wanting...something. Absolution, forgiveness, a spectacular argument—any of that would do. He had bitterness to burn and Angelique had never been one to shirk from confrontation. The stoking of old embers—that too might satisfy.

What was it Angelique had said earlier? *If their attraction had been allowed to run its course, it would be done and dusted by now.* Or words to that effect. But it hadn't, and it wasn't, and maybe it *was* time to explore what they'd started all those years ago. Put it properly to bed. He needed no royal wife any more, no paragon of virtue and mother to his children. Why *not* pick up with Angelique where they'd left off and see where it took them?

He stood and studied the half-dozen long tables set up in a banquet hall that sparkled and shone the way only a

Liesendaach banquet hall could. He spotted Angelique at the other side of the room, seated with Benedict and her brother and a professional polo player whose on-field play he liked a whole lot more than the easy smile the man was sharing with Angelique. 'Ah. There she is.' He turned to her sister. 'And here you are, and, as diverting as our conversation is, it's time you returned to your designated seat and let Angelique take hers. Shall you send her over or will I collect her?'

But Luciana had been forced to stand when he had, and her drawling ennui looked to have been replaced by temper, fierce and somewhat familiar. 'I'll be nice,' she said through gritted teeth. 'I'll be positively delightful. Baiting you is boring anyway. And in return you're going to leave my sister be.'

'No. That's not going to work for me. I'm feeling reckless, you see.' Reckless, cornered and somewhat defeated. It wasn't a good combination. He bowed like the good little Courtier King he was. 'Get a move on, Luciana, and send your sister to me. You're in the wrong seat.'

She left without further comment.

CHAPTER THREE

ANGELIQUE WATCHED FROM afar as Queen Consort Moriana waylaid the grumpy King of Thallasia. Valentine was ready to leave, anyone with a discerning eye could see that. She spared a glance for Luciana, who was gliding back towards the seat Angelique currently occupied. So much for the last-minute sister-swap agreement. Angelique hastily excused herself and rose to meet Lucia halfway. As always, they drew glances, especially once they stood together. Heated gazes grew longer and more covetous as she and Lucia became *those* women—the beautiful, untameable Cordova twins with their Spanish blood and fierce tempers and faces that could make poets weep. Scorned by most women and desired by so many men, and she was used to it, had taken the stereotype imprinted on her and turned it into a weapon. But God help her she was tired of wielding it. 'What happened?'

'Your handsome King is in a very bad mood. Being denied what he wants doesn't seem to agree with him.'

'What does he want?'

'You. And I don't think running away is going to do anything but rouse his hunting instinct. You need to shut him down, turn him away, and there is no time like now. Come, we shall both walk over and pretend to be up to our old twin tricks again. We shall be infamous for daring to fool yet another king, and then I shall draw the lovely Moriana away and you'll take your seat and be charmingly indifferent. And then we'll go home and rethink how invested in Carlos' new world we want to be. I for one could use a change of scenery.' She bared her teeth at a nearby ogler. 'Keep your eyes in your head, Grandpa. You can't afford us.'

'That's *definitely* not going to help,' murmured Angelique as she steered her sister away from the old man's impending apoplexy. It took a while for her and Lucia to reach their targets. Along the way they collected a retired opera star who couldn't wear enough diamonds to fully cover her papered, wrinkly flesh, but by heaven she tried, and Angelique respected that. And then somehow the opera Grand Dame, Queen Consort Moriana, Lucia and Angelique all ended up in a standing circle with a glowering Valentine, while they peppered the space with smiles and laughter and airy greetings. Social lubrication at its finest.

'Finally, my seat,' she said to the older man standing awkwardly across the table from her. 'I was quite caught up on the other side of the room until my sister came for me.'

'He knows you're lying.' It was Valentine's voice in her ear. Valentine who pulled out her chair and then deliberately seated himself, forcing all those around him to sit. 'He's simply too polite to say so.'

The others wandered away, still mingling, bright birds picking up scattered seed, and it was well done, the social efforts that had detained a king and allowed him time to settle once more to the part expected of him.

He turned to study her, his gaze an almost tangible press against her soul and skin. 'I didn't think you'd come.'

'Well, you were about to leave before the meal had even begun. I could have been blamed, as I so often am when there's a scandal in the making. And rather than see all my fine work infiltrating Theo's court go to waste, I decided to co-operate. So here I am. Honoured to be dining at your side. I'll try to remember to use the right fork.'

He hurt her eyes with all his finery. The medals. The sash. And on his finger a heavy-looking gold ring that she'd never seen up close. The royal signet ring of Thallasia, once worn by his father and now worn by him.

The King.

His face was formidable, not a trace of the boy she'd once known so well in the hard planes of his cheek and jaw. No sign of laughter in his fathomless black eyes. But then, rumour had it he had little to smile about. 'I hear you no longer have a fiancée—is that true?'

'Correct.'

'My condolences.' Nope, she didn't sound even the slightest bit sincere, and his raised eyebrow told her he'd clocked it too. Jealousy was a chore, but in for a penny... 'The two of you were so photogenic together. All her pale, aristocratic reserve and your brutal indifference. Who'd have thought it wouldn't last?'

His eyes glinted pure and heady challenge. 'I'm sure some of us must have had our doubts. But enough about me. Are you seeing anyone?'

'Several someones, as always.' Never mind that her

workday reality begged to differ. She saw a lot of people every day. And dated none of them.

'Name them. Or do you prefer them married, and are thus unable to speak their names?'

'No, you're thinking of Lucia. I prefer them generous, open, and laughing.' She paused while a waiter whisked away the half-filled water glass in front of her and a full one took its place. The moment he left, another attendant offered wine. She chose the white and murmured her thanks. 'I also prefer them not ashamed to be seen with me. Guess that rules you out.'

'Not at all.' He leaned back in his chair, his attention all for her. 'We're here in public right now. And there are many eyes upon us.'

'Probably because you want to make a new headline to overshadow your failed engagement and broken heart. And while I'm sure our salacious past and my wild reputation could help you there, I'm not feeling generous enough to accommodate you. I have no taste for the public feeding frenzy that would descend once you cast me aside. Again.'

'I might keep you this time.'

'You couldn't afford me.'

He countered with a look that suggested he could probably afford just about anything. 'You never know. What is it you want?'

'Your heart in my hands, bloody and dripping.'

'Ah.' He almost smiled. 'Revenge. I can work with that.'

'No, you can't. And as flattered as I am to have been seated next to you this evening—was that your idea?'

'Theo's.'

'Right.' So Valentine had been blindsided by the

change to the seating plans as well. 'So, King Theodosius thought to seat you next to the one person you don't
want to spend time with. Are you feuding with him?'

'Not yet. I rather think our host thought he was helping. He wants us to make amends.'

'And you? What do you want?'

His long, strong fingers toyed with the stem of his
wine glass, and then he downed the drink in one go. Not
the action of a king who could generally be counted on
to make a glass of wine last all night. Not that she knew
such things about him. Not that she'd been watching him
from afar for years.

She looked at him, really looked at him. The shadows
beneath his eyes that spoke of too little sleep, the tension
lines bracketing his mouth, and as for his eyes themselves, the inky brown-black of them, they held an empti-
ness she'd never seen in him before. Maybe he *had* cared
for his former fiancée more than he'd ever let on. She
hated that thought but couldn't discount it. 'I don't want
to give you the impression of caring one way or another,
but are you all right? Because you seem a little…off.'

'Off?'

'Unwell. Out of sorts. It's like…you don't seem yourself.'

He smiled, but it did not reach his eyes. 'Because you
know me so well.'

She had once. She'd swum in his soul and he knew it.
He was the first to look away. The first to start a conversation with the man seated opposite him. She reached for
her drink and turned to introduce herself to the young
gentleman on her other side. She could do this. Make light
of her unease, turn away from him with every evidence

of civility. No drinking in every little thing about him or worrying about what tomorrow would bring.

There would be no better way to have his adoring public think he was careening wildly towards the edge of sanity than for him to pursue her again.

He *knew* this, surely.

The meal came and went. Angelique didn't slurp her soup, drop her fork or start an argument. Doubtless, some people were disappointed. Instead, she talked with a Minister of Agriculture about water rights, and chatted with the young man next to her about horses—Cordova horses specifically—and the very long waiting list for one. At some point she might have been goaded into offering Valentine the use of a polo pony for the weekend's festivities, should he choose to ride. She drank very little and tried not to pay attention to Valentine's every movement. She shifted restlessly beneath the prick of borrowed jewels at her neck and the agony of time passing too slowly. She wanted nothing more than to go and check on her horses—horses that were already magnificently stabled and in the care of grooms who knew what they were doing—but the dancing was about to begin and she *knew* what she needed to do next, and that was dance with Valentine and feign indifference and then leave him to get on with whatever existential crisis he was having.

Because it was quite apparent to her and plenty of others that he was having one.

She turned to find him studying her. Again. 'Is my face not to your liking?'

'I like it better without the make-up, yes.'

'I always wear make-up.' Coloured sun-protection cream at the very least. Protective gloss for her lips. Her eyelashes were thick and dark and rarely needed mascara, though, and physical labour throughout the day tended to bring warm colour to her cheeks.

'Then I like you better with less.'

'I suspect this is simply a setting you've never pictured me in before.'

'Angelique, I say with complete confidence that I've pictured you in practically every setting imaginable. And you have always conquered it.'

Oh. Well. That was very... 'Kind of you,' she murmured.

'What are your thoughts on children?' he asked next, and she blinked.

'Are you usually all over the place with your conversation?' Because she hadn't remembered that about him.

'Humour me.'

'I really, really am.'

'Then what are your thoughts on having children?' he repeated.

'I don't have any children. You might have noticed.' Not that she didn't want to be a mother one day, maybe, but a relationship with someone special came first. A marriage the likes of which her parents had. Not dull, never that, but strongly nurturing, loving and secure. And *that* kind of relationship had never happened her way. 'What about you? Regretting the loss of your fiancée already? You should have married her earlier. Got some little heirs on the ground, created your happy family. Of course, you're still young so your lack of children isn't such a problem. Take your time.'

He smiled grimly. 'You're being obnoxious.'

Better he thought her obnoxious than overly sensitive, defensive and way out of her comfort zone. 'I haven't deliberately spilled anything on you yet and caused an out-rage. *I* think I'm being very restrained. That's because I'm worried about you.'

'Dance with me.' It wasn't a request.

'You really want that headline tomorrow, don't you? The one saying you've lost your mind and are once again consorting with the help.'

'I want nothing of the kind. Doesn't change the fact that I'll get it anyway. May as well go big.'

'You *are* bitter.'

'Don't forget twisted. Either dance with me or walk away, Angelique. Either way it'll make the news. You know that as well as I do.'

There was no humour in him. None. And again, con-cern for him plagued her. 'What happened to you?'

'I grew up. I'm growing old waiting to see if you'll dance with me, as is customary given the seating arrange-ments imposed on us.'

'One dance and done?'

'One and done. If that's what you want.'

'What else would I want?'

So many eyes on them as she placed her hand on the sleeve of his dress jacket and allowed him to escort her onto the dance floor. By tomorrow the gossip columns would be full of stories about the Thallasian King, his broken engagement, and his childhood whore—that would be her—but she couldn't care about that right now. All she cared about was making it through this dance without getting carried away by his nearness and his touch.

Some people danced stiffly or clumsily with one an-other. Some never quite meshed, unable to truly sink into the moment and just let go.

That had never been their problem.

His hand at her waist, warm and possessive. Her hand on his shoulder—no shoulder pads for him, just the seeping warmth of his skin beneath the finest of cloth. The brush of his hips, the huff of his breath against her hair as he dipped his head towards hers and they began to move. They'd never danced like this before, not formally, in a ballroom.

And still, it felt as if they'd already done it a thousand times over.

'I've missed you,' he murmured, and she faltered in her steps, causing him to step in closer to steady her. 'My greatest fear has always been that no other woman would ever satisfy me the way you did.'

'But they have.' She tried to sound confident. 'I'm sure.'

'Don't be so sure.' His fingers tightened fractionally around hers and his cheek brushed hers. She could have sworn her heart was beating in time with his. 'Want to run away with me, Angelique, while I turn my back on my family, my duty and my country?'

'Don't be stupid.' But when she looked him in the eyes, she didn't see a man who'd spoken teasing words. All she saw was a man in the deepest, darkest despair. 'What's wrong?' She might not have spoken to him in years, but she'd watched him from afar and she could still pick up on his moods, heaven help her she could. 'What's going on?'

A touch of concern, the slightest bit of care. Angelique in his arms again and he was ready to spill all his secret hopes and fears. Same as he'd done all those years ago amongst the hay in the feed loft or the shadows of a stable door. They'd grown closer while dancing, because together they became magnetic. Spin one way and they would repel each other. Spin them the other and they became as one.

He was a breath away from crushing her lips beneath his, and only a lifetime of having courtly protocols beaten into him kept him in check. 'I want to see you again.'

He wanted his hands on her and hers on him and the thought that she didn't seem to want children shouldn't have buoyed him as much as it did. But what if? What if he *could* now have this with her?

She stared at him as if searching for a catch. 'Why now? Why, after a dozen years, am I suddenly of interest to you? Nothing has changed. You're a king. I'm still me. And if you think I can't tell there's something else going on with you, you are sadly mistaken.'

She was too perceptive. Could read his moods better than he knew them himself. 'I'm a free man and I'd like to get to know you again. Which part don't you understand?' The dancing spun to an end and Angelique stepped away, out of his arms with insulting swiftness.

'I don't understand any of it. And the answer's no. You don't know me. You never did.'

'Your favourite wine was Spanish white, your favourite meal your mother's seafood rice, and your father was the best horseman you'd ever seen and probably still is. I know what you told me, what you showed me back then. It was a gift I've not forgotten.'

'You don't smile any more,' was what she said.

She could help with that. But first she had to want what he offered and nothing about her behaviour tonight suggested she did. Manners carried Valentine to the completion of their farce as he escorted her to the sidelines of the dance floor, bowed and took his leave. Let the gossipmongers talk as he headed for the exit and the privacy of his guest rooms. Let him be taken to task for not dancing with other, more acceptable women. Let them say he was in thrall once more to the stable hand.

He didn't care.

CHAPTER FOUR

'DID YOU SEE THIS?' Angelique's brother, Carlos, sat in the courtyard of the royal quarters he shared with Prince Benedict of Liesendaach. Their quarters were situated on the ground floor of the west wing of the royal palace. Given that Angelique had been up with the dawn to tend polo ponies and was only now returning for breakfast, it was a fair call to say she had no idea what her brother was talking about.

'What is it you want me to see?'

'Thallasia's national newspaper. Front page. Above the fold.'

'And?' She leaned over his shoulder and plucked a sweet roll from the basket. No need for butter; she liked them plain and warm and slightly sticky on top and the kitchen here did not disappoint.'

'"Scandal Rocks the Thallasian Throne as King Valentine Threatens to Quit."'

'What?' She almost choked on her roll.

'It mentions you too.'

'It does not!'

'Yes, you were seen having a spirited conversation with him in the stables.'

'Ah. Well, yes.'

'And again during the banquet.'

'That was very cordial.'

'Cosy was the word used. And then there was the dancing.'

'It was *one* dance.'

'Shockingly intimate, I think you'll find, and then he left and then you left—'

'To tend the horses. As many, *many* people can confirm.' She reached for the coffee pot and hoped the coffee in it was sufficiently strong and hot. 'Why's he threatening to quit the throne?'

'Oh, that's your fault too. His people won't accept you as his Queen—'

'True enough.'

'—and you've given him an ultimatum. Make an honest woman of you or your rekindled romance is dead.'

Angelique sighed. 'So much for being able to do my job today with *that* rumour flying around.'

'Unless, of course, you consider it your job to bring about the downfall of kings.' Carlos sipped his coffee and kept on reading. 'There's a quote from a billionaire.'

'Oh, you mean the one who can't ride?'

'The very one. He fears for Valentine's mental health, what with being in thrall to a shrew like you.'

'I'm never going to be invited back here again, am I? They're going to say, *"By all means bring your Cordova ponies to the picnic, but please leave that king-slaying shrew behind."* Father's going to ask me how this went and I'm going to have to say I've stuffed it up again. It wasn't my fault but, hey, who cares?'

'It's not that bad.'

'Speak for *yourself*, Carlos. It's bad enough.'

Carlos regarded her patiently. 'Why don't you give an

interview?' He gestured towards the paper. 'Set things straight.'

'Because no one wants to *hear* my side of the story. People want the scandal, not the truth.' She nibbled on her suddenly tasteless breakfast roll and her brother silently pushed a bowl of marmalade in her direction. She had a sweet tooth when stressed. She ripped her roll in half and slathered a generous supply of marmalade on both halves before jamming it back together again. 'Last night's civility was supposed to *fix* things, not stir all those old stories up again.'

'It's possible we miscalculated.'

'Oh, *you think*?'

Carlos regarded her steadily. 'I'll help you with the horses today. That'll shield you from the worst of it.'

'I'll let Lucia know to brace herself. Maybe she can wear a name tag.'

'She would never.' Carlos smiled fondly. 'We're Cordovas. Family solidarity is our strength.'

She nodded and rubbed at her temple with the heel of her palm. 'I told Valentine he could ride our horses today.'

'Why on earth did you tell him that?'

'Because I'm weak and pitiful and thought it might help. Nothing to see here, no feuds of old. Just regular people going about their business. Wonder if I can take it back?' But she knew she wouldn't, just as she knew Valentine would ride a Cordova horse today regardless of the hatchet job they'd done on him in the press, or maybe because of it. It was a matter of pride.

'There's one more thing they're speculating about in this article.'

'What *now*?' But the sudden rough gravity in her brother's voice made her uneasy.

'Not about you. It's about Valentine and his recent illness.'

She didn't even know he'd been ill, but it explained a lot.

'They're saying it made him infertile.'

'They're saying *what*?'

'No children for the King of Thallasia. No direct heirs. No need for him to take a wife or even for him to stay in power. He may step down.'

Suddenly Valentine's behaviour of yesterday and last night began to make sense. His reckless defiance. His interest in *her*. He didn't need to marry well any more. If he couldn't sire children, he didn't need to marry at all... 'That ratfink bastard!'

Her brother's eyebrows rose. 'Not quite the reaction I was expecting.'

'He's going slumming.' She waved the hand with her sweet roll in the air to emphasise her point. 'Sniffing around me all of a sudden because he's got it in his head he's only half a man now and no respectable woman will want him. Why *not* have me now, after all these years? He has nothing to lose!'

'To be fair, his thought process might be a little more nuanced than that.'

'All last night I worried about him.' Carlos was giving the man way too much credit. 'Twice, I asked him what was wrong, *three* times, but did he answer me? No. He couldn't even give me honesty! She waved her food in her brother's face and he leaned back and gently pushed it sideways. 'I'm going to castrate him.'

'Don't threaten with your food. Also, if this report is to be believed, he's already been unmanned. Give him a break.'

'You do *not* get to take his side in this.' Maybe she would want to eat her roll eventually, but as of this moment she'd quite lost her appetite. 'I'm right and he's an imbecile who can't come to terms with his new world order and is feeling *sorry* for himself. Boo hoo!'

'Are you done?'

'Would you like me to continue?' Because she could. 'Spoilt, self-obsessed, delusional, irritating…' *Hurting…* 'Don't you dare tell me he's not.'

'I wouldn't dream of it.' Anyone would think Carlos was used to such outbursts from her and knew exactly how to slide his way around them. 'But are we letting him on a horse?'

If there was one thing a man could count on in this world, it was Cordova family solidarity, decided Valentine as he stepped inside Theo's royal stables and headed for the Cordova horses. Carlos and Luciana had both joined Angelique in tending to their mounts today; preparing them for riders, making them look like the wildly expensive animals they doubtless were.

Carlos was point man, by the look of things, meaning anyone waiting for a horse dealt with him. Angelique and Luciana stayed in the background, glamorous and unattainable as they readied the animals for handover. Didn't matter to Valentine if he had to wait to be served, like everyone else. Didn't matter if Angelique had glared at him when he'd first arrived and then ignored him. He was here for Cordova horses to play polo on, because last night she'd made that offer and he was damned if he'd let his country's gutter press bleed every last vestige of pleasure from his existence.

'Angelique,' Carlos barked. 'Get the King's horse.'

Guess they weren't intending to keep him standing in line after all.

Carlos sent him a measuring stare and then gestured with his head for Valentine to pass through the invisible line Carlos had so effectively drawn to keep people away from his sisters. 'You're getting our very best today. All of them are bred for endurance, agility and speed, but these ones are special. Fit for a king.' Fine words, when every line in the other man's body conveyed a very different message. *Screw this up and we're done.* 'Interesting article in the paper this morning.'

'You read that?' Who was he trying to fool? Everyone he'd met so far this morning had read the salacious 'interview'. Interview with whom? Not him. Not Theo, the other King had been quick to inform him. No, the piece had the air of an article that had been a while in the making, with the distinct sniff of leaks from his own court. His personal secretary had his suspicions and had already set a trap. It wasn't the first time someone in his inner circle had chosen money over honour. It wouldn't be the last. The billionaire shipping magnate's quote had been nothing more than an opportunistic addition.

'Any of it true?' asked Carlos, and at least the man was blunt about it.

'The bit about your sister being a good horsewoman is true.' Valentine supposed more openness wouldn't go amiss at this point but he still couldn't bring himself to address other parts of the interview or clarify their truth. 'My apologies for bringing your family under scrutiny again.'

'We're used to it.'

'Doesn't mean you have to like it.'

'Can't imagine you like it much either.' Carlos

shrugged. A tall, wiry man, he had the beauty of face for which the Cordovas were famed and an air of calm that his sisters definitely lacked. Given that he'd taken up with Benedict, Prince of Liesendaach, and yet another temperamental diva, Valentine had to assume that other people's fireworks bothered him not. 'Angelique's convinced that if she gives you her mare to ride you'll score a dozen goals and show everyone you're more than the sum of that interview. Then she's going to rip you a new one for not being honest with her about your problems.'

The other man's words set Valentine back some. There was a lot to unpack and no time to do it in. 'I have no problems.'

'Ride well, Your Majesty.'

Angelique met him halfway across the stable yard, a stunning grey mare walking alongside her. The horse had keen, intelligent eyes and stood ready to ride. 'This is Armonía,' she said by way of greeting. 'It means Harmony in Spanish. She's fast on the turn and fearless when riding to the shoulder. She'll play best at number two, but so do you. I think you'll do well together.'

'Your brother says you're angry with me.' She met his gaze and smiled, tight and hard. 'It wasn't my intention to put you in the headlines again.'

'I couldn't care less what they say about me. Is it true you can no longer sire children?'

He nodded, just once. Which was more than anyone else had got from him on the subject.

'Do you have sperm frozen somewhere that you can use? Semen straws like we do for horses?'

'I'm not a horse, Angel. And, no, I put nothing aside. My mistake.'

'Could you adopt a child?'

'No.' He was a king, with all that his royal bloodline entailed. Why raise a child to understand the monarchy when they could never fully be part of it? 'I'm not that cruel.' Fatherhood of any kind was beyond him now. He was dealing with it. Not well, but still. 'If you pity me, I will never forgive you.'

'Why would I pity you? You're still a king, with access to untold wealth and resources. Still prettier than every other man here.' She waved an arm around as if to reduce all others in the vicinity to nothing. 'Still sexually functional—' his eyebrows rose '—I assume. Still desired by many, many women who would become your Queen and forgo having children. Still an ass, but let's not go there. I can be an ass too, given that I thought for a while that you might be turning your attentions to me once more because you figured you'd fallen so far in everyone's estimation why *not* consort with the help? Then I realised you hadn't actually *made* a move on me last night and then I got angry all over again because I couldn't tempt you, even when you were feeling unworthy. You can see my dilemma.'

'Er…'

'You can't see my dilemma? Probably for the best.' Her smile mocked him.

'About the horse…'

'Ah, yes. She needs to warm up. You need to get used to her. I suggest you check your towering self-pity at the door and get on with it. You *can* still ride, can't you?'

'What *towering self-pity*?'

'You can't see it? Rest assured, everyone else can. Tell your detractors to eat dirt and that you're staying on the throne because you're brilliant at what you do. Tell your people your twin sister has several children and the royal bloodline is secure and the necessary changes will be made as to who will rule next. And then love as you will.'

If only everything were that simple. 'You'd make a terrible royal adviser.'

She tossed her head, a picture of defiance. 'I'm much better with horses, this is true.'

She'd made him smile—and given the morning he'd had this was quite an accomplishment. 'Thank you.'

'For what? Giving bad advice?' She waved him away. 'Go. Go make my horse look good.'

The Angelique of his youth had been naïve, too trusting and wholly ignorant of the life he was being trained to. This one was jaded, politically aware and brutally honest—with herself as well as him. She was magnificent. 'I will.'

She nodded, once. 'Might make you look good too.'

Angelique made a point of watching every game in which Cordova horses played. She didn't trust second-hand accounts of the play and considered her presence a business requirement rather than a pleasure. Some games were excruciating to watch, like the one yesterday, but this game was different. Competitive, professional, sportsmanlike and thrilling.

Valentine, infertile King of Thallasia, rode as if he'd ridden her mare for years. Strong. Confident. Devastatingly effective. Merciless against his opposition, and beneath it all the skill to keep his mount safe and engaged, rested when the opportunity arose and all too willing when riding for goal. Even Lucia clapped his latest goal, appreciation for his skill outweighing years of dislike.

'You're clapping him,' Angelique observed with outright astonishment.

'I can't help it. Did you see that goal? He rides like you.'

'You mean he rides like he has something to prove?' She was enjoying the way her favourite mare shone beneath his guidance. No one could deny Valentine's expertise, his skill, his fairness. He looked *good* out there. Not sick or struggling or anything less than overwhelmingly *virile*. 'He thinks I pity him.'

'You have to admit it's quite a blow for a king to be sterile. If it's true.'

'It's true. I just asked him.'

Lucia grimaced. 'Poor man.'

'He's not poor! Or suddenly incompetent or incapable of ruling his country. Look at him!'

'I'm looking.' The slightest hint of indulgence had crept into Lucia's voice. 'Great seat, strong legs, *very* nice goal. Your "tough love" approach seems to be working for him. We should clap again.'

'He infuriates me.' In all fairness, he was playing exceptionally well. 'I don't know what to do with him.'

Lucia turned her attention from the polo match to Angelique. 'Last night you wanted nothing to do with him.'

And today it was different.

'You still want him. That's just fact.' Lucia didn't wait for any comment. 'And now he's no longer obliged to marry a Thallasian noblewoman and provide children for his throne you think you can have him? Is that what you think?'

'I—' She knew it was crazy and unhealthy and wrong, but, 'Yes.'

'What about children?' Her sister never had been one to mince words, and these ones were designed to provoke, to make her think. Maybe even to make her hurt.

Because she did hurt at the thought of missing out on

being part of a traditional family one day. Did she really want to forgo the chance to hold her son or daughter in her arms, to love beyond measure and watch her children grow? And for what? A man who might never even acknowledge a relationship with her, let alone her sacrifice?

And yet…

If she came to love Valentine, truly love him, and he loved and valued her too, and children weren't for him…

'What about them?'

CHAPTER FIVE

King Valentine of Thallasia played four consecutive chukkas, rode two more of her horses, and then the mare Armonía again at the last, and secured his team six goals and the competition win. It had been a masterful performance and everyone knew it. He weathered Theo's ribbing and the congratulations of his teammates with a shrug and a faintly pleased grin. Arrogance personified, she might have once said. Right up until he caught her eye and let the briefest glimpse of vulnerability show in his flashing black eyes.

Have I pleased you? Did I ride well?

And then the bright flare of relief when she responded by inclining her head in a wordless gesture of approval.

And then it was time for her to take the mare and for him to disappear, only he somehow stayed behind when the others moved on.

'You do realise everyone's watching us,' she murmured.

'I'm aware.'

'But you don't care? Still in self-destruct mode, then? Planning on going out with a bang?'

'I'll give you four million euros for the mare,' he countered, at which point Angelique all but tripped over her own feet. At best, the mare would fetch eight hundred thousand euros and that was assuming the buyer had no common sense and money to burn. An offer of four million was ridiculous.

'How much?'

'Four million euros. But there's a catch.'

'And I can't wait to hear it, but you should probably cool down before you make any rash offers.' Valentine was fresh off the field and flush with the endorphins that came with riding an animal that had catered to his every whim. It wouldn't be fair to take advantage of him.

Unfair, yet still altogether tempting.

She took the mare's reins and let Valentine fall into step beside her as they walked along the sidelines to cool the horse down.

'Four million for the mare and the catch is I want one month of your time. One month, and you'll live in my palace, rejuvenate Thallasia's royal horse-breeding programme and breakfast with me daily.'

'I'm not a breakfast person.' She tossed her head and glared at an over-curious group of spectators heading towards them. 'Besides, the Cordovas no longer sell horses to Thallasia.'

'So I've noticed,' he drawled. 'And I want that embargo lifted.'

'Then you need to speak with my father.'

'And I will. With your permission.' He seemed intent on walking them far from the spectator crowd. 'Did I mention the part about you coming to Thallasia and using your horse-breeding expertise for my benefit?'

'Isn't Alessandro still with you?' She knew for a fact he was. Over the years the old horseman had stayed in regular contact with her father about the progress of the foals she'd left behind.

'He is, and I'm sure he'd appreciate your input.'

In her experience, men who considered themselves experts in their field rarely appreciated any input. And then there was the whole 'I told you so' element of meeting the old horsemaster again after so thoroughly ignoring his advice to stay away from Valentine all those years ago. She still felt a healthy dose of shame for the way she'd jeopardised the man's career, and time hadn't lessened it. 'The point *being* that if Alessandro wants advice about the Cordova bloodlines in his care, all he has to do is pick up the phone and call my father.' Just because her father would sell no more horses to Valentine, didn't mean he wasn't still fully invested in the care of the horses he'd already parted with. 'You don't need me staying under your roof for that.'

'Then consider this offer my way of saying I want to see you again, and, given that I can't come to you, I'm quite prepared to pay you to come to me.'

'You want a mistress. For a month.' Was that his goal?

'No.'

Then she didn't understand. The horse shifted restlessly beneath her hand. Time to turn around and make their way back to the stables.

'Is it so hard to believe that I want to get to know you all over again, slowly and with no commitment on either side beyond a certain willingness to see where it leads?' His eyes were guarded, his stride relaxed. Jodhpurs did amazing things to his thighs and the thin sheen of sweat on his forearms brought corded muscles and veins into strong relief. He set her senses aflame just as easily today as he had last night, there was no denying it. Always had. Probably always would. And if anyone had made her feel *half* the attraction she felt for him, she might not have been nearly so willing to listen to his offer, but no one ever had.

'You know my limitations,' he muttered. 'No children, no need to marry. That's me. And if you're not interested, say so now and that will be the end of it.'

They kept walking. Angelique tried to find her voice, her pride, something to shake her from her stupor, but silence ruled. Silence and a world of what if.

'Offer for the horse, by all means,' she said finally. 'My father might indulge you if you're persuasive enough. I couldn't say.' She smiled lopsidedly. 'Safe to say I find you attractive. That hasn't changed. But I don't want some made-up job that takes me away from my real work, and I won't put my life on hold for you. What I *am* prepared to do is try and find a way to make our lives intersect more.'

'Angelique, if you're expecting me to travel, the planning and security alone—'

'Stop. Hear me out.' She knew who he was. She didn't expect miracles. 'My family has been looking to buy or lease horse-training facilities in Liesendaach. We've not looked towards Thallasia, but maybe we could. And then we could see to unfinished business. Slake our thirst, and, when that's done, I'll still have a career I love and a fulfilling life to be going on with that doesn't include you. You do not monopolise my time. When it comes to your royal duties, you're on your own. And when this…' she gestured between them '…this unfinished sexual attraction between us has run its course we finish it.'

'Just like that?'

'No, not just like that.' She could see the split now and

it would be messy and altogether too public and everyone would say I told you so, and she would be that woman— the one who kept coming back for more punishment and humiliation at the hands of a man who did not deserve her love. 'I have one more demand of you and it's to do with what happens once our time has run its course.'

'You seem so very sure it will.'

'Aren't you?' How could he possibly think otherwise? 'I know my reputation probably can't get any worse, but when we walk away, I want your respect. If someone I don't even know condemns me in public so be it, but you—you who know me and are about to know my friends and family—I want your word that you won't bad-mouth me to them. You do what you failed to do before, and that's stand up for my honour and my right to enter and exit a relationship with dignity, and without being called a conniving whore.'

He looked shell-shocked. Maybe because her words had come from a place of such deep hurt and she'd spoken them openly.

Maybe she fully expected him to turn and walk away and relieve her of the burden of willingly entering into such a foolish agreement with him. But he didn't go, and she couldn't breathe.

'I'm sorry.' She barely heard his raspy words. 'I owe you an apology, not just for the fallout and loss of reputation you endured, but for compromising you in the first place. I should have known better. But I'm not that man any more and I will never allow anyone to speak ill of you in my presence. You have my word.'

An apology. Years too late and just as anguished and heartfelt as she could have ever imagined.

She had no idea what to say next. 'How much land do

you need?' Fortunately for her, he turned to more practical matters.

'Three to five hundred acres, plus stables for at least
thirty horses, and a house for me to live in.'

'What kind of house?'

'Nothing fancy.'

'What kind of price?' he asked.

'Depends on the place. Leasing's also an option. I can't
imagine you wanting me within reach for ever.'

'You've made it very clear you don't want to be within
reach for ever.' He gave her a long, level look. 'I'll see if
I hold any land suitable for your needs.'

'You do that.' She let the silence envelop them, rich
with possibilities. 'So we're really going to do this? You
and me?'

'Looks like.'

'We're both mad. You know this, right?'

His laughter rang out, and, oh, how she'd missed it. 'I
know this.' He smiled, warm and wide, and she'd missed
that too. 'Yes.'

CHAPTER SIX

THE WEEKS THAT followed were, without doubt, some of the most brutal Valentine had ever experienced, and that included his years in the military and the dark months surrounding his father's demise. Secure the crown. Stabilise the country. Vala and his advisors, neighbouring kings included, had persuaded him to stay on as monarch and bring the issue of heirs to the throne to the forefront of national conversation. His publicity team had worked triple time trying to secure positive press for the crown as Thallasia rumbled and roiled its way around to recognising that his twin sister—younger by a matter of mere minutes—was now permanently first in line to the throne, and that his niece Juliana was the next generation's heir apparent.

As to the matter of his broken engagement, speculation was rife as to whether he would ever marry now that heirs were no longer part of the deal. The headlines spun the stories and he lost track of the reactions the press bestowed on him. Everything from *Suicidal* to *Free and Easy* got a run, never mind that he was neither. He'd been linked to no fewer than nine different women this past week alone—and it didn't seem to matter that he hadn't seen three of them in over a decade. His media team had deemed it prudent to create a standard letter of apology for him to dispense as needed. Four supposed illegitimate heirs had been revealed by tabloid journalists. All had been investigated and debunked, but still they took their toll on the nation's faith in his leadership.

Today's article was a recap of his history with Angelique, and a list of her accomplishments since then. Many of those accomplishments were on the sordid side. A list of men she'd been associated with—Theo included. Her longstanding on and off relationship with Benedict— which Valentine now knew had been nothing more than a cover for Benedict hooking up with her brother. Didn't stop the press from salivating over pictures of her and Benedict dancing on some outdoor nightclub stage. Or speculating on the sloppy, intimate smile Benedict had been sending someone over her shoulder. They'd been indulging in a wild threesome that night, according to the article. Just another regular night out for Angelique.

The recap then went on to discuss a night out in Mallorca that had ended with several arrests, Angelique's included—although she'd later been cleared of all charges. A stint on an All-Stars Polo team, complete with luxury watch ambassadorship deal. The accompanying picture was a beauty. Angelique in riding gear, with a fierce expression, a thoroughbred horse beside her and an expensive timepiece on her wrist. It was a smouldering, sexy, challenging approach, guaranteed to fire the blood and make a man want all those expensive things that lay just out of ordinary reach. The promise being that if you were rich enough, remarkable enough, lucky enough, you too might be able to possess such power, precision and beauty.

She seemed to be wanted and vilified in the same

breath, for the same reasons. He knew full well that the press was going to make a meal out of her when he entered the picture again. Kinder all round to leave her alone, but he simply couldn't do it. Just like all those years ago when he hadn't been able to stay away, no matter how dire the warning.

He had to believe that things were different this time. That change happened from the top down and that this time he could protect her from those who would seek to destroy her simply because they could.

To have her exit a relationship with him more beaten up than when she went into it was unthinkable.

Respect had to start from the top.

She had to enter his domain cloaked in as much honour and respect for her needs as he could give her.

It took him two days to identify a duchy and manor house suitable for Angelique's needs. But it took him another two weeks to set up a meeting with Angelique's father at the family estate in Spain, and that meant travel and security arrangements and no small expense, and having to explain his actions to his sister, who was already irritated by her newfound celebrity. She'd gone from being happy spare to scrutinised heir, and she was up to the task, no question. He'd never doubted it.

Didn't mean she had to like it.

'I'm filling in for you at the most important royal banquet of the year because you're going where?' His sister's voice was dangerously mild and completely at odds with the hard glint in her eyes.

'Spain, to meet with the Cordova patriarch and offer him the use of a duchy.'

'You see, that's what I thought you said. At which

point I immediately thought I must be mistaken. Is this about a horse?'

'No. It's about apologising to the father of the woman I wronged many years ago.'

'Valentine. Dearest.' Her sister sat back in the library chair she'd commandeered, elbows on the arm rests and her fingers steepled in front of her. She wore a simple blue shift with silver trim, diamonds at her ears and on her wrist, and her hair had been woven in a complex weave once favoured by the likes of Grace Kelly. No one who looked hard enough would ever doubt the razor-sharp ability to read people that lurked beneath her surface beauty. 'Trust me when I say you've wronged more than one woman in your lifetime and dare I suggest you'll do so again before you're dead? You start giving spare duchies to every one of them, we're going to run out of land.'

Okay, so perhaps he did have a few small reparations to make but who didn't? He'd get to them.

'I'm not bestowing the duchy. I'm offering to let the Cordova family company lease it for a modest sum in return for their collaboration when it comes to the breeding programme for Thallasia's royal horses. We're falling behind in the prize horse stakes. I don't like falling behind.'

'Horses.' His sister saw straight through that particular excuse.

'The Cordovas do specialise in horses, yes.'

'But it's not really about horses, is it? This is about Angelique.'

'She does factor into the calculation, yes.'

'God help us, not again.'

'Why not?' If Vala wanted an argument, he'd give

her one. 'It's not as if she'll ever be the future mother of my children.'

'Do you *know* how insulting you're being?'

When would he learn not to lead with that argument when there was no winning with it? 'And by that, I mean she won't be subject to the kind of scrutiny any wife of mine would receive. If I were to take up with Angelique in an unofficial capacity, no labels required, surely she would escape that dubious honour?'

'Don't be so sure.'

'Or I could keep any relationship with her low-key and therefore of little interest to others.'

'Because that worked so well for you last time you tried it,' his sister snapped, standing up and putting her hands on her hips. How anyone could spend time with her these days and think her a lightweight with no real authority or inclination to wield it was beyond him. She was the mother of three young children, including four-year-old twins. She'd been wielding authority effectively for years. Over them. Over her husband. And all too often now, over him. 'Honestly, Valentine, don't you ever learn? If you want to be with Angelique, at least do her and everyone else the service of publicly and proudly admitting it.'

He could do that. 'All right. This is me, owning my desire. I want Angelique in my bed and in my life and, the way I see it, apologising to her family for my sins against her and them is the first step towards me getting what I want. I'm trying to make amends. I don't need your permission.'

His sister scowled. 'Way to get me onside.'

'I do want you onside. Also at my side, ready to step up and rule if need be.'

His sister winced, her discomfort obvious. 'Don't leave me holding the crown, Val. I won't do it justice. The polls want you to stay on as King.' And hadn't that been a pleasant surprise, in amongst the daily headlines? 'I know you were thinking about other options.'

'I made a deal with myself,' he admitted gruffly. 'Stay and serve and in return I get to try and carve out a personal life that pleases me.'

'Has your heart really stayed true to the little stable girl all these years?'

He shrugged, uncomfortable with the question. 'What does it matter? That girl no longer exists. But the woman she became is almost within reach, and I want to get to know her better. I'm not going to compromise her. This time I can protect her and I intend to.'

'All right. Your happiness is important to me, never doubt it.' His sister's voice was no longer deceptively light and airy. Instead, it weighed heavy with comfort and understanding. 'Let's bring her within reach.'

It was easy to be impressed by the Cordova family estate in the northernmost reaches of Spain. The lush green pastures and mountain backdrop catered beautifully to the raising of horses. Mile upon mile of immaculate wooden fencing, laneways and shelters crisscrossed the hillsides and valleys. Stables made of tile and stone dotted the landscape, and the main house was set low and wide against a natural escarpment that allowed for views that seemed to stretch on for ever. An aura of quiet wealth, contentment, and sensitive stewardship stirred the air here. A maze of stone-walled gardens surrounded the main house and pushed visitors towards a U-shaped entrance driveway.

Eduardo Cordova was there to meet him as he got out of the car. Valentine's security detail had preceded him by minutes and were now spread like points of the compass, barely visible but there all the same. The Cordova patriarch regarded him thoughtfully, seemingly untroubled by the cavalcade. Given the list of royalty and billionaire families he regularly sold horses to, he was probably used to it.

'Señor Cordova.' Valentine held out his hand, not wanting or waiting for awkwardness to arrive. 'Thank you for agreeing to see me.' He counted it a win when the other man nodded and shook his outstretched hand before gesturing towards an archway to the left of the large main doors.

'My office. This is not my family's first encounter with those who travel with bodyguards. Your people have assured me our meeting place meets their needs. They can protect you from there and sight you as well.' The archway led to a modest outdoor area with a central tree laden with lemons, a pond full of water plants, ample outdoor seating, and access to the house via glass doors that opened up one wall of a long library room almost completely. Two of Valentine's guards were already in residence, one in the courtyard, another just inside a closed door that led further inside the house. 'Come.'

The older man headed towards a cluster of low tables and tan leather club chairs. One of the tables had been set with refreshments for two. 'Please, take a seat. Tell me, do kings still use poison tasters?'

Valentine took a seat that afforded him a view of the courtyard and the interior door both. 'Not that I know of.'

Angelique's father smiled and sat opposite. 'Coffee?'

'Please.' He watched as the other man poured.

'I have to say, I'm puzzled as to why you're here.' The older man settled back into his chair and made no move towards the fragrant brew he'd just served. 'I've already told you that the mare you want is not for sale.'

'And yet you've sold horses out from beneath your daughter before.'

'Not ones of this calibre. You're wasting your time if that's all you came for.'

'That's not all I came for.'

The old man's gaze didn't leave his face. 'I don't read minds.'

No one said making this apology was going to be easy. 'I wish to extend my sincere apology for the treatment I afforded your daughter, and by extension your family, all those years ago. I was young, foolish and arrogant and I regret my part in your family's fall from grace.'

'And there it is. The arrogance of kings,' the other man murmured. 'My family did not fall from grace. We merely stopped having anything to do with you.'

'My loss, certainly. To that end, I wish to offer Angelique, and by extension your family business, leasehold access to a modest duchy situated on the Thallasia-Liesendaach border. It consists of a manor house, the surrounding grazing land and forests and several smaller dwellings. A gatehouse, a hunting lodge, a groundskeeper's cottage. It has a manager, a gardener and a housekeeper—all paid for by the income from the estate. Some of the land is currently used for cropping, some of it for grazing. All of it perfect for horses. There is no duke or duchess—the title has been rotated out of use and remains with the crown. There are no plans to resurrect it.'

'And what makes you think we could ever afford a lease on such an estate?'

'A hundred thousand Euros per annum and Cordova consultancy services when it comes to reinvigorating the bloodlines of the royal horses of Thallasia says you probably can.' It was barely enough to cover the cost of the people already in place and who would stay in place to serve Angelique.

'And what's in it for you?'

'A chance to get to know Angelique on her terms. Nothing more, nothing less.'

'Not exactly a salesman, are you?'

'No, I'm a king.'

'You realise that my blessing is not all you need for your endeavour to succeed? You need my daughter's agreement as well.'

'I already have it.'

'Oh, *do* you?'

'More or less.' Possibly less.

The older man finally picked up his coffee and set it to his lips. Weathered, lean and wiry, he somehow managed to project a far bigger presence than his small stature afforded him. 'So, assuming you do manage to persuade my daughter within reach, what then? Do you intend to marry her?'

'No.'

'And children are not for you either, so I'm given to understand.'

'True.'

'You don't have much to offer her, do you?'

Valentine leaned towards his coffee cup, taking his time to add two cubes of sugar and stir well before lifting the fragrant brew to his lips. He had no arguments to counter the other man's observations. He knew Angelique deserved more and yet here he was. 'I have the arrogance of kings. That and the sure belief that if your daughter had wanted marriage to a man who loved her and children to complete that pretty picture, she would have had that by now.'

'She's young. She can still have all that.'

Although not if she takes up with you.

Those words sat there between them, unspoken but present. 'True. But not with me. She knows that.' The coffee was good. Best he'd ever tasted. Perhaps it was the pure mountain air and lack of bull. The fact that Angelique's father was giving him no quarter at all.

'My children have a tendency to love as they will,' the older man said at last. 'My son loves a man. Damn near broke my heart but here I am, heart-whole and thriving and my son is the happiest I've ever seen him. He loves without reservation and is loved just as much in return, and I am content. Love is love, isn't that the phrase?' He nodded to himself. 'If my daughter decides she loves you, with all the complexities involved, do you have the heart to love her in return?'

Not for a moment did he hesitate, and it wasn't just the arrogance of kings. 'I will cut out my heart before I hurt her again.'

Three weeks later, Angelique and thirty-six of the Cordova family's finest horses moved into Valentine's spare estate. Valentine had made his offer the day after he'd visited her father, and what they had spoken of neither would say, but her father had backed her decision to take on the lease, and the property really was perfect for their needs. Less travel for the polo ponies. Beautiful facilities. She could even repurpose part of the huge expanse of manicured lawn as a polo field, although the gardener would likely need resuscitating.

She'd searched her heart and decided to take a chance on this new chapter in her life. No marriage or babies on her horizon but an eventful and privileged future no less. She'd said yes to the lease. Yes to whatever might eventuate between her and Valentine. Yes to the crazy bad portrayal of her in the press, just as soon as they got wind of the transaction between the Thallasian monarchy and the Cordova horsemasters. Just yes.

Her whole family descended on the day she moved in. Her brother, Carlos, and Benedict, Luciana, and her parents. Even Queen Consort Moriana, along with Moriana's favourite lady-in-waiting and one extremely good-looking guardsman of Liesendaach, had snuck in to help Angelique take possession. Never had Angelique imagined the immaculately put-together Moriana tucking into three different kinds of paella, plus salads, and then plain old *natillas*—or custard—for dessert, elbow to elbow with Angelique's family and her employees. Never underestimate the woman, that was the take home.

Angelique had yet to understand why Moriana was even there.

'But this is wonderful.' Moriana sighed her contentment. 'Theo will be so sad to have missed this.'

'The slumming?' Angelique teased, and waited to see how the other woman would take it.

'Hardly.' Moriana waved her hand towards the rest of the hall with its fourteen bedrooms and umpteen sitting rooms and dining areas. 'The freedom to be with you all and not be on our best royal behaviour. I dripped paella on my napkin. I have opened up rooms for airing. Directed a hay truck down to the stables.'

'Raided Valentine's wine cellar,' murmured Benedict with a benevolent smile.

'You suggested it,' Angelique reminded him dryly. 'And I swear, you will be replacing it, because I'm damn sure I haven't a hope of buying any of these bottles again. This one's twenty years old and comes from a monastery I've never heard of.'

'And where *is* Valentine this weekend?' Moriana asked. 'I half expected him to put in an appearance.'

She wasn't the only one. 'I did invite him.' Angelique held up her hands in all innocence. 'Not for a meal, mind, but he knew we were coming in this weekend and that we'd all be here. I told him he was free to drop in any time. Not that kings drop in.'

'They don't?' said a voice from the doorway, and there stood Valentine in what for him counted as casual clothes. Dark trousers, perfectly pressed. A dove-grey business shirt, rolled to the sleeves and with the top buttons undone. No security detail in sight, although presumably they were around somewhere. 'I did knock. And when no one came to the door, I followed the noise.'

'Valentine!' Moriana was the only one there who was anywhere near his equal in rank, and when she stood immediately, everyone else began to, whether they'd finished their meal or not.

'Don't.' He held up his hand for everyone to stop. 'Please. Finish your meals. I've come at an inconvenient time.'

'Or you could pull up a chair and have some paella and drink some of your wine,' Angelique offered, and meant every word of it. 'What happens at Raven Hall stays at Raven Hall. It's the new rule.'

She could see him assessing everyone in the room. Her

parents, Luciana, Carlos and Benedict, Moriana and her retinue. 'No Theo?' he murmured, and Moriana waved a dismissive hand.

'His loss.'

Carlos dragged a chair across and placed it between himself and their father. Lucia snorted inelegantly and Angelique bit back a smile. Had the very fine-looking King of Thallasia ever been subjected to a Spanish family's intimidation tactics? She doubted it, even as she rose to get him a glass for the wine and a plate and utensils for the food on the table. 'It's serve yourself, although Carlos might be persuaded to fill your glass. It's yours, by the way, the wine.'

'That was my doing.' Benedict came clean, and Angelique laughed outright.

'What's this I hear? Is that your conscience speaking?'

'Only because I owe you.'

'So very much,' Lucia murmured.

And Carlos raised his glass and said, 'I'll drink to that,' so everyone did and it became a toast and then conversation resumed between Moriana and Lucia, between Benedict and her mother, between Carlos and her father as they talked straight through Valentine, who looked at his empty plate and then at her and then picked up a serving spoon and dug into her mother's monster pan of seafood paella.

'Good choice,' said Carlos, and Valentine nodded and glanced Angelique's way again.

'So I hear.'

'Nice place you have here,' said her father.

'Yes.'

'Rent it out often?' asked Benedict, full of barbs and

doublespeak, and Angelique aimed a well-deserved kick at him beneath the table. 'Ouch! You kicked me.'

'Did I hit anything important?' Own your actions, an old lesson learned well. She smiled sweetly, and winked at Valentine, the poor outnumbered soul.

Who was he when he wasn't being a king? She truly didn't know.

It was hard to say if even *he* knew, but he was no stranger to social situations and general awkwardness, that much was clear as he picked food as a topic and drew her parents into a conversation about their favourite meals and memories, and places too, until soon everyone was joining in, and it was fun to simply sit and watch him watching them.

After dinner Carlos, Benedict and her father drew him away to one of the sitting rooms while she and Lucia stayed back and helped clear the table. Moriana stayed too, a queen doing dishes, and she laughed and said she had the better of the deal, so Lucia opened another bottle of wine for them all.

'He wants you,' Moriana said to Angelique, and no one needed to put a name to those words.

'I know.'

'Are you going to let him have you?'

'I think so. I don't need marriage. I'm not interested in status. I don't care that he can't give me children. And if he wants to make waves and annoy those in his court who sought to bring him down, I'm just the woman to help him make a statement.'

'True,' said Moriana. 'I like it.'

'I don't.' Lucia pointed a clean wooden spoon in Angelique's direction. 'That's ninety per cent bravado talking, and ten per cent delusion. You're going to fall for him all over again and there'll be so many pieces to pick up at the end that we won't be able to find them all.'

'Lucia's a bit of a pessimist,' her mother explained to Moriana, and then it was on.

'Me? *Me* the pessimist?' This from Lucia and she had a wooden spoon in her hand and Angelique started running. Around the table and through the doorway and straight into the arms of the man they'd all been talking about. Thankfully, he was alone.

'And stay out!' Luciana's voice followed them from the doorway, as Angelique disengaged her elbow from his solar plexus and her cheek from his chest.

'Sisterly love?' he asked, and she could feel the deep rumble of his voice through his chest, because her hand was still on it, and she had two choices. She could either snatch her hand back and step away or she could stay right where she was and start smoothing him out. She chose the latter.

If his lazy grin was anything to go by, it was the right choice. 'I left your men in the study with my liquor. Let me know when you need more cellar supplies and I'll have it restocked. Especially if you take to entertaining Liesendaach royalty on a regular basis. Will your family be here often?'

'No, they're only here to help me move in. They have their own lives.'

'But you do seem close.'

'They're my strength.' They'd had their spats, but they'd also had to close ranks over and over again through the years. First when Angelique had run afoul of the Thallasian monarchy, and again when Carlos took up with Benedict.

'Should I expect a chaperone every time I visit?'

'Hardly.' Though Lucia would probably find it fun to watch his frustration grow. 'My family will remain silent if you wish for any association between you and me to remain a secret. You only have to look to my brother's relationship with Benedict to see that they can. That's been going on for the last seven, no, eight years.'

His lips tightened. 'With you as the beard.'

She shrugged, because basically yes. 'Sometimes Lucia pretending to be me, but yes. The fact is, my family is discreet.'

'What if I don't want to hide my relationship with you? Are you interested at all in being seen with me in public?'

'To step into the limelight with you all over again and have your country's gutter press tear into me like a pack of mountain wolves? Why not?' She would be playing to type, after all. 'It's my specialty. Part of my appeal. The unsuitable woman, no?'

'No.'

Her steps faltered and she slid him a sideways glance. The hallway sconces threw his features into stark relief. Beauty and shadows, always the shadows with him. 'You're not intending to use my wanton reputation to shore up your poor beleaguered masculinity?'

'No.'

'Oh.' Now she was just plain confused.

'Let's just say that while I don't want to hide my interest in you, nor do I intend to throw you to the wolves. I'd rather protect you. The way I never did before.'

She frowned.

'The national art gallery is opening a new exhibition area on Thursday and I'm saying a few words and staying on for a couple of hours afterwards. I'd like you to accompany me. It will draw comment, of that I have no doubt. Your leasing of this place may be unearthed. But the sooner I indicate my official interest in you and bring the palace's media machine on board, the better for you. I have no intention of treating you like a dirty secret. Not this time. Never again. Let's aim to do this right.'

His sincerity was her undoing. They could never re-write the past, but the future looked promising.

'We good?' he asked.

'Get your people to send me a brief—and by that I mean what you'll be wearing to the gallery opening, what others will be wearing, and who the main dignitaries are. It's the kind of brief Moriana makes up for Carlos and Benedict all the time. Works a treat.'

'That woman…' He shook his head.

'Inspiring, isn't she? You'd best say goodbye to her and the others in the kitchen if you're taking your leave. Of course, you could always stay. No one has taken pos-session of the master bedroom yet. It's free.'

'Why did no one take the master?'

'Could have something to do with the bear rug in front of the hearth and the stuffed leopard looking down from the ceiling joists. And then there's the monkeys.'

'Monkeys?' he repeated.

'You've never stayed here before, have you?'

'No. Can't say I'm familiar with the layout of the place beyond what's on a set of plans back at the palace.'

The perils of heading a monarchy. And, boy, was he in for a treat. 'Let me give you the tour.'

CHAPTER SEVEN

THERE WAS SOMETHING surreal about having Angelique give him a tour of a manor house he owned. He'd come to visit her on a whim, not intending to pursue her before she'd even settled in, but his desire to see her again had overridden common sense. She was nearby and he'd sped through all his work for the day and was at a loose end. In his imagination she had been alone and half expecting him. A diaphanous nightgown and a sultry smile had featured heavily in his daydream. She'd been wearing them when she opened the door to him...

His libido had clearly not died along with his ability to procreate.

Nor, apparently, had his imagination.

In reality, he'd knocked on the huge manor house doors and when no one had responded he'd gone round the back and, led by the noise, had let himself into the wet room and followed the scent of food through to the kitchen door. He'd somehow found himself sitting down to what amounted to a Cordova family dinner. Shedding his kingly persona bit by bit as the evening wore on, watching Moriana let her hair down with no little astonishment, enjoying Benedict's razor-sharp tongue and Carlos' calming presence in a room full of volatile people. Luciana and

Angelique so *different* from one another underneath their near identical features. The Cordova matriarch so beloved by them all, and Eduardo Cordova presiding proudly at the head of the table. A generous, gregarious man, with a steady hand on the reins of his family and an air of unwavering love and support.

For Valentine, whose family life had never been nurturing, it was like stepping into a whole new world.

After dinner, he'd made sure the drawing room had been stocked with the best the cellar could provide and had then made up some flimsy excuse to seek out Angelique. Fortunately, he'd found her alone, and now she was giving him the tour, her face flushed and her saunter relaxed. Her jeans, high boots and floral cotton top with a drawstring loose around her neck suited the informality of the evening and showcased her generous curves. He definitely had a thing for boots, he decided, and mentally shredded the diaphanous nightgown.

Only to have his brain helpfully replace it with an image of Angelique wearing boots and lacy pink lingerie with little bows.

The manor house had not been made for comfort or for nesting. Ceilings soared, bedrooms were huge and the dining rooms gilded with thick golden drapes of crushed velvet. Stone lined the floors, a mixture of grey and mossy green slate. The floor rugs were threadbare and the furniture heavy hand-carved dark wood. The entire manor had a faded, medieval air about it.

And then came the master bedroom—a circus from start to finish, what with the leopard prints and the zebra stripes and the ruby-red drapes and various stuffed animals. The leopard prowling the ceiling beams, as promised. A stuffed monkey hanging from the ceiling light. 'Moriana saw this?' he asked.

'Sure did. She said you win on the mad décor front, although her brother has a round room for courtesans that takes some beating. It has a trapeze.' She eyed the manacles bolted to a nearby wall. 'I didn't ask if it had restraints. Who used to live here?'

'A duke, a hundred years ago. Change whatever you want. There's likely an attic full of spare furniture somewhere.'

'There is, and we've already raided it. I only intend to occupy half a dozen rooms at most, and we spent the weekend making them comfortable. And the horse facilities are everything we could ask for and more. We're happy with the move and so we should be.' Her eyes drifted towards the ceiling and another stuffed monkey occupying a beam. 'Monkeys included. Plus I've had a few more minutes to think about being your date for the art gallery opening, and I'm happy with that too. I'm ready for you.' The look she sent him was pure smoulder.

'So if I was to kiss you right now, before I take my leave, that would be an acceptable end to the evening?'

'Yes.'

He'd kissed her before, all those years ago. He thought he remembered her passion and sweetness but it was nothing compared to what he tasted now. He let himself sink, undone, overwhelmed. He wanted nothing more than to pull her down onto the bed and take all the time in the world to discover her all over again. But there were monkeys overhead, and her family just down the hall and he wouldn't put it past any of them to go looking for her. He could wait. He'd waited this long, after all. They had time.

'Come back here after the gallery opening,' she murmured and drew him down for another kiss. 'Can that be arranged beforehand?'

'Presumptuous.'

'Yes, I am. I know enough about kings to know that spontaneity is hard to come by. So let's plan. Or am I moving too fast for you?'

Oh, challenge accepted. 'Your room. Now.'

He'd never seen her move so swiftly in the other direction. 'With my parents in the house? Never.'

It felt so good to laugh and pretend to be that carefree boy again—the one who had played and loved without reservation. Fearless, in a way he'd never been since. 'I'll see myself out, shall I?'

'I can walk you to the door.' She looked around. 'If I can find it.'

They found it together. His security team filtered in from their positions and she clocked them all and nodded but said nothing. 'Thank you for the meal,' he offered.

'What did you think of the paella?'

It wasn't just the food. It was the atmosphere around the table that made the meal so memorable, the warmth and wit and welcome extended to him. 'I've never tasted better.'

CHAPTER EIGHT

FOUR DAYS LATER, Valentine stood on the steps of the art gallery and watched Angelique alight from the vehicle he'd sent to collect her. He'd worked long hours all week so he could take tomorrow morning off, and he had every intention of enjoying himself this evening. If Angelique's presence at his side caused a stir, so be it. The people of Thallasia would simply have to get used to it.

She wore scarlet—of course she did, and her shoulders were bare and her hair had been artfully piled on top of her head and held in place by pins tipped with pearls to match the three-strand pearl choker at her neck. That choker had a leash on it—he had no idea what else to call it—that dangled down her back to rest just above the curve of her utterly perfect rear. He could pick it up and reel her in and his hand itched to take hold of it.

She saw him moments later and put her arms out and twirled. 'Will I do?'

'What exactly are you aiming for?'

'Well, the exhibition's called *The Downfall of Man*— it's an inspired first-date choice, by the way. I thought I'd stick to theme.'

'Good job.'

'Although there's really only one man whose downfall I wish to be associated with, and that's yours.'

'Still with the revenge theme.'

Her megawatt smile almost blinded him. 'That's what they'll say, and I do aim to please.'

He held out his arm for her to take, and felt a jolt of possessive satisfaction when her slender hand covered his arm. 'You certainly do. Do you need a powder room before we're announced?'

'Wouldn't hurt.'

'Are you nervous?' She didn't look it.

'I'd be mad not to be. But there's a difference between nervous and ready, and I'm ready.'

They caused a stir on entry to the exhibition as he had known they would, and she bore it all with a flair for mischief that shouldn't have surprised him as much as it did. She genuinely enjoyed the exhibition, it seemed, and stayed attentive during the speeches. She didn't simper, cling, or go out of her way to impress. At one point she winked at him and almost derailed his speech.

The ease with which she navigated his world surprised him, though perhaps it shouldn't have. They'd spent years travelling in similar circles, overlapping, rarely meeting.

His sister was in attendance and made a point of joining Angelique to view several of the paintings together. Enough to imply approval of his choice of guest for the evening. He nodded his thanks and she raised a brow and excused herself from Angelique's side and began to work the room in earnest—backing up the efforts he'd already put in. Not just the spare to be sidelined, she'd stepped up to present a united front alongside him and begun to let people glimpse the formidable intellect beneath the looks she'd always relied on to impress them.

Angelique welcomed him with a smile as he held out his arm for her to take and moved them on to the next picture.

'Kind of your sister to publicly endorse me,' she murmured. 'Did you put her up to it?'

'No. She likes that I'm falling in favour and that her power is rising. I'm giving her more responsibility, and for all that she may not have wanted it, she wields it beautifully. Makes it easier for me to move over.'

'You're still considering abdication?'

'Not any more. No. But it doesn't hurt people to see King Valentine with his twin at his side. They're getting two for the price of one. They should be pleased. Anyone give you trouble here this evening?'

'With you here watching them, and me, like a hawk? Who would dare?'

'Oh, I think you'll find that the papers tomorrow will dare.'

She shrugged dismissively. 'Don't expect me to care. My family is the foundation on which I stand, and they know who I am.' She looked so beautiful with her flashing black eyes and the scarlet draping her curves. 'I'm more worried about the fallout you'll face.'

'It can hardly be worse than being rendered less than a man and a failure as a king for being unable to provide an heir. "You had one job…"' he began, and she laughed, because, seriously, who knew he could do voices?

But it wasn't just the voices. He was beginning to accept his new limits and move forward, and she respected him for that.

And wanted to undress him very soon.

It wasn't a normal date, by any means, and when it ended and his driver took them to her place, which was technically his place, his security detail checking through the house put an end to all thoughts of ravishing him the moment they stepped through the doors. Still, there was a certain satisfaction in seeing him methodically unwind after being on show for the evening. They started in the study her visitors seemed to favour—the one with the deep library chairs and the side bar stuffed full of spirits and cut-glass crystal. She watched as he removed his jacket and slung it over the back of a chair before loosening his tie and then removing his cufflinks one by one before making a beeline for the drinks.

He'd been offered champagne on arrival at the gallery and had taken a flute full and carried it around for some time before handing the half-full glass off to a waiter and refusing another. So that other guests could feel free to pick up and carry a drink, he'd murmured at the time, but there had been no more drinking on his part and she'd stuck to two drinks, although contrary to him she'd finished both. Waste not want not, and all that.

'So it's not that you don't drink.' She set her clutch on a side table and silently admired the sheer beauty of him in the lamplight. 'But rather that you don't drink when on duty.'

'Exactly. May I pour you a nightcap?'

She asked for limoncello. He opted for a Scotch that might have been older than her. Would they sit down to dissect the evening and predict tomorrow's headlines, was that how this went? Because, boring.

But he didn't start there. Instead he flung himself down in the middle of a sturdy love seat, set his drink down and beckoned her closer with the crook of his finger and a smile that the devil would have been proud of. The whole display was pure arrogance and pantomime.

She loved it. 'Very smooth.'

'The drink?' He made a fine show of taking a sip and then dangling the crystal tumbler carelessly from finger and thumb. 'Yes.'

'The undressing and making yourself at home too. Why don't you let me get your tie?' She made a great show of leaning over to gently pull it apart and then flip his collar up and slide the tie free of his very fine shirt. Tut-tut. The poor man's shirt buttons were positively strangling him, so she attended to them too. 'Is this what a valet would do for you?'

'No.'

Such a delicious rasp to his voice.

'How fond of that gown are you?'

'Extremely fond.' Didn't mean she had a burning desire to keep it on. 'Why?'

'Because I'd like you to sit with me.' He put the glass down and patted his well-formed thighs. 'On me...'

'Ride you?' He had the best ideas.

Crushed velvet seemed such a small price to pay for the pleasure of straddling firm thighs and putting her hands to a warm chest clothed in finest cotton. He kept his hands to himself and maybe he liked it when she tilted his head the better to brush her lips against his. She wasn't a dominant soul, not really, but this acquiescence of his was starting to work for her in ways that went straight to her centre, pulling and twisting and teasing, such a lovely, teasing mouth he had on him, and kisses that smiled.

Where was his tie when she needed it? But the two sides of his collar would have to do as she grasped the fabric and deepened the kiss, even as he shifted to press the steel of his erection against her heated folds. He'd been a cocky teen and for good reason, long and thick, and she couldn't help but set up a rhythm that pleased her. Tiny circles against the generous wedge of him. 'I hope you remember how to use that,' she murmured against his lips and brought forth another smile.

Sex could be teasing, and playful and fun before turning white hot with passion. He'd taught her that and she saw no reason to abandon such teachings now. Sex could be urgent and messy or lazy and sated. Never just the one thing, you had to direct it. Feel your way. 'I remember you, you know. Your kisses. Your hands. Vividly,' she murmured.

'You should. You had me at my best. Maybe not my smoothest…' His fingers were feeling their way beneath her panties right now, sliding into her with unerring accuracy as his moistened thumb found her nub and circled again and again. 'But definitely at my most committed.'

There was nothing quite like a firm and knowing touch and none had ever been as knowing as his. Truth to say, she'd never allowed it. For all her hedonistic talents she'd never opened to any other man the way she had to him and for a passionate woman—which she was—it had been a very long time between drinks. She was about to embarrass herself, no question, what with his touch and his scent and the whisper of stubble on his jaw doing her in. 'We could slow down some.'

'Why?'

Because I'm almost already there, she could have confessed.

Because my memories of what was and what is are twining together to create an irresistible mix, she could have mentioned.

Because I'm not and never have been easy, she could have said, and it would have been the truth.

Only him.

Only this.

She closed her eyes and let him drive her higher, signalling her pleasure with drugging kisses, unable to stop her body from following where he led, but she wanted him sheathed in her when she crested.

'Put it inside.' Words she whispered as she fumbled to undo his belt and then the buttons—who did buttons with a member like his?—and then there was underwear and she nearly keened her relief when he halted his ministrations to lift his hips and push his clothes down and out of the way, and she knew exactly what to do with what was left.

Slowly, she positioned herself against his tip and bore down with a gasp. It was just as fulfilling as she remembered as he inched his way inside her…*slowly does it*… until they were a perfect fit. How? How did that fit where it did and still manage to feel so good?

'Size Queen,' he murmured, as if reading her thoughts, and maybe it was true.

'I've missed you *so much*.' And if that was a ridiculous reply he took as referencing his girth, well who was she to correct him?

'Missed you too.'

The things they'd learned together, about each other, seemed to stand the test of time. That place at his jaw, just before his ear, that made him curse when she grazed it with her teeth and then soothed it with her tongue. The way he dived into a kiss and wouldn't be satisfied until they were both blue for breath and gasping at the end of it. The sheer joy of slick bodies pressing, pressing against each other, rise and fall, empires could fall in that moment and there would still be no stopping them. Rise and fall. Rise and fall and climb and plead and beg.

'I need—'

He knew exactly what she needed. Less clothing, more flesh, hands on her body and her nipple in his mouth. Just like that, yet it wasn't the way it had been all those years ago in the hunting cabin. They had plenty of time now and somewhere along the way he'd taken a masterclass in finesse.

Nothing between them but the air they breathed and the searching, seeking slide of flesh within flesh. The velvet of the couch beneath them. The dim light and the way his gaze didn't leave her face, fierce and glittering, and she wondered, with what little brain she had left, how she'd gone so long without this kind of connection.

Such a deliciously deep connection.

'Hello again,' she whispered against the curve of his neck, and prayed their indulgence wouldn't cost them as much as it had last time. 'Is this what you want from me?'

His answer was yes, and yes again as she set up a tiny rocking motion with her pelvis that had him groaning and laughing and setting his busy hands to her hips and clamping her to stillness.

'Too soon.' And this time his kisses were set to soothe. 'Slow down. Long and slow, Angelique. I've waited so long. Let me learn you all over again.'

He stayed the night and most of the following morning.

And in this he was a man of his word.

He couldn't get enough of her.

Valentine knew he was ignoring the terms of their

loosely discussed agreement—especially when it came
to keeping Angelique separate from the duties imposed
on him by the monarchy, but it was such a little transgres-
sion to begin with. He'd stayed overnight at the manor,
again, and had a morning appointment with a charity he
personally supported. He'd told her about it over breakfast and she'd seemed so interested in what they did, and
what he did to amplify their reach, that he asked her if
she wanted to come with him.

Foolish, foolish man, because it had quickly turned
into a public relations disaster, and, in hindsight, Valentine took full responsibility. He hadn't briefed her properly, for starters. He hadn't told the organisers he was
bringing a guest.

He'd sprung the trip on her one morning as he played
house with her, his stomach full of bacon and mush-
rooms and sourdough toast, and his mind still clouded
by their activities of the previous night. He'd wanted to
stay with her just that little bit longer, eke out a couple
more hours spent soaking in her warmth, so he'd asked
her to accompany him on a job.

She'd been dressed too casually, for starters. Flat
shoes, neat trousers, a collared cotton shirt with the
sleeves rolled up to sit just below her elbows. No jewel-
lery to speak of, except for the watch she wore on an everyday basis. The charity they had visited tackled adult
literacy. As an adult for whom Thallasian was not her
first language, Angelique had been genuinely interested
in the classes and the teaching materials provided.

Her enthusiasm for their work had been everything
he could have asked for.

When one of the organisers had asked if she minded
being filmed reading from one of the beginner texts,

she hadn't minded a bit and Valentine had nodded yes. She'd mangled the story, of course. Her spoken Thallasian was far in advance of her ability to read it. It was her fourth language behind her native Spanish, Liesend-aachish and English.

The video had gone live on social media and the press had feasted on her ignorance.

Not only had the King's whore been shabbily dressed, she'd pimped an expensive watch brand she was ambassador for—thus monetising her association with His Majesty the King of Thallasia—and she had the reading skills of the average Thallasian eight-year-old.

All the good work of the charity had been buried beneath an avalanche of criticism, unsubtle innuendo about what the King saw in his foreign mistress, and the prediction that she couldn't possibly hold his interest for much longer.

All of it was his fault for deviating from the carefully curated script the palace had laid out for him.

Get your head out of the clouds and *protect* the woman, his sister had berated him, and rightly so.

Benedict—once upon a time the Crown Prince of scandalous headlines involving Angelique—had phoned to ask if Valentine had any other tips to impart when it came to ruining a woman's reputation. Not a good move on Benedict's part because it afforded Valentine the opportunity to vent about how little care Benedict and Carlos had had for Angelique's reputation—using her to hide their relationship behind for years and years, letting them say those things about her, and Benedict had said pot, kettle, black, and hung up on him.

Only to call back an hour later to say that he and Carlos had decided to grant a glossy magazine an interview in which they intended to emphasise Angelique's generosity and willingness to put her brother's happiness first as he navigated not only coming out but being in a serious relationship with a royal family member.

Not that Angelique would likely care one way or another about the article, or any other articles written about her, Benedict had warned.

Angelique cared a great deal about what her tight circle of friends and family thought of her, and beyond that, people could say what they liked. She truly didn't care, and it wasn't a front, although it might have started out as a kind of defence.

And maybe that was a fine quality for a king's mistress to have, but Benedict rather thought not, which meant Valentine, and Benedict, and others around her needed to lift their game and protect what she would not. This was what Benedict had phoned to say before they'd embarked on their blame game.

And this time, Valentine listened intently, and after work that day, when he joined her for dinner and Angelique barely spared the articles a glance, he asked her why she wasn't more upset and settled back against the chair in the manor kitchen and listened.

'I have my work.' She swirled the burgundy wine around in her glass and took an appreciative sip before continuing. 'I've spent all day on this beautiful estate, largely cut off from the rest of the country, and my horses care nothing for the words of people who live to find fault. I have a wonderful life here.'

'The tabloids are calling you dim.'

'Do you think I'm dim? I truly hope not.' She shook her head as if to dismiss the notion. 'Me and my family were blooded in this type of warfare years ago and know to ignore it. It doesn't bother me. I expect no less from the press hounds of Thallasia. Do you truly expect them to love me? She studied him curiously. 'Because if you do, you're dreaming.'

'It truly doesn't bother you, this rubbish they print about you?' he asked.

'No. Does what they say about you bother you?'

'Yes. I have a team of people dedicated to ensuring that the bulk of my press stays favourable. I can do more good when I'm seen to be above reproach.'

She snorted inelegantly. 'I get it. I do. But your relationship with me is never going to be above reproach.'

'People accepted my infertility, my broken engagement and my desire not to marry. Not at first, this is true, but they're coming around to realising that my will to serve my country remains true. If we—I—made a point of emphasising the real you, maybe they'd accept you too.'

'You'd do all this groundwork for a fling?'

'What fling?' He might as well bury that notion along with every last remnant of his pride. 'I don't know about you, but this is the happiest I've ever been and it's because you're in my world. I want to continue with this… whatever it is that we're doing—do we really need to define it? But whatever it is, it's not a fling. You're important to me. The way Thallasia sees you is important to me.'

Now would be the time for Angelique to say the same to him, but she said nothing. Instead she raised her glass to her lips, but she was still here and listening and he came by his reputation for strong powers of persuasion honestly. 'To that end—

'What are they saying about me today?'

It was the first time he'd been interrupted in…for ever, and the hint of a smile on her lips suggested she probably knew that already. He picked up the paper in front of him and made a great show of shaking it out. 'You're about to reveal the whereabouts of the secret love child you bore me all those years ago.'

'I see.' She lowered her glass but kept her fingers on the slender stem. 'That's a new one. They're assuming your father wouldn't have taken care of that in the most brutal way possible. You lot have very short memories.' The minute she said it, her expression changed to one of contrition. 'Sorry. That comment was out of line. I don't equate your father with all Thallasians, you know. I don't see him in you.'

'Maybe that's because I've spent a lot of time and effort stamping him out. He's not a man I wish to emulate. His behaviour towards you all those years ago brought that home most vividly. Even so, I still see parts of him in me. My temper. My…arrogance. For all that I'm more aware of it than I once was, it still rises when I'm challenged.'

'Doesn't everyone's?'

'I would not know,' he murmured. 'People tend not to have temper tantrums when I'm around.' People were deferential to him. It came with the king thing and probably did him no favours at all. 'I don't need that from you. I like when we talk like this, when you interrupt my pontificating.' Hell yes, she *had* known exactly how that might wind him up, her smirk said as much. 'I need you to be able to speak your truth and not apologise for it—even if you're speaking ill of my father.'

She tossed her raven mane and fixed him with a haughty stare. 'I'll apologise if I want to, and don't you forget it. And now...' She flicked a quick glance at the tabloid on the table before pushing the mess aside and planting her pert behind in its place. 'If we've finished examining my press for the day, perhaps we might move on to other, more important matters. You could stop looking at the newspapers and destress instead.' A kiss for the edge of his lips, undemanding as far as kisses went, but with the promise of more if he wanted it. 'Would you like me to help you with that?'

'Absolutely, by all means, help me destress.'

Everything Angelique offered only served to make him hungrier for more of her. He resented having to parcel out his time with her like a miser, having to carefully vet where he could be seen with her, and even then the ludicrous articles about her just kept coming...

'But first I want you to consider doing an interview about literacy, about the languages you do speak, about the fact that you're unapologetically learning to read and write Thallasian. You can do it here, but the palace will style you and organise the interview.'

'About that arrogance,' she murmured, but he silenced her with a kiss.

'Please.' He who so rarely had to justify his demands.

'Why feed the beast? That article about me being dim will be forgotten soon enough. As for styling me, you need to stop thinking of my looks as something to be harnessed and used to make people like me. It doesn't work like that. Usually, it makes others wary or resentful.'

'A statement from you, then.' He could be flexible. 'The palace will release it.'

She 'hmm-ed' against his cheek. 'How about, "I'm working hard to improve my verbal and written Thallasian, and have already started using the learning strategies shared by the adult literacy teachers and students of Loannault Community House. Next time I attend, I hope they'll see an improvement." Will that do?'

'You're good at this.'

'For what? Staying on message?'

'For putting up with everything that comes of being seen with me.' He pulled away a little, the better to see her eyes. How could she stay so serene when strangers made it their mission to pick her apart in order to score a headline? But she didn't look stressed or indignant. She looked as if she'd put it out of her head altogether and moved on to contemplating far more favourable things.

Namely him.

One elegant eyebrow rose and her lips curved in a satisfied smile.

Definitely him. 'Am I wearing too many clothes?' he asked.

'In my considered opinion, always.'

She made him laugh, this woman others thought so far beneath him. She made him think there could be a safe place for him far away from palace doors, and he'd never thought that before.

'Shirt buttons. Hurry up.' She reached for the top one and set it free. 'Must I do everything?'

Could he ask to lie back and be loved by her? 'Is that an offer?'

Her fingers stilled on button three as she paused to glance at his face. 'Oh,' she said softly, as realisation kicked in. 'You'd like me to lead tonight.'

'Yes.' The minute she said it, he wanted exactly that. Ached for it. Longed to lay the burden of leadership at her feet, if only for a night, and if such a request made him weak, so be it. 'Please.'

She caught his lips in a kiss that plundered first and then promised heaven. Mischief lurked in the curve of her mouth and the way she nibbled at the bow of his upper lip. 'You realise Moriana's been telling me about the round room Sera set up for King Augustus. The one with the trapeze and the owls and the big round carpet and the bathing area? I say we start this pamper Valentine session in a bathroom. There's a big spa bath here off the main bedroom, and, while it's not big enough for two, there are water jets, there's a sitting step for anyone who doesn't intend getting in, and it won't take long to fill.'

Water had so often been his punishment when his late father had wanted to toughen him up or punish him. Perhaps this time it could soothe him. 'Is that so?'

'Mmm-hmm. So why don't we head that way—bring your drink—and let me see what I can do for you?'

He was shivering by the time he sank naked into the steaming, scented water but it wasn't from the cold. She'd lit candles and kept the lights low, and maybe for someone else it would be romantic, but the cavern beneath the palace had always been poorly lit too, the water running swift and black through what his father had euphemistically called a pool. A rock overhang had covered the mouth of the river at one end and a steel grate formed the other end of the pool, letting water through the grid but not a person, and it had been fun to be pinned against it when the river ran sluggish and peaceful, and no fun at all when the river became a torrent.

'No jets,' he murmured, when Angelique went to turn them on, and maybe that was him taking control again when he didn't mean to, but he couldn't stand the thought of them. Angelique didn't question his request, merely picked up a flannel, loaded it with soap scrub and began to wash him down. This he could do. This firm and thorough touch that became more massage than tease, and relaxed muscles he didn't know he had.

'Lean forward,' she instructed, so he did, allowing her to start in on his back, slow circular movements, and then she set the flannel and soap aside, sluiced him down with water from her cupped hands and then smeared those hands with oil and began rubbing the tension from his shoulders.

She'd had her hands all over him before, but he doubted she'd ever seen his back the way she could now, and he wondered whether the dim light would conceal his shame or not. He could barely feel the whip welts any more, where his father had broken the skin, but he'd been told they were still visible if one looked closely enough, silvery lines on otherwise smooth olive skin.

She dug her thumbs in and slid them up his spine, all the way to the base of his neck, and he shuddered again, leaving old memories behind in favour of groaning his appreciation.

'Who did this to you?' she asked finally.

'My father.'

'Why?' Straight to the point, no surprise at his words. Had everyone seen his father so much more clearly than him?

'I displeased him.'

Her hands worked him over, gentler than they had been. 'When you were a child?'

'Why does it matter?' Everything about those marks on his back shamed him. That his first stumbling steps towards being a man of honour had been met with a whip. That he'd been too surprised to defend himself.

That Vala hadn't been able to meet his gaze as she'd tended him afterwards with salve she'd stolen from the kitchen's first-aid kit. 'It happened. It made me examine the kind of man I was and wanted to be. It made me seek my leadership role models elsewhere. In the armed forces for several years. In neighbouring monarchs and elder statesmen after that. I'm not proud of those whip marks on my back, don't get me wrong. But they forced a reckoning, not with my father, but within me. For that I'm grateful.'

She was silent for a long time after that, but her hands kept moving, and when more words came, they were halting. 'Valentine, did I cause this?'

'No.' He could say that with certainty, even if his liaison with her had been at the root of it. 'Let it go, Angelique. I've made my peace with them. There's no point reopening old wounds.'

She replied by crawling into the bath behind him and setting her lips to his scarred skin and he wanted to weep at her silent understanding. 'Relax,' she said. 'No more questions. Just feel.'

Not until every part of his body had been loosened did she urge him from the bath and towel him down and lead him to her bed. Fresh sheets and lazy kisses as he closed his eyes and let his hunger for her rise. Sank into her touch and let it build and build until he was a mass of writhing sensation and his head was filled with nothing but gratitude for every caress.

He'd never felt more naked than when, finally, she straddled him and took him in, took him apart, and in her own good time remade him.

He slept after that, fell hard and deep into oblivion, and when he woke and reached for her in the night she was there right beside him, warm and willing and this time he led. Giving back, getting lost all over again but he didn't care. It was too good and yet never enough and he prayed she would be strong enough to stay with him across the years and be content.

Or you could marry her and afford her the protections she deserves, a little voice whispered.

But that would be the end of her freedom, and for all that he was the son of a tyrant and a hard man in his own right, he wouldn't wish that role on her. This arrangement here was working for her. She had a career she could continue to grow and he had ready access to her, and if he missed her more and more whenever he was away from her, so be it. If the press flayed her for daring to claim some of his time, he had better get used to defending her.

'Be happy with me,' he whispered against her hair, big spoon to her little one, and she stirred in her sleep, and he stilled until she settled once more before adding a silent please.

Surely he could claim this small happiness.

Okay, not small, call it what it was. Surely, this deep, all-encompassing contentment in his bones and in his heart could be his.

Please.

CHAPTER NINE

THREE MONTHS LATER, happy beyond all reckoning, Angelique came to another reckoning while retching over the laundry sink because the smell of her morning coffee made her sick. It was the third time in a week, and the smart thing to do would be to swap out the coffee for a cup of something less fragrant, and she intended to, cross her heart. Morning sickness problem solved.

Morning.

Sickness.

'Madre de Dios.'

She couldn't be pregnant. Could she? Because Valentine couldn't have children and she sure as eggs wasn't sleeping with anyone else. Eggs. Terrible breakfast food that it was, she hadn't made any this morning for fear they would set her off. No food at all because she had a tummy bug.

Just a tummy bug.

She retched again, pitiful and groaning with the effort of bringing up nothing more than bile. She reached for the tap and let the water swirl. She washed her mouth out and splashed her face and finally leaned back against the wet-room wall and dug in her coat for her phone. Stables first—she got hold of her head groom and told him she was ill and staying away from them all for a day or so. They talked about the exercise needs of various horses and her groom told her they had everything under control and to get well soon, and that he'd call again this afternoon.

The worry in his voice had not been feigned. She was a Cordova, and Cordovas had to be half dead before they neglected their horses. Three quarters dead, at the very least.

That or unexpectedly pregnant to an infertile king.

She called Luciana next, after having slid down the wall to sit on the floor. She had her forehead to her knees, the jodhpur material warm and familiar against her skin.

'Hey,' she murmured when Lucia picked up. 'Can you do me a favour?'

'It's not even six a.m.,' her sister grumbled. 'I can do you a favour by not yelling at you for waking me up. How does that sound?'

'Sorry. Very sorry.' She closed her eyes as nausea churned again. 'I'll call you back. Give me a time that's good for you.'

'What do you want?' Her sister's voice held a hint of worry in it now.

She took a deep breath, held if for a slow count of five and then let it back out. 'A pregnancy test.'

Silence.

'I'd buy one myself but if the press got wind of it…' She didn't want to think what would happen if the press got wind of it before she'd had a chance to speak with Valentine.

'How can you possibly be pregnant?' Lucia argued. 'You can't be.'

'I *know*. But it's been months since I last bled, and,

while that's not uncommon if I work hard and drop weight, I have neither dropped weight nor worked myself ragged recently. My breasts are sensitive, my hair is thicker, and the smell of coffee makes me retch. Tell me that doesn't sound like I'm pregnant.'

'Are you glowing? Pregnant women glow.'

'Don't make fun of me, Lucia. Please. I think I'm pregnant, I'm terrified, and I need a pregnancy test. Or two. Maybe three in case I don't believe the results of the first two.'

'Oh, hell. How? No, scrap that question, I know how. But how the hell did they get Valentine's diagnosis so bloody wrong? Doesn't he have the best of the best physicians? If there'd been the tiniest chance of him siring an heir wouldn't he and the doctors have been all over that possibility?'

'You'd think so.' She didn't know what to think.

'Do you have a belly?'

'No!' Not yet. Did she? Riding horses all day made a person toned enough that she would know. She ran a hand over the area in question. 'I don't think so? No one's said anything. But the breasts, Lucia. The breasts!'

'What about mood swings? Are you feeling all hormonal these days?'

Was she? Hard to say. She could be a little highly strung on the best of days. 'Nothing more than usual.' She tried to sound confident about that and vowed to ask her grooms if she'd been more difficult than usual recently. 'Can you post me a test? Or three?' Valentine had a permanent security detail at the manor these days, and he justified it because of the amount of times he visited. They also checked her mail. She'd have to hover and get the parcel before they did, but it could be done.

She was almost sure it could be done.

'No.' From her sister's mouth to her ears, and it shocked her into speechlessness. Lucia had always come through for her. 'You're not doing this alone. I'll be there by this evening and I'll bring a batch of tests with me.'

Inexplicably, her eyes filled with tears. 'I don't know what I'd do without you. I love you so much. You're the other half of my heart, with me every step of the way and I would be desolate without you. Desolate!'

Silence greeted her tearful declaration.

'Luciana?'

'Oh, my God, you're pregnant.'

The day passed excruciatingly slowly and when Luciana emerged through the airport arrivals door Angelique was hard pressed not to fling herself into her arms and drag her to the nearest restroom. Her sister took one look at her, enfolded her in a hug and muttered, 'Bathroom. Now.'

Being a twin with the near psychic ability to know what the other was thinking had never been more glorious.

They went into adjoining cubicles and Lucia passed a package full of pregnancy tests beneath the door before seeing to her own needs. If they were monitoring cubicles on film, a security person would likely be waiting for them when they exited. That was the thought she chose to occupy her mind as she peed on a stick and waited.

And then did it again.

Upon exiting, she met Lucia's eyes in the mirror and didn't have to say a thing.

'Dios mio.'

Oh, my God. Lucia had said it for her.

They ate a late meal at the village near the manor. Valentine rang, and, when he heard she was with Lucia, decided against coming over.

Luciana smirked as he told them to enjoy their catch-up and that he'd likely see them tomorrow. 'That man is scared of me. As he should be. When are you going to tell him?'

The food in her mouth suddenly tasted like ash.

'You should do it while I'm here.'

And have Lucia witness his disbelief and never, ever forgive him if things did, in fact, work out okay? 'I think it needs to be a private conversation.'

'Suit yourself.'

'Maybe I could do it by phone.'

'And deny yourself the look on his face or his temper while he sorts out other people's mistakes surrounding his diagnosis? That could work.'

But she did want to see his face, that was the problem. 'This arrangement that we have…it doesn't involve children. Valentine's not going to *want* a child.' And at her sister's raised brow. 'He's not going to want a child with *me*. If he's all fixed and fertile he'll be off to find a proper princess to marry. One his country will accept without reservation.'

'Why are you even with him if that's what you think he's going to do? Don't you trust him to do right by you at all?'

Angelique's hesitation spoke volumes. 'He's a king. I trust him to serve his country, first and always.'

'Then he's a fool.'

'Maybe so.'

Her sister eyed her speculatively. 'Would you marry

him if he asked you to? Spend the rest of your life as a civil servant with pretty clothes and tiaras and a child who might one day sit on a foreign country's throne?'

She bowed her head and tried to picture all the rigmarole that happened every time they stepped out somewhere together multiplied a hundredfold. Every day planned down to the last second. Almost every evening spoken for in one way or another. Patronages and responsibilities eating into her time with the horses. The horses… The family business… Goodbye to all she'd worked for.

On the other hand, waking up to Valentine in bed beside her every morning was a vision she could embrace. 'I don't know. I doubt he'll ask.'

'Oh, he'll ask,' Luciana muttered grimly. 'What a mess.'

Angelique lowered her fork; she couldn't eat any more. Couldn't even take a sip of the wine Lucia had ordered for them both, just in case any reporters had spotted them. Champagne for breakfast and bottles of wine with every meal. Man-eating sirens, both. They had reputations to uphold.

'Eat,' Lucia urged, but she shook her head, tears threatening to fall, and if this emotional cresting and cratering was what she had to look forward to for the next six to nine months she'd be a wreck before the child even took its first breath.

And then a flash went off nearby, and her sister swore, and tossed her napkin on the table and rose, looking every inch the avenging devil. 'Let's get out of here.'

Heaven knew where that photo would end up. Probably in tomorrow's news cycle alongside a heading declaring her desolate because Valentine had tossed her over.

Which might just be true.

'Keys.' Angelique handed them over and let her sister drive them to the manor.

By the time the gate guard nodded to them and waved them in, she had herself under control and even managed a smile. Luciana went one better and lifted her finger from the steering wheel in acknowledgement, all smiles and credible good cheer.

All this luxury. All the beautiful pastures and training facilities for the horses were wholly dependent on the whims of a king who'd only ever taken up with her because he couldn't have children. The entire foundation on which they'd based their relationship lay in tatters at the feet of her newly pregnant self. 'I think I'll take that third test when we get inside. Just in case the other two were faulty.'

'And when you've done that, I'll give you the next three packets,' her sister murmured sagely.

'How many did you bring?'

'Twelve.'

Angelique huffed a laugh. Slight overkill, but, then again, one could never have too many pregnancy tests when carrying the bastard child of an infertile king. 'Thank you.'

'We'll figure it out,' her sister reassured her. 'We're Cordovas. We always do.'

Valentine strode towards the royal stables with his niece in tow and a spring in his step that had nothing to do with the perfect blue sky or the happily skipping Princess at his side, and everything to do with the woman they were going to meet. Ask him if happiness came in the shape of a woman and a year ago he would have said no. Ask him if contentment meant sharing a simple meal at a kitchen table and he would have asked why?

Why would a woman's smile and hot temper and sharp observations of the world around them energise him so?

But they did, and continued to do so in spite of so many around him hoping his fascination for Angelique Cordova would fade. He didn't shove her presence down anyone's throat these days. They'd agreed she would accompany him to one royal event each month and the rest he would attend alone. Enough to let people know they were still seeing each other. Little enough to keep the worst of the press hounds away from her. Meanwhile, behind the scenes, he and Angelique became ever more entwined. This latest project—a pony for his horse-obsessed niece—had without question required Angelique's expertise. She'd said to leave it with her, because she had a pony in mind but her father might take some convincing to let the little gelding go.

The cost of the ageing gelding had not been insignificant, even for him.

Alessandro, his stable master, had been disappointed it hadn't been a breeding mare, preferably in foal.

Angelique had laughed when he'd told her that, and muttered, 'He can dream. He and my father are cooking up something between them, you know. Be prepared to open your wallet even more when they present it to you. That or bargain. You have a mare my father wants. Cordova bloodlines a few generations back. I tell you this to help you in your upcoming negotiations.'

He'd teased her about putting him before family and she'd huffed and told him loftily that she'd deny it with her dying breath, and then there'd been sex.

Which wasn't something he needed to be thinking

about as he made his way into the stables, with Juliana skipping at his side.

Angelique was already there and so was the horse, and there was no contest as to which of them drew his attention first. Call it a kink but he loved seeing this woman in shiny black riding boots, tight jodhpurs and that little collared work shirt with the silhouette of running horses and mountains making up the bottom third of the shirt. He wondered who had thought it better to put the picture low on the hip area rather than across the chest. Regardless, it drew his eye to the perfection of the body beneath.

'Afternoon, Horsemaster Cordova,' he said for Juliana's benefit. 'What have we here?'

'Your Majesty, Princess—may I introduce you to Girar? Although in English we call him Twist. When he was a little foal he used to turn and turn and turn.'

'Girar,' said Juliana, mangling the pronunciation, but Angelique nodded.

'Almost. You want a soft G and to cut off the R. Chop!' Another hand motion. Her hands often spoke for her. 'Girar. Say it.' And when Juliana did… 'Yes! Again. And again. That's it. You learn very quickly. He will like you, I know it.'

He hadn't expected her to have so much time for Juliana after her comments on not being cut out for motherhood. But his niece was entranced, and Angelique seemed equally happy to lavish attention on the girl.

'Shall I tell you a secret?' Angelique continued. 'All the children of the grooms in our Spanish stables get to learn from Girar. They are put on the back of the horses at a very young age, of course, but from ages six through to eight, they get him. And do you want to know why?'

His niece nodded, eyes shining.

'Because he is the best. If you lose a stirrup he will stop. If he's going too fast and you clutch at his mane, he will stop.' She suited mime to words and made his niece laugh. 'If you yell *para* really loud Girar will stop.'

'You taught the horse Spanish verbal commands? Not English?'

Angelique met his gaze and shrugged. 'Girar is one of our best. Hand-picked, hand-reared, and countless hours of training have gone into him. More than our usual standard of excellence. Normally we keep our best.' She dug into her pocket, produced a slightly crumpled, folded sheet of paper and handed it to Juliana. 'The boy who learned to ride on him most recently wrote you a note. It's in Spanish so you might need help reading it, but it tells you all the things Girar likes best. The boy is of the opinion only very special people are worthy of this pony, and I quite agree.'

'I'll write to him,' Juliana promised solemnly. 'I'll draw him a picture of Girar doing all his favourite things.'

'He'd like that.'

'Come,' Valentine commanded. 'Let us see this paragon of equine perfection that we are so very lucky to receive. Can he be used for polo at all?'

Angelique snorted. 'Are you deliberately trying to insult me?'

'No?' He hadn't been. Had he? 'I'm merely wondering how far his training extends beyond teaching people to ride.'

'Trust me, the horse knows the difference between a learner rider and a professional. You want to play polo on him, he will not disappoint. Careful, though. He turns on the head of a pin.'

The horse was perfectly formed, superbly conditioned

and altogether happy to be fussed over by an enchanted little girl.

'He has a beautiful temperament,' she said as they stood back and watched Juliana brush the horse, under Alessandro's watchful tuition. 'He really is the best of our best for this purpose.'

'Thank you.' He'd asked for a horse and expected a good one. He hadn't expected quite this level of sacrifice in order to accommodate him. 'Have you eaten?' She often didn't stop for food once she started her workday. He didn't know how she did it.

Her stomach chose that exact moment to betray her with a loud rumble, but she countered with a grimace. 'You had to talk about food. I'm not hungry. Really.'

'You sure about that?'

'Very.' She seemed subdued now that Juliana was otherwise occupied. 'Look, can we talk privately? I want to give Juliana a lesson on the horse but after that, can I come and find you?'

Something was wrong. And it wasn't that he read other people particularly well, but he knew what contentment looked like on her these days and this wasn't it. 'All right. Mind if I stay and watch the lesson?'

'Would it matter if I did?'

'Is there something wrong?' Might as well be direct.

'God,' she muttered. 'I just—' He suddenly found himself with an armful of woman who clung to him as if she'd never see him again after this. She trembled in his arms, her face buried somewhere in his chest, and he hoped to God the choked noise she made was a laugh and not a sob, because a crying Angelique would render him utterly lost.

'Any time.' He tightened his arms around her. 'You can just—any time.'

There was the laugh he'd been hoping for, and if it was a little bit wet, he was all for ignoring it. 'Let me get Girar's saddle and bridle and this excited little girl sorted and then let's do that again.'

He let her go reluctantly, aware of several pairs of eyes upon them. They normally didn't do displays of affection in public. Standard protocol for him, no matter what kind of relationship he might be in. Self-preservation for her, because the last thing she needed was to draw attention to all the ways she wasn't a suitable paramour for a king. She walked a fine line between ignoring the judgment of others and accepting that the easiest pathway to acceptance of her position in his life was to keep her head down.

Not since the literacy reading had she put a foot wrong, and, of all the stories about her wild, wild ways, not one of the people involved had a bad word to say about her.

The polo player who, when asked about his debauched weekend with her, laughed himself to tears before saying she was an absolute slave-driver and his arse would never be the same again, but his forward game was one hundred per cent better for knowing her. The soccer player she'd spent a weekend with, helping his four-year-old daughter overcome her fear of horses. The racing-car driver who'd wined and dined her, and had, on their second date, introduced her to his *nonna* who'd promptly forbidden him to corrupt her because she was far too good for the likes of him. She still kept in touch with the *nonna*, and with the driver, even though he was now happily married to someone else.

The more the press dug, the more the picture emerged that the Cordova family as a whole were tight-knit, supremely loyal to each other, and had a habit of collecting a wide circle of friends and keeping them. 'Go do your work. I'll wait.'

All she'd done was buy herself some time. Angelique smiled absently at Valentine's earnest young niece, and then shook her head to clear it of all thoughts of babies and betrayal. Right now, she held an eager young girl's heart in her hands and that was what she should be concentrating on. Quietly, Angelique began to explaining Girar's regular routine, and showed Juliana how to get the horse to lower his head so a not-so-tall person could put his bridle on and do it up without assistance. She put the girl on the horse and walked along beside them as they walked a lap of the round yard, her instructions warm and clear as she ran Juliana through lesson number one when it came to riding a Cordova pony, and all the while Valentine watched them from a distance, radiating a warmth and approval she could feel from anywhere in the training yard.

Maybe he'd understand. Maybe he'd realise that it was no one's fault and perhaps even think it a miracle that she was pregnant at all. Maybe he'd want her and the baby both, and Valentine would gain an heir even as she lost the lifestyle she'd worked so hard to build. Either way, with a pregnancy now in play, her work with the horses would soon be restricted to teaching and advising rather than riding.

Maybe—if wishes counted for anything—happiness would ensue.

* * *

She had the patience and enthusiasm reserved for only the finest of teachers. Valentine watched as his niece soaked up the attention like a sponge, her riding confidence improving a hundred times over as Angelique set about building trust between rider and horse. Angelique was good with children, generous and inspiring, and he wondered why that surprised him so much. She'd indicated so early on that having children of her own didn't interest her. She was with *him* now and knew full well he could not oblige her with that. She'd made her choice.

And still…

Watching her with Juliana made his heart ache, just a little.

His sister appeared beside him and together they watched the lesson in silence for several more minutes as Angelique ran through the commands for the horse to stop.

'This is the wildly expensive pony you're spoiling my firstborn with?' his sister asked finally.

'Not just your firstborn.' It was for his younger nephews too, never mind that they were still too young for the saddle. They'd grow. 'It's for all of them.' He tried another tack. 'And you too.'

Vala snorted inelegantly. 'You don't fool me, you know. Never have, never will.' She eyed the horse some more. 'He's well trained, I'll give you that. Is Angelique staying on for dinner? And if so, are you both dining with us or would you like me to tell the staff to provide a table for two in your quarters this evening?'

'Not sure yet.' Angelique hadn't exactly jumped at the idea of food. 'But I'll let you know.'

'She's welcome at my table. Just so *you* know.'

It was quite the acknowledgement. His sister's acceptance of Angelique into their inner circle. 'Thank you.'

She shrugged. 'How long will the lesson go on for? Because if you're waiting for my daughter to get sick of riding her new pony, you'll be waiting the rest of the day. More to the point, I need my daughter back. Her tutor's waiting.'

Ah. His habit of collecting Juliana whenever he had a spare moment to spend on her was beginning to rub his sister the wrong way. Easily fixed. 'Okay, ladies. Time's up. Juliana, you've other lessons to see to.'

Getting the child off the horse wasn't hard once she spotted her mother. He watched them return towards the castle, his solemn little niece talking nineteen to the dozen, and he didn't regret spoiling her one little bit. Not in this way, given all the extra tutoring in place now that the child was in line to inherit the throne. Angelique handed the horse off to Alessandro and he walked up to join them. 'Very instructive,' he offered.

'I hope so.' She seemed calmer now. Less agitated.

'Vala has invited us to dine with her and her family this evening, should you decide to stay on.'

'Oh.' She looked trapped, hunted. 'That's very kind of her.'

'Or we could dine in my quarters. It's not a big deal.'

She allowed him a tight smile. 'Let's talk first.'

But she didn't seem to have anything at all to say as they strode beneath the deep blue sky towards the palace. He took her through the back entrance to his quarters, up three flights of steps carved into stone and circling round and round until they reached a door that led directly into his bedroom via a hidden passageway and wall panel.

She stepped through and looked around, then looked back towards the tunnel that led to the stairs. 'Handy,' she murmured.

'Shall I send for refreshments?'

'I'm probably not staying.'

'Any particular reason why?'

She nodded, took a deep breath. 'I'm pregnant.'

'Excuse me?'

'Pregnant.'

He had no words.

'To you,' she added and lifted her chin.

'That's impossible.'

'Well, clearly it's not!'

But he couldn't comprehend a word she was saying. He turned away, a hand to his hair, and began to pace.

'I know what you're thinking,' she murmured.

'You have no damn idea what I'm thinking.' He *wasn't* thinking. His brain had stopped, hung up on that one little word. He couldn't… It wasn't… His.

'Who is he?' He saw her wince out of the side of his eye and he didn't care. How could she possibly think to fool him?

'You.' With only the barest tremble to testify to the lie. 'I don't know how far along I am—I haven't seen a doctor yet, but there's no other man in my life. It *has* to be yours, and I'll take any kind of DNA test you like in order to prove it. Whether you want to claim it as yours is the bigger question.'

But he was nowhere near accepting her words at face value. 'I'm not fertile.'

She shrugged with a helplessness he'd never before seen, her body suddenly too slender for him to even contemplate her carrying a child. His child. 'I don't know what to say to you,' she offered. 'You said you couldn't have children and I believed you. Why would you lie? We didn't use protection because of that very reason, yet here I am. Expecting. Take the test again.'

'*You* take the test again,' he shot back.

'I have. Too many times and the result never changes. *I'm pregnant!*'

'*Keep your voice down!*'

He couldn't look at her, couldn't stop running his hands through his hair and if it had been long enough to grab fistfuls and pull he'd doubtless be doing that too. How could his physicians have got it so wrong? Weren't they supposed to be the best? Had it all been some kind of plot to unseat him? A mix-up with the results? How the hell could a bunch of experts get it so wrong? 'You're sure about the pregnancy?'

'I took a pharmacy test.'

Bah. 'It's wrong.'

'Six of them. And while it's true I haven't seen a doctor yet, that's only because I wanted to do you the courtesy of telling you first.'

'It's not mine.' How could it be? He came to a halt in front of her. 'Whose is it? One of your grooms? One of my guards? One of your polo-playing swains?'

She held his gaze but he couldn't hold hers. 'Is that what you want me to say?' she asked at last.

'I want the truth!' he spat, hot temper getting the better of him.

'And when it turns out to be yours? What then? Or can your tiny brain not think that far ahead?'

He couldn't stay; he had to get out of there before the shadow of his father rose up and pushed him towards behaviours he'd sworn never to emulate. 'Stay here.'

While he headed for the door. 'If you leave, I will hunt you down.'

He didn't wait for her reply as he left the room and started calling for guards. Two for the door to his quarters. Another for the door to the hidden stairs that would take her to the garden. God only knew when he'd feel calm enough to return and she wasn't going anywhere.

'Where are you going?'

He heard her words but his stride didn't slow. 'Away from you.'

Down, down, past the dungeons to the underground caverns where his forefathers had discovered a river and waterfall, where the water would be icy cold and exactly what he needed and where his body would take a pounding beneath the forceful torrent and if he let the current take him he would wash up against the grate. If he fought the current and swam, his body would soon exhaust itself but his tension and anger would be gone, buried beneath the primal urge to simply survive. He could thank his father for this particular coping method. He'd been a child when his father had pushed him to the edge of the waterfall and ordered him to jump.

Because he was too hot-headed and undisciplined even then.

Jump and cool the hell off.

The icy water helped. The pounding water beneath the fall pummelled his temper into submission, although there would be bruises tomorrow and an aching body to go with them. It would give him something to hold onto besides anger.

'There are easier ways to die, you know.' The voice was light and languid, but the mind behind it was sharper than most people knew. He turned to face his sister—younger than him by mere minutes. She'd escaped their father's notice and much of his wrath simply by being beautiful, outwardly obedient and second in line to the throne rather than first. 'Our head of security tells me there's a Cordova locked in your bedroom.'

'Locked is a strong word.'

'Is there another word you'd like me to use? Are you sure you don't want to get out of the water yet?'

'Positive.'

'Because your skin is turning blue.'

'Five more minutes.'

'That's four minutes too many. Because I really don't want to be crowned Queen any time soon—any time at all, if we're being honest.'

'Angelique's pregnant.'

Valentine had the dubious pleasure of seeing his sister rendered speechless.

'She says it's mine.'

'And you believe her?'

God help him, he wanted to. 'She says she'll take any test I want her to have.'

His sister began to smile. 'But what marvellous news.'

'Really? *Really?* Angelique Cordova—a woman Thallasia loves to hate—is having my baby and you call that a *good* thing?'

'Don't *you*?'

'Yes. God forsake me, I want this so much it hurts.' He closed his eyes and stuck his head beneath the fall of water again. Fear and anger and hope and tears and pain, and this time he let it all come out with an animal roar.

Then he felt a slender hand wrap around his biceps and pull, hard, and he opened his eyes to find his sister, fully dressed and soaking wet, tugging him towards the edge of the pool.

'I swear, people who say you got all the brains and I got all the beauty got it wrong,' she muttered. 'I've always been of the opinion that we're both too stupid for words. Hoist me up.'

He hoisted her up.

'It's simple,' she said from the edge of the pool as she reached down to haul him up beside her, and he tried to help himself out, he really did, but he barely had the strength for it. Maybe she'd been right to urge him out of the water, not that he'd ever tell her that. Not that he needed to say it, given the way he was gasping and shivering, and, yes, slightly blue.

'What's s-simple?' he chattered.

'The solution. Marry the woman you've never stopped loving, cherish the child you've created together, and close ranks in such a way as to protect them both until there comes a time when our misguided public value Angelique as much as you do. It'll happen eventually, and probably sooner than you think if she gives you an heir.'

'If they believe it's mine.'

'Like you said, there are tests for that. They'll believe once they're forced to. Look at what our beloved public think of me. At the beginning of the year I was nothing more than a faded socialite birdbrain. Don't look at me like that, you know that's what they thought. And I have changed not one hair on my faded socialite head, yet all of a sudden I'm a fount of wisdom, fortitude and ageless beauty. The point is, you want this, don't you? If you could have any woman at your side, mother to your children, who would it be but her?'

'And what will I woo her with exactly? A public who is going to crucify her for her wild reputation—'

'Augustus of Arun married a *concubine*. How, exactly, is this any worse?'

'And she's a foreigner.'

'Cas's foreign Queen can guide her through the worst of it. And I can… I don't know…teach her how to handle your moods.'

'I'm not moody.'

'Please.' She made the most dismissive noise she could. 'You put me to shame.' His sister reached for his hand. 'Here you are with the gift of family right in front of you—and all you need to claim it is a willing heart, an *open* heart, and a thimbleful of understanding and instead you choose punishing rage?'

'I'm not *choosing* it. I came down here to get rid of it! Don't you understand? All those bits of him that are in me, this is where I come to drown them, so that I can go back up those stairs and offer a terrified mother-to-be my support with an open heart!'

Rage at his sister. Rage at the hand life had dealt him and the pressure to perform to standards he could never quite reach. Just rage. 'I don't even know if Angelique wants this child. It wasn't exactly planned. What if she says no to everything? To me.'

Now his sister was turning away from him, standing and walking over to the nearby pile of towels, and then she was back with a towel that she wrapped around his shivering frame and holding him tight and he closed his eyes and took comfort from the only person who'd always had his back—even when he sometimes hadn't been able to see it.

'How can I help?' she murmured gently. 'What do you need me to do?'

'Just…' He had no idea. 'If it doesn't go smoothly. If Angelique says no, and I start to turn into someone you don't like… If I start behaving like him…our father. Protect her.'

'I can,' she murmured. 'I will.'

CHAPTER TEN

IF ANYONE HAD asked Angelique how she'd thought her meeting with Valentine would go and they'd said, he's going to lock you in his quarters and walk away, she'd have dismissed it as crazy talk, and yet here she was. All locked in, with guards at all the entrances, and quite decidedly alone.

Valentine's suite consisted of a bedroom decked out in dark blues and deep brown mahogany, a white marble bathroom, a dressing room the size of an average home and a sitting room full of books, several deep-seated library chairs and a sideboard laden with sliced fruits, nuts, pastries, water and juice. The food had arrived ten minutes ago, when she'd also been told that His Majesty would be with her soon. Trying to brush past the guard had resulted in him crowding her deftly back inside the room and closing the door. Yelling and banging on the door had brought a staff member with more food and a calming tea—none of which she'd touched.

The huge arched windows did not open. If there was another secret passageway—and what respectable king's bedroom didn't have more than one secret exit?—she had yet to find it. Valentine showed up five minutes later, his hair damp and his dark eyes raking her from head to toe.

'You left me locked in here to go for a *swim*?' she asked incredulously. He'd barely stepped inside the door, but she couldn't help but lash out. Fear and anxiety were riding her too hard.

'Needs must.' He surveyed the groaning table of untouched food. 'You haven't eaten.'

She laughed, tightly incredulous. 'Help yourself.'

He did just that, but not before handing her a sheet of thick, creamy coloured paper with a crest embossed on the top. 'Sign this.'

'What is it?' She couldn't read the language but a signature had already been scrawled on one side of the paper.

'Our wedding contract.'

He took his time spreading soft cheese on crusty bread, and topped it with a slice of fresh fig. 'Our what?'

'Dated today. There's no other way.'

'There's not marrying you. That's definitely an option.'

'You are sadly mistaken.'

'You can't just take what you want!' she snapped. 'There are rules. Laws.'

'And they will favour me.' He shrugged. 'If—as you say—the child is mine, you're carrying a future heir to the Thallasian throne, provided the baby is born within wedlock.' He smiled crookedly, wholly without mirth. 'Sign the papers. You're not leaving until you do.'

'Valentine, please. We do have other options.'

'What? Squirrel you away somewhere until you have the child? Pretend it doesn't exist? Adoption? Abortion? Letting a child of royal blood be born outside wedlock? I will tolerate none of those options. You will give me an heir. I will give you a crown and a lifetime of service. You lose—don't think I don't know that. Welcome to royal life.'

'Walk away,' she challenged him doggedly. She'd seen his utter disbelief and horror at the news they'd conceived a child together. He hadn't believed her. Hadn't wanted to believe her, and now all of a sudden he wanted to marry her?

'No.'

'You don't want this. *I saw you lose your mind at the thought.*'

'I found it again.'

'You can't possibly want to marry me. Your people will never accept me.'

'We'll see.' He ate the tiny snack he'd created, his manners neat, his hands already busy creating the next.

'Valentine, think.' She marshalled her arguments. 'You can have a proper wife, one who could help you rule—like Moriana does Theo, or Sera with the King of Arun. I'm not trained to do this. I know about horses. I won't do you any good.'

He ate again, poured a glass of water and then another and kept her waiting. 'Drink?' he asked finally.

'I don't want to be your brood mare.'

He picked up a plump date. Ate it.

'I am wholly unsuited to be the mother of future rulers!'

'You wouldn't be the first.' He looked at her, his lips twisted in a bitter little smile. 'C'mon, Angelique. I'm not a magician. I can't make your pregnancy unhappen, even if I wanted to—which given my circumstances I sure as hell don't. This is a gift for me. A second chance at a role I thought lost to me for ever. Did you seriously think I wouldn't take it?'

'If it turns out that you test fertile again—which you must be—you can marry well and have children you actually want. Why stick with me?' She voiced her deepest fear and watched as he went pale and his eyes glittered, first with shock and then thinly hidden fury.

'Is that truly what you think of me?'

'No!' Yes. 'Maybe.' Honesty was important. 'I think getting me pregnant with your child is not an outcome you would have wanted for your country.'

He turned away, jammed his hands into the pockets of his trousers and began to pace. 'Maybe you're right. But Valentine the man is ecstatic. You at my side and a family we've created—it's been my go-to fantasy for more years than I care to confess, so don't you dare think I don't want this. Us. A baby. I just never thought I could have it. Never dared reach for it might be a better description, but you're here for the taking, you *and* a chance at fatherhood. We've been happy these past few months, haven't we? I know I have. Marry me and we can continue with that. What's stopping us?'

She had to laugh at his arrogance. 'Your crown?'

He waved a hand. 'The people of Thallasia got over my inability to produce an heir. What's to say they won't honour you for giving me one?'

'Or call me a liar, you a dupe, and the child someone else's—no matter what the tests say.'

'Are we caring about that?'

'Aren't you?' Hard to believe he wouldn't.

But he shot her a glance and just kept pacing. 'I've been emasculated, called suicidal, and my rule has come into question—all in the last few months. If some want to add cuckolded husband to that list, let them. I want a real marriage with you. Your passion, your anger, your problems and your dreams—I want it all. In return you get me and all my flaws exposed for you to see. In this we would be equal. I'll do my best to be a good father and husband. You will have horses. Helpers. Access to your family. Things to help you and our child be happy. It wouldn't be like it was during my father's reign. You have my word.'

'Where did you go? When you left me just now? What did you do?'

'As you say, I went for a swim to cool down and clear my head. And I have.'

Which was all well and good to say, but whether he really had or not was anyone's guess. 'You're sure you wouldn't like to, oh, I don't know, sleep on it? Take advice? Wait?' She stared at the blurry words on the paper. 'I can't even read this.'

'Turn it over. It's repeated in English on the other side.'

It was a simple enough contract. His offer of marriage, signed and witnessed. Her acceptance, still to be signed and witnessed. 'Is this even a legal document?'

'It is.'

'I'll bear witness.' The voice from the doorway came from Valentine's twin, a woman reputed to be flighty and none too smart. A woman obsessed with beauty and fashion and maintaining a perfect complexion. Except that wasn't how Angelique remembered Vala at all. Instead she remembered a girl who'd held her tongue when her brother had fallen for the stable girl. The sister who'd covered for her brother's unexplained absences more than once. A young woman who'd been outclassed on the polo field nine times out of ten but who'd taken her falls and got back up and dusted herself off with a sigh or a sob, and then gone to tend her horse, no matter her backside covered in grass stains or her hair full of dirt or the waiting stable hands whose job it was to care for the horses. She was not what the public made her out to be, this woman. Not by a long way. 'Hello, Angelique. Has he convinced you of his undying devotion yet?'

Um...

'Give it time,' Vala said into the silence. 'Do I need to witness this signature or not? I'm on a schedule.'

'I'm not signing it.'

'And I'm not leaving your side until you do,' he said.

Valentine had a pen. Inside pocket of his perfectly cut blazer. He held it out to her in silent challenge and she crossed her arms and stared him down. 'At least wait until you know it's yours. Get the tests done. Go see a doctor so you know what's going on with your *health*. Why did they call you infertile in the first place?'

'I fell ill last year with a childhood illness I had no immunity to. I recovered. My sperm count did not.'

'Can your fertility come back?'

'They said not.'

'Not ever?'

'Do you think either of us would be in this position had they said yes?'

No, no they would not. He would never have spent his royal sperm so unwisely if he'd thought his fertility might come back over time. 'I don't know what to say.'

'Say yes and sign the paper,' he urged.

'No. Can't we just...?'

'Just *what*?'

Frustration lit his words.

'Just wait and get the tests done and then *think* about this a little bit more.' She glanced at the paper he wanted her to sign. 'See if we can come up with a solution that isn't so…so…'

'Permanent?' He sneered. 'You're having my child. What the *hell* did you expect?'

She wrapped her hands tightly around her waist and looked away, unable to bear the confused despair in his eyes. 'I didn't ever expect to be in this position. Actually.'

And wasn't that the long and short of it?

'Right, well.' Vala clapped her hands as if to banish the heavy sorrow in the air. 'Leaving the paperwork and wedding plans aside, for now, let's bring a medical team in to examine both of you, shall we?'

'Not the usual ones,' Valentine warned her, and her schoolmarmish expression softened.

'I quite agree. Not the same set of incompetent, addle-headed buffoons you dealt with before—of that I'm sure.'

They believed her. Oh, he hadn't at first, but here he was now willing to marry her before he was even sure the baby was his and that had to count for something, didn't it?

Vala turned towards her. 'Angelique, I'll have a room made up for you—'

'She's staying with me.'

'I thought I'd head back to the manor.' Might as well put it out there as an option.

'I don't think you quite understand.' Valentine's voice came hard and implacable enough for her to glance up, only to be immediately ensared by his unfathomable black gaze. 'Until you sign that piece of paper, you're not going anywhere.'

Dinner was served in Valentine's quarters. A succulent roast with tender roasted vegetables and delicately buttered beans. Angelique barely ate any of it. Valentine's impeccable manners ruled every interaction, no sign whatsoever of the playful, laughing man who felt comfortable enough with her to truly let his guard down. No wryly revealing comments about the global news of the day. No snippets of personal information, sparingly spoken, but she'd hoarded them carefully and when bundled together they'd revealed a picture of a smart, passionate man with a deeply playful streak that he only allowed close friends and family to see.

Painstakingly built over that deeply private core was an impenetrable public persona of stern politeness, and it was this he showed her now. Asking her how her food was and did she need any additional fixings. Opting against having a glass of wine himself because she was not drinking or for some other reason he didn't care to share with her. Mentioning how pleased he was with Girar, the horse she'd delivered for his niece. Saying out of the blue, 'You're good with children.'

It was enough to make her fork clatter against the fine bone-china porcelain of the plate, and she winced, and muttered sorry, because clearly her table talk and manners were no match for his, and she couldn't read him at all. He probably had no idea what she was thinking either and it was all so wrong that she wanted to weep.

'Will you show me that place where you swam, earlier?' she asked after dinner, and it was partly because she wanted to get out of his suite and partly because walking, or swimming, might give them something to do besides brood and grow ever more distant with each passing minute.

She'd never been more grateful for the massive vastness of palaces as he led her down through the levels, past the storage cellars in the kitchen and lower still until they came to a door that pushed inwards into deep inky blackness. The flick of a switch revealed dozens of wall sconces, a long and skinny natural cave, and a turbulent, fast-flowing river running from one end of it to the other, entering through huge iron grills that someone small enough could probably pass through. Rough-hewn steps led to and from each end of the pool, only it wasn't like any pool she'd ever seen, it was a torrent. '*This* is where you swim?'

'It's more appealing on a good day.' He stood to one side of her, watching the water. 'Some days it can be quite gentle.'

'Are there things in it? Fish?' Sharks… Bodies… Lost city of Atlantis…

He shrugged.

'And you swim in this? Just to be clear.'

He ran his hand around the back of his neck and shrugged again. 'I was six the first time my father brought me here. It was two days after my mother had died and I was too quiet and withdrawn for his liking. He told me to strip down to underwear and took me to the edge of those steps over there. Said she was dead but I was still alive and he would have no more moping from me and that I needed to toughen up. He said swim. And he pushed me in.'

She gasped. Couldn't help but cover her mouth.

'It was worse than it is now and by the time I'd surfaced I was halfway down the cave. I tried swimming to the side but ended up pinned against the exit grid before I got there. It was hell getting over to the steps and out of the water but I did it, and then I lay there on my back and I laughed, with my body full of endorphins, and I

laughed, because it was either that or cry and I sure as
hell didn't want to be thrown in again. My father seemed
pleased with me.'

He couldn't be serious.

But he was.

And Angelique bit her lip and with it her horrified
protest and tried her best to understand this complex,
deeply wounded King.

'My father thought he was toughening me up. From
my perspective, I'd discovered a whole new way to deal
with emotions that were too big for me to hold inside.
Grief, rage, isolation. A boy in a towering temper went
into the water at that end, got pummelled by fear, and
came out the other end calm again with all those dark,
destructive emotions washed away.'

'That's horrific.' She had to say it.

'Works for me.' He straightened and turned to look
her dead in the eye. 'I'm sorry I reacted badly to your
news. That's not who I want to be.'

Such honesty demanded an equally honest reply. 'As
a child my passions ruled me completely. I was so highly
strung that sometimes my presence alone could upset the
horses. The number of times my father ordered me out
of the stables to go and sit on that rock till I'd cleared my
mind...' She shook her head, remembering. 'But medita-
tion never completely worked for me, and I doubt your
river swims will either. Right now I have all these feelings churning around inside me with nowhere to go. The
thought of marrying you scares me. I'd be such a liability.'
She turned away, couldn't even hold his gaze.

And then he stepped up behind her, close enough that
she could feel the heat of his chest through the layers
of his clothes and hers. His hands settled lightly on her

shoulders, his thumbs rubbing faint circles into the back of her neck. Too tentative for a massage. His touch had never been tentative before and it was just one more reminder of the way things had changed with the creation of a child.

Where was the joy?

'I never meant to trap you,' he offered quietly. 'I only ever wanted to love you.'

A sob rose up and tore through her throat, and then another, and then she cried, hard and ugly, and he turned her around and wrapped her in his arms where she repaid his steadfast support by drenching his shirt in a waterfall of tears. He held her until she was all cried out. Until she felt as if she'd swum that pitch-black river at her back and crawled up those jagged, wicked-looking stone steps, exhausted and empty.

'Right. So. Each to their own.' He put a finger beneath her chin and tilted her head until she met his gaze head-on. 'Feeling better yet?'

'Yes.' *Dios*, this man. 'Yes.'

Angelique never expected Valentine to be the one to break the news of her pregnancy to her father, but he was. She hadn't expected him to return to the manor with her, but he did. She couldn't sit without him asking her if she needed some food, or a drink, or a pillow for her back. She couldn't work in the stables without him ordering grooms to do her work. He stayed with her for days, no mention of his own work, as he not so subtly fortified the security around the estate.

Vala had indeed arranged a raft of medical specialists to attend them both. Angelique had been poked, prodded and had undergone a paternity test and the results had confirmed what she already knew. The baby was Valentine's.

As for Valentine's medical tests, they told him his viable sperm count remained next to non-existent, but there were clearly some that could… One that had…

She had an ultrasound done, with Valentine present, and she had to laugh because although she wasn't as far along as she'd thought—eight weeks or so rather than twelve—she'd be getting bigger in a hurry.

She was having twins.

If she thought Valentine fussed over her *before* he heard this news, it was nothing compared to his compulsive desire for her to be seated on a chaise longue for ever, with a bunch of grapes in hand, *after* he realised she was eating for three.

She bluntly told him that maybe he didn't have to return to the manor to tuck her in each night, or bear witness to her pale face and uneasy stomach of a morning.

His sister was pushing for him to break the news of his impending fatherhood and upcoming nuptials. 'Get out there and sell it,' she'd pleaded during her last visit. 'God help me, Valentine, you're not doing yourself any favours by neglecting your duties and holing up here, and if you think you're protecting Angelique by squirrelling her away, think again. The press know you're here, they know you've had medical specialists in. The stories about you and Angelique are getting wilder.'

'Have I poisoned him yet?' asked Angelique.

'No, you've had a riding fall and are at death's door. That or you're undergoing artificial insemination with my brother's teenage sperm—that you kept *frozen for years* in a facility meant for horse sperm—'

'Ew…'

'I hear you.' Valentine threw up his hands. 'I'll prepare a statement and have the palace announce it tomorrow.' He glanced her way, his expression shuttered. 'I could announce our engagement and upcoming wedding at the same time as well.'

'I haven't said yes.'

And there it was. Happy-clappy noises on the surface and a deep unease about stepping fully into his world underneath.

'You're stuck with me either way, you realise.'

'But he would, of course, prefer his heirs *legitimate*,' Vala emphasised, with a glare for them both.

'I'm working on it,' he replied coolly. 'Butt out, Vala. And, Angelique, brace yourself.'

'I'm ready.' She summoned a smile.

'Liar.'

Hard to deny. 'Are you willing to deny paternity?'

'Never.' His eyes flashed dark warning. 'You know this.'

'Then I'm ready.'

The news did not go down a treat. It was one thing to make the foreign horsemaster with the terrible reputation and sultry good looks his mistress. It was quite another to inform a nation they had twins on the way.

Angelique said very little beyond, 'Told you.'

If it bothered her more than that, she didn't let it show. Her family closed ranks. No comment from any of them or any of their employees. Not one leak from the house of Cordova and that in itself was impressive. No lovers coming forward to spill the beans. Angelique had responded to that with a funny little smile and words that held the sting of hidden truth. 'I've only ever had one lover, so if you want to give an interview, go ahead. The rest of my reputation is pure fabrication—some of it planted by me for reasons I thought valid at the time. For protection, even. It protects me still, in that if I'm never given a chance to succeed, I can never try to win the hearts of your people and fail.'

'That's your approach?'

'What's yours?' she enquired politely, far too politely for it to be anything but a warning. 'Ram me down people's necks until they swallow?'

Yes. Faint heart would get him nowhere. 'Yes! We run positive press to counter the negative. We stand united. I go on record more often to express my joy at the thought of starting a family with you. We get married. Do you know how many articles here are calling me out for not offering to marry you? Dozens! What good a king who rules by example not being prepared to stand up and protect his family? And don't even start with the "we're not good together" line, because I won't believe you. I'm yours. You're mine. Across time. You know it's true. Why won't you even consider it?'

It was the closest he'd ever come to begging.

'Can't you see I'm a liability?' she countered. 'It will take years, a lifetime, before I am fully accepted by the good people of Thallasia. Maybe on my death bed, at which point I will hopefully be unable to raise my middle finger in response to such largess, but I will be thinking it and you will know it and laugh and kiss me and tell me your life has been richer than you ever imagined it could be. That you never regretted loving me—not for one minute. That you're proud of our children who are wonderful people. That you'll think of me every day with joy. *That's* what I will consider a life well lived.

Not what your papers think of me today or tomorrow or after the birth of two more souls for your royal machinery to shape. Who wants to inflict a life of service onto their children? Not me!'

'It's not all *bad*, Angelique. Yes, there are constraints, but we can still be royal and raise children who are wonderful people. It's not all tyranny and tiaras and nothing else. You could do such good. *As my wife*. Why won't you let others see you the way I do?'

'Hear! Hear!' said a male voice from the doorway, and there stood Theo with Moriana next to him. 'Is this a bad time to call?'

'Kings,' muttered Angelique, but then turned and curtseyed and hardly blushed at all. Nothing like airing dirty laundry. Valentine suspected his colour was a dull red too.

Moriana smiled brightly and flowed into the room, a vision of modern elegance, and Valentine could clock the difference between her and Angelique, of course he could, and he'd still choose Angelique's heart and passion and fire every time. Didn't she *know* what she brought to his table?

'Theo thought we might, oh, I don't know, go cavorting with you both in public. Somewhere with horses or children or fluffy kittens.' Moriana glanced at her husband. 'To show our support for you both, no matter what kind of union you choose.'

'She also mentioned piles and piles of leftover paella,' added Theo. 'It's the only reason I'm here. Valentine didn't call for reinforcements against the future mother of his children who has misguided thoughts of ignoring her public image. At all. We didn't drop everything to get here.'

'Well, thank God for that,' muttered Valentine and strode forward to clasp hands with Theo and embrace Moriana. 'Otherwise I'd owe you both a favour, and that never ends well.'

'You mean never ends well for you,' murmured Moriana. 'I vote we all ride the grounds of this estate and then return for a private dinner between friends that may or may not involve leftover paella made by Angelique's mother.'

'But Angelique's pregnant. With twins.'

Moriana looked at Valentine blankly. 'I know. Everyone knows. Bravo.'

'He thinks I shouldn't ride,' Angelique supplied helpfully.

'Oh, for—' Whatever Moriana had been going to say was cut off by her husband's elbow to her ribs. 'Ow.'

'A drive, then,' said Theo. 'Very civilised. Or a buggy ride. I love a good buggy ride.'

The man was very clearly mad, but a buggy was duly found and royal horses trucked in from the palace. A photographer arrived too, and the following day a series of happy photographs appeared online to help sway public opinion. Wedding or not, King Valentine of Thallasia had welcomed the Cordova woman into his inner circle.

Angelique read the half a dozen news articles about her that now turned up on the kitchen table every day, courtesy of the father of her unborn children. In truth, it had been no hardship, sitting in the open carriage and listening to tales from the daily horseback processions that had proceeded Moriana's wedding to Theo. The ridiculous pageantry they'd endured in the lead-up to their wedding. A cavalcade of horses, the black steeds of Arun against Liesendaach's greys. The village welcomes, the charities they'd arranged to visit every single day. The medieval-style tournaments at the end of each day that had brought spectators by the thousands and money into every place they'd stayed. Angelique had never laughed so hard as she had at Moriana doing her 'Ice Queen with ants in her pants while sitting astride a horse at the end of a long day and she simply had to pee' impersonation, but there was no peeing yet because she still had to listen to an earnest city mayor announce her by every title she held, and then welcome her to their very beautiful city, and *then* list the name of every last person who'd helped them prepare for her.

'But you did get to pee, eventually,' Theo had drawled.

And when Moriana had replied, 'Like a horse,' that had been the end of Angelique's composure.

Their visit seemed to relax Valentine, and for the next few days he backed off, just a little, when it came to treating Angelique like a priceless porcelain doll.

Pregnant, yes. Slow to start some mornings. But she was real, and warm and they were in this together.

And during those nights when he held her close and passion got the better of them, she thought that maybe, just maybe, she could be what he needed.

CHAPTER ELEVEN

'Yes,' she said, one evening a few days later when they were back in his palace and getting ready for bed. 'I want a small wedding, and by that I mean tiny, with only your family, my family, and one or two others present, and I want to have it in the little tiny chapel here, the one with the stained-glass window that catches the setting of the sun, but yes. I'll marry you.'

The look on his face.

The lovemaking that followed.

No matter what the world served up as punishment for daring to think she could be enough.

She'd never forget.

Confusion ruled Valentine in the time leading up to the wedding. It turned out that sex was an excellent antidote to actually addressing the issues likely to plague them once Angelique became his Queen. The limitations she would have to accept. The knowledge she'd have to absorb if she wanted to represent the crown and do so without fault. He could protect her from the worst of it, he knew he could. But first she had to listen to him and at the very least acknowledge that, in regard to all things royal, his experience would serve her well.

She knew the news articles about her—and him—were brutal, but had told him she didn't read them. She missed horse-riding but never mentioned it in front of him. His head of security informed him that she'd taken up jogging through the woodlands as part of her daily exercise routine.

Their wedding banns went out, and instead of a formal picture his publicity team had shown one of Angelique teaching Juliana how to ride and sharing a smile, while he looked on from a few steps away. They'd chosen it because Juliana's delight and Angelique's pride in the young girl's achievement had made him look happy and approachable. A man rather than a king, and a novel approach for his publicity team to take, but it seemed to be working.

Sometimes.

On occasion.

In between the more vitriolic pieces in the press.

Protocol lessons began for Angelique, and folders full of rules now sat on her work desk alongside breeding logs and bloodline registers.

'It's okay,' she would say to him. 'I've got this.'

Moriana and his sister tossed the rule books aside in favour of offering Angelique practical lessons in palace etiquette. They took her under their wings, only to have her emerge hours later, pale faced and subdued, with eyes lit from within by worry rather than happiness.

'Nothing to it,' she'd deadpan, only her hand would be shaking when he enfolded it in his, and she'd sag against him as if hoping for strength, and then he'd go berserk with wondering if she'd been on her feet too long and end up sweeping her into his arms and depositing her on the nearest soft surface while he buried his face in her neck and simply breathed her in.

He could give her everything but her freedom.

'Let's go riding,' he said the following morning as they lay in a tangle of rumpled sheets and sunbeams, and she edged up onto her elbows, her dark hair a messy cloud and her expression still warm and open—not yet shutting down beneath the demands of the day.

'Did you not ban me from horse riding? With the full approval of my traitorous parents?'

He had. Not one of his more logical decisions. 'I was thinking you could borrow Juliana's pony and I could ride a quiet horse to match and we could go to the hunting lodge for the day. Just like old times.'

Absolutely nothing like old times, her arched eyebrow told him.

'I'll throw in an open fire and a catered meal when we get there,' he added.

'I'll take it,' she said. 'With one condition.'

'Name it.'

'I need help with the list of charities your sister left for me to look at. I'm supposed to pick half a dozen and become their patron. And, sure, I can put a tick beside half a dozen of them in ten seconds flat, but what will it *mean*?'

Which was how two days later they ended up in a sitting room stuffed with velvet furniture, velvet drapes and heavy carved wood tables, throwing goose-down pillows in a circle in front of a dancing fire and asking for hot coffee, tea and chocolate for three, as his niece and Angelique spread out on their stomachs on the pillows and looked to him and the dozen or so files full of paperwork for answers.

'Should you be lying on your stomach?' he asked Angelique, because, what about the babies?

'It's very comfortable at this point in time, Your Majesty,' she replied with a wink towards his niece. 'Would you care to join us?'

Surrender seemed inevitable. He sank onto a cushion, legs crossed in front of him, unbuttoned his blazer rearranged his cuffs and straightened his tie. 'Presentation matters,' he began. 'It makes others feel that you're making an effort for them. It's a way of showing that you value them and those things they stand for. Will you value me?'

Juliana sat up immediately. Angelique followed. 'Who *are* you?' she murmured. 'Do I know you?'

'As His Majesty the King? No, I don't believe you do. But just as I discovered another you when in the presence of your family, it's time for you to see another side of me. Who am I, Juliana?'

'King Valentine II, by the Grace of God, King of Thallasia, Defender of the Faith,' the young girl answered immediately.

'And what do I do?'

'You govern Thallasia according to the laws and customs of the land. You offer law, justice and mercy in all your judgments, in the name of God.'

'And?' he prompted, while Angelique looked on.

'And you do so willingly, with a glad heart, a sound mind, and a spirit of...' The little girl faltered.

'Service,' he offered quietly. 'We live to serve.' Heavy concepts for a seven-year-old. Parroting the words back at him was only the start of coming to terms with what they meant. 'And there are very few circumstances where we can decide not to do that and just walk away.' He held Angelique's gaze. 'Even if we fall madly in love with someone and want to do whatever makes them happy, we still can't walk away from our duty. That's why only very special people choose to marry us, and even when we rejoice that they *want* to marry us we worry we'll break them, because it's hard to serve this country day after day, year after year, decade after decade, and sometimes the criticisms outweigh the thank-yous. And when that happens and people start saying bad things about us, what do we do?'

'Cry?' said Juliana. 'Because that's okay, but not in front of people. Only some people, like you or Mama or nanny Chloe.'

'Maybe,' he murmured. 'Maybe we do cry in front of our special people, but then we wash our faces and see if what the people are saying is true and we really can do better next time. And the time after that and the time after that until we're doing a much better job a lot of the time and people don't say nearly as many bad things about us any more. But sometimes that takes years.'

'I have years,' Angelique promised quietly, and in that moment his heart truly did break for her, because he loved this woman so much, and he really had put her in an untenable position.

'They're crucifying you.'

'I have you,' she said next, and he wanted to cry on his own behalf now, because he wasn't enough, he would never be enough to counter all the freedoms she would lose. 'You're right here, telling me about the things that drive and inspire you, and I have our babies in my belly, and members of your family to get to know and I will learn how to do what you do, and it won't always be enough but it will always be my best. This I promise you.'

He cleared his throat of its sudden tightness and reached for the first folder. 'I'll read them out and you can say yes, no or maybe. Juliana, this goes for you too.

And then we can examine those options you like in depth. Number one. Libraries and literacy for children?'

'Me!' said Juliana, and he nodded and placed the folder in front of her.

'And why might Angelique not want that one also?'

'Because she's a grown-up?'

'Because she can barely read Thallasian?' Angelique offered. 'Maybe adult literacy is my jam.'

Valentine nodded his approval. 'Next. Mobility for the disabled. Including therapy horses and the roles they play in rehabilitation?'

Juliana's hand was up in the air and she looked fit to burst.

Angelique raised her hand too. 'Could we both become patrons of this one? Because I have some ideas and I'd like to know more. Horses or not.'

He created a middle pile. 'Heart Foundation? Rare Cancer Awareness? Alzheimer's research? The medical ones are always hard to choose from because the need to shine a light on their research goals is always there. But what we can do is make connections. We raised funds for the national college of music by tasking them with performing in small groups for Alzheimer patients and filming those concerts. Charitable donations went up thirty per cent for both causes that year. Performing throughout the elderly community became a permanent outreach programme for the orchestra. Some of the young musicians we showcased *still* visit those nursing homes to play for old friends, and once a year, Juliana, your mother invites the musicians and carers and doctors and researchers to a big luncheon in the blue ballroom. That's just one of the things you can do when you decide to lend the might of your royal name to a cause. And the trick, if it's a trick, is to make people feel good about helping others, and to say "I see what you did there" and "thank you". It can be about connecting people who can help each other. It's not always about raising money.'

'What's your hardest patronage portfolio? The one you work hardest at but never seem to get anywhere?' asked Angelique, and he didn't have to think twice for an answer.

'Domestic violence.' Darkness lived there. He'd barely scraped the surface with his own father. It could have been worse. It *was* worse for so many people.

'Then I want that one too,' Angelique said. 'I've never lived it, but I want to share that load with you. Will you let me?'

'I'll have it sent to you.'

She shouldn't smile at him as if he'd given her the world.

'Would you like to run away with me to your hunting lodge and get married tomorrow?' she asked. 'It would solve a lot of internal debate about empire waistlines versus regency ones.'

'Sorry. We need the spectacle.'

She sighed. 'What *are* your thoughts on empire waists versus regency ones?'

'They're very convoluted thoughts.' He had no idea what she was even talking about.

'Do you have a tiara?' the little Princess wanted to know.

'No. But I do have a mantilla,' Angelique replied. 'It's a lace veil that's been in my family for many years, and it has a special comb that goes with it that makes it sit up just so.'

'There are tiaras available for—' he began.

'No.' It was a very cool no, even if accompanied by a softening smile. 'I will not deny my heritage and I will not disappoint. You just need to trust me on this.' She gave Juliana a wink. 'I am on the lookout for the perfect pair of earrings, though. Diamonds.'

They both turned to look at him, and he obliged with a theatrical sigh. 'I suspect I can help you there. What about a necklace?'

Angelique shook her head. 'No need. The neckline of the dress I'm partial to is too high.'

'Bracelet?'

'The sleeves are too low.'

'Is there any skin on show?'

'Not a lot, no. It's a gown of many buttons. Very demure. And don't say, "You? Demure?" because that would be the wrong reply altogether.'

He did have some tact. 'Doesn't matter how modest the gown, it's you I'll be looking at.'

She searched his eyes as if looking for the truth in his words. 'Are you sure?'

Because you don't have to go through with this, her own eyes seemed to say.

Every so often she touched on this with him as if to gauge whether the publicity had grown savage enough or her ignorance of royal protocols was problematic enough that he might wake up one morning and think no.

She was a mad mix of 'I've got this' coupled with 'I know this isn't what you signed on for'.

Surely her insecurities would fade once they were married? Or maybe her baby-making hormones were holding her hostage to doubt and it would take longer.

Until then he'd simply have to be sure for her. 'I'm sure.'

* * *

They were doing okay on the 'we're getting married in a few days' time' front. Valentine, for all his fiery emotions when first hearing he was to be a father, and the mad protectiveness in the weeks thereafter, had managed to find some kind of balance that allowed him to be supportive without being overbearing. Loving without being smothering. Encouraging without being condescending. He seemed happy with his lot, with *her*, and his confidence in her ability to be the Queen Consort he needed her to be never wavered.

No pressure.

She tried not to let the pressure get to her, but the closer she got to her wedding day, the more Angelique knew something had to give. She couldn't keep learning how to be a royal wife, and a royal patron, and give Juliana riding lessons, and run her own stable from afar, and be a mother to twins once they arrived.

She had to let go of her old life in order to fully embrace this new one.

'I'm heading to Spain on Friday to tie up some business commitments,' she told Valentine when he arrived at the manor after spending yet another evening at a charity banquet without her. He attended so many, and he did not complain, but sometimes when shedding his uniform or dinner suit he seemed to shed his strength along with it, nothing left in the tank for her but a smile and silence until they hit the sheets and he lost himself in her warmth.

He worked harder than anyone she knew—including her father. He had very little downtime now that he was fully back at work. Trying to have an everyday conversation with him often felt like loading him up unnecessarily. And yet she wasn't one to hold back when it came to sharing the parts of her life that he wasn't involved with.

He lay stretched out on her bed, still half dressed, with half his face buried in a pillow, his one visible eye closed, dark lashes fanning across his perfect features, and he might not have been looking at her but his ears still worked and his groan said a lot.

'No.' One word, muffled but unmistakable, and then he rolled onto his back, his eyes mere slits as he regarded her with a frown. 'I can't get away.'

'You don't have to get away. I'll go alone. I'm only going home.'

'No.' He put the heels of his hands to his eyes as if he had a headache brewing.

'If it's a security issue, I'm sure I'll be—'

'Fine? No. There'll be no leaving the country without me. Bring your work here.'

'But the horses and the people are there.'

'I *said* no. You'll stay in Thallasia until the babies are born, and after that there will *still* be no leaving the country without me.' He levied himself to a sitting position on one edge of the majestic bed. 'That's just the way it is.'

'But…what do you think is going to happen?'

He didn't answer her.

'Do you think I won't return?' He wouldn't look at her. 'Valentine?'

'It's about risk management, nothing more.' He still wouldn't look at her.

'Because I will return, if that's what you're worried about.' They were getting married in less than a week.

'It's not.'

'I've given you no cause to doubt me.'

This earned her a sullen stare. 'Like I said, it's a risk-analysis decision, not an emotional one. I've commitments here and cannot accompany you, therefore you cannot go. Sorry.' He didn't sound sorry. He sounded resolute. 'Surely you realise this is how it goes?'

'I realise this is how you want it to go,' she offered mildly. 'But engaged, married, or soon-to-be parents— we're still individuals. I don't expect to accompany you every time you pop over the border for a business meeting. Do you expect me to?'

'No.'

'Didn't think so.' They stared at each other in stony silence.

'Humour me,' he said finally.

'You don't think I'm going to return.' How could he possibly think that?

His silence was telling.

'You're having second thoughts,' she said next.

'No.' He was quick with his answer. 'No. But you might be, now that you know what marriage to me is going to take.'

'I signed your piece of paper. I gave you my word. I'm not leaving you.'

He said nothing. Still waters, this man. And very deep, very turbulent emotions. An image of his underground river flashed before her. He would cope with her absence, of that she had no doubt, but he would do so with the coping mechanisms available to him.

'Okay, let's make a deal. I stay here for you, you do something for me.'

His eyes narrowed even further. 'I trust you to know how far you can push me.'

Big of him. 'I want permission for my family to visit here or at the palace any time they or I choose.' She needed them in her life. Always had, always would. 'If I can't get to them, they need to be able to come to me. They're my strength and I'm going to need them.'

'Done.'

'And I want Carlos, Benedict, Luciana and your sister to be godparents to our children.'

'Absolutely not.' He reared up onto his elbows. 'Three of them are terrors. I'd say all four were unsuitable, but I don't know your brother well enough to tell.'

Snort. Her brother was the most centred of the lot, this was true. 'You don't think our children will be high spirited and in need of guidance from those who know exactly what they'll likely get up to? These are *our* children we're talking about.'

'Point. I'll consider it.'

But she was already shaking her head. 'Not good enough. The power in our relationship can't rest wholly with you. I will bend on the matter of not returning to Spain. I'll give you the peace of mind you seem to need. And in return you'll do the same for me.'

He could push the matter if he wanted to. Refuse her request and limit her freedom. Keep the upper hand and be every bit the man his father had been when it came to personal relationships and authoritarian rule.

But in the end, he chose differently.

'Done,' he murmured. He might have preferred to choose differently, more strategically, and cut her family out of selection. But unconditional love and a sense of belonging mattered too, and, from what he'd experienced, the people she'd chosen would provide it. 'I accept your choice of godparents.'

Her brilliant smile made him shake his head and smile. He'd wanted a woman who would challenge and impassion him, he reminded himself silently. One who had no hesitation when it came to calling out his insecurities and insisting on fair treatment. He could do this—learn to accommodate her as they went through life together. Learn to trust her opinions and instincts and be ready to bend if they disagreed. He wanted his people to value her as he did, and if that meant leading the way, then lead he would.

'You'll need to take my best security detail with you, and I'll still worry from the moment you leave until the moment you're back in my arms, but if your business in Spain is that important that you need to be there, you can go.'

He had an armful of Angelique moments later, her eyes shining with tears as she let loose a string of impassioned Spanish, and he had no idea what she was saying—but it was likely something along the lines of 'You wonderful, complicated, fascinating, treasure of a man. I love you.'

She kissed him hard and fast, and then again, and that second time felt like a thank you. 'You fool!'

Oh. So… Not even close.

'I love you,' she said next, and that was more like it. It was the first time she'd said it. He would hear more of it. Embrace it. Commit to a lifetime of loving her too.

'My future Queen and mother of my child, I'm all in. No matter what it takes, I love you too.'

CHAPTER TWELVE

ANGELIQUE DIDN'T GO to Spain—she brought the horses and buyers to her. World-class polo players were an odd lot, but tell them she was selling her first and second string polo ponies—twelve altogether, preferably to be sold in two groups of six—and she was stunned by how many of them were willing to travel to see her.

Her father, who usually conducted sale negotiations, would always be on the other end of the phone for her and they knew it. But the horses were hers—selected and brought on by her, not to sell, that hadn't been what she'd meant to do with them at all, but with children on the horizon and queenly duties to contend with, and Valentine to make time for, something had to give. She'd always been a trainer first and a rider second. Those invitations to try out for World Championship events had been gratifying but not the end game where Cordova ponies and reputations were concerned.

She'd even fielded an enquiry from the newly minted billionaire who couldn't ride.

He'd been taking riding lessons, he said.

He'd offered her an apology for his behaviour, no excuses. His sister had threatened to disown him if he didn't stop treating people like they were mud on the bottom of his overpriced shoes, he'd said. Having money had not made him a better person, he'd confessed. And even if she had no desire to sell him any Cordova ponies, or to accept his apology, he was indebted to her for speaking out as she did when no one else around him would.

It made her think. It made her examine her own hot-headed responses and realise that she needed other ways to make her point if she was to stand at Valentine's side and do good.

She'd always been altogether willing to call out poor horsemanship, but maybe there was another way of pushing for change that didn't involve arguing with insecure billionaire shipping magnates in public. Give the man riding lessons. She almost choked on the thought, but what if she'd encouraged him to improve rather than humiliating the man?

She penned a reply before she could overthink it. The horses were in all likelihood already sold to professional players, but he was welcome to visit the Cordova estate in Spain. She was offering a tour of the facilities there, either her father or their head groom would see to that, and insight into how Cordova ponies were trained. She'd been placed on the back of a horse before she could walk. Becoming a skilled practitioner in any sport took time and if he really had caught the polo bug she knew good people who could help him on his way.

Her old self scoffed, figuring he was playing her and all he wanted was to buy her horses.

Her new self thought life journeys took so many twists and turns that giving a person the benefit of the doubt might just be a good thing.

'I have to become a better person than I am,' she told Valentine later that evening.

'For the babies?' he asked, and she hadn't even *thought* of that angle.

'Yes. For the babies, and for you and for all the people who are going to have to rely on me now to know how things work and do the right thing and not lose my temper at the slightest provocation. Oh, this is bad. I'm two minutes into the mere thought of self-improvement and already I'm failing!'

Valentine set a steaming cup of green tea in front of her, and she liked green tea, but wanted to weep at the thought of limiting her caffeine intake for months on end.

'Hormones have a lot to answer for,' he murmured. 'No one is saying you have to be perfect. No one ever is.'

She wrapped her hands around the warm cup. 'You're kind of perfect.'

'It's official. Baby brain is real. You've lost your mind.'

'I'm scared.'

'I know.'

'I don't want to let anyone down.'

'I know that too.'

'We get married on Sunday.'

'Yes.' He gathered her in, ran his hands over her body. 'Do you need me to distract you?'

'Yes.' Please God, yes, before she drowned beneath the weight of a foreign crown and her ever growing insecurities. 'I want you to do your very best.'

She found a buyer for her top six horses in an old friend from Argentina. His name was Enrique, horses were his life, and he was currently the number two ranked polo player in the world. He'd tumbled Carlos ten years or so ago now, before Benedict, and he and her brother had not remained friends afterwards. He'd always been civil to Angelique and Luciana though—even at the height of their notoriety. She had a soft spot for him and he had the money to buy and the weight of his international polo club behind him. Her horses would thrive in his care and shine on the field. He was the perfect match for her beloved ponies, no question.

He was married now with two young children and a partner he loved to distraction. His phone was full of pictures of his ranch and family. Benedict—her brother's partner—was a brilliant, complex prince of a man, and she liked him for her brother very much, but this man could have been her brother-in-law had the world turned a little differently, and she wouldn't have been disappointed.

She was practically selling her horses to family.

This was what she told herself as she shook hands on a deal that would put more money in her pocket than she'd ever earned before, and then she had to go and spoil her professional persona by choking on hot tears. He saw her struggle, he was standing right in front of her, and wrapped her in his arms in an instant. He was a confident, compassionate married man giving comfort without thought.

It didn't look that way the following morning with a full colour picture of her and Enrique embracing and a headline to go with it that made a mockery of the truth, of her values, and of Valentine, King of Thallasia.

The Real Father Revealed!

A headline for the ages, and the words beneath it weren't much better. Never mind Enrique's loving family. Never mind her upcoming wedding at the weekend.

She was the worst kind of soulless schemer and Valentine was the worst kind of fool. She tried to set the paper aside and get on with her day, but Valentine had been staying at the palace these past two days on account of a water management convention being held in the capital that he'd attended, and she hadn't been able to get hold of him this morning.

He'd *know* it was a lie, wouldn't he? Berate her for letting another man hug her in public, maybe, and for feeding the negative-publicity machine, but it hadn't been deliberate. The photo had to have been taken by one of the grooms or the security staff. An opportunist looking to make a quick killing, nothing more. Or maybe she should read significantly more into it—a last-ditch attempt by palace courtiers to derail her marriage to their King. The thought made her want to throw up, or maybe morning sickness was the reason. Nothing she could do to stop her twenty-minute visit to the bathroom.

She was sitting on the restroom tiles, her back against the wall and a porcelain toilet bowl her closest companion, when her phone rang in the other room and she almost let it ring out but it might be Valentine, so she got to her feet and made a dash for it, hoping her stomach wouldn't choose this moment to revolt. Nothing left in it anyway.

It wasn't Valentine. It was Carlos. She could picture him reading the same paper she'd just read, Benedict seated opposite, both of them baffled by her naiveté. They'd taught her better than this.

She hadn't expected her brother's anger, but it spat down the phone line. 'What on *earth* do you think you're doing?' he asked icily, and she closed her eyes and took herself back to the bathroom and sat back down against the wall.

'This is about the article in the paper?'

'Enrique? Seriously? I know you've always had time for him, but what the hell was he doing anywhere near you? Why? Why would you let yourself be photographed with him like that just days before your wedding to a king who's fighting for the right to be with you with every breath he takes?'

'I know. I know. I didn't mean to, it was just a mistake.' She took a deep breath and hoped he would understand. 'I sold my horses. All of them.' Eyes closed, with her head in her hand, the phone to her ear and her voice small. 'I figured I needed to commit to being Queen Consort completely, so I sold all my horses to a brilliant polo player and an honourable man, and then I cried like a baby at the loss of an identity I've worked my whole life for.'

Silence greeted her words, and then Carlos swore, and she cut the call and threw the phone across the floor. It came to rest on white tile, the screen now shattered, just one more visual reminder of how thoroughly unsuitable she was to be anyone's queen. Too fiery and emotional. Too stupid to keep her head down and not bring shame upon the people who loved her.

So many rules, and she didn't know them all and might never know them all and it mattered now more than ever because she wasn't just representing herself any more. She *knew* that.

Valentine would have every right to be furious with her.

Carlos was. The brother she'd driven her tattered reputation into the ground for hadn't even thought enough of her to listen when faced with a picture of her in his old lover's arms.

She spent forty more minutes in the bathroom, alternating bouts of tearful self-pity with the dry heaves of morning sickness. Her stomach settled eventually, and she stripped off to take her second shower of the morning and start the day afresh. She couldn't face heading down to the stables today and the work would be all but finished anyway. She'd say goodbye to her horses tomorrow night when everyone had left for the day so there'd be no one around to witness her tears.

But if not jodhpurs, what would she wear? She stared into the closet full of demure new clothes carefully selected with her new role in mind and couldn't even choose one that wouldn't make her feel like a fraud. In the end she reached out and randomly plucked a dusky pink dress from the hanger—its feminine colour muted by simple lines, a modest crossover neckline, a fitted waist and a flared skirt that ended just below her knees.

She plaited her hair and rolled it into a bun and added the moonstone and white gold earrings her parents had given her for her twenty-first birthday and a matching bracelet that had come from Luciana. A pendant necklace from Carlos completed the set and she put that on too, with shaking hands. He had to be looking at that photo with different eyes now, surely? He had to know how much the sale of her horses had cost her. He'd come round.

She tried not to dwell on how badly his criticism had shaken her. The rest of the world could go hang, but her people, the ones who knew her inside out, when they acted up she trembled.

As for what Valentine might think...

She reached for the engagement ring he insisted she wear whenever they were in public. A priceless diamond from the bowels of the royal vaults, to be sure. An enormous glittering bauble and a total pain to wear and maybe once she was married and had a perfectly plain wedding ring to wear, she could set it aside and only wear it on special occasions.

If she got married.

The news article she refused to glance at again had truly done a number on her. Gold-digger, schemer, conscienceless liar, foreign filth. The King's Downfall.

Maybe she wouldn't be getting married after all.

Valentine knew something was afoot when his head of palace affairs swept into his quarters at a quarter past seven with Vala hot on his heels. Neither looked pleased to be there.

'Problems?' he asked. 'Because I'm due at the conference at nine to introduce the British delegation.' He'd planned to spend most of the day there—hopefully soaking up information like a sponge. One swift glance at the newspaper on the tray his secretary held out towards him made a mockery of that plan.

The headline was hard enough to swallow, but the accompanying picture landed like a blow to his heart. Angelique enfolded in the arms of another man, clinging to him as if he was her everything. 'Who is he?'

'A polo player,' his sister said.

He recognised the background. They were on the grounds of the duchy Angelique rented from him. She'd brought another man inside the manor. 'When was he there?'

'Yesterday.'

'And who took the photo?'

His secretary grimaced. 'One of our security personnel. They've been relieved of their post, Your Majesty.'

Betrayed by someone whose job it had been to protect him and Angelique. It had happened to him before and would happen again. Never got any easier to bear. 'Good. Cancel my conference duties and tell my driver I'm going to see Angelique this morning.'

'Your Majesty, shall I alert Ms Cordova as to your imminent arrival?'

'No.'

'I can accompany you,' his sister began.

'No.'

'But—'

'I'm not angry.' He spoke true. 'I'm disappointed by the gross invasion of privacy, but it happens. People get greedy. As for the insinuation that I'm not the one who is the father, those rumours have been circulating since the beginning.' He waved his hand towards the paper. 'Take it away. There's nothing new to see.' Except Angelique's spectacularly bad judgment and choice of friends to snuggle into, a little voice inside his head suggested helpfully. And the jealousy threatening to cloud his eyesight with a blood-red haze if he had to look at the picture for one more second.

His secretary beat a hasty retreat. His sister stayed, her gaze concerned. 'Do I have to remind you that our father's temper was not his best feature?' she asked, and that itself was warning enough.

'Do you see me frothing at the mouth?'

'No, but I see the look in your eyes. Are you sure you wouldn't rather cool down before you speak with Angelique?'

Go take yet another dip in surging, freezing cold water in an attempt to get a handle on his emotions? He wasn't angry. Not in the hot-headed way that usually assailed him. This anger was cold and patient and aimed directly at those who would destroy the best thing that had ever happened to him. 'No.'

'Should I come with you?'

'To see my beloved?' That earned him a hard glare. 'No.'

'Just don't say anything you're going to regret.'

'You mean like ask why she placed herself in such a compromising position in the first place?' He mirrored his sister's dark glare right back at her. 'She doesn't know life beneath the microscope yet. As you say…she'll learn.'

Angelique was sitting at her dressing table of her small side bedroom when he arrived, and he stood in the doorway a moment and watched as she played with the engagement ring he'd given her weeks ago. She looked as beautiful as he'd ever seen her, all soft femininity and flawless features. Beautiful and unutterably sad at the sight of his ring.

Any small sliver of anger at the thought of her hugging the polo player evaporated, replaced by concern for her well-being. If she'd seen this morning's paper she already knew what her unscripted hug had cost them.

He watched as her gaze found his in the mirror, full of misery and wordless apology.

Guess she had seen it.

'Put it on,' he said, and she shook her head as if she would deny him.

He softened his voice and vowed to keep his cool. 'Put it on and tell me what happened, and if I can fix it, I will.'

'You can't fix it. You'd have to fix me.' Her eyes filled with tears. 'I didn't mean to get so upset that Enrique felt he had to comfort me.' She still hadn't put the ring on. 'He's a good player. With them, he'll be the best. They couldn't have gone to a better home.'

'What are you talking about?'

'I sold my polo ponies.'

He didn't understand.

'Didn't make sense to keep them.' Her smile wobbled. 'I'm pregnant. I'm going to be something else from now on. What use did I have for them? I just didn't think it'd be so hard. I was there when every one of them were born. I delivered half of them, nurtured them. All my father's knowledge and mine went into selecting them to keep. They were my companions and my confidants. My identity. Mine. All gone. Paid for in cash by the highest suitable bidder.'

Her sacrifice threatened to split him open with the force of his feelings. She'd given up everything for him, to be with him, even her beloved horses, and his people had repaid her with slander and rejection. 'You didn't have to sell them.'

'Yes, I did.' She put the ring on and took a deep breath and turned to stand and face him, beautiful and elegant in all her fine clothes. He barely recognised her, she was so tightly composed. He'd done this to her. Stripped her of everything she held dear. 'Aren't you supposed to be somewhere else this morning?'

'No.' He took her in his arms and felt her sag against him. Such a slight woman for all her wiry strength. 'You didn't have to. We'll get them back for you, and you can—'

'I can what? Compete? Stay a horsemaster? You know I can't.'

'You can if I abdicate.' He meant it. 'Marry on Sunday, put Vala on the throne on Monday and walk away. Say the word and I'll do it. I love you. Quite desperately. You have to know that.'

She buried her face in his neck and clung. 'I thought the article would send you into a temper.'

'It did, but not in the way you're thinking. Thallasia doesn't deserve you and nor do I, but I plan to spend the rest of my life convincing you I do.'

'You're not angry with me about the photo?'

'I'm extremely angry about the photo.' He would not lie. 'But not with you. And seeing as I'm about to try and buy your horses back from your handsome polo player I'd best not turn on him either.'

She pulled back to look him in the eye. 'They're not going to stop writing terrible articles about me.'

'Not for a while, no. But, Angelique, I know they're rubbish. I know your heart, and it's mine, and whether I deserve you or not I'm not letting you go. So pick a road and watch me walk it with you.'

He couldn't stand it when she cried, and she cried long and hard, another waterfall to drench the front of his snow-white shirt. Maybe there was something wrong with him, but he far preferred their emotions out than in. This bedroom—their private places—were not for stoicism or secrets. They were for loving and being loved and letting feelings flow.

Finally, she stepped away and wiped at her eyes and looked at her fingers and hiccoughed a laugh. 'They always say the mascara is waterproof and it never is.'

The streaks on his shirt seemed to prove her theory

correct, as she turned back to the mirror and reached for a tissue and wiped the make-up away. She picked up a mascara tube as if to start all over again, and then met his gaze in the mirror. 'You really love me enough to walk away from your duty?'

'It's breaking you. And, yes.' If that was what it took to make her whole again, then yes.

She ran her finger over the engagement ring and shook her head as if to object. He'd never seen anything more beautiful than a tear-drenched Angelique Cordova reaching for her inner strength.

'I'm not broken.' Her mouth firmed. 'I'm hormonally challenged because I'm pregnant and I'm coming to terms with a new way forward. That's all it is. And you don't need to relinquish your crown in order to prop me up. Not now. Not ever. I'll learn, we'll learn, together, and maybe one day we'll laugh about our mistakes, because you know what?' She flung the words at him like a challenge.

'Tell me.' He played the part she offered him with a keen sense of anticipation.

'I'm going to be the best Queen Consort your country has ever had.'

CHAPTER THIRTEEN

THE KING OF THALLASIA's wedding day bloomed warm and bright, with a blue sky overhead and the scent of roses, sweet peas, and the faintest hint of jasmine of the night wafting through the air. The press reports were encouraging. There was nothing like a royal wedding to make a nation hope for the best. The modest chapel located deep inside Valentine's palace walls had been dressed with flowers from the heartlands of Thallasia and the far mountain regions of Spain, and framed the entrance to the place of prayer with splashes of green, soft whites and creams, and deepest crimson.

Valentine fidgeted, and his sister tutted and swiped at his hand to stop him fussing with his cufflinks once again. Vala had taken on the role of groomsman, because if a king was going to break tradition and marry in private why not go all out and have a woman to attend him?

He wanted no other to stand with him, no matter her gender. She was his twin.

The chapel only had room for a dozen or so guests—the seating consisted of one long pew on either side of a central aisle, repeated so as to be only three rows deep. Where to sit three kings, their queens, assorted children, and the immediate family members of the bride had been a problem, but Vala had sorted it, and that result too eschewed tradition. Vala's husband, daughter and twins in the first pew closest to him. Angelique's mother with King Theodosius on the other side, with room for Angelique's father once he delivered her to the altar. Moriana in the pew behind them, glowing with late pregnancy, with Benedict and Carlos alongside her. Queen Consorts Ana of Byzenmaach and Sera of Arun sat across the aisle from them, with Ana's little girl nearest the aisle for the better view. A couple of kings stood sentry at the rear, one on either side of the door, ready to open it as soon as directed to. Give them something to do other than stand there and look pretty, Vala had said, and she'd got away with it too. Luciana, in her role of bridal attendant, would slip in beside whichever king she chose, after making sure Angelique's bridal veil and train were just so and following along behind her sister and father on the way to the altar. A simple wedding.

A beautiful day for it.

Prayer candles sat in wall sconces carved from stone a thousand years ago. A single stained-glass window with the picture of a sun in the sky and a castle and verdant farmlands beneath it took the full force of the late afternoon sun, sending scattered light patterns across the walls.

Private. Intimate. Perfect.

So perfectly right, his decision to take this woman as his bride. To serve at his side. To brighten his day and warm his nights. To love beyond measure for as long as he drew breath.

And every last person in the room knew without doubt that his vow to do just that would hold.

He'd loved this woman since they were both eighteen years old, and this time he would love, honour and cherish her.

There was no music to announce the arrival of the bride. The music would come later, when they had their first dance as man and wife and then everyone gathered around a perfectly informal round table for a wedding feast prepared by the mother of the bride. The most glorious cooking smells had assaulted his senses every time he'd drifted past the kitchen that morning.

The fact that the wedding feast table had been dressed with a king's ransom in bejewelled and golden tableware only added to the feeling that this blending of cultures and ancestry and families was something truly special.

He'd been pacing the halls all day, waiting for the morning, and then lunch, and then the afternoon to pass so he could get to the getting married part of the day and beyond.

Whoever had decided a sunset marriage would be just the thing for him to bear clearly had a master's degree in psychological warfare.

Vala and Moriana had suggested the time, if memory served correct.

Figured.

But that time was upon them now, and, at the faintest of knocks, Cas and Augustus reached for the chapel doors and pulled them open, and there stood Angelique, bathed by the light of the setting sun filtered through precious stained glass.

He wasn't the only one to gasp and hold his breath.

He might have been the only one to hold his breath until Angelique took her first step forward.

And then more steps, until her father handed her over and stepped back, and then it was only the two of them and the archbishop and repeating words and vows that described all the love he had to give. To have, to hold, to honour, serve and protect. To love, deeply and wisely, and he knew, when he finally raised the veil to reveal his wife, and the sun shone down on them and bathed them in a golden glow, that his choice had been the right one and that he had permission from above to love as he would.

The kiss, when it came, was as reverent as he could make it, what with the aching need to sweep Angelique into his arms and carry her off, into that sunset, on a pair of horses bound for the hunting lodge, but he resisted.

That was for later. Her horse had been decked out with a flower harness. His stallion was the fastest one in his stables, Alessandro had assured him.

Guess they'd find out later if that was true or not.

He resisted the urge to sweep her away as they ventured hand in hand down the aisle and braved a rainfall of rose petals flung at them by kings who did silly, spontaneous things in private that they'd never do in public.

Resisted through the first dance in a near empty ballroom before someone bribed the string group to play heavy metal.

Resisted through the lone photographer's plea for fifteen minutes of their time, and the resulting selection of half a dozen photographs to release to the press that evening.

Relaxed through the dinner, and, by the time the speeches came, he tossed the one he'd laboured over and simply spoke from the heart.

'To my family and friends who have stuck by me all these years and lent their support to my choices…

'To my wife's family, my thanks for gracing me with one of their own…

'To the people outside these walls who are counting on me to rule wisely, with compassion and love, and in the name of duty to the crown… I will not let them down.

'And to my wife, whose love, and grace, and tolerance make me a better man. Angelique, there are some new horses in the stables. Enrique helped me choose them and so did your father and Alessandro. They tell me they show promise. Their bloodlines are magnificent. They will delight and challenge you, so I'm told. Never feel guilty about spending time with them. Nurture them, take joy in them, because I want you to have passions that will sustain you. Besides me.' Ad libbing had its flaws, the sniggers that followed reminded him so. The arrogance of kings, tamed, and bent towards love. 'They are my gift to you because, although together we will endure, I will not allow the weight of the crown to swallow who you are. A toast.' He raised his glass. 'To my wife. Horsemaster Cordova.'

Not a traditional toast by any stretch, but necessary, here and now amongst this lot, so many of them who knew what it was like to lose track of themselves in service to crown and country.

There were more toasts.

And dancing. Dear heaven, the ridiculous dancing. Who needed a million-dollar DJ and a warehouse full of smoke machines and chemical stimulation when you had this lot?

Benedict had ordered a disco ball and it turned out they had one. They put *Pulp Fiction* to shame, and no one died but bribery material was collected for the ages.

The photographer had been banished hours earlier and the children had all been tucked up in bed. Which begged the thought, 'Are you by any chance ready for bed?'

His glowing bride bestowed on him a wicked smile that promised heaven, and said, 'I've practised wedding goodbyes for three days solid. I've memorised titles, compliments, invitations for people to join us that I know won't clash with their calendars. Moriana helped.'

'Of course, she did.' That woman was a menace to royalty everywhere.

'I reckon I've got it down to three minutes solid if no one interrupts.'

'Hey, everyone!' He held his hand high. 'Thank you for coming. We need three minutes of your time and then we're gone.'

Angelique had never spoken so fast. She'd forgotten about all the hugs people insisted on giving her, but they were out of the room in five minutes.

Angelique had never been so happy.

Valentine, on the other hand, was tugging her in the wrong direction. 'Where are we going?'

'The hunting lodge.'

'Now?' She was all for surprises but there was a perfectly good turret and a king's bedroom two storeys up in the other direction. It had candles and chocolates and champagne and white bedding in it. A vase stood ready for her wedding bouquet and her bridal nightgown had been set out in all its glory in his dressing room. She'd arranged everything.

'The hunting lodge is all set up for our wedding night.' His grin promised a good one. 'Palace staff have been there all afternoon getting it ready. There are no stuffed monkeys anywhere in it, I promise.'

His staff had clearly been very, very busy, what with getting two places ready. They really had to work on coordinating their surprises.

She walked with him through the palace doors and nearest gardens. Two horses stood waiting at the edge of the herb garden, one of them with what looked like a whole carrot plant in its mouth and a garland made of flowers around her neck.

She knew that horse as she knew her own reflection.

It was her favourite mare. The one Valentine had ridden so successfully a few months back. The first of her first string of polo ponies that she'd sold to Enrique. The other horse was big and black, a stallion, Thallasian bred, no question.

'She's yours again, with Enrique's blessing,' he whispered in her ear. 'But is she faster than my fastest stallion? That's the question.'

This gorgeous, generous man in front of her was hers, and she was his.

And the journey beckoned.

EPILOGUE

HE WAS NEVER having sex again. The fact that he'd said this aloud in a birthing room filled with far too many people…okay, four other people…meaning Angelique, Luciana, a midwife and a royal physician, as well as him, served only to show him how truly panicked he was. Because King Valentine of Thallasia was a cool, calm and considered monarch, not prone to blurting out the first thought to enter his head. Even if he was currently sitting behind Angelique, on a birthing bed, so as to provide a bulwark for her to lean on and hands for her to crush every time the midwife said push.

'I swear—'

'No swearing in front of the babies,' Angelique's twin said cheerfully, although he noted a certain tenseness around Lucia's eyes that suggested she wasn't exactly unaffected by the longest labour in the world either. 'What do you think, Angelique? Do you intend to hold him to the no-sex-ever-again plan?'

Angelique looked up at him, long strands of silky black hair sticking to her neck and forehead. Escapees from the plait she'd pulled her hair back into several decades ago.

It sure as hell felt like several decades ago.

'I mean, it could be the only thing he has going for him,' Luciana added, wicked to the end, but if it made Angelique smile—which it did—he would forgive her twin the overreach.

'No sniping,' Angelique told them.

'But it keeps me sane.' Luciana strode to the business end of things, took one look, paled, and walked briskly back to her sister's side.

'I agree. It's our thing. The bedrock on which we base our friendship,' he added. Anything to avoid thinking about what might be happening, or not happening, and he just wanted someone to *do* something to ease Angelique's pain. 'Take the sniping away and we'll be mute.' He played his part, silently scanning Luciana's face for reassurance she couldn't give.

He had no idea what was happening other than his wife was in pain and had been for an eternity.

'Okay, mama,' the midwife said from way down where he was never going again. 'This is the one. Imagine the rolling waves pushing the little seashell further up the sandy beach each time. Gentle rolling waves, and if a big fat wave comes along, don't fight it, go with it, because it's going to push that little seashell right to your feet.'

Possibly not the best time to remind the woman that this was a landlocked country or mention that the river running beneath the castle was a ferocious, tumultuous beast with a history of being used for punishment. Besides, Angelique's homeland had azure beaches, gentle waves and sunshine, so who was he to deny her the pretty imagery? Whatever worked, right? Because something had to work for her soon. They'd been at this for over twelve hours already.

He couldn't take much more.

'Deep breath,' said the midwife suddenly, and there was an air of command in her voice that had never been there before. 'Hold it… And push hard, *now*!'

Angelique pushed, her teeth clenched and her eyes tightly closed, as if directing all her energy southward. Too tense, the midwife had told her when they were only a couple of hours in. Still tense, he thought, and trying to stay in control.

'I'll roar if you will,' he whispered. 'I'll start.' Who cared if the first noise his children heard was their father screaming for them to come out and face his wrath for giving their mother such a hard birthing time?

He was a protective man. Very.

They'd find out soon enough.

Luciana met his gaze and he wondered if he looked as terrified as she did. She nodded, and rallied around his challenge. 'I'd like to see that.'

He pressed his lips against Angelique's temple for a moment, tightened his hold, flung his head back and roared. Full volume, holding nothing back. Not the pain nor the joy of living and loving as he would, not the agony of seeing the woman he loved in pain. Suffering, for him.

Luciana joined in.

'You're both mad.' But Angelique pushed and joined her voice with theirs and twenty seconds later his daughter was born.

'Well, that's one way of doing it,' offered the midwife dryly as she handed the baby to the doctor and went back for seconds.

Not three minutes after that, his son arrived in the world, his voice almost as loud as the rest of his family's. Someone placed his daughter on Angelique's chest, skin to skin, and it was an image he would carry with him for ever. There were tears. Some of them might have been his.

Then the midwife was ordering him to stand up and take his shirt off, and Angelique lay smiling, and Luciana started laughing like a loon before leaning over to kiss her sister's cheek before stepping away. 'I'm out of here to tell the family the good news.' They were all out there—every last Cordova, and Benedict too, and Valentine's sister and her family and probably the ghosts of all the rulers of Thallasia. 'A future queen for Thallasia. How about that?'

How about that, as the midwife showed him how to hold his son and cradle him to his chest.

'Don't drop them,' said Luciana, and then she was gone.

'I'm going to kill her,' Valentine announced, now terrified of dropping his baby. 'Are they healthy, the babies?' And hot on the heels of that thought, he turned to Angelique. 'Are you okay? Is my wife okay?'

Angelique's 'I'm okay' got lost beneath the midwife's answer that she was doing very well.

He couldn't stop looking at the two tiny miracles in their arms. 'They're so beautiful.' He should have expected as much, given the gene combinations involved. God knew, he and his sister had been feted for their looks from the moment they were born, and still were. As for Angelique, some would say her looks had been her downfall. 'How do we make them plainer?'

'We don't.' His birth-battle-hardened wife smirked at him. 'We all have our burdens to bear. Take me, for example: I have a husband who's never having sex again.'

About that... 'I could be persuaded to revisit that particular edict.'

'You do that.'

'I love you, you know.' The words came from deep down inside. 'You're everything I've always wanted. You. Them.' He nodded towards the babies. 'Us. I'm never letting this go.'

Smiling eyes regarded him fondly. 'Good thing I'm in it for the long haul, then.'

A fact for which he was eternally grateful. 'Together, then.' So many blessings had been bestowed upon him. 'Let's go rule the world.'

* * * * *

MILLS & BOON

Coming next month

SECRETS OF CINDERELLA'S AWAKENING
Sharon Kendrick

Almost as if he'd read her mind, Leon caught hold of her and turned her round, his hands on either side of her waist. She held her breath because his touch felt *electric* and he studied her upturned face for what felt like a long time, before lowering his head to kiss her.

It was...dynamite.

It was...life-changing.

Marnie swayed in disbelief, her limbs growing instantly boneless. How was it possible for a kiss to feel this *good*? How could *anything* feel this good? At first there was barely any contact between them – just the intoxicating graze of his mouth over hers.

He deepened the kiss and began to stroke one of her breasts. Her nipple was pushing against her baggy T-shirt dress towards the enticing circling of his thumb. Was it that which made her writhe her hips against his with instinctive hunger, causing him to utter something in Greek which sounded almost *despairing*?

The sound broke the spell and she drew back – though in the faint light all she could see was the hectic glitter of his eyes. 'What...what did you just say?'

'I said that you set my blood on fire, *agape mou*. And that I want you very much. But you already know that.'

Well, she knew he wanted her, yes. She wasn't actually sure about the blood-on-fire bit because nobody had ever said anything like that to her before. And although she liked it her instinct was not to believe him because even if they were true, she knew compliments always came with a price.

Yet what was the *point* of all this if she was just going to pepper the experience with her usual doubts, and spoil it? Couldn't she have a holiday from her normal self and shake off all the worries which had been weighing her down for so long? Couldn't she be a different Marnie tonight – one who was seeking nothing but uncomplicated pleasure? She had always been the responsible one. The one who looked out for other people – with one eye on the distance, preparing for the shadows which inevitably hovered there. Wasn't it time to articulate what *she* wanted for a change?

She cleared her throat. 'Would you mind speaking in English so I can understand what you're saying?'

She could hear the amusement which deepened his voice.

'Are we planning to do a lot of talking then, Marnie? Is that what turns you on?'

Something warned her she'd be straying into dangerous territory if she told him she didn't *know* what turned her on because she'd never given herself the chance to find out. But while she didn't want to lie to him, that didn't mean she couldn't tell a different kind of truth.

'*You* turn me on,' she said boldly and something about the breathless rush of her words made his powerful body tense.

'Oh, *do* I?' he questioned, tilting her chin with his fingers so that their darkened gazes clashed. 'So what are we going to do about that, I wonder?'

Continue reading
SECRETS OF CINDERELLA'S AWAKENING
Sharon Kendrick

Available next month
www.millsandboon.co.uk

COMING SOON!

We really hope you enjoyed reading this book.
If you're looking for more romance, be sure to
head to the shops when new books are
available on

Thursday 10th
June

LET'S TALK
Romance

For exclusive extracts, competitions
and special offers, find us online:

MILLS & BOON

THE HEART OF ROMANCE

A ROMANCE FOR EVERY READER

ODERN

Prepare to be swept off your feet by sophisticated, sexy and seductive heroes, in some of the world's most glamourous and romantic locations, where power and passion collide.

TORICAL

Escape with historical heroes from time gone by. Whether your passion is for wicked Regency Rakes, muscled Vikings or rugged Highlanders, awaken the romance of the past.

EDICAL

Set your pulse racing with dedicated, delectable doctors in the high-pressure world of medicine, where emotions run high and passion, comfort and love are the best medicine.

ue Love

Celebrate true love with tender stories of heartfelt romance, from the rush of falling in love to the joy a new baby can bring, and a focus on the emotional heart of a relationship.

Desire

Indulge in secrets and scandal, intense drama and plenty of sizzling hot action with powerful and passionate heroes who have it all: wealth, status, good looks…everything but the right woman.

EROES

Experience all the excitement of a gripping thriller, with an intense romance at its heart. Resourceful, true-to-life women and strong, fearless men face danger and desire - a killer combination!

To see which titles are coming soon, please visit

millsandboon.co.uk/nextmonth

JOIN US ON SOCIAL MEDIA!

Stay up to date with our latest releases, author
news and gossip, special offers and discounts, and
all the behind-the-scenes action
from Mills & Boon...

 millsandboon

 millsandboonuk

 millsandboon

It might just be true love...